High Praise for

"Count on Jill Shalvis for a witty, steamy, unputdownable love story."

— Robyn Carr, *New York Times* bestselling author

"Shalvis [has a] knack for creating witty, humorous, warmhearted characters dealing with complex emotional situations." — *Library Journal*

"Jill Shalvis's books are funny, warm, charming and unforgettable."

— RaeAnne Thayne, *New York Times* bestselling author

"Jill Shalvis has a unique talent making you want to spend time with her characters right off the bat."

— Kristen Ashley, *New York Times* bestselling author

Once in a Lifetime

"Scores big with a delicate love story and red-hot passion. Fans of smalltown contemporaries will savor this delicious and heartwarming story, a refreshingly realistic romance between two great characters."

— *Publishers Weekly*, starred review

"Shalvis never disappoints with her witty, comical, and überromantic reads. Fans of contemporary romance will fall in love with Aubrey and Ben and find their sexual tension electrifying. Sweet and spicy—what more could you ask for?" — *RT Book Reviews*

It's in His Kiss

"Shalvis's command of contemporary romance is again on display. Shalvis combines humor, sparkling repartee, believable characters, and highly sensual sex scenes to make this book work on every level."

—*Publishers Weekly*, starred review

Luck at
First Sight

Also by Jill Shalvis

The Cedar Ridge Series

Second Chance Summer
My Kind of Wonderful
Nobody but You

The Lucky Harbor Series

Simply Irresistible
The Sweetest Thing
Heating Up the Kitchen (cookbook)
Christmas in Lucky Harbor (omnibus)
Small Town Christmas (anthology)
At Last
Forever and a Day
"Under the Mistletoe" (short story)
It Had to Be You
Always on My Mind
A Christmas to Remember (anthology)
Once in a Lifetime
It's in His Kiss
He's So Fine
One in a Million
"Merry Christmas, Baby" (short story)

Other Novels

White Heat
Blue Flame
Seeing Red
Her Sexiest Mistake

Luck at First Sight

**2-in-1 Edition with
Once in a Lifetime *and*
It's in His Kiss**

JILL SHALVIS

FOREVER

NEW YORK   BOSTON

Forever
Hachette Book Group
1290 Avenue of the Americas, New York, NY 10104
read-forever.com
twitter.com/readforeverpub

Once in a Lifetime and *It's in His Kiss* originally published in 2014 by Forever.
First 2-in-1 edition: September 2023

Forever is an imprint of Grand Central Publishing. The Forever name and logo are trademarks of Hachette Book Group, Inc.

The publisher is not responsible for websites (or their content) that are not owned by the publisher.

The Hachette Speakers Bureau provides a wide range of authors for speaking events. To find out more, go to hachettespeakersbureau.com or email HachetteSpeakers@hbgusa.com.

Forever books may be purchased in bulk for business, educational, or promotional use. For information, please contact your local bookseller or the Hachette Book Group Special Markets Department at special.markets@hbgusa.com.

ISBN: 9781538742549 (paperback 2-in-1)

Printed in the United States of America

LSC-C

Printing 1, 2023

Luck at
First Sight

Once in a Lifetime

To Alex Logan, because I can't imagine writing Lucky Harbor without you in my court. Thanks for all you've done and continue to do for me.

Chapter 1

♥

There was one universal truth in Lucky Harbor, Washington—you could hide a pot of gold in broad daylight and no one would steal it, but you couldn't hide a secret.

There'd been a lot of secrets in Aubrey Wellington's colorful life, and nearly all of them had been uncovered and gleefully discussed ad nauseam.

And yet here she was, still in this small Pacific West Coast town she'd grown up in. She didn't quite know what that said about her other than that she was stubborn as hell.

In any case, she was fairly used to bad days by the time she walked to Lucky Harbor's only bar and grill, but today had taken the cake. Ted Marshall, ex–town clerk, ex-boss, and also, embarrassingly enough, her ex-lover, was self-publishing his own tell-all. And since he'd ever so thoughtfully given her an advance reading copy, she knew he was planning on informing the entire world that, among other things, she was a bitchy, money-hungry man-eater.

She'd give him the money-hungry part. She was sinking much of her savings into her aunt's bookstore, the Book & Bean, a sentimental attempt at bringing back the one happy childhood memory she had. The effort was leaving her far too close to broke for comfort. She'd even give him the bitchy part—at least on certain days of the month.

But man-eater? Just because she didn't believe in happily-ever-afters, or even a happily-for-now, didn't mean she was a man-eater. She simply didn't see the need to invite a man all the way into her life when he wouldn't be staying.

Because they never stayed.

She shrugged off the little voice that said *That's your own fault* and entered the Love Shack. Stepping inside the bar and grill was like going back a hundred years into an old western saloon. The walls were a deep, sinful bordello red and lined with old mining tools. The ceiling was covered with exposed beams, and lanterns hung over the scarred bench-style tables, now filled with the late dinner crowd. The air hummed with busy chatter, loud laughter, and music blaring out of the jukebox against the far wall.

Aubrey headed straight for the bar. "Something that'll make my bad day go away," she said to the bartender.

Ford Walker smiled and reached for a tumbler. He'd been five years ahead of Aubrey in school, and was one of the nice ones. He'd gone off and achieved fame and fortune racing sailboats around the world, and yet he'd chosen to come back to Lucky Harbor to settle down.

She decided to take heart in that.

He slid her a vodka cranberry. "Satisfaction guaranteed," he promised.

Aubrey wrapped her fingers around the glass, but before she could bring it to her lips, someone nudged her shoulder.

Ted, the ex-everything.

"Excuse me," he began before recognition hit and the "Oh, shit" look came into his eyes. He immediately started to move away, but she grabbed his arm.

"Wait," she said. "I need to talk to you. Did you get my messages?"

"Yeah," he said. "All twenty-five of them." Ted had been born with an innate charm that usually did a real good job of hiding the snake that lay beneath it. Even now, he kept his face set in an expression of easy amusement, exuding charisma like a movie star. With a wry smile for anyone watching, he leaned in close. "I didn't know there were that many different words for *asshole*."

"And you still wouldn't if you'd have called me back even once," she said through her teeth. "Why are you doing this? Why did you say those things about me in your book? And in chapter one!" She'd stopped reading after that and maybe had tossed the book, with great satisfaction, into a Dumpster.

Ted shrugged and leaned back. "I need the money."

"Am I supposed to believe anyone's going to buy your book?"

"Hey, if the only buyers are Lucky Harbor residents, I still make five grand, baby."

"Are you kidding me?"

"Not even a little bit," he said. "What's the big deal,

anyway? Everyone writes a book nowadays. And besides, it's not like you're known for being an angel."

Aubrey knew exactly who she was. She even knew why. She didn't need him to tell her a damn thing about herself. "The big deal is that *you're* the one who wronged people," she said. It was a huge effort to keep her voice down. She wasn't as good at charm and charisma as he was. "*You* two-timed me—along with just about every other woman in town, including the mayor's wife! On top of that, you let her steal fifty grand of the town's funds—and yet somehow, *I'm* the bad guy."

"Hey," he said. "You were the town clerk's admin. If anyone should have known what had happened to that money, it was you, babe."

How had she ever worked for this guy? How had she ever *slept* with him? Her friend Ali had told her that every woman had at least one notch on her bedpost she secretly regretted. But there was no secret to Aubrey's regret. She gripped her tumbler so tight that she was surprised it didn't shatter. "You said things about me that had nothing to do with the money."

He smiled. "So the book needed a little…titillation."

Shaking with fury, she stood. "You know what you are?"

"A great guy?"

Her arm bypassed her brain and capped off her no-good very bad day by tossing her vodka cranberry in his smug face.

But though he was indeed *at least* twenty-five kinds of an asshole, he was also fast as a whip. He ducked, and her drink hit the man on the other side of him.

Straightening, Ted chortled in delight as Aubrey got a look at the man she'd inadvertently drenched. She stopped breathing. Oh, God. Had she really thought her day couldn't get any worse? Why would she tempt fate by even thinking that? Because of course things had gotten worse. They always did.

Ben McDaniel slowly stood up from his bar stool, dripping vodka from his hair, eyelashes, nose…he was six-feet-plus of hard muscles and brute strength on a body that didn't carry a single extra ounce of fat. For the past five years, he'd been in and out of a variety of Third World countries, designing and building water systems with the Army Corps of Engineers. His last venture had been for the Department of Defense in Iraq, which Aubrey only knew because Lucky Harbor's Facebook page was good as gospel.

Ted was already at the door like a thief in the night, the weasel. But not Ben. He swiped his face with his arm, deceptively chill and laid-back.

In truth, he was about as badass as they came.

Aubrey should know; she'd seen him in action. But she managed to meet his gaze. Cool, casual, even. One had to be with Ben: The man could spot weakness a mile away. "I'm sorry," she said.

"Are you?"

She felt herself flush. He'd always seemed to see right through her. And she was pretty sure he'd never cared for her. He had good reason for that, she reminded herself. He just didn't know the half of it.

"Yes, I am sorry," she said. Her heart was pounding so loudly she was surprised she could hear herself speak. "Are you okay?"

He ran his fingers through a sexy disorder of sun-streaked brown hair. His eyes were the same color—light milk chocolate marbled with gold caramel. It was difficult to make such a warmly colored gaze seem hard, but Ben managed it with no effort at all. "Need to work on your aim," he said.

"No doubt." She offered a tight smile. It was all she could do—she hadn't taken a breath since she'd hit him with the drink. "Again, I'm…sorry." And with little spots of anxiety dancing in her vision, she backed away, heading straight for the door.

Outside, the night was blessedly cold, tendrils of the icy air brushing her hot cheeks. Lucky Harbor was basically a tiny little bowl sitting on the rocky Washington State coast, walled in by majestic peaks and lush forest. It was all an inky shadow now. Aubrey stood still a moment, hand to her thundering heart. It was still threatening to burst out of her rib cage as she worked on sucking in air so chilly it burned her lungs.

Behind her the door opened again. Panicked that it might be Ben, and not nearly ready for another face-to-face, she hightailed it out of the parking lot. In her three-inch high-heeled boots, she wasn't exactly stealthy, with the loud *click-click-click* of her heels, but she was fast. In two minutes, she'd rounded the block and finally slowed some, straining to hear any sounds that didn't belong to the night.

Like footsteps.

Damn it. He was following her. She quickened her pace again until she passed a church. The building, like nearly all the buildings in Lucky Harbor, was a restored Victorian from the late 1800s. It was a pale pink with blue-and-white trim and lit from the inside. The front door was wide open and inviting, at least compared to the rest of the night around her.

Aubrey wasn't a churchgoer. Her surgeon father hadn't believed in anything other than what could be found in a science book. Cold, hard facts. As a result, churches always held a sort of morbid fascination for her, one she'd never given in to. But with Ben possibly still on her trail, she hurried up the walk and stepped inside. Trying to catch her breath, she turned around to see if she'd been followed.

"Good evening," a man said behind her.

She jumped and looked around. He was in his thirties, average height and build, wearing jeans, a cable-knit sweater, and a smile that was as welcoming as the building itself.

But Aubrey didn't trust welcoming much.

"Can I help you?" he asked.

"No, thanks." Unable to resist, she once again peered outside.

No sign of Ben. That was only a slight relief. She felt like the fly who'd lost track of the spider.

"Are you sure you're okay?" the man asked. "You seem...troubled."

She resisted the urge to sigh. She was sure he was very nice, but what was it with the male species? Why was it so hard to believe she didn't need a man's help? Or a man, period? "Please don't take this personally, but I'm giving up men. Forever."

If he was fazed by her abruptness, it didn't show. Instead, his eyes crinkled in good humor as he slid his hands into his pockets and rocked back on his heels. "I'm the pastor here. Pastor Mike," he said. "A happily married man," he added with an easy smile.

If that didn't cap off her evening—realizing she'd been rude to a man of God for having the audacity to be nice to her. "I'm sorry." It didn't escape her notice that this was now the *second* time tonight she'd said those two very foreign words. "My life's in the toilet today…well, every day this week so far, really."

His eyes were warm and sympathetic. The opposite, she couldn't help but note, of the way Ben's had been.

"We all have rough patches," he said. "Is there anything I can do?"

She shook her head. "No. It's all me. I just need to stop making the same mistakes over and over." She took another peek into the night. The coast seemed clear. "Okay, I'm out. I'm going home to have the stiff drink I missed out on earlier at the bar."

"What's your name?" Pastor Mike asked.

She considered lying, but didn't want to further tempt fate—or God, or whoever was in charge of such things. "Aubrey."

"You don't have to be alone, Aubrey," he said very kindly, managing to sound gentle and in charge at the same time. "You're in a good place here."

She didn't have a chance to reply before he'd gently nudged her into a meeting room where about ten people were seated in a circle.

A woman was standing, wringing her hands. "My name's Kathy," she said to the group, "and it's been an hour since I last craved a drink."

The entire group said in unison, "Hi, Kathy."

An AA meeting, Aubrey realized, swallowing what

would have been a half-hysterical laugh as Pastor Mike gestured to a few empty chairs. He sat next to her and handed her a pamphlet. One glance told her it was a list of the twelve steps to recovery.

Step one: We admitted we were powerless over alcohol—that our lives had become unmanageable.

Oh, boy. Aubrey could probably get on board with the unmanageable life part, but really, what was she doing here? What would she possibly say to these people if she were asked to speak? *Hi, my name is Aubrey, and I'm a bitchaholic?*

Kathy began to speak about step eight, about how she was making a list of the people she'd wronged and making amends. After she finished and sat down, a man stood. Ryan, he told them. Ryan talked about something called his fearless moral inventory and how he, too, was working on step eight, making amends to the people he'd wronged.

Aubrey bit her lip. She'd never taken a fearless moral inventory, but it sounded daunting. Nor did she have a list of people she'd wronged, but if she did, it would be long. Horrifyingly long.

Ryan continued to talk with heartbreaking earnestness, and somehow, in spite of herself, she couldn't help but soak it all in, unbearably moved by his bravery. He'd come back from a military stint overseas angry and withdrawn and had driven his family away. He'd lost his job, his home, everything, until he'd found himself homeless on the street, begging strangers for money to buy booze. He spoke of how much he regretted hurting the people in his life and how he hadn't been able to obtain forgiveness from them. At least not yet, but he was still trying.

Aubrey found herself truly listening and marveling at his courage. She didn't even realize that she was so transfixed until Mike gently patted her hand. "You see?" he asked quietly. "It's never too late."

Aubrey stared at him, wondering if that could really be true. "You don't know for sure."

"I do." He said this with such conviction that she had no choice but to believe.

She thought about that as the meeting ended and she walked home to her loft above the Book & Bean. Her aunt Gwen had run the bookstore until her death last year, and her uncle—the building's owner—hadn't been able to bring himself to lease the space to anyone else. He was dating someone new these days, but the bookstore was still very sentimental to him.

Then, last month, Aubrey had left her job at the town hall after what she referred to as the Ted Incident. Restless, needing more from her life but not sure what, she'd signed a lease, both as an homage to her aunt Gwen—the bookstore had been a refuge for Aubrey as a troubled teen—and because she was determined to bring the bookstore back to its former glory.

The Book & Bean had been unofficially open for a week now, so it could start bringing in some desperately needed income, and in a month—after some renovations—she had plans to celebrate with a big grand opening party.

She was working on that.

And maybe she should be working on other things as well, such as her karma. That was heavy on her mind now after the AA meeting. Hearing people's problems and how they were trying to change things up for themselves had been extremely intimate and extremely uncomfortable—and yet somehow inspiring at the same time. She wasn't an alcoholic, but she had to admit the whole step eight thing had really intrigued her.

Could it be as easy as that, as making a list? Checking it twice? Trying to find out if she could pass on naughty and move on to nice?

Skipping the front entrance of the bookstore, she walked around to the back of the building and let herself in without turning on any lights. Inside, she headed up the narrow stairs to the loft.

Meow.

She flipped on a light and eyed Gus, an old, overweight gray cat who thought he was king of the mountain. She'd inherited him with the store. She knew nothing about cats, and in return, he acted like he knew nothing about humans, so they were even. "Hey," she said. "How was your evening?"

Gus turned around and presented her with his back.

"You know," she said, "I understand that some cats actually greet their people when they come home."

They'd had this talk before, and as always, this prompted no response from Gus.

"A dog would greet me," she said. "Maybe I should get a dog."

At this threat, Gus yawned.

Aubrey dropped her purse, hung up her coat, and took her first real breath in the past few hours. The place was tiny but cozy, and it was all hers ever since she'd filled it with an assortment of vintage—a.k.a. garage-sale and thrift-store—furniture. Her favorite part was the dartboard she'd gotten for a buck. It was a great stress reliever, especially when she pictured Ted's smug face as the bull's-eye.

Her kitchen table was covered with the drawings she'd made—her ideas for changing the layout of the store below.

Now that the other two storefronts in this building held flourishing businesses—a flower shop and a bakery—she had high hopes her bookstore would do well, too. A pipe dream. She was working against the odds, she knew. After all, this was the age of Kindle, Nook, and Kobo. Most people thought she was crazy for facing off against the digital world. But Aubrey had made a lifelong habit of facing off against the world, so why stop now, right? Besides, there was still a place for print books; she believed that with all her heart. And it was a statement of fact that sales in indie bookstores were up about 8 percent this year.

She was going to take heart in that. She pulled the pamphlet from her pocket and thought about her karma, which undoubtedly could use a little boost. Grabbing the small notepad she used for list making, she began a new list—of people she'd wronged.

Meow, Gus said, bumping her arm.

Reaching down, she stroked his soft fur, which he tolerated even though they both knew he just wanted dinner. She poured him a small cup of the low-calorie dry food the vet had insisted she switch to.

Gus stared at her balefully.

"I promised the doc," she said.

Huffing out a sigh, Gus heaved himself off to bed.

Aubrey went back to her list. It took her a while, and when she was done, she eyeballed the length of it. Surely it would've been a lot easier to simply stand tall and face Ben tonight rather than run into Pastor Mike.

But though Aubrey had a lot of faults, being lazy wasn't one of them. She was doing this, making amends, come hell or high water.

And there was a good chance she'd face both before this was over.

Kicking off her boots, she leaned back, staring at the list. Specifically at one item in particular.

Ben.

And he wasn't on it because she'd tossed her drink in his face.

Chapter 2

♥

It was early when Ben walked out of Lucky Harbor's deliciously warm bakery and into the icy morning. His breath crystallized in front of his face as he took a bite from his fresh bear claw.

As close to heaven as he was going to get.

He glanced back inside the big picture window to wave his thanks, but pastry chef Leah currently had her arms and lips entangled with her fiancé, who happened to be Ben's cousin Jack.

Jack looked to be pretty busy himself, with his tongue down Leah's throat. Turning his back to the window, Ben watched the morning instead as he ate his bear claw. Tendrils of fog had glided in off the water, lingering in long, silvery fingers.

After a few minutes, the bakery door opened behind him, and then Jack was standing at his side. He was in uniform for work, which meant that every woman driving down the street slowed down to get a look at him in his firefighter gear.

"Why are you dressed?" Ben asked.

"Because when I'm naked, I actually cause riots," Jack said, sliding on his sunglasses.

"You know what I mean." Not too long ago, Jack had made the change from firefighting to being the fire marshal, and he no longer suited up to respond to calls.

Jack shrugged. "I'm working a shift today for Ian, who's down with the flu." He pulled his own breakfast choice out of a bakery bag.

Ben took one look at the cheese croissant and shook his head. "Pussy breakfast."

Unperturbed by this, Jack stuffed it into his mouth. "You're just still grumpy because a pretty lady tossed her drink in your face last night."

Ben didn't react to this, because Jack was watching him carefully, and Jack, unlike anyone else, could read Ben like a book. But yeah, Aubrey had nailed him—and not in a good way.

Not that he wanted the sexy-as-hell blonde to nail him. Well, okay, maybe she'd occasionally done just that in a few of his late-night fantasies, but that was it. Fantasy. Because the reality was that he and Aubrey wouldn't mix well. He liked quiet, serene, calm. Aubrey didn't know the meaning of any of those things.

"It was an accident," he finally said.

"Oh, I know that," Jack said. "Just checking to see if you know it, too."

Ben looked at his watch. "Luke's late."

The three of them had been tight since age twelve, when Ben's mom, unable to take care of him any longer, had dropped him on her sister's doorstep—Jack's mom, Dee Harper. Luke had lived next door. The three boys had spent their teen years terrorizing the neighborhood and giving Ben's aunt Dee lots of gray hair.

"Luke's not late," Jack said. "He's here. He's in the flower shop trying to get into Ali's back pocket. Guess that's what you do when you're engaged."

Ben didn't say anything to this, and Jack blew out a breath. "Sorry."

Ben shook his head. "Been a long time."

"Yeah," Jack said. "But some things never stop hurting."

Maybe not. But it really had been forever ago that Ben had been engaged and then married. He and Hannah had had a solid marriage.

Until she'd died five years ago.

Ben went after his second bear claw while Jack looked down at his vibrating phone. "Shit. I've gotta go. Tell Luke he's an asshole."

"Will do." When he was alone again, Ben washed down his breakfast with icy cold chocolate milk. *You drink too much caffeine*, Leah had told him, all bossy and sweet at the same time, handing him the milk instead of a mug of coffee.

He planned to stop at the convenience store next for that coffee, and she'd never know. It was early, not close to seven yet, but Ben liked early. Fewer people. Quiet air. Or maybe that was just Lucky Harbor. Either way, he found he was nearly content—coffee would probably tip the scales *all the way* to content. The feeling felt...odd, like he was wearing an ill-fitting coat, so, as he did with all uncomfortable emotions, he shoved it aside.

A few snowflakes floated lazily out of the low, dense clouds. One block over, the Pacific Ocean carved into the harbor, which was surrounded by rugged, three-story-high bluffs teeming with the untouched forestland that was the Olympic Mountains. Around him, the oak-lined streets were strung with white lights, shining brightly through the morning gloom. Peaceful. Still.

A month ago, he'd been in the Middle East, elbows deep in a project to rebuild a water system for a war-torn land. Before that, he'd been in Haiti. And before that, Africa. And before that...Indonesia? Hell, it might have been another planet for all he remembered. It was all rolling together.

He went to places after disaster hit, whether man-made or natural, and he saw people at their very worst moments. Sometimes he changed lives, sometimes he improved them, but at some point over the past five years he'd become numb to it. So much so that when he'd gone to check out a new job site at the wrong place, only to have the right place blown to bits by a suicide bomber just before he got there, he'd finally realized something.

He didn't always have to be the guy on the front line. He could design and plan water systems for devastated countries from anywhere. Hell, he could become a consultant instead. Five years of wading knee deep in crap, both figuratively and literally, was enough for anyone. He didn't want to be in the *right* hellhole next time.

So he'd come home, with no idea what was next.

Polishing off his second bear claw, Ben sucked the sugar off his thumb. Turning to head toward his truck, he stopped short at the realization that someone stood watching him.

Aubrey. When he caught her eye, she said, "It *is* you," and dropped the things in her hands.

Her tone of voice had suggested she'd just stepped in dog shit with her fancy high-heeled boots. This didn't surprise Ben. She'd been two years behind him in school. In those years, he'd either been on the basketball court, trouble-seeking with Jack, or spending time with Hannah.

Aubrey had been the Hot Girl. He didn't know why, but there'd always been an instinctive mistrust between them, as if they both recognized that they were two kindred souls—*troubled* souls. He remembered that when she'd first entered high school she'd had more than a few run-ins with the mean girls. Then she became a mean girl. Crouching down, he reached to help her with the stuff she'd dropped.

"I've got it," she snapped, squatting next to him, pushing his hands away. "I'm fine."

She certainly looked the part of fine. Her long blonde hair was loose and shiny, held back from her face by a pale blue knit cap. A matching scarf was wrapped around her neck and tucked into a white wool coat that covered her from her chin to a few inches above her knees. Leather boots met those knees, leaving some bare skin below the hem of her coat. She looked sophisticated and hot as hell. Certainly perfectly put together. In fact, she was always purposefully put together.

It made him want to ruffle her up. A crazy thought.

Even crazier, she smelled so good he wanted to just sniff her for about five days. Also, he wanted to know what she was wearing beneath that coat. "Where did you come from?" he asked, as no car had pulled up.

"The building."

There were three storefronts in the building, one of the oldest in town—the flower shop, the bakery, and the bookstore. She hadn't come out of the flower shop or the bakery, he knew that much. He glanced at the bookstore. "It's not open yet."

The windows were no longer boarded up, he realized, and through the glass panes, he could see that the old bookstore was now a new bookstore, as shiny and clean and pretty as the woman before him.

She scooped up a pen and a lipstick, and he grabbed a fallen notebook.

"That's mine," she said.

"I wasn't going to take it, Aubrey," he said, and then, with no idea of what came over him—maybe her flashing eyes—he held the notebook just out of her reach as he looked at it. It was small and, like Aubrey herself, neat and tidy. Just a regular pad of paper, spiral bound, opened to a page she'd written on.

"Give it to me, Ben."

The notebook was nothing special, but clearly his holding on to it was making her uncomfortable. If it had been any other woman on the planet, he'd have handed it right over. But he didn't.

She narrowed her sharp, hazel eyes at him as she waggled impatient fingers. "It's just my grocery list."

Grocery list his ass. It was a list of names, and there was a Ben on it. "Is this me?"

"Wow," she said. "Egocentric much?"

"It says Ben."

"No, it doesn't." She tried to snatch at it again, but if there was one thing that living in Third World countries did for you it was give you quick instincts.

"Look here," he said, pointing to item number four. "*Ben.*"

"It's Ben and Jerry's. *Ice cream*," she informed him. "Shorthand. Give me the damn notepad."

Hmm. He might've been inclined to believe her, except there was that slight panic in her gaze, the one she hadn't been able to hide quickly enough. Straightening, he skimmed the names and realized he recognized a few. "Cathy Wheaton," he said, frowning. "Why do I remember that name?"

"You don't." Straightening as well, Aubrey tried to crawl up his body to reach the pad.

Ben wasn't too ashamed to admit he liked that. A lot.

His jacket was open. Frustrated, she fisted a hand in the material of his shirt, right over his heart. "Damn it, Ben—"

"Wait…I remember," he said, wincing, since she now had a few chest hairs in a tight grip. "Cathy…she was the grade in between us, right? A little skinny? Okay, a *lot* skinny. Nice girl."

Keeping her hold of him, Aubrey went still as stone, and Ben watched her carefully. Yeah, he was right about Cathy, and he went back to the list. "Mrs. Cappernackle." He looked at her again. "The librarian?"

With her free hand, Aubrey pulled her phone from her pocket and looked pointedly at the time.

He ignored this, because once his curiosity was piqued, he was like a dog with a bone, and his curiosity was definitely tweaked. "Sue Henderson." He paused, thinking. Remembering. "Wasn't she your neighbor when you were growing up? That bitchy DA who had you arrested when you put food coloring in her pool and turned it green?"

Aubrey's eyes were fascinating. Hazel fire. "Give. Me. My. List."

Oh, hell, no, this was just getting good—"Ouch!"

She'd twisted the grip she'd had on his shirt, yanking out the few hairs she'd fisted. She also got a better grip on the pad so that now they were tug-o-warring over it. "You could just tell me what this is about," he said.

"It's none of your business," she said, fighting him. "That's what it is."

"But it *is* my business when you're carrying around a list with my name on it."

"You know what? Google the name Ben and see how many there are. Now let go!" she demanded, just as the door to the flower shop opened and a uniformed officer walked out.

Luke, with his impeccable timing, as always. Eyeing the tussle before him, he raised a brow. "What's up, kids?"

"Officer," Aubrey said, voice cool, eyes cooler, as she jerked the pad from Ben's fingers. She shoved it into her purse, zipped it, and tugged it higher up on her shoulder. "This man"—she broke off to stab a finger in Ben's direction, as if there were any question about which man she meant—"is bothering me."

"Lucky Harbor's beloved troublemaker Ben McDaniel is bothering you?" Luke grinned. "I could arrest him for you."

"Could you maybe just shoot him?" she asked hopefully.

Luke's grin widened as he gave Ben a speculative glance. "Sure, but there'd be a bunch of paperwork, and I hate paperwork. How about I just beat him up a little bit?"

Aubrey looked as though this idea worked for her.

Ben gave her a long, steely look, and she rolled her eyes. "Oh, never mind." Still hugging her purse to herself, she turned, unlocked the bookstore, and vanished back inside it, slamming the door behind her.

"I thought the store was closed," Ben said, absently rubbing his chest where he was missing those few hairs.

"It was," Luke said. "Mr. Lyons is her uncle, and she rented the place from him and reopened the store. She's gone with a soft opening for now because she needs the income from the store, but she's wants to have a grand opening when the renovations are finished."

"How do you know so much?" Ben asked.

"Because I know all. And because Mr. Lyons called. He needs a carpenter, so I gave him your number."

"Mine?" Ben asked.

Luke shrugged. "Everyone in town knows you're good with a hammer."

"Yeah." Ben's phone rang, and he looked at the unfamiliar local number.

Luke looked, too. "That's him," he said. "Mr. Lyons."

Ben resisted the urge to do his usual and hit IGNORE. "McDaniel," he answered.

"Don't say no yet," Mr. Lyons immediately said. "I need a carpenter."

Ben slid Luke a look. "So I've heard. I'm not a carpenter. I'm an engineer."

"You know damn well before you got all dark and mysterious and broody that you were also handy with a set of tools," Mr. Lyons said.

Luke, who could hear Mr. Lyons's booming voice, grinned like the Cheshire cat and nodded, pointing at Ben.

Ben flipped him off. An older woman driving down the street rolled down her window and tsked at him. He waved at her in apology but she just waggled her bony finger at him. "Why not hire Jax?" he asked Lyons. "He's the best carpenter in town."

"He's got a line of customers from Lucky Harbor to Seattle, and I don't want to wait. My niece Aubrey needs help renovating the bookstore, and she needs someone good. That's you. Now I know damn well she can't afford you, so I'm paying, in my sweet Gwen's memory."

Well, shit.

"Oh, and don't give Aubrey the bill," Mr. Lyons said. "I don't want her worrying about it. She's going through some stuff, and I want to do this for her. For both my girls."

Ah, hell, Ben thought, feeling himself soften. He was such a sucker. "You should be asking me for a bid," he said.

"I trust you."

Jesus. "You shouldn't," Ben said firmly. "You—"

"Just start the damn work, McDaniel. Shelves. Paint. Hang stuff. Move a few walls, whatever she wants. She said something about how the place is too closed-in and dark, so figure it out. I'm going on a month-long cruise with my new girl, Elsie, and I need to know before I leave. You in or not?"

Ben wanted to say no. *Hell, no.* Being closed up in that bookstore with the beautiful, bitchy Aubrey for days and days? The reality of that didn't escape him. If he did this, surely one of them would kill the other before the work was done.

"Ben?"

"Yeah," he said, facing the inevitable. "I'll do it."

Whether he'd survive it was another thing entirely.

Chapter 3

♥

Two days later, Audrey opened her bookstore bright and early, much to Gus's annoyance. He liked to sleep in. Ignoring the curmudgeonly cat's dirty look, she took a moment to just look around. Despite her efforts, the store was still too closed-in and stuffy. She wanted to open it up by moving shelves back against the walls and adding a coffee and tea station. Definitely an Internet café and a comfortable seating area for a variety of reading and social clubs that she'd host here.

She wanted it more spacious. Sunny. Bright.

And God, please, *successful*...

Half an hour later, she welcomed her first customers of the day—a van of senior citizens. She'd coaxed the senior center into driving them over here two mornings a week for their book club.

"Hey, chickie," Mr. Elroy said, leaning heavily on his cane. He was decades past a midlife crisis, but he still managed to be quite the lothario at the senior center. "Which aisle has the sex stuff?"

He meant the how-to manuals. Anticipating him, she'd hidden any and all books on sex on the bottom shelf of the self-help aisle. No one ever went to that aisle. "Sorry," she said. "Don't have any."

"Really? Didn't anyone ever tell you that sex sells?"

Mr. Wykowski had come in behind Mr. Elroy. "You need a manual?" he asked Mr. Elroy. "All I need is a little blue pill."

And so went the morning.

When the seniors were gone, a bus full of kids showed up, as Aubrey had also made a deal with the elementary school.

The kids managed to find the sex manuals. Luckily, Aubrey was quick on the uptake and confiscated the explicit reading material before a single book spine got cracked. By the time they left, she was exhausted. In the past week, she'd learned several vital facts. One: Seniors and kids were a lot alike. And two: She wasn't making enough money for this.

By lunchtime she was back to daydreaming about the "bean" part of Book & Bean. Right now she was using a back corner, which was really a storage closet, to make tea and coffee. She wanted to remove the door and wall and replace them with a curved, waist-high counter that would create a coffee and reading niche. She ate a PB&J while perusing the Internet for affordable bar stools for the spot.

But for now, most everything she wanted was out of her budget. She knew she could ask her father for help, but she'd have to choke on her own pride to call him, and she wasn't good at that.

So instead she'd gone to the local hardware store and bought a book on renovation. She'd read it from beginning to end and thought she could handle some of the easy stuff on her own. She planned to tear out the closet herself, and she'd brought in the crowbar from the back of her car to do just that.

Clearly, it'd be far easier to suck it up and call her dad, but she rarely took the easy route. Her parents had divorced when she'd been ten and her sister, Carla, eight. Her father, William, retired from being an orthopedic surgeon, was a consultant now, but still he had a hard time talking to mere mortals. Not her mom. Tammy was an ex–beauty queen working as a manicurist at the local beauty shop, and she loved to talk. In the divorce, she'd gotten Aubrey, and William had taken the child prodigy, Carla.

An unorthodox custody arrangement, but it'd allowed the divorced couple to stay away from each other and avoid arguments. It'd also alienated Aubrey from her father, who'd recently remarried and had two new daughters now. Plus Carla had followed in his footsteps and was a first-year resident at the hospital, heading toward the same brilliant career path as her dad.

And then there was Aubrey. Living with Tammy had meant that the pressure of an Ivy League school and a medical career were off the table, but there'd been other pressures. Tammy had been the ultimate beauty queen and had turned into a beauty-queen mom, entering Aubrey in every beauty pageant and talent competition she could afford. There'd been many—at least until Aubrey had gotten old enough to put her foot down and refuse to put on one more tiara. She'd been thirteen when that had happened.

That's when the pressure to be a model had begun, but after a few disastrous auditions, even Tammy had been forced to admit defeat. Not that she'd ever given up impressing upon Aubrey the importance of beauty, the right lipstick color, and posture. Aubrey had taken every dance class known to man and also gone to grace school. Yes, there really was a school for that. Her mother'd had to work two jobs to pay for it all, but she'd been happy to do it. Or so she'd claimed every single night when she'd come home, kick off her shoes, and sag in exhaustion onto the couch.

Sugar, could you make Mama a gin and tonic?

Aubrey had hated those classes. Hated. But her mom had given up so much for her, so she'd done it. She'd learned early how to primp, walk with a thick book on top of her head—even if she'd rather be reading it—and look ready for the camera in fifteen minutes. And in spite of herself, she'd even managed to get a BA degree in liberal studies from an online institution. She had the tuition loans to prove it.

The last time she'd talked to her dad, he'd questioned her as though she were a three-year-old. "A bookstore, Aubrey? In today's day and age? Why don't you find a better use of your money—say, like shredding it?"

But she loved books. Maybe she wasn't exactly a traditional bookworm, but she could quote Robert Louis Stevenson poems, and she loved mysteries. She'd always been a big reader, back from when she'd been a child and had come here after school.

Her aunt would serve her tea and cookies and let Aubrey curl up in a corner and just be free—free of wondering why she wasn't good enough to be wanted by her own father, free of her mom's pressure to look perfect and be something she wasn't. Free of trying to fit in at school and failing. Back then, she'd huddled here in this warm place and inhaled books to escape. She'd started with the classics but had quickly found thrillers and horror, which she still loved to this day.

But back then, being here, being left in peace and quiet...it'd been her idea of heaven.

And maybe, just a little bit, she'd reopened the store hoping for that same safe place to curl up and lick her wounds.

Not exactly the smartest reason to open a bookstore. She knew better than anyone that memories and sentiment didn't a business plan make, and that a business certainly shouldn't be run from the heart.

But Aubrey had rarely, if ever, operated from her heart, and it hadn't gotten her anywhere. Time to try something new. The bookstore was new thing number one.

Her list was number two.

The door to the store opened, and Aubrey smiled a greeting at the woman who entered. "Can I help you?"

"I'm looking for some fiction. Historical fiction."

In one short week, Aubrey had learned that "historical fiction" didn't usually mean the classics. Instead, it almost always meant the romance section. She pointed the way and, a few minutes later, sold a copy of the Fifty Shades trilogy.

During a late-afternoon lull in business, Aubrey went to work on demolishing the closet wall.

Halfway through, the bell above her door rang. Naturally. Dusting herself off, she moved into view just as another woman came in.

"I'm looking for something to take with me on vacay next week," she told Aubrey.

"What do you like to read?"

"Oh," she said, "a little of everything…"

Aubrey knew this *also* meant the romance section, so she again pointed the way.

The woman leaned in close and whispered, "Do you carry that *Fifty Shades* book? And maybe…book covers?"

Aubrey was back to attempting to demolish the back wall when the bell rang again.

A woman entered with her three little kids and one of those tiny dogs that looked like a drowned rat in her shoulder bag. The thing was yapping as though his life were in mortal danger.

From his perch in a nook beneath the stairs, Gus, three times the size of the dog, growled low in his throat.

The dog immediately shut up. Probably terrified that the cat was going to sit on him. Aubrey gave Gus a warning look. They'd had this talk. There would be no bitch-slapping the customers, even the four-legged ones.

Gus stalked off all stiff-legged, with his tail swishing in the air. Aubrey reached out and stroked the little dog's head, and he pushed closer for more.

For just about all her life, she'd wanted a dog, preferably a puppy—one of the big breeds. She'd begged and pleaded her case, but her dad—pre-divorce—had always been firm.

Puppies make noise.

Puppies are messy.

No puppies, he'd always said. Ever. For a while there, Aubrey had actually believed she could get him to change his mind. She'd even rescued a dog once and brought it home, convinced her father wouldn't be able to turn away a stray.

The puppy had been gone the next day. "The owners came and got him," her dad had said. "He's living on a farm in the country."

After her mom had divorced her dad, Aubrey had gone to work on her mom. Tammy loved dogs and was on board. But they'd lived in a pet-unfriendly building, and that had never changed.

Aubrey had never gotten her puppy.

And now she had a fat, old-man cat named Gus.

Her customer, looking harassed and exhausted, sent the kids to the children's section and smiled wanly at Aubrey. "What would you recommend for me to read?"

"What do you like?"

"Anything."

Aubrey nodded. She'd found that this was rarely actually true: In fact, it usually meant that the person wasn't a reader at all. "What's the last book you read and enjoyed?" she asked, looking for a hint just in case she was wrong.

"Uh...I can't remember."

Nope, not wrong. Aubrey directed her to the latest Nicholas Sparks. After the sale, she went back to the demolition.

The other day, she'd put a bucket of books just outside the store. They were gently used cookbooks, encyclopedias, and miscellaneous nonfiction. The cookbooks had vanished almost immediately. The other books still sat out there, and despite the fact that she had a big FREE sign posted, every day at least one person would stick his or her head in the door and yell, "Are these really free?"

Today it was a twentysomething guy wearing a ski cap, down jacket, bright yellow biker shorts, and round purple sunglasses, à la John Lennon. Mikey had been a couple of years behind Aubrey in school, and by the looks of things, was still a complete stoner.

"Dude," he said. "Are these books really free?"

"Yep," she told him.

His brow went up, and he surveyed the store. "So...is everything free?"

"Nope."

"'Kay. Thanks, dude."

At the end of the day, Aubrey tallied the sales, got the day's new arrivals stocked and shelved, and locked up. Seeing the lights still on in the flower shop, she moved down two doors and knocked on the back door.

Ali opened up, wearing a T-shirt, jeans, an apron, and lots of flower petals. She smiled and pulled Aubrey in. "You're just in time. Leah brought over her leftovers, and I'm about to inhale them all by myself."

Leah operated the bakery between Aubrey's bookstore and Ali's flower shop. She was sitting on the counter near Ali's work space, licking chocolate off her fingers. "Better hurry," she said. "Ali wasn't kidding. There's two kinds of people here, the quick and the hungry."

Not needing to be told twice, Aubrey moved toward the bakery box and helped herself to a mini chocolate croissant. No one made them like Leah. "Oh, my God," she said on a moan after her first bite. "*So* good. I've been tearing up that back wall and am starving."

"I hate you," Leah said.

Aubrey felt herself go still and, out of a lifetime habit of hiding her feelings, schooled her features into a cool expression that she knew was often mistaken for bitchiness. "What?"

"You just worked for hours without getting a speck of dirt on you?"

Aubrey looked down at herself. "Well—"

"And your hair is perfect," Ali broke in, taking in Aubrey's appearance. "I hate that about you."

Leah nodded.

Both of them had businesses running in the black, hot-as-hell boyfriends who loved them madly, and their lives on track. And they were jealous. Of her.

It was just about the nicest compliment they could pay her, and she went back to breathing. She should have known they weren't being mean—neither of them had a mean bone in her body. "Lifelong habit," she said. "Being perfect."

Leah laughed and offered another goody from the bakery box. "You could at least get chunky. Or a little dirty, just once in a while."

"I don't usually get dirty."

Ali shook her head. "Back to hating you, Wellington."

Aubrey smiled now and reached for the last mini croissant at the same time as Ali. "I'll totally fight you for it," she said.

Ali grinned. "I could kick your skinny ass, but since the croissant will just go straight to my hips, it's all yours."

Aubrey took a bite of the croissant, licked her fingers clean, and then pulled her laptop out of her bag. "I finally got Internet, and I'm trying to decide what to name my Wi-Fi. I'm torn between FBI Security Van and Guy in Your Tree. Any opinions?"

Leah snorted chocolate milk out her nose.

"How about Pay for Your Own Effing Wi-Fi, You Cheap Ass?" Ali asked.

They laughed for a few minutes, cleaned up their croissant crumbs, and then Leah dropped the bomb. "Heard about Ben," she said.

Aubrey nearly dropped her laptop. "Um...what?" Her heart was thundering, but she was telling herself that they couldn't know. *No one* knew. Not even Ben himself.

Leah was looking at her oddly. "The whole tossing-your-drink-in-his-face thing at the Love Shack the other night," she said.

Oh, *that.* Aubrey relaxed. "It was an accident. I was aiming for Ted." She took a side look at Ali because one of the most weaselly, shitty things Ted had done was sleep with *both* Ali and Aubrey while letting them each think that he was single. And they hadn't been the only women he'd done that to, either.

Aubrey had recovered quickly because...well, she knew men were jerks.

Ali had been thrown for an emotional loop, and, clearly remembering just that, she smiled grimly. "I hope you ordered a second drink and corrected your error."

Aubrey shook her head. "I got...discombobulated."

"You?" Ali asked. "Pissed off, yes. But discombobulated? That's not like you."

Yeah, Aubrey was *real* good at the tough-girl facade. But then again, she'd had a lifetime of practice. "Hard to keep it together when you toss a drink in the wrong guy's face."

"And not just any wrong guy," Leah said with a laugh.

"Ben McDaniel. Lucky Harbor's favorite son. How'd he take it?"

Aubrey shook her head at the memory. "He didn't even flinch."

"He wouldn't," Leah said. "He's pretty badass."

He hadn't always been like that. In school, he'd been the first to land himself in trouble, but he'd been fun-seeking, not tough as nails and impenetrable. Even through college. Afterward, he'd been an engineer for the city and had led a nice normal life.

Then his wife had died, and he'd taken off like a bat out of hell, living a life of adrenaline and danger as if survivor's guilt had driven his every move.

"It was his job," Leah said. "He saw and did things that changed him."

Ali was watching Aubrey carefully. "Maybe you should try to make it up to him."

Aubrey could see a certain light—a matchmaking light—in her eyes, so she headed to the door.

"Where you going?" Leah asked.

"Things to do."

"Or you're chicken," Ali called after her with a laugh.

Or that…But the truth was, Aubrey wasn't chicken. She was realistic. Nothing would, or could, ever happen between her and Ben.

No matter how much she might secretly wish otherwise.

Two minutes later, she was in her car. It was time to face the names on her list. Up first was her sister, Carla.

They weren't close. Growing up in two separate households had done that. Living with parents who didn't speak to each other had done that. Carla being told that she had gotten all the brains had done that.

But eight years ago, Carla had needed a favor. She'd found herself needing to be at her job at the same time as she'd needed to sign some documents to accept a very important internship, so she'd asked her look-alike sister to go sign for her.

Aubrey had been working her butt off full-time and trying to keep full-time school hours as well. Busy, exhausted, hungry, and admittedly bitchy, Aubrey had agreed to the favor, even though she'd known it would be a real crunch to get there in time. She'd left a little later than she should have, gotten stuck in traffic, showed up late, and lost Carla the internship.

Carla had been forced to ask their dad to step in, and she still hadn't forgiven Aubrey.

Sighing at the memory, Aubrey parked at the hospital where Carla worked and asked for her sister at the front desk. Aubrey was kept cooling her heels for twenty-five minutes, though when Carla finally showed up in the reception area in scrubs and a doctor's coat with a stethoscope around her neck, she seemed genuinely exhausted and surprised. "Hey," she said. "What's wrong? Mom?"

"Everything's fine," Aubrey said. "I just wanted to talk to you."

Carla nodded but gave her watch a quick, not-so-discreet glance. "About?"

Aubrey drew a deep breath and then let it go. "Remember the time you asked me for a favor and I screwed it up?"

Carla's gaze was moving around the room, taking in the people waiting to be called by the hospital's various departments. "Uh-huh."

"Well, I want to apologize," Aubrey said, "and find a way to make it up to you."

Carla looked at her watch again. "Wait—which time was this again?"

"The one and only time I screwed up," Aubrey said a little tightly.

Carla's gaze landed on Aubrey then, looking a little amused now. She pulled a protein bar from her pocket and offered half to Aubrey, but since it looked like cardboard, Aubrey shook her head. "It was when I was supposed to sign those documents for your internship," Aubrey said. "And I got there late."

Carla chewed her cardboard bar. "Oh, that's right. You were probably busy with Mom, having your hair or nails done. That was your life, right? Dressing up and being a beauty queen, while I had to go to the toughest school and study all the time."

Aubrey had been operating under the assumption that *she* was the jealous sister. And she *was* jealous as hell and always had been, because Carla had had it all: brains, the big fancy medical degree, not to mention their father's pride and adoration. But in feeding her green monster over the years, it'd somehow escaped her attention that Carla might have been jealous as well.

She didn't know what to make of that.

"I lost the internship," Carla said, "and had to wait an entire year to get another shot at it. Dad was fit to be tied. He'd set the interview up in the first place. He said—" She broke off, clearly tempering herself.

"What?" Aubrey asked. "He said what?"

"That I'd acted like you."

Aubrey absorbed the unexpected hit and nodded.

"Well, then, I imagine he was quite pleased to know it was me who screwed up and not you."

Carla's smile was brittle, and Aubrey wondered if she smiled like that, too. "I never told him," Carla said. "How could I? I'd gone on and on about how you were changing, how you were maturing. How I could *count on you.*"

Aubrey winced. "I'm sorry," she said quietly. "I'd like to make it up to you."

Carla gave a small laugh. "How? How could you possibly do that?"

"I don't know," Aubrey said. "We still look like twins. Maybe you have another conflict of interest, and I could—"

"What? Operate for me? Meet a patient and discuss treatment?"

Aubrey met her sister's eyes. They were hazel, like her own, magnified slightly from the glasses Carla had worn since grade school. They only added to the smart image.

She wasn't going to get forgiveness—she could see that now. And she probably didn't deserve it anyway. "No," she said quietly. "I can't do any of those things. We both know that."

And there was the problem. The big flaw in her grand scheme—and there was always a flaw. She didn't know *how* to make things right. And anyway, who would forgive her? She certain didn't deserve forgiveness. Holding in the despair that this thought brought, she turned to go.

Carla didn't stop her.

It was dark outside when she got back to the Book & Bean, and she stopped short just outside the door. She'd locked up when she left and turned off the lights.

But the door was unlocked now, and the lights were

on. She went still, then pulled out her phone and dialed 911. She didn't hit SEND, but kept her thumb hovered over CALL. Taking a step inside, she paused. "Hello?"

"Hey."

The low, slightly rough voice wasn't what had her heart pumping. That honor went to the fact that there was a man on a ladder in the back of her store.

Ben.

He was in jeans, wearing a tool belt slung low on his hips, his T-shirt clinging to him. He seemed a little irritated, a little sweaty, and just looking at him Aubrey got a whole lot hot and bothered in places that had no business being hot and bothered by this man at all. "What are you doing in here?" she asked.

"I work here."

"What are you talking about? Get out."

"Sorry, Sunshine." He wasn't even looking at her, but using some sort of long, clawlike tool to pull down a ceiling tile above the wall she'd been working on. And his tool worked way better than hers.

His movements were agile and surprisingly graceful for a guy his size. Not that he was bulky in any way. Nope: That tall, built body was all lean, tough muscle, and it screamed power. And with each subtle movement, his body made it clear that it knew exactly what to do with all that power. "The owner of this building hired me," he said. "Said you were making a mess of things because your pride was bigger than your wallet."

This caught her completely off guard, both the insult and the information. "My uncle owns this building," she said.

He smiled thinly. "Yep. Happy birthday."

"It's not my birthday."

"Then happy you've-got-a-great-uncle day."

She pulled out her phone and punched in her uncle's number.

"He left on a month-long cruise with Elsie," Ben said.

Damn it. That was true. He'd just recently started dating again and was seeing Leah's grandma Elsie. Aubrey tossed her phone and purse aside and went hands on hips, giving off the intimidation vibe that worked with just about everyone. Except, apparently, Ben, who didn't even take a bit of notice. Instead, he reached down with that claw tool in his hand. "Hold this a minute," he said.

Was he kidding? "I don't take orders from you."

"I imagine not, since you don't know the meaning of taking orders."

She opened her mouth, but before she could speak, he gave the tool a very slight jiggle in her direction.

The motion was filled with such authority and innate demand that she walked toward him to take the thing before she even realized her feet were moving. It was heavy, and she let it fall to her side as he pulled himself up with nothing more than his biceps and vanished.

She stared up into the space. "Hey."

He didn't answer, and she got worried. "Ben?"

There was a slight rainfall of debris, and then he was back, lowering himself out of the hole like an Avenger, shoulder and arm and back muscles bulging and defined as he dropped lithely to his feet.

She let out a breath.

He brushed off his hands and turned, and then nearly tripped over Gus.

Meow.

"Watch out," Aubrey said. "He doesn't like—"

Ben squatted low and stroked the cat. Gus plopped onto his back with a grunt, exposing his belly for a rub.

"—to be touched much," Aubrey finished, and then rolled her eyes as Gus soaked up Ben's affection, even sending Aubrey a "be jealous, bee-yotch" look from slitty eyes.

Her cat was a man ho.

When Ben stood again, he looked at Aubrey for the first time. The briefest of frowns flashed on his face. Still dirty, still a little damp, and still complete sex on a stick, he took a step toward her.

Thinking he wanted the tool, she thrust it out at him. But he didn't take it. Instead, he stepped into her personal space and crowded her both physically and mentally.

"What's wrong?" he asked.

Chapter 4

♥

If Ben knew anything about Aubrey Wellington, it was that she was one cool, tough, hard customer. He'd once seen her stare down an entire pack of mean girls at school with no fear—at least none showing. She didn't back down from much.

But she backed away from him and turned so he couldn't see her face. She definitely wasn't on her game at the moment. In fact, if he wasn't mistaken, she'd been...crying? Unable to imagine what could have rattled her so badly, much less bring her to tears, he moved closer to take the tool from her, tossing it aside as he turned her to face him. "You've been crying."

She looked away. He put a finger under her chin and brought her face back to his. "You've been crying," he said again.

She blew out a sigh and slapped his hand away. "You're a man. You're not supposed to notice," she said.

He took another step toward her, and he had no idea

why. Maybe because those usually razor-sharp hazel eyes were soft now. Soft and maybe even warm. She was vulnerable, and it was bringing out some crazy instinct in him to try to soothe or comfort her. And then there was the fact that he'd clearly affected her. When he'd come close, her breathing had hitched audibly.

Awareness?

Frustration?

Irritation?

A combination of all of them, no doubt, but he'd take it over her usual indifference. "Talk to me, Aubrey."

She let out a sound that might have been a laugh or a sob, and her eyes went suspiciously shiny. "I just have something in my eye, that's all."

He'd spent his formative teenage years under the authority of his aunt Dee, who'd cried at the drop of a hat. He wasn't fond of a woman's tears, but they didn't scare him. He waited her out with a pointed look.

She sucked in a breath and put her hands on his chest. The touch gave him a pure electrical jolt that stunned him stupid. He had no idea where this sexual tension was coming from, but he liked it. He didn't get a chance to figure it out before she gave him a little nudge that was actually more like a shove.

He didn't budge, and this time there was no mistaking the sound she made. Pure temper. "You're breathing on me," she snapped, and walked by him, shoulder-checking him hard enough to make him smile.

Whatever her problem, she no longer felt like crying—which worked for him.

"I can't afford you," she said.

"Your uncle's paying. Whatever you need."

That had her step faltering for the briefest second, but she caught herself. Looking touched, she said, "I'm going to pay him back."

"Not my deal."

She strode to the makeshift worktable he'd set up. Two sawhorses with a four-by-eight piece of plywood across them. He'd unrolled the set of plans he'd drawn up based on what Mr. Lyons had told him needed to be done. It was a fairly big job, actually, one that would take his mind off his own life for a while. Just what he needed.

Aubrey stared at the plans for a long moment. "This is wrong," she said, pointing to the shelving. "I want open shelves, four feet tall max, in wide rows. And this." She dragged her fingers across the half wall that her uncle had suggested to break up the room. "I want it open. And here…" She tapped a long finger on the tiny kitchen area in the back, which she'd started to demolish herself and made a mess of. "I want the half wall here."

"Half-walled shelves severely limit your product space," he said. "And without a wall there"—he nudged her finger with his, bringing it to the spot he was indicating—"your store will be noisy. And why do you want the serving area exposed to your customers?"

"Not that it's any of your business," she said, "but this is going to be more than a bookstore. It's going to be a gathering spot, where the lonely can come and make friends, where book clubs and knitting clubs alike can use the space for their meetings, where drinks and goodies can be easily served in comfy chairs and sofas while my customers read."

"How do you intend to make any money if you let them read here instead of buying?"

She shot him a grim smile that was sheer determination and grit. "Don't tell me I won't make it work," she said. "Because I will."

He looked down into her face for a long moment, then nodded. "I wouldn't bet against you."

She went still, and that's when he realized how close they were standing to each other. So close that he could see her eyes weren't just a mix of brown and green; gold swirled in their depths as well. If she'd been wearing any lip color, she'd long ago chewed it off, leaving her full mouth naked and bare—and tantalizing.

She was staring at his mouth, too, with an expression that gave nothing away, but he'd have sworn he'd seen the briefest flash of yearning. "Aubrey."

She blinked, as if coming out of some sort of dream, and cleared her throat as she tapped the plans again. "You'll have to redo these."

Shocked at how badly he suddenly wanted to taste her, he shook it off. "Anything else I should know?"

"Yeah." She crossed her arms. "I need the work done yesterday, but I don't want the work to be too intrusive on business. And also, it's probably best if our paths steer clear of each other as much as possible."

"You trying to piss me off so I'll keep my distance?" he asked.

"Would it work?"

It sure as hell should. Keeping his distance from Aubrey Wellington was of utmost importance. Wasn't it? Suddenly he couldn't remember why that was, exactly.

A tall figure appeared in the open doorway. Jack. He knocked on the doorjamb twice and then propped it up with a broad shoulder. "Ready?" he asked Ben with all his perfection of timing.

The two of them were meeting Luke for dinner. Ben shook off whatever was going on between him and Aubrey, although it took a surprising amount of effort to do so. "Ready," he said, and without another word grabbed the sweatshirt he'd left draped over the back of a couch.

"Hey," Aubrey called after him. "You never answered me."

"Because I don't answer to you, Sunshine." But yeah, he knew he'd work early and late to avoid as much inter-action with her as possible.

Jack watched Ben shut the bookstore front door and then check to make sure it was locked. "Huh," he said.

"Huh what?"

"Nothing," Jack said.

"It's something."

"Okay. You've been back a month and you're already bored?"

Ben shrugged.

"'Cause if you are," Jack said, "I need help."

"With what?"

"As fire marshal, I inherited all these pet projects for town council and the like. And in all the monthly meet-ings, everyone always says they'll help, but then they don't answer my calls."

"What do you need?"

"Everything. There's the senior center—"

"Pass," Ben said quickly. "Those old ladies are sexu-ally depraved miscreants."

"Afraid of Lucille?"

Lucille was a gazillion years old, and there were ru-

mors that she'd been the first person to inhabit Lucky
Harbor, around the time of the dinosaur age. She was still
in town, running an art gallery and the gossip mill with
equal fervor. "Hell, yeah, I'm afraid of her," Ben said.

"Me, too," Jack admitted. "Okay, no to the senior center. How about a project at the rec center? It's called Craft
Corner." He smiled. "Should be right up your alley. You
supervise after-school crafts twice a week."

"Crafts?" Ben asked in disbelief. "Do I look like a
crafts kind of guy to you?"

Jack grinned. "You're a builder at heart, man. Figure it
out. The kids really need someone, and you've got a lot
of knowledge to impart."

"Uh-huh."

"And the principal of the school is a really hot, single
brunette. How long has it been since you had a hot
woman look at you?"

About three minutes... "Maybe," Ben said noncom-
mittally.

Commercial Row was lined with shops, including the
requisite grocery store, post office, and gas station. A few
patches of snow and more than a few patches of ice lin-
gered here and there from the last storm. With the dark
had come an icy chill that had Ben shoving his hands in
his pockets. The temperature tended to drop the moment
the sun did.

When Jack spoke next, his voice was void of his usual
good humor. "So. Aubrey Wellington? Really? You sure
about that?"

"What about her?"

"You know what. She's trouble with a capital *T*."

Yeah, Jack was right. Ben already knew.

"Tell me you got that," Jack said.

"I got that."

There was a full minute of silence between them as they continued to walk toward the Love Shack. But then Jack, who'd never been real good at leaving anything alone, said, "There was something in the air between you two."

"Animosity?" Ben asked.

Jack laughed. "Not exactly."

"What, then?"

Jack shrugged, but Ben knew this wasn't necessarily an I-don't-know shrug. Because Jack knew.

Ben knew, too. But he held his tongue. It was natural for him to do so, and plus, as an added bonus, it drove Jack wild. Jack couldn't handle silences any more than he could handle leaving things alone.

And sure enough, after another minute, Jack started whistling. He couldn't whistle worth shit, and he was completely tone-deaf—which meant that hearing him whistle was far better than hearing him sing. But still, Ben wasn't in the mood for either. Especially since Jack only sang when he was being obnoxious. It was his own special brand of torture.

"Spit it out," Ben said.

Jack shook his head. "Nothing to spit out."

Ben looked at him, but Jack went silent. It was a first.

"I'm just working on the bookstore," Ben finally said.

Jack blew on his hands and shoved them into his front pockets as they continued to walk.

"You know damn well her uncle hired me," Ben said.

Jack nodded and squared his shoulders against the evening's wind.

"And we're not even going to be in the shop at the same time," Ben said.

Jack snorted.

"Damn it." Impressed that his own techniques had been used against him—and that it'd worked—Ben caved like a cheap suitcase. "Okay, so there *was* a weird vibe between us. But it's nothing."

"It was way more than nothing," Jack said. "The two of you practically melted the place down." He paused. "Do I need to give you the birds-and-the-bees talk?"

At that, Ben had to laugh. "Shut up. I lost my cherry two years before you did."

"Yeah, well, you were a real ho back then."

This was true. Ben had discovered women early. And then in high school, he'd tangled with the pretty, smart, and funny Hannah, and he'd fallen hard. He'd drawn her over to the dark side, and she'd loved it. Right up until she'd dumped him just before college.

Two years later, they'd run into each other at a party. She'd grown up a lot, and so had he. They'd gotten back together, and he'd put a ring on her finger so as not to lose her again. Then he'd lost her anyway when a drunk driver had crossed the center line and hit her car head-on.

He'd not gone back to his bad boy ways. Instead, he'd quit his nine-to-five engineering desk job and gone off the grid with the Army Corps and then the DOD.

As if reading his mind, Jack's smile faded. "It's been a while for you. With a woman."

Yeah, it'd been a while. But not as long as Jack thought. "I've been with women since Hannah."

If this was news to Jack, he didn't show it. "Just hookups."

"Yeah," Ben said. "So?"

"So what I saw back there in the bookstore didn't feel like it'd be a quick hookup."

"You're wrong," Ben said.

Jack was quiet a moment. "No one would blame you if you went for it again. For love. No one. It's just…Aubrey Wellington?"

The doubt in his voice pissed Ben off. Which was asinine. No one knew Ben better than Jack—no one alive, anyway. He knew what Ben had gone through after Hannah's death.

He knew Ben had loved her. The real kind of love. The once-in-a-lifetime, forever kind. For a guy who'd been pretty much dumped by his own parents and dropped at his aunt Dee's house at the age of twelve, it shouldn't have been possible for him to feel it at all. But his aunt Dee had mothered him relentlessly. And Jack's father—before his untimely, heroic death fighting a fire—had been a real dad to Ben. Jack had been a brother. Between the three of them, they'd taught Ben love.

And he'd had it with Hannah—a solid, soul-deep, comfortable love.

But it was long gone now, and while he missed it, he didn't want to risk it again.

Jack was looking at him, waiting for a response or reaction, and Ben shook his head. "You're reading too much into things," he said. "I'm just working at her bookstore."

"That's it?"

"That's it." And he one hundred percent meant it.

Okay, maybe ninety percent…

Chapter 5

A few days later, Ben got up early and went for a hard run. He was met at the halfway point—the pier—by Sam Brody. Sam was an old high school buddy. The two of them had landed here in Lucky Harbor under shitty circumstances—Ben because his mom had dumped him and Sam because he'd been sent to yet another foster home.

And though Ben'd had Jack and Dee and a whole bunch of people who cared, none of them had ever quite understood where he'd come from.

Sam had understood.

Sam had come from worse.

They nodded at each other and fell into step, a hard, fast pace that suited the both of them. They didn't talk. They often never said a word while running. Ben wasn't a big talker anyway, although next to Sam he looked like Chatty Cathy.

Still, the silence was always comfortable, like an old

shoe. Three miles later, on the outskirts of the county, they finally slowed to their usual cool-down pace and headed back.

"How's it going with the latest boat?" Ben asked. Sam built boats by hand, and his workmanship was amazing.

"It's going," Sam said simply. "How's it going at the bookstore?"

"Just making shelves."

Sam snorted, the sound managing to convey a sarcastic "Yeah, right" and "Good luck with Aubrey, buddy" all in one.

At the pier, they separated with a fist bump, each to go on with his own day.

After a shower, Ben headed out. He and Jack shared a downtown duplex. Jack was out front walking his 150-pound black and white Great Dane, Kevin. Kevin didn't like to exert a lot of energy, so they never walked far. And mostly, his favorite walk was to his food bowl and back. But sometimes in the mornings, Kevin liked to check things out—like which dogs had peed near his territory. Kevin did his business, and then he and Jack headed off to the fire station for work.

Ben drove to his aunt Dee's house. She was working hard at recovering from breast cancer. And though it had kicked her ass, she was now kicking the cancer's ass. But sometimes she was too tired to take care of herself, and on those days, Ben and Jack took turns doing it for her. It was only fair, since she'd taken care of the both of them for the better part of their lives.

As he'd been doing several times a week, Ben let himself into her place and headed straight for the kitchen, where he'd drum up a nice, protein-rich meal.

But in the kitchen doorway, he stopped short in surprise.

Retired fire marshal Ronald McVane stood flipping sausages at the range top where Ben had created some of his best work.

Dee sat at the table, serenely sipping tea.

When Jack's dad died, a little part of Dee had died with him. Okay, a big part. In the years since, she'd battled depression and anxiety. Not once in all that time had she dated anyone.

But she was dating now. She was dating Ronald and had been for the past month, very casually. What Ben hadn't realized was that the casual part of the program had changed, because Ronald was barefoot and his shirt was unbuttoned. And, most telling of all, Dee was still in her bathrobe, with her hair more than a little wild. Not bed-head hair.

Sex hair.

He tried not to shudder at the thought of the only mother figure he'd ever known having sex.

Dee, reading his mind, smiled sweetly. "Baby, I left you a text that I was doing okay this morning."

Ronald glanced over at her, a private smile hovering about his mouth.

Dee returned the smile.

And Ben threw up a little in his mouth. "Yeah, well, you didn't define *okay*."

"Not sure you'd have liked my definition," Dee said, still all sweet-like.

Aw, Christ, Ben thought, and scrubbed a hand over his eyes.

Taking pity on him, Dee laughed, rose, and gave him a kiss on the cheek. "How about some breakfast?"

Hell, no. "That's okay, thanks." He waved vaguely at the door. "I've got a thing—"

"I heard you're helping Aubrey Wellington get her bookstore ready," Dee said.

Ben stopped. "How the hell did you hear that already?"

Dee smiled. "Do you really have to ask? It's Lucky Harbor, after all. And everyone here loves you so much. They're all so glad to have you back. You're a common topic on the Lucky Harbor Facebook page. But about Aubrey—"

"It's just some bookshelves and renovation stuff," he said quickly, not wanting to hear from anyone else what a bad idea it was. "That's it."

"Hmm," she said, not commenting on that directly. "I was just going to say, if you need any tools, you know I still have all of Jack senior's in the garage."

"Say the rest," he said.

"What?"

"The part you're dying to say. That she's a bad idea for me."

"Well, of course she is." She met Ben's gaze. "But you already know that."

He blew out a breath. "Yeah."

"She's not exactly your type."

"No one's been my type."

"She's got a reputation."

"Maybe she's changed."

She cocked her head at him. "Well, you're a big boy now. You'll have to decide that for yourself."

"But you don't like it."

"I don't." She cupped his face. "Baby, no one is ever

going to be good enough for you. Not in my eyes. You know that." She snagged a quick, hard hug and then let him go.

Ben left there like his ass was on fire. He trusted Dee with his life, but it wasn't her business whom he saw.

Or didn't see...

Back on the road, he found his zone. He liked Aubrey's plan for the bookstore, but he couldn't shut off his engineering brain. He could think of several ways to improve her vision.

Not that she'd thank him for it.

Nope—he'd have to finesse the situation, make her think everything was all her idea. He was playing around with that, working it as he would any puzzle, when two figures dashed out into the street right in front of him. "*Jesus.*" He stomped on the brakes, and thankfully his truck stopped on a dime.

He couldn't say the same for his heart.

Or his coffee, which went flying, spilling everywhere.

Out in the middle of the street, the two kids had gone still as statues. Two little girls. He threw the truck into park and ran to them, crouching down to their level. "Are you okay?"

"Yes," one said while the other just stared up at him, eyes as big as saucers. They were clearly twins, maybe five years old, one wearing all pink and the other a mishmash of mismatching colors. They shared the same crazy, wild hair the color of a copper penny, which flew around their thin, angular faces. Stark blue eyes. Skinny as toothpicks.

"What are you doing in the street?" Ben asked, craning his neck, trying to figure out whom they belonged to, but the area was quiet. This was a low-income neighborhood. Yards were neglected, houses were small and close together. There was no one in sight. The hardworking blue-collar class had already left for work.

"We're supposed to stay on the sidewalk," the pink one said. "But there's lots of cracks. We're sorry, mister."

When he just looked at her blankly, trying to understand what the hell she meant about the cracks, she pointed at her sister. "Kendra's afraid of them. The cracks." She leaned in a little, like she was departing with a state secret. "She thinks trolls live in the cracks, and if she steps on one, they'll get her."

Kendra stuck her thumb in her mouth and nodded.

Ben blew out a breath and shuddered to think what might have happened to them if he hadn't seen them in time. "What's your name?" he asked Pink.

She opened her mouth, but Kendra pulled on her twin's sweater and gave her a quick head shake. Pink rolled her lips inward and looked down at her shoes—which were untied. "We're not supposed to tell strangers our names," she said softly.

Ben leaned in to tie her shoe for her before realizing that the reason it was untied was because the string had broken off on one side. "That's a most excellent rule," he said, straightening, nudging them to the side of the road. "Which house is yours? I'll see you home."

"We're not going home. We're going to school," she said.

"By yourselves?" He hated that idea. They were so young, so vulnerable.

"Billy's supposed to walk us, but he never does," Pink said. "Sometimes Joey or Nina stays with us, but today they ran ahead real fast 'cause the mean kids were chucking rocks. Kendra couldn't keep up, so I stayed with her."

Ben craned his neck and looked around, ready to rumble with whatever little asshole punk was throwing rocks at these two little girls. He couldn't believe they were on their own. The elementary school was at least another mile away. Letting out a breath, he scrubbed a hand over his jaw. "I want to talk to your mom."

"We don't got one," Pink said.

Well, if anyone understood that short sentence, it was Ben himself. "Who's in charge of you?"

Pink bit her lower lip.

Ben crouched down low again, getting as small as he could. Not easy on a six-foot-two frame. "Talk to me, Pink."

She smiled at the nickname, then sneaked a peek at a house about a hundred yards back, the corner house.

"Come on," he said, and headed that way.

"But mister, we'll be late."

"Ben," he said. "Call me Ben."

"Okay. But mister, Suzie don't like it when we're late, 'cause then the school calls her and she gets in trouble."

Then Suzie should have damn well driven them, Ben thought grimly. He walked up the narrow path and rapped his knuckles on the front door.

A fiftyish woman answered, looking harassed. "Yes?" she asked, and then frowned down at the two girls. "Oh, Lord. What did you two do now?"

"They didn't do anything," Ben said. "Though I nearly ran them over when they were in the street."

"In the street!" she gasped and glared them. "What in

the world? You know better, both of you! And now you're going to be late for school!"

"They're too young to walk to school alone," Ben said.

Suzie sent him a mind-your-own-business gaze. "They *weren't* alone. There's five of them, and the others are all older."

"Someone was throwing rocks at them," Ben told her. "The others ran ahead."

The woman heaved out a heavy sigh. "They have to learn to fight their own battles."

"They're too young to fight any battles," Ben said, beginning to get real pissed off.

"I know you," she said. "You're dating that bitchy Aubrey Wellington, not that anyone can figure out why. And you went to school with my son Dennis. You took his point-guard spot on the varsity basketball team. I know everyone thinks you're all that, but you're not."

Her son Dennis had been a first-class asshole, and he'd sucked at basketball, to boot. Ben hadn't. "The girls," he said tightly. "Can you drive them to school or not?"

"If you're so worried about them, do it yourself."

"I don't have—"

The door slammed.

"—car seats." Well, hell. Ben looked down at the two rug rats.

They looked right back, their eyes filled with worry.

"Okay," he said, making a snap decision. "Let's go." Against his better judgment, he loaded them carefully into the backseat of his truck, cinching the seat belts tight to their skinny frames and hoping to God he didn't get arrested trying to do the right thing.

"Wow," Pink said, looking around. "This is the coolest truck ever!"

His truck was a twelve-year-old Ford, and, granted, he'd had it lovingly taken care of by Jack when he'd been gone, but it wasn't *cool* by any stretch. It was functional, just the way he liked it.

In the backseat, Pink was holding her sister's hand and kicking her feet, as though her energy couldn't be contained. "Mister, are you married?"

"It's Ben," he reminded her. He pulled cautiously out into the street, not wanting to mess with his precious cargo. "And no, I'm not married."

"Why not?"

Since responding with "Well, I *was* married, but she died" wasn't exactly appropriate, he ignored the question. Not difficult, as Pink had a thousand more questions.

"You spilled your coffee?" she asked.

"Yep."

"All these tools yours?"

"Yep." Thankfully, a mile went pretty fast, and in a couple of minutes, he was pulling up to the drop-off lane in front of the elementary school. He started to get out of the truck, but Pink had herself and her sister unbuckled and out the door before he could.

"Thanks, mister!" she yelled back. "I hope you get another cup of coffee!"

Ben nodded and waved, meeting Kendra's big eyes as she gave him one last look.

She still hadn't spoken a word.

As soon as the two little redheads vanished inside the school, Ben pulled out his phone and called Luke to give him the lowdown. "What's up with that foster home?"

"It's better than most," came Luke's surprising answer.

Ben wrestled with that for a moment, knowing that if it hadn't been for Aunt Dee, he'd have ended up in a situation just like the two girls. Or worse. There were plenty of people who never got to have an Aunt Dee. Like Sam...

"Tell me you're kidding," he finally said.

"You have no idea."

Ben sighed.

"Listen," Luke said. "The kids are safe; they get a roof over their heads and three squares."

And what went unsaid...it was more than a lot of kids got. "Shit," Ben said, and hung up.

He drove himself to the car wash and took care of the spilled coffee situation. He was halfway through a three-egg-and-cheese omelet and a not-so-short stack of pancakes at Eat Me when Luke slid into his booth.

"Just heard that we're looking for an engineer to work on the new water systems for the county," Luke said.

Ben looked at him and then kept eating.

"Interested?"

"That was my old job, before I left," Ben said.

"Duh. They need an overhaul and want you back to head up the team. Are you interested or not?"

Ben shrugged.

"Let me phrase this another way," Luke said casually. "You *are* interested."

Ben's brows went up. "Is that right?"

"Yes, damn it."

"Because it'd keep me here in Lucky Harbor?"

"Your aunt and Jack missed you. And Kevin. Kevin missed you, too."

"Kevin didn't know me. Jack just got him last year."

"Whatever, man."

Ben smiled. "*You* missed me. Admit it."

"Shut up." Luke snatched Ben's plate of pancakes and pulled it toward him. He doubled the amount of syrup on the plate and dug in. "You should know that you've already turned in your résumé."

"Did I?"

"Yeah. Stole it off your laptop. They expect you to stop by this week."

"Thanks, Mom."

"Smart-ass."

It was early the next day when Ben pointed his truck in the direction of the bookstore. Halfway there he stopped at a four-way stop and saw a woman standing on the sidewalk in front of a town-house complex. She was staring at a lower unit, looking unsettled and anxious. Normally, this wouldn't necessarily have caught his interest, but the willowy, well-dressed blonde wasn't just any woman.

It was Aubrey.

She shook her head, muttered something to herself, and then began walking away. She turned the corner.

There were no cars behind him, so Ben remained there a moment, a little thrown by having seen her look so off her axis not just once, but twice now.

And then, suddenly, she was back, retracing her steps so that she once again stood on the sidewalk staring at the town house.

"What the hell?" he murmured, and pulled over.

Aubrey stood in front of a small, narrow town house, taking mental notes. The place was clearly well taken care of—lovingly so—with flowers lining the windowsills and freshly painted shutters.

You're not here to notice the care of the building. Drawing a deep breath, she looked at the list in her hand, then back at the town house.

But still, she hesitated. Yesterday she'd have said she had courage in spades, but the truth was that her encounter with the first person on her list hadn't gone so smoothly, and she was still smarting. What if this one didn't go any better?

Just do it, she told herself. Like the Nike commercials. She drew in a big breath and started forward—

"What are you up to?" asked an unbearably familiar male voice.

She nearly jumped right out of her skin. Instead, she forced herself to calmly turn.

Ben was in his truck, window down, idling at the curb, dark lenses hiding his eyes from her, looking effortlessly big and badass.

The way she wished she felt.

Chapter 6

♥

Before Aubrey could formulate an articulate answer, Ben turned off the engine and ambled out of the truck.

Damn it. Cursing herself for getting cornered, she narrowed her eyes at him. "What are you doing here?"

"Wondering the same thing about you," he said calmly. He glanced at the building. "You seem a little fixated on number forty-three. Who lives there?"

"None of your business."

As if he had all the time in the world, Ben leisurely pulled out his phone and thumbed the screen for a moment. "Huh," he said, sounding fascinated. Then he lifted his head. "I knew this place was familiar. Mrs. Cappernackle lives here. The school librarian."

Like she didn't know. "How did you do that?"

"I have ways," he said mysteriously. "Didn't you and she have an incident? What was it?" He paused, thinking, and then nodded. "I remember now. You stole some books from the library, and she busted you for it."

No. No, no, no, that *wasn't* what had happened. Well, not exactly, anyway. "Stop it," she said. "Go away. Go put in a water system in Nigeria or something."

He actually smiled. "Already done."

Show-off.

"Why are you at the home of someone on your list?"

She went still. *Shit.* He had the memory of an elephant. And he was relentless.

And as nosy as any of the old ladies in town.

"Again," she managed to say through her teeth, "none of your business."

"You planning to off the people on that list or what?"

She whipped around to stare at him. He pulled his sunglasses off, and that's when she saw the light of amusement in his eyes. He was teasing.

Sort of.

Because the smile wasn't quite real. He didn't understand her. He was confused by her.

Well, join my club, she thought.

"Because if you are," he said, shifting closer, lowering his voice to a conspirator's whisper that shouldn't be so sexy, but totally was, "then you should be scoping the place out at night, not in broad daylight. And you should be in a vehicle with night-vision and heat-seeking goggles."

"I'm afraid to ask how you know all this," she said.

"I'd tell you, but..."

"You'd have to kill me?"

His smile went slightly more real, but his eyes were still laser sharp. "What's going on, Aubrey?"

She shook her head. What was going on was that she'd lost her mind if she thought she could really pull this off.

A million years ago, or so it seemed now, Mrs. Cappernackle, the high school librarian—the woman who lived in the town house—had tattled on Aubrey. Her claim was that Aubrey'd had sex in the reference section of the library with the principal's son.

And though Aubrey certainly had been guilty of being in the wrong place with the wrong guy before, she hadn't been that time, and not with the boy in question, either.

But in spite of her innocence, she'd gotten in big trouble, and because Mrs. Cappernackle falsely claimed she'd stolen books while she was at it, she was suspended. So when a few weeks later Aubrey realized she'd actually forgotten to return a library book she'd legitimately borrowed, she did a really stupid, juvenile thing. She claimed she *had* returned it but that Mrs. Cappernackle had only said she hadn't because the librarian had it out for her. Aubrey even managed to produce real tears and must have been convincing enough, because she'd gotten away with it, and Mrs. Cappernackle had been written up by the superintendent.

Mrs. Cappernackle had retired later that same year, and Aubrey had always felt guilty, like she'd had something to do with it.

Now, more than a decade later, Aubrey had the book she'd stolen in her purse. It wasn't the original, of course, but a new copy from her store. She wanted to hand it over as a peace offering. Or such had been her plan, but it seemed stupid now. "I'm asking you nicely," she said to Ben, "to go away."

This was hard for her, very hard, and some of that must have been conveyed, because he studied her with those assessing eyes for one long moment, then nodded and walked back to his truck.

And then he was gone.

She wasn't hopeful enough to think he'd actually completely vanish from her life, but that he'd left for now was good enough. Drawing in a deep breath, she marched up to the town house and forced herself to knock.

A moment later, Mrs. Cappernackle opened the door. She was tall, thin, and using the cane she'd once wielded to enforce her reign of terror in the library. If you got that cane pointed at your nose, you knew you were in deep trouble. Aubrey'd been at the wrong end of it often enough to vividly remember the bone-quaking, knee-shaking fear it could evoke.

Mrs. Cappernackle had aged in the past decade, and she'd been old to start with. But she took one look at Aubrey, and her expression puckered as if she'd just sucked on a sour ball. "Well, look what the cat dragged in."

"You don't have a cat, Martha," said another woman's voice, and then she poked her head around Mrs. Cappernackle.

It was Lucille. She was a senior, too, and though Aubrey had never personally had any run-ins with Lucille, the woman's gossiping prowess was legendary. So was her soft heart and kind soul. Aubrey was banking on both. "Hi," she said. *You can do this.* "Mrs. Cappernackle, I was hoping for a moment of your time."

"I have no time for you," Mrs. Cappernackle said. "And stay away from Ben McDaniel. You don't deserve him." And then she slammed the door on Aubrey's nose.

Aubrey stared at the closed door and felt her inner strength wobble a bit. Two for two...she turned to walk away, but the door opened again.

It was Lucille. Glancing back over her shoulder as if

checking for a tail, she tiptoed out and grabbed Aubrey's hand. "Honey, don't take that personally."

"Hard to take it any other way," Aubrey said.

Lucille paused as if she wanted to say something, but changed her mind. "It's not a good day," she said carefully. "Will you do me a favor and try again, real soon?"

"Sure," Aubrey said softly, managing a smile when Lucille gently patted her arm.

"You're a good girl," she said, and then vanished before Aubrey could tell her she wasn't a good girl at all.

Not even close.

Three days later, after a very long ten hours at the bookstore, Aubrey closed up shop and was dragged to a wine tasting and spa event at the local B and B with Ali and Leah. While having a free paraffin hand treatment by the spa's owner and sheriff's wife—a very lovely, very pregnant Chloe Thompson—Aubrey dodged her friends' questions about Ben. She did this because, one, she didn't want to talk about her feelings for Ben, and, two, she didn't even know what her feelings were.

Liar, liar.

On the way home, she stopped and picked up some color samples from the hardware store for the paint she couldn't possibly have been able to afford if not for her incredibly generous uncle. She'd spoken to him yesterday via Skype from his cruise and got a lump in her throat just thinking about it. He knew his wife had loved the bookstore, and he loved Aubrey enough to give her a shot at it.

It meant the world to her, but she wasn't going to spend more than was absolutely, strictly necessary. And she'd repay every penny.

The moment she parked next to Ben's truck at the bookstore, she nearly chickened out and retreated to her loft apartment for the night instead. But she wasn't a chicken, she told herself, and she forced herself to enter via the front door.

"How much do I owe you?" she heard Ben ask.

She moved in far enough to see him. He had his back to her. He held a bag of something delicious-smelling in one hand and was shoving his other hand in his pocket.

Another guy stood in front of him in a bike helmet, army fatigues, and a black T-shirt that read EAT ME DE-LIVERS. Aubrey recognized him as the man who'd been at AA the other night.

Ryan.

Ryan shook his head vehemently at Ben. "Nothing, man. You owe the diner nothing. It's on me." He paused, and his voice was filled with emotion. "It's good to see you home. Safe. Everyone's so happy to have you back." Then he stepped close to Ben and enveloped him in one of those masculine, back-slapping hugs, holding Ben for a long beat, as though he was incredibly precious to him.

Ben let out a breath and hugged him back, and Aubrey felt another lump in her throat, this one the size of a regulation football. Uncomfortable with the emotion, she let her heels click on the floor, and both men turned to face her.

Ben met her gaze, his giving nothing away.

Ryan looked at her as well, and it was clear from the way he gave one slow, surprised blink that he remembered her from the AA meeting. She braced herself for questions, but he didn't say a word. He merely turned back to Ben, clapped him on the shoulder once more, nodded at Aubrey, and then was gone.

"You know Ryan?" Ben asked into the silence.

"No."

"Sure? It seemed like you two might know each other."

"No," Aubrey said again, and bent to pet Gus, who'd come close to wrapping himself around her ankles.

Meow, he said a little forcefully and accusatorily.

She was late with his dinner.

Aubrey fed him and glanced at Ben. He was back in his tool belt, which was made of leather and crinkled all male-like when he moved. Plus, it forced his jeans a little low on his hips. She couldn't stop staring, because there was something about the way he wore his clothes that suggested he'd look even better without them.

And then she noticed...he had cat hair all over his jeans. That shouldn't make her melt, right? Swallowing hard, she forced herself to turn away. But her eyes had a mind of their own and needed one more peek, and she pivoted back.

And bumped right into him.

Chest to chest.

Thigh to thigh.

And everything in between. He'd moved silently, coming right up on her. "Did you talk to Mrs. Cappernackle?" he asked. "Did you apologize for whatever it is you did?"

She went still, then forced herself to relax. "You think you know something," she said. "But you don't." She turned to leave, but he wrapped his hand around her wrist and pulled her back.

"I don't want to talk about it," she said. Once again he was close. Too close. *So damn close.* "At all," she added, hearing with some alarm that her voice had softened.

Everything had softened, at just his proximity. "Ever," she whispered, and found her gaze locked on his mouth.

He had a really great mouth.

"I don't want to talk, either," that mouth said very seriously. And then he lowered his head. They shared a breath for a beat, just long enough for her to know what was going to happen and feel the anticipation wash over her.

Then he kissed her, deep and slow and utterly mesmerizing. His hands were firm on her back. Needing an anchor, she reached out and grasped his shirt and leaned into him. He was warm and solid, so very solid, emitting the kind of strength that she herself was a pint low on today. Leaning in more, she felt his body respond.

Someone moaned. *I did*, she realized, swamped with the sensation of being wanted, even just physically. She took in the delicious taste of him, the feel of him, the sound of his very male groan when she stroked her tongue to his.

Things got a little hazy then. A lot hazy. She felt his hands move over her, melting her bones away. She touched him, too. Her hands wandered all over his body—and good Lord, what a body.

She had no idea how long they kissed—*and kissed*—but she didn't think about stopping until she ran out of air. Breathing hard, she slowly opened her eyes and stared directly into his.

They'd heated. Darkened. And something else. He wasn't looking so relaxed now. In fact, he was looking the opposite of relaxed. He looked...feral.

And she was his prey.

It made her quiver in arousal, which was crazy, but she couldn't look away. He was still holding her. In fact, he was holding her up. And having his hands on her was doing a number on her heart rate. "I have paint samples," she said inanely.

"Paint samples," he repeated.

"Yes."

"You were thinking about paint samples just now?"

No. She was thinking about the temptation of his hard body and how he might feel on top of her, holding her down while he did all sorts of delicious things with all that...*hardness*. Not that he needed to know that. "Yes," she lied. "I was thinking about paint samples."

His lips swept along her jawline to her ear. "I could make you forget about them."

No doubt in her mind. "I don't think so," she said, having to lock her knees, what with her bones melted and all. Her palms were damp. Other places on her body were damp, too. Damn him. Realizing she was still fisting his shirt, she loosened her hands, stroking her fingers over the wrinkles she'd left.

He stepped back and let out a small smile. "I know better than to compete with paint samples." He dropped his tool belt and headed to the door.

She stared after him. "Where are you going?"

"For air."

"But...there's work to do."

"Yeah. You and your paint samples should get on it."

And then he was gone.

Meow.

Gus was still hungry. *Starving*, if his vehemence said anything.

Aubrey was hungry, too. Just not for food.

Chapter 7

Ben was halfway down the street with absolutely no destination in mind when his phone vibrated.

"Don't forget," Jack said when Ben answered. "Craft Corner starts tomorrow. You need to be at the rec center between the elementary school and high school by three fifteen."

Shit. He'd completely forgotten. His brain was currently on overload.

Kiss overload.

And yeah, it'd been a while since he'd kissed a woman, but he was pretty sure a kiss had never fogged up his head the way that Aubrey's kiss just had.

It was her mouth, he decided. It was a pretty damn great mouth. "And if I've changed my mind?" Ben asked.

"I'll change it back for you," Jack said.

Ben laughed, because this was just bullshit posturing on his cousin's part. Probably. Either way, he wasn't all that worried, since he could fight mean and dirty as a snake when he had to.

But…he'd taught Jack everything he knew. "What the hell am I supposed to do with a bunch of kids at some stupid Craft Corner?" he asked.

"You've got a truck full of tools; you'll figure it out," Jack said, and then hung up.

Great. He was so *not* busy that he'd been reduced to playing arts and crafts with teenagers. He went home and barely slept—when he wasn't fantasizing about Aubrey's mouth.

He got up early and ran a few miles with Sam. "Do I look bored to you?" he asked Sam.

Sam's lips twitched. "If you're asking, you're bored."

Yeah. Shit. After he got home and showered, he formally applied for the job with the county, just to get Luke off his ass.

That afternoon, he pulled up to the rec center just as the school bus was dumping a load of kids off.

These weren't high school kids; they were much younger. Elementary school kids. Some looked as though they could be in kindergarten.

Then he saw Pink and Kendra, and he got a very bad feeling. He whipped out his cell phone and called Jack.

He didn't pick up. Fucker, he thought. Surely the older kids were already here, and that's who he'd be working with. No one, especially Jack, would think to put *him* in charge of little kids. He walked to the back of his truck. He'd loaded up a crate full of tools, figuring they'd wing it.

Pink squealed at the sight of him and ran up close,

dragging Kendra behind her. "Mister! Hi! Whatcha doing here?"

"Teaching Craft Corner."

She squealed again, confirming all his suspicions before she let out a "Yay! That's where we're headed, too!"

They walked into the classroom assigned to Craft Corner, hanging on him like they owned the place because they knew the teacher. Ben set down his crate of saws and hammers and chisels and soldering tools, and one of the grade school teachers—apparently a few of them volunteered here after school—gave him a horrified look. "What is *that*?" she asked.

"Stuff for Craft Corner." He paused. "For high school kids, right?"

The girls were jumping up and down at his side, clapping their hands in uncontained joy and excitement.

The teacher shook her head. "No. This is Craft Corner for ages five to seven."

Jack, you bastard…

The teacher heaved a put-upon sigh, pulled out a set of keys, and went to a closet. She unlocked a cabinet and gestured to it.

"What's that?" Ben asked.

"Spare materials."

He stared at the shelves stocked with things like buckets of glitter glue and popsicle sticks. "What do I do with all this?"

"I don't care, as long as you keep them busy for an hour and a half."

And then she was gone.

Ben had once been in a remote area of Somalia with two other engineers when they'd been surrounded by a group of starving rebels. They'd rounded up Ben and his two co-workers, stolen everything they had, beaten the shit out of them for good measure, and left them for dead.

That had been less painful than this—being with a group of twenty kids staring at him with excitement and hope that he was about to do something cool. Because he had nothing. To stall, he dumped out the bucket of popsicle sticks, spread them around. Did the same with the glue.

Pink tugged on the hem of his T-shirt. "So what are we doing, mister? Making something really neat, right?"

"Right." He shoved things around in the supply cabinet, looking for something—anything—to help him.

"Are we going to do it today?" she asked.

He turned to her, but she appeared to be utterly unconcerned over the long look he gave her, the one that would've had a grown man cowering in his boots. She just met his gaze straight on and smiled.

Last year in Thailand, he'd had a group of local teenagers assigned to assist him on a project. They'd been quick studies, smart as hell, and, best of all, resourceful. During their off time, they'd shown Ben how to weave. Baskets, hats, even shoes. An engineer to the bone, Ben had taken their weaving techniques one step further. He'd taught them how to extract lumber from the piles and piles of debris that lay everywhere. What had worked in their favor was the humidity, which made the wet scraps they found thin, malleable, and easy to work with. They'd been able to weave effectively with no tools at all. Using building skills they learned from Ben, they'd made a bunch of aesthetically pleasing baskets. What had started out as a fun project to cure boredom and stimulate the teens had turned into a viable way for them to actually make a living—to trade the baskets for the things they needed to survive. Ben had left there knowing that he'd truly given something back.

He held no such illusions here. These kids weren't going to remember him or these stupid sticks. But he still had an hour and twenty-eight minutes on the clock, so he had to do something. "Okay, we're going to make a picture frame."

"What will we put in the frame?" Pink asked, her cute little face upturned to his.

Good question. They didn't care about getting a photo printed. These kids had cell phones and iPads and all sorts of shit on which they could bring up a picture at the touch of a thumb. "I meant a collage," he said. "We're going to make a collage."

"What's that?" someone wanted to know.

"Stuff you collect."

"What'll we collect?" another kid asked.

He smiled as the idea came to him.

Five minutes later, he had all the kids in the rec center parking lot, finding "treasures" from his truck. Kendra was cradling a few quarters and Oreos. Another girl had claimed all the chocolate-kiss candy wrappers he'd tossed in the back. One of the other kids had found a baseball cap and a pair of flip-flops; Ben had no idea whom they belonged to. Yet another kid went through the glove compartment, making Ben damn glad he no longer kept condoms in there. But his maintenance records were now officially someone's art project. Several of the boys had gathered up the rest of his change and were making a mint off of him. One of them held up a ten-dollar bill with a whoop. Ben winced over the loss.

"Hey, this is a pretty napkin," Pink said of the—surprise—*pink* napkin she'd found. It had seven digits on it. A few weeks back, a waitress had scribbled down her number and shoved it in Ben's pocket, and he'd forgotten about it. "Uh…" he said, but Pink was cradling it as though it were gold, so he let it go.

Someone else had found several coffee cups and a parking ticket. Ben winced again. He'd forgotten about that ticket…

An hour and twenty-six minutes later, they were done. Each kid had a frame made by hand out of popsicle sticks, and inside each one was an assemblage of things they'd collected—from his now-clean truck.

Win-win, he thought.

When he'd been relieved by Ms. Uptight Teacher, he headed back to his blissfully empty truck. He slid behind the wheel and started to turn the key when he saw two familiar little redheads walking down the street.

Alone.

Shit. "Don't do it," he said to himself. But he put the truck back into park, pocketed his keys, and got out. "Hey."

Pink, holding her sister's hand, whipped around. When she caught sight of him, she beamed. "Mr. Teacher!"

"You're walking home," he said.

"Well, yeah. But on the next block we run, 'cause that's where Kelly and the mean dog live."

He sighed grimly. "Get in."

She beamed.

Kendra beamed.

And the next thing Ben knew, he'd put them both in his truck, cinched down by seat belts, legs swinging, smiles across their faces.

He pulled up to their foster home and idled a minute. "How long have you lived here?"

They both shrugged. "A while," Pink declared. "Since all the bad stuff."

He was afraid to ask, but as it turned out, he didn't have to. Pink didn't have a filter. "Our grandma died," she said. "And our daddy's up for the big one, so he couldn't take us to live with him."

Ben craned around to stare at her. "The big one?"

She shrugged again. "I'm not real sure what that means, but he's very busy doing it because he hasn't come to see us."

Ben was pretty sure he knew exactly what it meant. The guy was in prison for murder. Not that Ben was going to explain *that* to a five-year-old. He got out of the truck, unbuckled them, and waited until they were both inside their house.

While he was still sitting there, Jack called him.

"You're a shithead," Ben said in lieu of a greeting.

"You made them clean out your truck?" Jack asked incredulously. "Seriously?"

"So I'm fired, right?" Ben asked hopefully.

Jack laughed. "You're going to have to do a lot worse than that. And don't even think about it. I need you there. The kids loved you. But Jesus, figure out a craft that doesn't involve cleaning out your truck."

Ben hung up on him and put the truck in gear. On the next street he saw a teenage boy slouched against a fence, a huge mutt on a leash in his hand. He pulled over and rolled down his window. "Kelly?"

The kid sneered. "What's it to ya?"

Ben smiled at the size of the balls on the little idiot. Then he got out of his truck.

Kelly gulped but stayed in place, straightening, trying to add some height.

Height wasn't going to help him. Only brains could save him, and Ben had his doubts about even that. "We need to talk."

Kelly gulped again. "'Bout?"

"Your dog," Ben said. "You let it terrify any more little kids, especially redheaded ones, and I'll introduce you to *my* dog. And my dog eats your dog's breed for lunch."

Kelly lost a whole lot of his belligerence but tried to keep his bravado up. "Who are you, the dog police?"

"Worse," Ben said. "I'm not the police at all." He leveled the teen with the same stare that hadn't intimidated Pink much.

It worked on Kelly. The kid nodded like a bobblehead. Ben got back into his truck and called Luke. "What's up with the girls' parents?"

"What girls?"

"The two sisters from the foster home. Kendra and..." Shit. He still didn't know Pink's real name. "The one who wears pink all the time."

Luke laughed softly. "The one who wears pink?"

"Yeah," Ben said impatiently. "From head to toe. You can't miss her. What's their story?"

"I don't know," Luke said.

"But you could find out."

"Well, yeah."

"Call me back when you do."

Luke paused. "You do remember you don't like kids, right?"

"It's all Jack's fault."

"Of course," Luke said without missing a beat. "It's always Jack's fault."

Ben disconnected and then, in need of fortitude, drove to the diner. He hadn't even gotten out of the truck when he saw the flash of a willowy blonde standing in front of the beauty salon.

Aubrey.

As he watched, she stuffed that damn notepad into her purse, turned, and walked away. Quick, sure steps. Determined. She walked the same way she'd kissed him.

A woman on a mission.

He couldn't imagine what she was up to, but he'd bet his last dollar it involved her list. The one with his name on it.

Aubrey stopped short, said something to herself, and walked back to the salon. She strode inside, back ramrod straight.

Fascinated, knowing he'd seen this game before, Ben waited. While he did, Luke called back.

"Records on the kids are sealed, so I went to the source," he said.

"Child services?" Ben asked.

"Lucille."

Ben had to laugh. If anything had happened in Lucky Harbor that Lucille didn't know about, it wasn't worth knowing. "And?"

"She knew their grandmother. The kids' mom is gone. Their grandmother died, too, in a car wreck. The girls were four at the time and in the car. Minor injuries only. Father's a mechanic in Seattle."

"What?" Ben asked. "He's not in prison?"

"Not according to Lucille."

Ben absorbed the unexpected shock—and the anger. Also a shock. But he *was* angry. He was furious. The girls had lost a mother and grandmother, and their prick of a father was working less than two hours away while letting them think he was in prison?

Aubrey came out of the beauty shop. "Gotta go," he said, and disconnected. He studied Aubrey. She didn't look devastated this time. She looked…well, he wasn't sure. He looked her over again and then realized what it was.

She was relieved. There was a lightness to her carriage, and damn if she wasn't almost smiling as she got into her car, without even looking his way, and drove off.

He had to try damn hard not to follow her.

Chapter 8

When the alarm went off several days later, Aubrey had trouble getting out of bed, and she hit SNOOZE on her alarm clock about four times. Finally, Gus sat on her chest and refused to budge until she promised to feed him immediately.

She'd gone to her mom's the night before and stayed late. They'd had dinner, and then Aubrey had helped paint Tammy's bathroom a sunshine yellow for "cheer," as her mom had called it. Aubrey thought it was okay, but if it'd been her bathroom, she'd need sunglasses to take a shower every morning.

She'd planned to beg off early, but then Carla hadn't showed up, which had saddened her mom. Carla was invited every week and rarely, if ever, showed up, but it still got to Tammy. So it'd been midnight before Aubrey had gotten home, and she'd been shocked to discover that in her absence, the renovation fairy had finished demolition of the closet area.

Ben had come back and worked, and standing there alone in her dark store, in the middle of the night, she'd smiled. And been so grateful.

And confused.

How was it she only liked Ben when he wasn't here, or when he had his tongue in her mouth?

Now, in the light of day, standing in the same spot, she looked around again. Already so many changes had been made. There was little left of Aunt Gwen's store—except the heart. The heart was here in spades.

Meow.

And Gus the cat.

Her phone buzzed, and she pulled it out of her purse. It was Leah.

"Why are you starting your day without stopping in?"

Leah and Ali had a morning ritual that involved Leah feeding Ali breakfast and Ali putting up a fresh bouquet in Leah's bakery. "I didn't know I was part of the equation," Aubrey said.

"Well, you are. So get your skinny ass over here. I've just created a brand-new batch of raspberry Danishes, and Ali's going to eat them all if you don't hurry."

"I don't have anything to give you in return."

Meow, Gus said.

"Well, except the cat," Aubrey said. "And I don't think you can have a cat in a bakery."

"I'd take that fat sweetheart in a hot minute if I could," Leah said.

Aubrey looked down into Gus's annoyed green eyes and felt her heart squeeze. Nope, even she couldn't give up the grumpy old man.

"And anyway," Leah said, "it's not about what you can

give us in return, though you do have books now. I can download right from your website to my e-reader, right?"

"Right," Aubrey said.

"Well, then, that makes you my new crack. Hurry." And then she disconnected.

One of the things Aubrey was most proud of was her website, where people could download books to read on any digital device. They could do it from right inside her store or from the comfort of their own homes. She walked out her back door, down the alley about fifteen feet, and into the back door of Leah's bakery.

Inside the kitchen, Ali was leaning against the workstation, double-fisting Danishes.

"See?" Leah said. "Oh, and be careful when you take one from the box. Sometimes she bites, and I don't know if she's had her shots."

"I've totally had my shots," Ali said. "And anyway, I only bite Luke."

Aubrey carefully took a Danish, keeping an eye on Ali just in case Leah wasn't kidding. She took a big bite and then realized both Ali and Leah were looking at her.

"Now," Ali said to Leah. "Ask her now. While she's sugar-loading. It's hard to dodge people when you're on a sugar high."

Leah nodded and turned to Aubrey. "So...you've been busy."

"Very," Aubrey said warily.

"Busy kissing Ben."

And just like that, Aubrey choked on the Danish.

Leah pushed away from the counter, went to the refrigerator, and poured Aubrey a tall glass of milk.

She drank down the milk. She was no longer choking.

Mostly she was stalling for time. "Went down the wrong pipe," she said.

Ali and Leah were both watching her, waiting, and she sighed and set down the remainder of her Danish. "So this wasn't really about including me as part of your morning ritual. You wanted to hear the gossip."

"Actually," Ali said, "we were hoping for both."

Leah nudged the Danishes back toward Aubrey. "You always going to be so defensive?"

"Maybe," Aubrey said, and then caved. "Okay, probably."

"Listen," Leah said. "You're a friend. I think you're going to be a really good friend. But…"

"But Ben is family," Aubrey finished. "You're marrying his cousin. I get that. You're worried about him."

"Always," Leah said. "Even though he's a big boy, and he's going to do whatever he wants to do."

She'd noticed.

"Actually, to be totally honest, we're a little more worried about you," Ali said.

This surprised her. "Why?"

"Ben's not exactly a long-term bet right now," Ali said.

"And you think I am?"

"Of course," Ali said. "You had a rough patch and an unfair deal over Asshat Teddy. We both did."

Leah nodded, and Aubrey realized that what they'd said was true: They were worried—for her. Touched, she set aside her glass. "It really was just a kiss." Even saying it made her wince a little bit on the inside. First of all, it *hadn't* been just a kiss. It'd been the kiss of all kisses. And second, she shouldn't have allowed it to happen. No matter what she'd told Ben, he *was* on her list. This meant she had to try to make amends with him, not kiss him. Because when he found out why he was on her list, he wasn't going to want to kiss her. He was going to want to never see her again…

"I saw the kiss," Ali said. "I just happened to be outside, on the front sidewalk, talking to Olivia, who runs that very lovely vintage clothing store down the street. And bee-tee-dub, that was no 'just a kiss' kiss," she said. "That was a…wow kiss. I went home and jumped Luke's bones."

Aubrey had to laugh. Ali was right: It *had* been a wow kiss. But it'd also been a fluke. "It's not happening again," she insisted, and faced both their doubt and her own. "It can't."

A few minutes later, Aubrey was back inside the Book & Bean. She unlocked the door, turned on all the lights, and flipped over her OPEN sign.

Gus, asleep in his bed beneath the stairs, cracked open one eye and meowed at her. The nocturnal creature was annoyed by daylight.

Aubrey went to stand in what would soon be her little service niche. Ben had cleaned up after the demolition, but she went over it, sweeping and dusting to keep the store spotless. When she was done, she stood looking at the place where Ben had pressed her up against his long, leanly muscled, warm body.

At just the thought, her lips tingled in memory of their kiss. And if she was being honest, other parts tingled, too. In the bright light of day, she couldn't imagine what the hell she'd been thinking to slide her hands up his chest and into his silky hair and pull his head down to hers for more.

Okay, so she hadn't been thinking…

It'd been a mistake, albeit a delicious one, and she needed to move on. She was good at that—moving on. And she'd proven it with the first success on her list. Smiling just thinking about it, she pulled the notebook from her purse, then took out a pen.

And then, with a smile she couldn't contain if she'd tried, she very carefully, very purposefully, crossed off number three.

Melissa.

Back in high school, the two of them had been rivals who'd gotten off on one-upping each other. Melissa had been pretty and funny and incredibly charismatic, and whenever she'd set her mind on a guy, she'd gotten him.

Even when Aubrey had wanted him.

Aubrey'd had the fattest crush on one guy in particular. Ben, of course. It didn't matter that he had a longtime high school sweetheart; she'd still yearned and burned for him. Secretly, of course. She hated to remember those days, when she'd been a lowly freshman, garnering a lot of unwanted attention from the junior and senior boys because of her looks. This had, in turn, made her a target for the popular girls, of course. Hannah being one of them. One time Aubrey had been in the school parking lot, surrounded by a couple of aggressive, obnoxious boys. Ben had chased them off, and Hannah had been with him.

"She asks for that attention, Ben," Hannah had said when a grateful Aubrey had started to walk away.

The humiliation of that had burned deep, but it was chased away by Ben's defense of her.

"No girl asks for that, Hannah," he'd said.

Aubrey had never forgotten it. It'd been the start of her terribly painful crush, that one moment of kindness, and she'd hated, *hated*, that he'd been with Hannah.

In any case, Melissa had sensed Aubrey's crush and loved to torment her about it. One summer night Melissa had a bonfire on the hidden beach past the pier, a spot only teenagers and the homeless ever bothered to hike to. Melissa had brought some alcohol that she'd pilfered from her parents and had plied Hannah with it until she'd fallen asleep by the fire. Melissa had then sat down next to Ben and pulled out every trick in Aubrey's own arsenal. The *I'm-so-cold* accidental snuggle. The *scared-of-the-dark* accidental snuggle. The *wow-you're-really-strong* accidental snuggle. By the time Melissa had moved on to the *there's-a-big-bug!* accidental snuggle, Ben was cranky from fending Melissa off, and Aubrey was cranky knowing she wasn't going to get a shot at Ben herself.

So she'd one-upped Melissa.

She'd dared everyone to go rock climbing on the cliffs and jump into the water—a stupid, dangerous stunt. She'd been neck and neck with Melissa all the way up to the top. They'd been neck and neck at the jump into the water, too. Aubrey had landed safely.

Not Melissa. A wave had slammed her up against a rock, and she'd broken her arm. They'd dumped her at the hospital and deserted her, not wanting to get in trouble for the illegal bonfire, the alcohol, or the cliff jumping.

Melissa had been treated and then cited for public intoxication and reckless endangerment.

Aubrey had gotten off scot-free.

She'd have written it off as a silly, juvenile stunt, but

Melissa had been on course to play softball at a junior college. But with her arm requiring two surgeries, she'd been dropped from the team.

She'd never gone to college.

Aubrey's path had crossed Melissa's a few times here and there. After all, Tammy worked at the same salon. But Aubrey and Melissa had never talked about that night, which had changed Melissa's life forever. But this morning, Aubrey had driven by the salon and got lucky, finding Melissa there early working on stock, and she brought up the past for the first time in all these years.

Melissa had told Aubrey that not too long after she'd broken her arm, her parents had cut her off because of her partying ways. It'd been a wake-up call. She'd gotten herself together, gone to beauty school, and was now running her own hair salon. She swore up and down that she was actually grateful for the path she'd ended up on. And happy.

Happy…

Aubrey shook her head in marvel. But Melissa had been sincere. She'd hugged Aubrey and told her to come in for a cut sometime and they'd talk about old times.

"Wow, she smiles."

Aubrey stifled her startled shriek. Ben stood in the doorway, propping up the doorjamb with a broad shoulder, arms crossed over his chest. A casual pose.

But there was nothing casual about the assessing look he was giving her. "I smile plenty," she said, irritated at herself. Just the sight of him used to remind her of her mistakes. Now the sight of him reminded her that he'd kissed her.

And he kissed amazingly…

That knowledge was damned distracting. She needed to find a way to get rid of it, but she couldn't. She thought about it every waking moment. And also during her sleeping moments, what few there'd been.

Meow.

Gus had gotten up for Ben. He never got up for Aubrey, but there he was, on all four legs, rubbing up against Ben as though he were catnip.

She was beginning to see how it was that Ben might have gotten cat hair on his pants.

Ben crouched low and gave the cat an allover body rub that had Gus rolling in ecstasy on the floor, the low, loud rumble of his rarely heard purr filling the room.

She rolled her eyes and then realized Ben was looking at her, really looking at her, and she went on guard. "We going to talk about it?" he finally asked, straightening.

"No." Hell, no.

He gave an almost smile, as if that had been the answer he'd expected, and yet there was a flash of something else as well. She dismissed it, because there could be no way he wanted to talk about it, either.

Another man came up behind Ben in the doorway. "Knock, knock," he said, rapping his knuckles on the doorjamb. "Am I interrupting?"

"Pastor Mike." Aubrey immediately looked around herself guiltily, as if she'd been caught doing something wrong. She stopped herself and added a mental head slap. *Good Lord, woman, get a grip.* "No, you're not interrupting anything. How can I help you? Do you need a book?"

"No, I don't need a book," he said. "But thank you."

Aubrey didn't know what to make of this. People came here for books. Or, in Ben's case, to drive her crazy.

"I just wanted to see how you were doing," Pastor Mike said, his smile casual. Easy.

"I'm..." She didn't dare look at Ben. "Good. Thank you." She had no idea why he was really here. Were there AA rules she didn't know about? She hadn't signed up for anything. She'd been careful not to make any commitments that night. She hadn't wanted anyone getting into her business.

And she especially didn't want *Ben* getting into her business.

Mike looked at Ben and held out a hand. "Good to see you home safe. There were lots of candles lit for you. Your aunt Dee lit one every week."

Ben shook Mike's hand. "She likes to hedge all her bets."

The pastor smiled. "It worked. Heard you were sticking around this time. You helping our girl out?"

Ben's mouth quirked at the "our girl." "Yeah. So you and Aubrey are close?" he asked Pastor Mike.

Aubrey jumped in before Pastor Mike could give her secret away, on purpose or otherwise. "Yeah, we're close," she said, moving toward Ben. "We're...buddies." She tried to nudge him out the door—to no avail, of course. The big lug couldn't be budged.

"What are you doing?" he asked, effortlessly resisting her efforts.

"You've. Got. To. Go."

"Do I?"

"Yes!" She flashed a we're-all-family-here smile over her shoulder to Mike. "He was just saying he had to go," she told the pastor. "He's a big sinner, you know. Maybe you should go with him. Keep him from sinning further today."

Pastor Mike laughed. Why he was laughing Aubrey had no idea, because this wasn't funny.

"I don't have to go," Ben said. "I've got all day."

Great. He had all day. "No, really. You're a busy guy, so—"

"I'm all yours," he said easily.

Oh, for God's sake.

"Aubrey," Mike said gently.

"Just a minute, Pastor." She gave up trying to shove Ben out the door and went hands on hips, blowing a strand of hair from her face. She gave him a dirty look before turning back to Mike.

"It's okay," he said quietly. "I can't stay. I really did just want to see how you were doing, or if you needed anything."

Oh. Well, that was a little sweet, she could admit. "I don't. I'm fine, thank you."

Mike looked as though he knew better than to believe that, but he didn't argue with her. He simply nodded. "You know where to find me if you need anything."

And with that, he was gone.

"So," Ben said into the silence. "You and Pastor Mike. You're...buddies."

"Yep."

"From...?" he asked.

She gave him a look. "Maybe I go to church every Sunday."

He flashed a heart-stopping grin, and she sighed. "Yeah, that was probably a stretch, believing I'm actually good enough to go to church."

His smile faded as his gaze touched over her features. "Good's way overrated," he said. "But you're doing okay, I'd say."

The combination of that and the way he was looking at her had her heart squeezing uncomfortably, so she took a few steps back. "What are you even doing here?"

"I work here," he reminded her.

She sighed. "And thanks for that, by the way. It's really amazing how much you got done last night. It looks good."

He nodded in acceptance. "My turn to ask a question now," he said, and pushed off the wall, closing the distance between them.

"Uh…okay. But maybe we should set limits—"

"No limits. Here's my question. When are you going to tell me what's going on with you?"

Oh, boy. "That's a pretty widely scoped question."

"You're right," he said. "Let me narrow it down for you. Start with the list, and why you're going around town talking to people. Did you become a Jehovah's Witness or something?"

That startled a laugh out of her. "I think that's two questions."

His eyes warmed a little. "And?"

"And…no. I'm not a Jehovah's Witness."

Chapter 9

Ben laughed, and when he did, Aubrey took another step back—right into the wall. She frowned at him as though it were his fault, which made him want to laugh again. Instead he studied her, a little surprised to realize that she was truly flustered by him.

This was fascinating. He knew it wasn't often that she allowed her feelings to show. Hell, he'd have said it wasn't often that she actually felt anything. She was one tough, smooth cookie. She always had been, all through school, even when she faced off against the mean girls or the stupid guys who thought she'd put out just because of how she looked.

She'd gotten even tougher. Inscrutable.

But then he'd kissed her. He'd had her in his arms, and he knew damn well she'd been feeling plenty.

So had he.

But today it was more than lust. He was making her

nervous, and he decided he liked that, too, much more than he should.

Mostly because she made him a whole hell of a lot of things, including—of all the ridiculous possibilities—jealous of a happily married pastor. He had to wonder what the connection was between Mike and Aubrey. The list?

And why did he care so much? The answer to that was unsettling, to say the least. She was getting under his skin—big-time.

He shouldn't have kissed her.

She was wearing a pretty dress, some silky forest green wraparound thing that hugged her curves and brought out her eyes.

And Christ, how it was that he was noticing such shit, he had no idea. She was a job to him right now, nothing more, nothing less.

Which didn't explain why he couldn't take his eyes off her mile-long legs when she turned and put some distance between them. She walked to the open space between the last row of bookshelves and the closet he'd removed and then squatted down and began to set out a bunch of squares.

A layout, he realized as she arranged them. She was working on a layout now that she had the funding she'd so desperately needed.

He looked around and realized something else. After he'd made a bit of a mess last night, she'd swept up. Dusted. And gotten rid of the last of the shit lying around from the old bookstore. She'd been working hard.

Really hard, he realized, getting a closer look at her, seeing the signs of exhaustion beneath her eyes and in the tightness of her mouth. Exhaustion and worry. "You've been busy," he said.

"Why do you sound surprised? It's my store."

He didn't know why he was surprised, exactly. "I guess I don't see you as the local friendly merchant type," he said.

"Should I even ask how you *do* see me?"

He knew better than to touch that one.

At his silence, she made a low sound of annoyance. "You don't know me, Ben," she said, making him feel like an ass as she went back to her little squares, toeing some things around, giving off an *I'm-very-busy* vibe.

But he did know her. Or he was starting to. He knew how very much this store seemed to mean to her. Knew that whatever that list was, it, too, meant a lot.

And he knew she kissed and tasted like heaven on earth.

Not that she wanted to hear any of *those* things from him. "Are you sure you want things so open?" he asked, and she jumped, clearly startled to realize he was right behind her now, looking over her shoulder down at the arrangement.

"I want to encourage socializing," she said stiffly. "I want people to have a place to go." She didn't look at him. "I want people to feel comfortable hanging out here so they won't be alone."

This made his heart squeeze, because he thought maybe she was the one who felt alone. "Why do you think people are so alone?" he finally asked, sincerely curious.

"Everyone's alone at some point." She glanced back at him. "You know that."

Because he'd lost Hannah. Holding her gaze, he gave a slow nod. "And you think a bookstore can make people feel...not alone?"

"I think having a place to go can help."

"Getting unlonely isn't about a physical place," he said.

"Well, I know that." Breaking eye contact, she once again went back to her layout. "But it's a start."

He watched her play with the arrangement of the squares for another moment. "Why such a wide path between the seating areas?" he asked. "You could have more merchandise in here if you close it up, even a little."

"I know what I'm doing."

"Yeah? Care to share?"

"I'm going to be hosting bingo night. And the knitting club. And the cookie and book exchange. And, I hope, a whole bunch of other stuff. A lot of that includes seniors, and they need the extra space to maneuver with canes and wheelchairs and things. The other day, Mr. Elroy took out an entire book display with his cane and then blamed in on Mr. Wykowski. They nearly came to blows, like a couple of twenty-year-olds, but Lucille stepped in, telling them they couldn't have any cookies if they didn't zip it."

Ben smiled. "Remember the time that you danced at the senior center and put three seniors into cardiac arrest?"

"*Near* cardiac arrest," she said, correcting him. "And it was a beauty pageant. I wasn't dancing. I was baton twirling for the talent competition."

He fought a smile and lost. "Whatever you say, Sunshine." He stepped into her space then, all the more amused when she went still, like Bambi in the headlights, unsure of whether to move clear, or stand firm.

She stood firm.

He pushed the squares around a bit. "How about this? You get an extra wall, which we'd make a half wall, as you wanted. That divides up the space so you can have two different groups at the same time and yet still gives you an open feel. Also, if you make the wall a shelving unit, you acquire additional product display or storage space."

She stared down at the squares for a long moment, saying nothing.

"Or not," he said with a shrug. "Your space."

"No, it's...good. You're good."

"Sometimes."

Her gaze jerked to his, and for a moment, hunger and yearning was heavy in the air between them.

Then she rolled her eyes. "And so modest, too."

He smiled, then pulled back the edge of the carpet, revealing what he'd discovered last night—hardwood floors beneath.

"Oh, my God," she said, and dropped to her knees, bending low to see the wood more closely. "Score!"

He eyed the way her dress pulled tight over her perfect ass and said, "Definitely." He tore his gaze off her. "I'll pull up the carpet for you tonight if you'd like."

"I'd like." She stood up, dusted her hands off, and pulled out a stack of paint samples. "I was thinking this one for the walls, and this one as an accent color."

He spread out the samples and nudged two colors over the top of her choices.

She stared down at them. "Lighter?"

"Yes. It'll make your space appear bigger."

"Warmer, too," she noted.

"You wanted comfy," he reminded her. "Your word, not mine."

She stared at his colors for a long moment. "You going to help me paint?"

"I can do it myself," he said, thinking a little space between them might be warranted.

"I want to be involved."

Perfect. "Painting's messy," he said.

"I'm good at painting."

He looked at her for a long moment, then shrugged. If she was willing to get burned, why the hell wasn't he?

"Besides," she said. "I don't tend to get messy."

He smiled, a real one. "Where's the fun in that?" he asked, and was rewarded by her blush.

The next night, Ben entered the bookstore after closing. He hadn't necessarily set out to avoid Aubrey.

Okay, he'd totally set out to avoid her.

As a result, he'd managed to go several hours today without thinking about her at all. Which was completely negated by the fact that she'd been starring in his dreams…

Yesterday, he'd pulled up the carpets in the bookstore. He'd swept afterward, but the hardwood had still needed some TLC. But as he looked the place over now, he realized Aubrey had scrubbed the hell out of the floors, getting up years of grime and scuffs. He didn't know what he'd expected from her, or why he'd assumed she'd have him do as much of the dirty work as possible, but she was working her ass off, and he found that…appealing. Wildly so.

"My aunt loved this place," she said from behind him. She was in sweats, eyes sleepy, as if maybe he'd woken her up. "I'd come here after school, and she'd have a snack waiting," she said. "She was always so busy, because she did all the work herself, but she made time for me. No matter what her day looked like. She'd put me in that big, soft chair"—she pointed to a huge overstuffed chair in the corner—"and then she'd bring me a stack of books to read, and for a little while, I'd escape."

"Escape what?" he asked.

She shrugged as if embarrassed and then looked out at the store. "I want to bring that magic to others."

He had no idea why his gut tightened, or why in that moment he wanted to give her whatever she needed. "We can do that," he said.

She turned to him. "We?"

"Your uncle hired me," he reminded her. "I don't leave a job just because the customer drives me insane."

She gave a little smile. "But why is this your job in the first place? Why are you even back in Lucky Harbor?"

Good question. Loaded question. Here felt like... home. Here was where he felt most like himself, but he shrugged. "Maybe I missed it," he said, testing the waters by saying it out loud.

"Sentimental, Ben? You?"

"You don't know me," he said, repeating the words she had said to him. "Or who I am."

She didn't smile, but she did nod in acknowledgement. "Is it getting easier?" she asked quietly. "Being here without her?"

He paused. No one ever asked him that. Where he'd been, most people had no idea he'd lost his wife. Only the people here in Lucky Harbor knew it. And the people here tended to tiptoe around the subject, not wanting to upset the grieving widower.

But five years was a long time, and he'd learned that as much as you loved someone, you couldn't keep her memory alive in your head for five years. Much as you loved someone, her laugh, her smile, her voice...it all faded a little with time. "I'm not on the edge of a cliff, if that's what you're asking," he finally said.

"What are you?"

He shrugged. "Tired, mostly."

"Given where you've been and what you've done, I can only imagine," she said softly.

Uncomfortable with this very real conversation, he turned away and walked the length of the room, pulling out his tape measure. "I bought the wood for the shelving units. I'll get more for the half wall if you want to go that route."

"I do," she said. "I scrubbed the floors, and since I like them scarred, I'm not going to do anything else to them. You're good at changing the subject, you know that?"

He did know that. She wanted to talk about the past five years, which made her as interested in him as he was in her.

She lifted a shoulder and gestured around her. "A bookstore is my favorite place. It shouldn't surprise you that I read—a lot. Research a lot. Your last project saved the lives of thousands, providing not only water for farmers and their crops but also giving them a means to keep providing those things on their own for generations to come."

His brows went up, both surprised and uncomfortable with the close scrutiny. "Are you actually giving me a compliment?"

"Maybe. Just a little bit."

"Why?"

"Why? What do you mean, why?"

He moved toward her, noting with some amusement that she sucked in a breath but held her own and stood firm.

They bumped. Front to front.

She appeared to stop breathing and tilted her head up, her gaze going to his mouth. "You know why," she whispered. "Because we're…attracted to each other."

"That's one word for it." Slowly he lifted a hand, watching her pupils dilate as he reached toward her…

And then past her to the counter, where he flipped open her notebook.

She blinked, whipping around to see what he was after, and went from soft and dreamy to pissed off in the blink of an eye. "Hey—"

"You've got someone crossed off," he said, teasing her. "Should I call the police?"

She narrowed her eyes. "Ha-ha." She snatched back her notebook. "Maybe you can be a funny carpenter and actually get some work done. I need those shelves, like, yesterday."

"What else do you need?"

She was at the door already but stopped to turn and look at him. "Excuse me?"

"A minute ago, it seemed like you needed a man."

"I don't *need* anyone," she said. "But if I did, it'd be someone...*sweet*," she said pointedly. "Sweet and... beta."

"Beta," he repeated.

"That's right," she said. "I'm over alpha men. And you, Ben McDaniel, are as alpha as they come."

Well, she had him there.

Chapter 10

♥

Two days later, Aubrey pulled up to her mom's house and checked herself out in the rearview mirror. Pale. Serious.

Stressed.

She put on some shiny lip gloss and then smiled—a big fake smile that didn't reach her eyes. One could fake anything, she knew, including happiness.

She was a pro at that.

But it was important to her that her mom really believe she was happy. Tammy had been through a lot in life—too much. So keeping the smile in place, Aubrey headed up the walk to her mom's condo. The evening was chilly but gorgeous. Clear and sharp, without a cloud in the sky. The stars lit her way.

She didn't even have to knock. With uncanny mom radar, Tammy sensed her daughter coming home to the fold and threw open the front door. "My baby!" she squealed with an ear-to-ear grin, yanking Aubrey in close for a tight hug. "Come in! I've got chicken frying, and now that you're here, I'll make mac and cheese, too, the way you love it, with the crusty bread crumbs and extra cheese on top."

Comfort food. Once upon a time, Aubrey had lived for such meals. Until the day she'd gone headfirst into puberty and couldn't fit into her jeans. After that, she'd secretly starved herself, pretending to eat her mom's food but really feeding it straight into the trash compactor.

Tammy had often expressed her pleasure at passing her "good metabolism" to her own flesh and blood, but the truth was Aubrey had her father's metabolism. She had to watch every calorie and work her ass off at the gym for every single indulgence she took. "I'm not hungry, Mom."

"Nonsense! You have to eat. I hope Carla comes tonight."

"Mom," Aubrey said slowly, not wanting her to be disappointed, as she always was. "Carla's not coming."

"Yes, I am." Carla came in behind Aubrey, still in scrubs. "But I've only got half an hour before I have to be back."

"Of course!" Tammy said, beaming at her two girls. "Your job's very important; I know that. Come in!"

Aubrey stepped into the living room. There was a lot of furniture there for the small space, but Tammy didn't like to throw anything away. And on every end table and coffee table there was…stuff. Candy dishes, frames, knickknacks. It was clustered and crowded, but to Aubrey, it was also home.

Carla had never spent much time here. She looked around now, and though she didn't say anything, Aubrey knew she was thinking that the place was a hoarder's dream.

And Aubrey could admit that they pretty much were a reality show waiting to happen.

Carla settled for sitting on a corner of a couch. Aubrey took the other far corner. "So…" She searched for a safe topic. "How are you?"

"Exhausted," her sister said, leaning back, closing her eyes. "Two straight shifts, and I'm a zombie. Haven't had time to go food shopping, get my mail, or water my poor plants, much less brush my hair. My neighbors probably think I'm dead."

Tammy tsked. "Honey, you've got to at least brush your hair. What will people think?"

Carla let out a low laugh. "They'll think I'm not dead after all, but that I do need a hairdresser."

"I could do those things for you," Aubrey said to her.

"What?" Carla asked. "Brush my hair? Or tell my neighbors I'm not dead?"

"Get you some groceries. Get your mail." Aubrey shrugged. "Water your poor plants."

"Why?"

"Because I'm your sister."

Carla opened her eyes and looked at her. "Is this about last week?"

"No," Aubrey said. But it was. A little. She had something to offer, damn it.

"That's so sweet of you to want to help, Aubrey," Tammy said. "Look at us, getting along like a real family."

"We *are* a real family, Mom," Aubrey said. She looked at Carla. *Tell her*, she said with her eyes. *Tell her we're a damn family*.

Carla met her gaze, paused, possibly rolled her eyes briefly, and then nodded at her mom. "We are family, Mom. We're just not always that good at it."

"Hey, we're better than some!" Tammy put her hand to her chest and her eyes filled. "No one move, do you hear me? I need a picture of this." She scrambled through the crap on the coffee table and came up with her phone. "Move closer to each other."

Aubrey and Carla shared an awkward grimace and then shifted closer.

"Yeah, like that. Perfect! Now hug." She gestured with one hand, the other holding the phone. "Oh, and smile! Goodness. This isn't a funeral."

Aubrey and Carla put their arms around each other, held the uncomfortable pose, and smiled.

And…smiled.

"Mom," Carla said, a little strained. "Take the picture already."

"I'm trying!" Tammy said, fumbling with her phone. "Crap! I can never find the damn camera on this thing."

Aubrey's smile was feeling more than a little brittle. "It's on your home page, Mom. Top left app. It says CAMERA."

"Oh." Tammy laughed. "Yes. Got it."

When Tammy finally took the shot and lowered the phone, Aubrey and Carla immediately broke apart.

They ate at the tiny table in the kitchen, practically elbow to elbow.

"Just like old times," Tammy said. "Remember when you'd come visit, Carla? We'd sit here just like this and talk about school. Hey, we could talk about work!"

"I live my work," Carla said. "I don't want to talk about it. How about yours?"

Aubrey watched as Tammy happily told Carla all about the salon and her clients. She remembered every single one, and every single thing they ever told her. It was part of what made her so popular.

"And you?" Carla asked Aubrey. "How are things at your work?"

"You know she's running her own business now," Tammy said, voice bursting with pride. "She took over Aunt Gwen's bookstore."

"You stopped working for the town hall?" Carla asked, surprised.

"Honey," Tammy said on a laugh. "Don't you ever read Facebook? Her boyfriend dumped her and she got fired."

"Well, not exactly," Aubrey said to a gaping Carla. "I dumped *him* and then *I* quit." Important difference, at least to her.

There was an awkward silence while everyone processed this.

"A bookstore," Carla finally said. "I thought those were all going out of business these days."

"This one's different," Aubrey said. "I'm selling digital books, too, and opening the place to all sorts of clubs, like knitting clubs and tea clubs…" She broke off because Carla wasn't looking impressed.

"How will that sell books?" she asked.

"Because it's going to be a place where people want to come and hang out. And buy their reading material," Aubrey said, trying to sound more positive than hopeful. "Don't you and your fellow surgical residents have a bunch of reading and studying to do? I could give you guys a place to meet and get together, and give you a discount on your materials."

"A discount," Tammy said. She loved a good bargain. "Well, isn't that nice?"

A few minutes later, Carla's cell phone buzzed. She read a text and stood. "Sorry, I have to get back." She looked at Aubrey. "I'll let people know about your store and the discount. We get together on Sunday nights and Wednesday mornings at the ass crack of dawn."

"My store is closed during those times, so you'd have the store exclusively."

Carla hesitated. "We meet in the cafeteria now, and it's not ideal. Their tea sucks."

"My tea never sucks, and I'll bring in goodies for you guys from the bakery next door," Aubrey said.

Carla nodded, and then was gone a few minutes later.

"That was really sweet of you, looking out for your sister like that," Tammy said. "You have such a big heart, honey."

Aubrey looked at her as if to say *Yeah, right.*

"No, it's true," Tammy insisted. "Carla may have gotten the brains, but you got all the heart."

Aubrey laughed. Okay, *that* she'd heard before, but there was no use in being insulted. Not when her mom meant it as the highest of compliments. Her gaze snagged on a stack of bills in the mess on the table. "How are you doing, Mom? Really?"

"I'm great, honey."

Aubrey tapped the stack of bills.

Tammy shrugged. "Oh, those," she said. "Don't you worry about those. They'll get paid in good time."

"I've got a little savings left," Aubrey said. Emphasis on *little*. "Let me—"

"No, no. I've got it, though you've proven my point

about heart." Tammy stroked Aubrey's hair. "You're still using that stuff I gave you from the salon, right? It's a miracle worker, isn't it?"

"Yes. Mom—"

"But you're not wearing any lipstick."

"I'm wearing gloss. And I was working."

"You should *always* have lipstick on beneath," Tammy said. "Especially when you're working. It gives you color and pizzazz."

"Carla wasn't wearing any," Aubrey said, "and you didn't bug her about it."

"Yes, well, I'm a little afraid of Carla, to be honest."

Aubrey laughed.

"Are you telling me she doesn't scare you?" Tammy asked, smiling.

"She scares the crap out of me," Aubrey admitted, and they *both* laughed. And then her mom went back to her favorite topic. "There's really no reason to slack off on how you look, you know. Even if you're working your tush off. How many times have I told you: If you look good, then life *is* good."

Aubrey suppressed her sigh. "I look *fine*."

Tammy looked pained at this. "You know how I feel about that word."

Fine was reserved for bad hair days. "I'm not on a modeling job, Mom."

"Well you *should* be," Tammy said. "You'd make a fortune. Goodness, you were on such a roll with the beauty contests. You could've gone all the way, honey. You could have become a model."

"I love what I'm doing now," Aubrey said, shuddering at the memory of her modeling days.

"That's wonderful," Tammy told her. "But I'm just saying. You're so pretty, baby. And your figure! You could have done catalogs. You could have been one of those angels for Victoria's Secret."

Aubrey laughed.

"I'm serious!"

Sad thing was, Tammy *was* serious. And she could have no idea, but Aubrey *had* given modeling a try. There'd been some lowbrow modeling, which had led to some lowerbrow modeling, which had led to some things that Aubrey tried very hard not to think about, though she had managed to pay for most of her college tuition that way. "Modeling isn't for me," she said firmly.

Tammy sighed. "If you say so."

"I do."

"I just want you to be taken care of," Tammy said.

"I'm perfectly taken care of, Mom. By myself."

Tammy smiled. "Oh, I know. You're so strong, Aubrey. So independent. I know you've had to be. Sometimes I worry we did the wrong thing, your dad and I, splitting you two up like we did the furniture and silver."

"You did what you had to," Aubrey said.

"For me," Tammy agreed. "I loved you both so much, but your father and I...we were on track to kill each other. I just figured the best thing was to split everything up, including you girls. And when it worked out so well, your sister with your daddy and you with me, it just got easy to not switch around so often."

"Or at all," Aubrey said mildly.

Tammy sighed. "Or at all."

"Dad wasn't much for following the rules."

"Your daddy isn't the only one at fault," Tammy said

softly. "I know it hurt you that he didn't have much time for you, but he was so busy working at the hospital, and his work was so important. Your sister is so much better suited to that life. I always meant to get me another man so you'd have a father figure, but that never really worked out."

"Mom, it's fine. It's all water under the bridge."

"Well, now, that's what I've always thought," Tammy said. "You were so popular at school."

More like notorious…

"You had boyfriends. And you dated in college. You always seemed to have a date."

Aubrey loved her mom, she truly did, but Aubrey had gone to college in Seattle while working at various admin jobs. Not very far away in the scheme of things, but since Tammy rarely—if ever—left Lucky Harbor, Aubrey might as well have been on the moon. In all honesty, Tammy had no idea what Aubrey's college life had been like.

"And then you got that fancy job at the town hall. I thought for sure you'd find yourself a fancy man to go with it and finally give me grandchildren."

"Mom—"

"No, honey, let me finish. Every job you've ever had, you excelled at. Anything you've ever wanted, you got for yourself. You're so capable. So strong. But you're acting like…what do they say? An island."

Every once in a while, a shockingly deep and wise kernel of wisdom came out of her mom's mouth. "There's nothing wrong with relying on myself," she said in response. She couldn't be disappointed in someone else that way. "I'm really okay, Mom. I promise."

"Well, I have eyes in my head, don't I? I can see that you're good. But it's okay to let someone in sometimes, you know. Being independent and strong and having to do everything yourself is one thing. But you shouldn't have to be all on your own, always. You can let people in, let down your guard. Have more friends. Be less stressed…"

Aubrey smiled. "I'm not stressed. I love the store. And I'm not alone, either. I have you."

"Aw, honey." Tammy's eyes went shiny, and she tilted her head back and blinked rapidly while waving a hand near her face. "Don't you dare make me cry—I'm not wearing waterproof mascara today."

Aubrey left her mom's place feeling like a stuffed sausage—reminiscent of a time years ago when she'd felt that way every night. She took the long way back to the shop, by way of the bluffs—which actually wasn't on her way home at all. It was at least ten miles out of her way.

The houses up here were expensive. Ritzy. Gorgeous.

Her dad lived at the end of a cul-de-sac in a huge, sprawling two-story house he'd had built to spec a few years ago, designed for his second wife.

Aubrey didn't pull all the way down to the end of the street; she didn't want to give herself away. Feeling like a ridiculous stalker, she eyed the lit-up house and felt her pulse kick. On the big front porch, with all the pretty hanging lights, sat a huge dollhouse. A big, perfect, gorgeous, fancy, clearly outrageously expensive dollhouse.

And it was forgotten on the porch, looking a little wet from the elements and dirty.

Her heart squeezed. Not hers, she told herself. Not anything like hers.

Hers had been much smaller, made of cheap plastic and cardboard. But she'd loved it. She'd loved it so much. Somehow it'd gotten lost in the divorce shuffle and subsequent move, and she'd mourned its loss more than the loss of her family's togetherness. How silly was that?

But seeing this perfect dollhouse, neglected, unloved, brought it all back. That's how she'd felt after the divorce, too. Neglected. Unloved.

Suddenly there was activity in the yard, which was lit by the house and porch lights, and she went still as stone, as though *that* would make her invisible.

But the three occupants on the frozen grass didn't so much as turn her way or pay the slightest bit of attention to her.

It was her dad and Aubrey's two half sisters, Brittney and Katrina, ages four and six. They were in matching dresses and wool coats. Her dad was in a suit and overcoat, looking neat and unruffled as ever, and they were all chasing around after a little puppy.

Aubrey felt sucker punched in the gut. She actually bent over with the pain, her hands on the steering wheel, her mouth open and gaping as though she were a hooked fish.

A dollhouse *and* a puppy. They had her dollhouse and her puppy. Okay, okay, not *hers*. But she felt as if part of her had just been stolen. Peals of laughter were coming from her half sisters, and then a sound she didn't recognize at first.

Her father's laugh.

By the time Aubrey got home, she was feeling the need to put on her ugliest sweats, swipe off all her makeup, and fill a Big Gulp cup with wine.

Make that vodka. She let herself in through the shop and inhaled the scent of freshly cut wood.

Then she heard Ben's clipped voice.

"Fuck that," he said. "The guy's working less than two hours away? At a decent-paying job? And yet he's not providing for his kids, much less even *seeing* them? They're rotting away in that foster home, Luke."

Aubrey stepped farther inside and found Ben at the far window, facing outside. He held the phone up to his ear with one hand while the other was shoved into his hair, holding it off his forehead. His feet were planted wide, in an aggressive stance that was dialed to pissed-off badass.

"No, I'm not backing off on this," he said, and then paused, clearly listening. Whatever he heard made him relax and let out a breath. "Say that to my face and we'll see how pretty your fiancée thinks you still are afterward," he growled, though now he sounded a whole lot less pissed off.

"At least contact the asshole," he said. "Those girls deserve that—yeah, yeah, I look at them and see me. Jesus. Neither of us needs a shrink to know that. But they're *five*, Luke. I was twelve, and already knew how it was. These girls, they're…*shit*. They have no idea. They need him. Tell the asshole that. They *need* him." He disconnected and shoved his phone in his pocket.

And didn't move. Just stared out into the night…

Aubrey didn't know what to do—an unusual feeling for her. She was intruding on a private moment, and yet this was *her* place. She dropped her purse to give him warning of her presence, and when he still didn't move—not a single, tense, muscled inch—she realized he'd known she was there all along.

"If you're looking for an argument," came his disembodied voice in the low light, "forget it. I'm not in the mood."

But that was a lie. He was absolutely in the mood for a fight, and that suited her just fine.

Because she was in the mood, too.

Chapter 11

♥

W hat's the problem?" Aubrey asked Ben.

"I said I wasn't in the mood for you, Aubrey."

Given the conversation she'd just overheard, she decided to cut him a break on the serious 'tude. "I can see that. Maybe you should cut out for the night."

At that, he turned to her, his gaze narrowing as he took in her face. "What's the matter?"

Unfortunately, she was still embarrassingly close to tears, so she didn't dare go there. "Just go home, Ben."

And to make sure he—or she—didn't do anything stupid, she left first. She walked to the small back hallway, which opened to an even smaller office space and a very narrow set of stairs that led to her loft.

She took the stairs at a quick pace, closed the door behind her, and stood in the middle of the room. The only light came from the moonlight slanting in through the slats of the window blinds. She didn't need to hit the light switch to see the four hundred square feet, which consisted of a love seat, a square table and two chairs, a kitchenette, and her one indulgence…a soft, plush bed piled with softer, plusher pillows.

She resisted, barely, the urge to throw herself face-down on it and assume her favorite thinking position.

Meow.

Oh, good. A purpose. Without so much as shedding her coat, she strode over to Gus, who was sitting by his empty bowl, staring at her accusatorily. She poured him a scoop and petted him while he ate.

"You ran away before you decided on colors."

With a gasp, she whirled. Ben was standing right there. Of course he was. He was in faded, loose jeans and a T-shirt, snug across his chest and arms. He looked a little dusty, a little sweaty, and his eyes glittered with the same temper she felt coursing through her.

"You need a damn bell around your neck," she said.

He didn't smile. He simply held out two color samples. "Pick one."

"There were more than two choices."

"There's only two *good* choices."

She'd picked out five decent colors, but decided not to push him. "What was your phone call about?"

"What call?"

"The one that pissed you off when I walked in."

He gave her an assessing look. "Why do you look like you've been crying?"

"What was your phone call about?"

"You first," he said.

She crossed her arms.

He gave her a grim smile. "Yeah, that's what I thought."

She sighed. "I don't like to talk about it."

He shook his head. "Listen, maybe I don't know what's going on. Maybe I can only guess it has something to do with your list. But have you considered that I might be worried about you?"

"Worried? Whatever for?"

"Maybe you're involved in something bad or dangerous."

She looked at him for a beat. His eyes were solemn, his mouth grim. He was serious. Dead serious.

He was worried about her. That had never crossed her mind. "I had dinner with my mother," she said. See? She could share. She wasn't always an island. "I ate enough comfort food for three people for a week. Then, for shits and giggles, and because I didn't feel bad enough about myself, I drove by my father's house and found him playing in the yard—in a suit, no less—with his new family and a puppy." She closed her eyes and admitted the most painful part. "And the girls had a dollhouse on the porch."

"A dollhouse."

"Yeah, like…I don't know." She gestured with a hand to waist height. "About this big. I had one when I was little, but when my parents divorced, somehow it got in with my sister's stuff. When I asked my dad for it back, he said it was Carla's." She laughed a little at herself. "It's dumb how much I loved and missed that thing."

"Why didn't you ask your sister for it back?"

"Because what if she loved it as much as I did?" Aubrey shook her head. "My mom felt really bad, but she couldn't afford to buy me one." She hated that memory and wished she'd never said anything. "It's silly, letting that get to me. It wasn't mine. It was a new one, a brand-new one, all pretty wood and fancy."

And unused...

Shaking it off, she said, "Your turn."

He just looked at her for a long beat. "You didn't say why you've been crying."

"Does it really matter?"

"You wouldn't think so," he said softly, coming close. He stroked a strand of hair from her temple, tucking it behind her ear. "And I'm not all that thrilled to tell you, but it does. Matter."

She closed her eyes. Not to savor his touch. Because it wasn't *his* touch she was reacting to, she assured herself. Anyone's touch would have reached her tonight.

Okay, that was a big fat lie.

"When I was growing up," she said softly, eyes still closed, "there was no playing in the yard with my dad, and he certainly never would have done so in his suit. He might've gotten dirty. And a puppy...well, I was more likely to take a spaceship to the moon than be allowed to have a pet."

"Ah," he said quietly. "Daddy issues."

Her eyes flew open, but there was no mockery in his face. Instead, he let out a long, slow breath. "I nearly hit two kids who ran out in the street in front of my truck last week," he said.

"Oh, my God."

"Yeah. Twin five-year-old girls. They were walking to school."

"Alone?" she asked.

"Well, not after I found them."

She felt her heart melt over this big tough guy facing

an emotion as sweet as protectiveness for two little girls he didn't even know.

"They're foster kids," he said. "And their foster mother is supposedly one of the better ones, but…" He shoved his hand through his hair and shook his head. "I saw them again later when I worked Craft Corner—"

"Wait," she said, stopping him. "*You're* working Craft Corner?"

He scowled. "Yeah. So?"

She smiled. "You're working Craft Corner," she said again, and laughed. "I'd like to see that. Mr. Tall, Dark, and Grumpy-Ass working with little kids."

"Now, see, how is it that everyone but me knew it was little kids? Jack conned me into it," he admitted.

She laughed again.

"Not funny."

"You being conned into anything is pretty funny."

"You think I'm impenetrable?"

"I think you're a fortress."

He blew out a breath, but didn't deny it. "Pink told me their mom is dead and their dad's in jail for the big one."

She was beginning to see why this had gotten to him. "Murder?" she asked.

"That's what I assumed. I had Luke run them."

"And?"

"And mom *is* dead, but their dad's working at an auto shop in Seattle."

She gaped at him. "That fucker."

"My thought exactly."

He looked extremely pissed off again. Unusual for him, but she understood now and ached for the girls *and* him. "I didn't have the greatest childhood," she said quietly. "But I know it could've been so much worse." She met his gaze, knowing that his childhood *had* been worse, maybe as bad as the girls'. After all, his dad was rumored to be in jail, too, and his mom had just dropped him off one day at his cousin Jack's and had never come back for him. She couldn't even imagine the ways that haunted him. "I know you had it rough," she said softly.

He met her gaze and then stepped into her a little bit more, so they were sharing air. "I don't feel like talking anymore."

His voice and proximity gave her a whole-body shiver. "Sure. What do you feel like doing?" she asked.

He just looked at her, eyes blazing.

"No," she said, lifting a hand, not sure if she was warding him off or really just trying to keep herself in check. "I meant what I said earlier."

He caught her hand in his. "When you said you didn't need a man, but if you did it wouldn't be me?" he asked. "When you said you wanted sweet? And...*beta*?" This last was said with more than a hint of mockery.

"That's right," she said, standing by her words, however stupid they sounded now. "Beta."

They were toe-to-toe now, and their bodies brushed. His was tough as nails. Hard. Warm.

Strong.

Male.

He smelled like freshly cut wood and like whatever soap he'd used. Like overheated man.

And everything within her tightened in desperate need, just to be...taken. To let go. To forget, just for an hour...

"You'd better say it again," he said very quietly.

"What?"

"That you don't want me." He gave a slow shake of his head. "Because you're looking at me like I'm dinner and you haven't eaten all day."

She let out a shaky breath, and her breasts brushed his chest.

His eyes darkened, but he didn't move. "Aubrey. Say it."

"I said I don't *need* a man," she said softly. "Need and want are two different things. I *don't* need a man." She blew out a breath. "But I want one. I want you. Damn it." She was so on edge that she was already trembling, dying for his first touch. For the taste of him.

For the oblivion she knew he'd bring.

But he still didn't move.

She raised her chin, looking him straight in the eye. "Don't play hard to get, Ben. It doesn't suit you."

His jaw tightened, and she couldn't help but be a little maliciously pleased at making him as frustrated as she was. "I've just said I want you," she murmured. "So what's the problem?"

"The problem is—" His eyes dropped to her coat, the one covering her from neck to thigh.

"Yes?"

"*Shit.*" He shoved his fingers through his hair again, the muscles in his arms taut as he stood before her, the image of hot and temperamental, with testosterone and pheromones pouring off of him, and her stomach cramped.

He was going to refuse her.

Reject her. She started to turn away, but he slapped both palms on the wall on either side of her head, caging her in. "I don't need you," he said succinctly.

"Already established," she managed, her body already

humming, yearning, aching for him. Her body was a hussy.

Still holding her caged against the wall, his gaze dropped to her mouth. "This changes nothing," he said. "We do this, we're over it."

"*So* over it."

He nodded, gaze on her mouth. His own quirked very slightly. "You want me."

"In spite of yourself," she said, annoyed all to hell. "Yes."

He stared down at her for what felt like an eternity. "Lose the coat."

Chapter 12

♥

Aubrey's bones liquefied. "What?"

"You heard me," Ben said, voice so low and rough as to be a growl.

She had no idea what it said about her that she reacted to this with a shudder that was a mere millimeter below orgasm. Not taking her eyes off Ben, she reached up and slowly began to unbutton her coat. There were a lot of buttons. Each one she popped open made his eyes darken further.

After the last one, she let the coat fall. Before it hit the ground, Ben slid a hand on the nape of her neck and drew her in, his mouth closing over hers. Soft, then sure and demanding, and the hunger consumed her, hot and terrifying.

As if he felt the same, he let out one low, mirthless laugh and whispered, "Damn, you drive me insane" against her mouth.

There was a note of dazed frustration to his tone, and Aubrey absolutely knew the feeling. He wasn't in her future, and yet he tasted better than her wildest fantasies. And God help her, but she wanted more.

Leaning in again, his mouth hovered near hers as his gaze raked down her body, sending sparks racing along every nerve ending. "In those fuck-me boots, you're as tall as I am," he said.

"Is that a problem?" she asked.

"Hell, no. I like it. We're all lined up." Proving it, he hauled her in against him, one hand sliding up to sink into her hair, the other low on her back, nudging her even closer. She let out a low moan at the contact, and his lips curved in a sinful smile. His mouth should be illegal in all fifty states, but she bet he could do things with it. Things she wanted.

Bad.

He nipped at her lower lip, and she parted for him, but then he bypassed her mouth, skimming along her jaw. She heard a needy whimper. Hers, of course. Her eyes fluttered closed as he kissed a hot path to her ear and ran the tip of his nose along her lobe. "You sure this is what you want?" he asked.

Was he kidding? She was clutching him, her hands fisted in his shirt, rubbing against him like a cat in heat.

"Aubrey."

She didn't know why, but the sound of her name on his lips did something to her. Something sinfully wicked, but more, too. She took a deep breath, wrapped her arms around his neck, and melted into the planes of his hard body. "Yes. This is what I want."

"I'm not sweet," he reminded her.

"Or beta," she said. "But I'm not looking for that kind of man right this very minute."

"What are you looking for?"

"You. This."

He traced her spine with his fingertips, leaving a trail of fire that she felt all the way to her toes. Holding her gaze prisoner, he brushed his lips across hers, his hands sliding with purpose from her back southward, until he was cupping a cheek in each hand, rocking her into a most impressive erection. There was a jolt of electricity as he skimmed further south, beneath the hem of her dress.

She arched back as his clever fingers traced the edge of her thong, teasing, stroking up, and then down, and then further, between her legs.

Less clothes. She needed less clothes between them and more full frontal contact. As if reading her mind, he gave a quick yank and her thong tore free and slithered to the floor.

His eyes were black with desire. "Do you have a condom?" he asked.

"Bathroom."

He scooped her up so that she could wrap her legs around him and carried her there. He set her on the counter and flicked on the light.

"Bottom drawer," she managed.

He found the box, not commenting on the fact that it hadn't been opened. In return, she didn't comment on the fact that he obviously didn't have a condom on him. She reached out to turn off the light but he put his hand over hers. "On," he said.

Contrary to what anyone might think, she hadn't actually done this in a while. She assumed it was like getting back on a bike, but just in case it wasn't, she wanted room for error. "Ben—"

"On," he said firmly, and before she could say another word, he pulled off his shirt and she found herself sighing in pleasure at the sight of him, all lean, tough planes delineated with muscle born of years of hard physical labor.

Watching her watch him, he kicked off his work boots and finished stripping with easy, economical movements.

He was hard.

Everywhere.

Okay, well, if *this* was her view, he was right—the light could absolutely stay on.

"We good?" he asked, clearly amused by the fact that he'd just caught her drooling over him.

Yeah, she was good. So damn good…"I didn't know I was going to be so attracted to you naked," she admitted.

"Liar."

Yeah, he was right. She *was* a big fancy liar. She'd known she was attracted to Ben for a very long time. Possibly forever.

"Now you," he said, reaching for the zipper on her dress.

She held him off. "Maybe we should move to my room." *Which would have more forgiving light than these harsh fluorescents…*

In answer, his mouth came down on hers. She opened to him completely, not that he gave her a chance to do anything less. Still kissing her, he shifted to stand between her legs, opening them wider, then wider still. She lost herself in the way he devoured her mouth, so that when her dress fell to her waist, she gasped in surprise. She opened her eyes and looked into his.

"I wish you could see yourself the way I'm seeing you," he said hoarsely. Her heart clenched because she caught something in his gaze she didn't often find when people looked at her.

Raw desire.

This worked for her, but there was something else as well, possibly affection—not that she wanted to acknowledge it. Still, it was there, as apparent as the racing of her pulse. Then he leaned down and brushed his lips across hers as his hands stroked her heated flesh.

Her plan had been to infiltrate his defenses, get him naked, and—she hoped—get an orgasm while she was at it.

Stick to the plan, Aubrey.

But…but what if this was his first time since Hannah? She opened her mouth to ask, but he kissed her until she lost her train of thought. He kissed her as though he knew *exactly* what he was doing. If he was just getting back on the bike, he was having no problems. "Ben?"

He dragged that hot, talented mouth down her throat, along her collarbone, to a breast. She stopped breathing. But when he sucked her nipple into his mouth at the same time he slid a hand between her thighs, she cried out, arching back, giving him full-pass access without even realizing what she was doing.

She completely forgot what she'd wanted to ask him.

He teased her until every thought left her brain, and then he dropped to his knees and ran his hands up the inside of her legs. Holding her in place right where he wanted her, he leaned in and continued the torture with his lips, his tongue, his teeth, groaning his approval when she gasped out his name and slid her fingers into his hair. Her eyes strained to stay open because there was something about seeing him get so turned on by pleasuring her. But her eyes drifted shut in sheer, lustful bliss.

"Watch," he said, and she tried to, but he did something diabolical in tandem with his tongue and fingers that had her writhing mindlessly into him. He was taking her apart one lick at a time, and she was already quivering, on the edge, toes curled. She knew that she could give herself a somewhat satisfying orgasm in about ten minutes. A man, when she chose one, could usually get her off in about twice that.

But Ben had her shuddering in less than five minutes.

She was still lost in the throes and thinking she'd never had such an erotic experience in her life when he entered her with one hard stroke and reminded her there was more.

So much more...

She opened her eyes to find him watching her, unwavering and intense. She slid her hands up his chest and around his neck, pulling him closer as they moved together.

Unbelievably, she started to tighten around him again, though she tried to hold back. She wasn't sure why, but before she could think about it, he stroked a thumb over her swollen, wet flesh and she was gone, gone, gone. Her cry of pleasure seemed to push him over the edge. Fisting one hand in her hair, the other on her ass, holding her in place, Ben buried his face in the crook of her neck and came with her.

She didn't move for a long moment, couldn't. Ben didn't, either, and she wondered if he was as stunned as she was by the sheer sexual power they held over each other. When she finally shifted to get up, he tightened his grip on her. Face still pressed against her throat, she felt him just breathe her in. After a few minutes, he gave her a slow, lazy nuzzle, then kissed her with surprising tenderness before raising his head.

She took stock. Her dress was bunched around her waist, her only item of clothing. Well, except for her footwear. "I'm still wearing my boots," she said inanely.

He smiled. "The memory of how you look, just like this, is going to fuel my dreams for a long time to come."

She gave him a little nudge. Taking the hint, he disentangled their bodies with care, but she couldn't control the needy little gasp that escaped her at the loss. He went still for a beat, but she nudged again. Her torn panties were useless, but she managed to twist her dress back into place.

Ben hadn't made a move to get dressed. He unselfconsciously dealt with the condom disposal and then offered her a hand to help her hop down from the counter.

Life was simple for guys, apparently. No complicated emotions to think about. They could walk around naked without worrying what they looked like.

Of course, she thought, Ben didn't have to worry. He looked...edible.

The bastard.

She bent for his clothes and shoved them at him.

Taking his sweet-ass time, he pulled on his pants and straightened, and she did her best not to stare at him. But she failed. She couldn't help it; he was just so damn...hot. She let her eyes soak him up, from his still-bare chest to the fact that though his pants were on, they were unbuttoned and riding low, and he was still semihard. He looked...dangerous, she decided. And primed for another round.

Her body was game.

He flashed her a smile. He knew what she was thinking. She turned her back while he finished getting dressed, which made him laugh softly and pull her around to face him again. "Okay?" he asked.

She swallowed her half-hysterical laugh. "Well, let's see. I just had wild monkey sex with a man I can't get along with to save my life, in the bathroom above my shop, no less—which, by the way, I don't even think is locked." She tossed up her hands. "Why wouldn't I be okay?"

He studied her a moment. "We got along just fine in the past hour, I'd say."

She felt the blush race up her face. "You know what I mean."

"Yeah, I suppose I do. Do we need to talk about it?"

"Hell, no."

He looked relieved. "We said this wasn't going to change anything," he said. "We both got what we wanted."

"Yeah," she said. But what if she suddenly couldn't remember what she'd wanted?

And suddenly, he wasn't looking so relieved. He was looking…wary. "Did you change your mind, Aubrey?"

"No." Not that she would admit it anyway, not even over the threat of death and dismemberment.

"Good," he said with quiet steel. "Because I don't want a committed relationship."

"Ever?"

He hesitated. "Not any time soon, anyway."

She absorbed the unexpected shock of disappointment, and, she hoped, kept it from her face. "Then we're good."

He paused again, as if searching that statement for

honesty. "I locked the shop before I came up here," he said. "The flower shop and bakery are long closed." He smiled, his voice light and teasing when he added, "So no worries. No one could have heard you."

Oh, hell, no, he didn't just say that. She opened her mouth to tell him that they'd *both* been loud, but she shut it again.

Because he was right. *She'd* been the noisy one.

Damn. She should really have orgasms with other people more often. She moved from the bathroom to the door of her loft and not so subtly opened it for him to leave.

Ben looked amused but didn't say one word as he crossed the room. As he came up even with her, he cupped her jaw and planted one hell of a kiss on her. If she hadn't still been trembling from what they'd just done, she'd have pushed him away. But as it was, she had to fight her limbs, which wanted to cling to him like Saran Wrap.

Lifting his head, he sent her one last look of wicked promise, and then he was gone.

Alone, she shut and locked her door and then leaned back against it. *What had she just done?* There was really only one man in town who had the power to hurt her. And she'd just had sex with him.

Chapter 13

♥

Ben dreamed about Aubrey writhing in ecstasy in his arms. Best dream ever. He was late getting out of bed, but it was worth it, he thought, hitting the road running as he headed along the harbor. The icy ocean air—so cold it felt like hell had frozen over—sucked the breath from his lungs, but the discomfort was nothing compared to what he'd felt in some of the places he'd been.

Sam was waiting for him at the pier, running in place, his breath puffing out in little white clouds. "Thought maybe you weren't coming," he said, and looked Ben over carefully. "Rough night?"

Yeah, not exactly. "I'm good," Ben said. And he was. Possibly a little too good.

Sam let it go, and they ran hard, as usual. No words necessary.

An hour later, Ben was in the bookstore when Aubrey stormed in with eyes flashing, boots clicking as she moved across the floor, anger coming off her in waves.

She was wearing yet another businessy dress, this one made of soft, sweater-like material that covered her from chin to knee but nicely hugged the curves he now knew intimately.

He was pretty damn sure he should have been over her enough not to get hard at the sight of her. "What's up?" he asked.

Like he didn't know...

"My car won't start," she said animatedly, furious and beautiful. "Something happened to it overnight."

Yeah. *He'd* happened to it. He'd pulled the coil wire late the night before after a drink with Luke. The coil wire was still in his pocket, as a matter of fact.

Aubrey stalked across the store, straight to Ben's still-steaming to-go cup of coffee, which Leah had poured for him. She drank from it as though it were her lifeline.

All without making eye contact with him. "Black. Blech." She sighed. "I don't know what I'm going to do. I can't afford a mechanic."

She wasn't going to need one.

"It's always something," she said, sounding tired. Frustrated. At the end of her rope.

Still not looking at him directly.

Another man might have felt guilty as hell, but Ben told himself he wasn't another man. He wanted to know what she was up to, what was wrong, and he'd meant it when he'd said he wanted to know if she was okay. And yeah, after last night, he was more curious than ever. There was no better way to figure her out than to drive her around. "Where do you need to go?" he asked.

She looked down at her phone, thumbing through screens with dizzying speed.

He put a hand on her. "It can't be far," he said. "You need to open the store in an hour and a half, right?"

She finally looked at him and then blushed. He figured that was the "wild monkey sex," as she'd called it. The best wild monkey bathroom sex he'd ever had. "Do you need a ride?" he asked.

"No," she said quickly. Too quickly.

"Look at you, lying so early in the morning."

She blew out a breath. "Okay, so I have a few…errands to run."

"I'll take you."

She drank some more of his coffee and just stared at him. "Why would you do that?" she finally asked.

Because he was a jerk. "It's the neighborly thing to do," he settled on.

"We're not neighbors."

"Okay, it's the thing to do for someone who screamed your name as she came."

She sputtered. "I so did *not* scream your name."

"The mirror practically shattered," he said.

"I can't believe—that is just so rude of you to say."

"I loved it," he said simply, and watched as a good amount of her defensiveness drained away. "Come on," he said. "Let's hit the road. I've got an errand, too. The stain came in for your shelves. Oh, and I need to buy more condoms."

"You do *not* need more condoms. Remember? We decided we were a one-time thing—" Then she seemed to finally catch his drift and realized, belatedly, that he was just yanking her chain. "Shut up," she said.

He gave her a slow, long, hot look, and the last of her temper appeared to vanish. She squirmed a little bit, and with that little telltale move, made his entire day—though he couldn't have said why to save his life.

"What are you going to do while I'm...doing my stuff?" she asked suspiciously.

"I've got my own stuff to do in the truck while I wait."

"Yeah?" she asked. "Like what?"

He pulled out his phone. "Like kicking Jack's ass on a game we're playing."

"*Call of Duty*, or something equally alpha and macho?"

"Something like that," he said.

She finished his coffee and handed him the empty cup. "Fine," she said. "Let's go. I need to hit the grocery store first."

Two minutes later they were on the road, huddled up to the heater vents in his truck.

"You need a newer vehicle," she said, squinting through the foggy windshield.

"Shh!" He lovingly stroked the dash of the truck. "Don't listen to her, baby. You're perfect just as you are."

Aubrey rolled her eyes. "A little attached, are we?"

"Very," he said. "This was my uncle Jack's truck, you know."

She glanced at him. "No, I didn't know."

"I helped him rebuild her."

"He died while fighting a fire, right?" she asked.

"Yeah." Ben and Jack junior had been fourteen at the time. It had devastated the both of them—Jack, who'd lost his dad, and Ben, who'd lost the only father figure he'd ever known. His aunt Dee had given Ben the truck, though officially he'd had to wait several years to be old enough to drive it.

Unofficially, though, he and Jack had used it to make

more than a few illegal and illicit late-night trips. The truck had seen him through some pretty hairy times. He'd never get rid of it.

"That must have been a terrible loss for you," Aubrey said quietly.

It hadn't been his first loss, and even at age fourteen, he'd known shit happened. But yeah, it'd sucked hard. "I had Dee," he said. "She kept me on the straight and narrow." Even when he'd only added to her grief, she'd never given up on him.

"I've met her," Aubrey said. "She's a wonderful woman. Strong, too."

Ben smiled. "She had to be to keep a rein on Jack and me."

"I bet," Aubrey said on a soft laugh. "I can only imagine the holy terrors you guys must have been. Are you in contact with your parents at all?"

"No." And what went unsaid was that his dad refused visitors and he didn't even know where his mom was.

Aubrey turned from him, looking out her passenger-side window. "I was raised mostly by my mom," she said quietly. "She was twenty-one when she had me. My dad was a few years older, but still not ready for a family—though he took my sister in the divorce."

Ben glanced over at her, but she still wasn't looking at him. "They split you up like two pieces of furniture?" he asked.

"Yep," she said lightly, but the tenseness in her shoulders gave her away.

"And you don't see him much, right?" he asked.

"No." She shrugged. "He's pretty busy," she said. "He has two new daughters now."

"And a puppy." He paused. "And a dollhouse."

She turned her head and met his gaze, looking surprised that he remembered.

Didn't people listen to her? Care about her? He hated the idea that it was probably far more likely that she rarely opened up and *let* anyone listen to her. "Parents can really suck," he said.

She choked out a short laugh. "Yeah."

The coil wire in his front pocket was starting to weigh him down now, big-time, but he pulled up to the grocery store.

"Be right back," she said.

Good as her word, five minutes later she was back with a mysterious brown bag, and then directed him to a town house complex. "Be right back," she said again.

When she reappeared a few minutes later, he once again slid his phone away and looked at her.

"What?" she asked. "Do I have something in my teeth?"

"Can't tell unless you smile."

She flashed him a very fake smile, and he made a big show of looking at her teeth. "Perfect," he said, and flashed her a *real* smile. "Are you going to cross a name off your list?"

She studied him a moment. "Not yet."

He looked at the town house she'd just come from. "Who lives there?"

"Carla. My sister."

"You bring your sister groceries?"

Aubrey shrugged, a little embarrassed, he thought. "She's a resident at the hospital and working crazy hours," she said. "She's exhausted and doesn't have time to do stuff like get food."

"That's…sweet of you."

She looked at him. "You and I both know I'm not sweet."

It was true that he'd never thought of her as particularly sweet, but he was beginning to change his mind. "Your boots are wet."

"I watered her plants."

Yeah, he was definitely changing his mind about her. "Where to now?" he asked.

She hesitated.

"We can just sit here if you'd rather."

She was turned away from him, staring out into the gray morning so that he couldn't see her face. He didn't have to; he could sense the eye roll. "The pier," she finally said. "And this time, *no questions*."

Aubrey's nerves were high and getting higher. She didn't wait for Ben to turn off the engine at the next stop. The moment he pulled into the pier parking lot, she slid out of the truck and then paused, glancing back at him. "You're waiting here, right?"

"Right."

She didn't trust him. "Promise?"

"What are you so worried I'm going to see?" he asked in that lazy, calm voice that made her want to crawl into his lap and cajole him into taking her to the same place he'd taken her last night in her bathroom.

But that wasn't going to happen. That had been a one-time thing.

The best one-time thing ever…

Shaking that off, she looked at him. It hadn't escaped her notice that he *hadn't* promised. He was in dark reflective glasses, so she couldn't see his eyes. His hair was finger-combed at best, and he had sawdust on his jeans from working at her bookstore. "I mean it, Ben," she said. "This is my business."

"Whatever you say, Sunshine." He pulled out his phone, presumably accessing whatever shoot 'em up, kill 'em game he was playing with Jack.

It was as close to a promise as she was going to get, and she knew it. She blew out a breath and then caught sight of his screen. Not a shoot 'em up, kill 'em game at all. "*Words with Friends*?" she asked. "*That's* the killer game you play?"

"It can be killer," he said lightly, his manhood apparently not threatened in the slightest. "Hey, do you know a seven-letter word that's got the letter *X* in it? I've got a triple-word opportunity here."

"Extinct," she said, "which is what I'm going to make you if you follow me." She shut the truck door on that ridiculous threat and walked off.

The Ferris wheel was lit up but not turning. It was icy cold outside, but she ignored the wind as she walked past the diner and then the arcade. Between the arcade and Ferris wheel were two kiosks. One sold ice cream, another sold locally made items.

Both were closed now. The ice cream shop was actually boarded up. The two brothers who ran the place didn't work during the winter months. One of them, Lance, suffered from cystic fibrosis, so they usually— providing Lance's health allowed it—took off somewhere south for warmer weather.

The other kiosk wasn't closed for the season. In fact, the woman who ran it was there right now, getting ready to open up for the day. She was busy flipping through a stack of receipts and not paying any attention to the pier around her until Aubrey stopped right in front of her.

Her name was Cathy, and she sold beautiful handmade scarves, hats, and throws she and a few other local women created.

Looking up with a friendly smile, Cathy said, "I'm still closed, but if you see something you like, I could probably be talked into a quick deal."

Aubrey reached out and ran her fingers over a knitted infinity scarf the color of a rich ruby. Soft as heaven. "It's beautiful. They're all beautiful," she said.

"That one would look good on you, with that coat and your golden hair."

Aubrey pulled it off the rack and draped it around her neck. She peered into one of the mirrors hanging on the side of the kiosk.

"Pretty," Cathy said.

Aubrey looked at her reflection and met Cathy's eyes in the mirror behind her. "You don't remember me."

"Oh, I remember you," Cathy said. "We were in PE together. And cooking class."

Aubrey let out a breath. "I came here to see you."

"Why?"

"Because I've never been able to forget how I teased you for being so skinny," Aubrey said quietly. "It was rude, and so wrong." It'd haunted her all these years.

"Well, I *was* skinny," Cathy said, and adjusted Aubrey's hair so it fell better over the scarf in the back. "And I've always thought you did it because you were jealous."

"Definitely jealous," Aubrey said. "I had to run off my

nightly junk food every single morning and I was *still* curvy. I was unbearably jealous of how you looked, but it's no excuse."

Cathy once again met her gaze in the mirror. "I was anorexic. Did you know that?"

"No." *God.* Aubrey closed her eyes. "I'm so sorry, Cathy."

"I was anorexic," Cathy said again. "And no one noticed that I was starving myself. Except you."

Aubrey opened her eyes and once again met Cathy's.

"You got me to eat one of the cheeseburgers we made for cooking class—do you remember?" Cathy asked. "It was our midterm, and we were required to eat what we cooked. I tried to throw mine away, but you told on me and then I had to eat the burger in front of the whole class."

Aubrey winced at the memory. "Yeah, I remember. I—"

"No, listen to me." Cathy's voice shook a little now. "I hadn't eaten in a week, Aubrey. That burger was the best thing I'd ever tasted. It helped me to start eating again."

Aubrey let out a breath. "I'm glad. So glad. But I shouldn't have done any of that to you. Not that I'm trying to excuse myself, but I was trying to lose weight. I needed to fit into a stupid pageant gown for an upcoming beauty contest, and I couldn't. I was starving myself, too, and so hungry and angry all the time—but I wasn't anorexic. I was just a bitch."

Cathy smiled. "Yeah. You were that." She cocked her head and studied Aubrey's reflection. "I was going to overcharge you for this scarf, you know. Because I'm a bitch, too." She smiled. "But you know? We didn't turn out so bad after all."

* * *

Ben was leaning against his truck, sipping the coffee he'd purchased from the diner with one hand and beating Jack's ass in *Words with Friends* with his other hand when Aubrey stepped off the pier and headed his way.

It'd only been about fifteen minutes, but she looked like she'd lost a little bit of the chip on her shoulder. He didn't say a word as he opened the door for her.

"Pretty scarf," he said, and watched her hand fly to the material now wrapped around her neck.

But she said nothing.

"How'd it go?" he asked.

More nothing.

"Do you have any gum?" he asked.

"Yes." She opened her purse, and he reached in and smoothly grabbed her notebook.

"*Hey*," she said.

He flipped it open. "We crossing anyone off yet?"

She snatched it back and hugged it to herself.

Reaching past her into the glove compartment, he pulled out a pen and handed it to her.

She glared at him for a beat and then snatched the pen. She opened her pad and very carefully crossed off number four.

Cathy.

He smiled at her. "Where to now?"

She reached for his coffee, but he got to it first, lifting it out of her reach. "You could do me next. Seeing as I'm sitting right here."

"I could *do* you? You think I'm going to *do* you right here in your truck?"

He had to work hard to keep from laughing. "I meant the list. I'm on your list."

"Oh." She narrowed her gaze at him, her cheeks flushed. "I've told you, you're *not* the Ben on my list."

"Prove it," he said.

"What?"

"If I'm not the Ben on your list, then who is?"

She just looked at him for a long moment. "You have a shovel?" she finally asked.

"In the back. Why?"

"Can you go back to the store?"

"Sure. On the drive there, you can tell me what your definition of 'do me' is."

She blushed some more and ignored him. At the store, she was gone for less than five minutes, and then she climbed back into the truck a little breathlessly. "Head out on Route Ten," she said.

"You should feel free to show me this bossy side of you in bed anytime."

She sent him a baleful glance as he pulled out of the parking lot and headed to Route 10. The highway turned inland—not up into the mountains, but east, to the far end of the county. The houses out here were few and far between. There were a few ranches, but mostly these places were older and run-down.

"Turn right," Aubrey said, looking down at her map app.

Ben followed her directions onto a dirt road, and then onto a dirty driveway. The mobile home there was a double-wide. Sitting on the porch was an old guy in a rocking chair.

Ben stopped the truck. "Is that...Mr. Wilford?"

"*Ben* Wilford," Aubrey said smugly.

"The mean old science teacher?"

"He's retired now, but yes. And mean is an understatement," she muttered under her breath.

"*This* is the Ben on your list?" he asked in disbelief.

"Yes, Mr. Egomaniac, this is the Ben on my list. Stay here," she said, and started to slide out of the truck.

He caught her arm. At the touch, she went still as if prodded with an electrical current.

He knew exactly, because he felt it as well. And it told him something, something he hadn't been prepared for. They *weren't* done with each other.

Not by a long shot.

This wasn't good news. Neither was the fact that he was playing with her. He'd tricked her into needing a ride from him and he'd justified it because he wanted to know what she was up to.

But the joke was on him, because he realized the truth—he just *wanted* to be with her.

That wasn't good news, either.

"What?" she asked.

More than a little unhappy with his epiphany, he shook his head. "Nothing." And then he let go of her, gesturing for her to have at it. Whatever "it" was.

She slid out of the truck and headed to the back to pull out his shovel. Then, carrying the shovel, she walked up to the double-wide in her fancy dress and coat, as though she belonged there.

Mr. Wilford stood, eyes narrowed and nearly hidden behind his white, bushy brows. Ben rolled down his window, but he still couldn't catch any words. He didn't have any trouble at all catching Mr. Wilford's bad attitude, though. Ben braced to get out of the truck, but the old man got up, limped to his front door, and vanished inside—but not before slamming the door, practically on Aubrey's nose.

Damn it, that pissed Ben off. But Aubrey merely squared her shoulders and vanished around the back of the trailer.

Ben waited a minute and then followed. He couldn't help it if he wanted to make sure she was okay. And that Mr. Wilford didn't shoot her for trespassing. He risked Aubrey clobbering him over the head with the shovel for not staying in the truck, but he'd deal with that when he got closer. He wasn't actually too worried, but he'd discovered something about his odd relationship with Aubrey. He preferred kissing her to arguing with her.

Not that he was exactly comfortable with that...

Chapter 14

♥

Twenty-five minutes later, Aubrey slid back into Ben's truck. The ground had been frozen and was almost impossible to break apart, forcing her to work her ass off. As a result, she was hot and sweaty, but she felt good about the morning's progress. Very good. Lowering the truck's sun visor, she studied her reflection in the small mirror there. Not too bad. She swiped at her slightly smudged mascara. Then she pulled out her notebook and, with great ceremony for the man seated next to her, she crossed off BEN. "There," she said to Ben. "All taken care of."

"Uh-huh," he said.

"Yep. Ben's off my list." It wasn't the *right* Ben, of course. The right Ben was seated next to her, but he didn't need to know that.

Nor did he need to know how much it was killing her, how she was sleeping less and less at night, worried about exactly that.

His being on her list.

Not to mention his reaction when he found out. She couldn't bring herself to tell him, not yet. He'd walk away, and even knowing that's what she deserved, she wasn't ready for it.

"Well, if you're righting your wrongs," he said—clearly fishing but coming so uncomfortably close to the truth that she held her breath—"then don't forget Kristan. Remember how mean you were to her in high school when she took your spot in the school play?"

Kristan wasn't on Aubrey's list. Nor would she be. "She tripped me at rehearsal, and I sprained my ankle so that I couldn't dance the lead. If I were making a list of wrongs to right, which I'm not"—she paused when he snorted, and she sent him a glare—"then *I* should be on *her* list." She swiped her sweaty brow and sat back, arms still trembling from exertion.

He started the truck and took them back to the highway. "You want to talk about it?" he asked casually.

No. She didn't want to talk about last night and the best sex she'd ever had. She was afraid she'd beg for more. "Talk about...?"

He glanced at her. "You were out there digging for something—or attempting to, anyway, since the ground was pretty frozen."

Damn it, he'd sneaked a peek. "A pumpkin patch," she admitted. She leaned back and sighed. "And if you were spying on me, the least you could have done was come help."

He gave her a slow, lazy grin that did things to her girl parts. Each and every one. And thanks to him, there were more of those parts than she'd remembered. "You looked like you were doing all right," he said.

Trying to ignore her annoying reaction to him, which she was helpless to prevent, she sighed. "Gee, thanks."

"So why were you digging Mr. Asshole a pumpkin patch in the off-season?"

She looked at him. "It's the off-season?"

He grinned. "Little bit, Sunshine."

Damn. She'd not even thought of that, and she hadn't looked at the seed packet when she'd bought it earlier at the grocery store. "How about I answer a question, and then you answer a question?" she suggested.

"Fine," he said. "You first. What the hell was that back there?"

She slid on her sunglasses. "Mr. Wilford gave me an F in eighth-grade science because he didn't like me."

"He didn't like anyone."

"But I'm the only one he failed. He said I was cheating when in fact I wasn't." She paused. "Okay, so I *was* cheating, but only to help Lance."

"The kid with cystic fibrosis? The one who runs the ice cream joint on the pier in the summer?"

"Yeah. He'd been going through a rough patch and had missed a week of school. He couldn't catch up, so I was feeding him the answers to the test. Mr. Wilford caught me." She'd never forget how he'd stood over her, those bushy brows—which were black then—bunched together. And how he'd said so harshly, *You're a selfish girl, Aubrey Wellington. No one likes a selfish girl.*

She'd heard *No one likes you,* and she'd reacted with predictable bad behavior. "Lance tried to tell Mr. Wilford the truth," she said, "but he wouldn't listen. He thought I was a bad seed, and his mind was made up. So he failed me."

She'd then been disqualified from two beauty contests that her mom had already paid for and bought gowns for, and it'd been a huge drama in the house. "I tried to talk to him about it after school," she said. "I found him in the school garden, working on his pumpkin patch with the garden club." She blew out a breath and a low laugh. "I can still see him standing there among his prize pupils and his equally prized pumpkins, pointing a dirty, bony finger in my direction. He said"—she adopted a low baritone—"*You, Aubrey Wellington, will* never *amount to anything.*"

"He thought we were all miscreants," Ben said quietly. "But he shouldn't have said that to you."

"Actually, in hindsight I probably deserved it," she said. "I was a total shit. But there was something in his tone that got me. And then he just walked away, like I wasn't worth his time."

"He spoke like Darth Vader," Ben said, "and walked like he had a stick up his ass."

She laughed. "Yes," she finally said. "But at the time I didn't think about that. I was embarrassed and humiliated." She paused and then admitted the rest. "I kicked one of his pumpkins and broke it loose from the stem. I didn't find out until the next day that it'd been one of his award-winning pumpkins, the one he'd planned on taking to the annual pumpkin contest—which had a thousand-dollar prize."

"Ouch," Ben said.

Aubrey sighed. "He cried. Mr. Wilford cried." She was still staring out the side window, so she was surprised when she felt his warm fingers close over hers.

"You were just a kid, Aubrey."

"Yeah, but not really. And I cost the school garden club that grand. I've always felt so bad about that."

"So you dug him a new pumpkin patch," Ben said. "What's your plan, to grow him another award-winning pumpkin?"

She bit her lower lip, and he laughed. "It is," he said, and laughed again.

"Stop that."

"It's cute," he said.

"Cute?" She almost choked on the word. No one had ever called her cute before, not ever. Her phone rang, and she pulled it out, frowning at the unknown number. "Hello?"

"Aubrey Wellington," said Darth Vader's voice. "What did you do to my backyard?"

"Mr. Wilford?" she asked, glancing over at Ben in shock.

"Well, how many other people's yards did you decimate today?" he asked testily. "What the hell did you do?"

"I...dug you a pumpkin patch," she said. "I planted pumpkin seeds."

Ben smiled.

"You *what*?" Mr. Wilford asked.

"I ruined your prize pumpkin all those years ago, remember? And how did you get my number?"

"Of course I remember what you did. You cost me a thousand bucks and ruined the best pumpkin I ever grew. And this is Lucky Harbor. It was easy to get your number; I called Lucille."

"I'm going to grow you new pumpkins," she said.

"Off-season?"

She sighed. "Okay, so I didn't plan that part so well.

But maybe one of them will be a prize pumpkin," she said. "It's my way of apologizing."

"Fat lot of good that's going to do me now," he said. "I'm too old to be worried about the watering."

Well, crap. She hadn't thought of that, either. "I'll do it," she said.

Ben laughed and then choked it off when she glared at him.

"*You're* going to water the pumpkins?" Mr. Wilford asked in disbelief. "You, Miss Fancy Pants?"

"Yes," she said through her teeth. "I am."

"Pumpkins like to be watered regularly," he warned.

"Fine. Um, how often is regular—" But he'd hung up. She slid her phone away.

Ben was still grinning.

"Not a word," she said, Googling "pumpkin patches." "Unless you know how often to water pumpkins."

That night, Aubrey closed up the bookstore after a decent business day and smiled as she walked across the scarred hardwood floors. They'd been a surprising find beneath the carpet. The wood was nice and light, and it seemed to open up the store.

Happy, she headed up to her loft. There, she pulled out her notebook and eyed the crossed-off items, including BEN.

She'd improvised there, and she thought maybe she'd actually pulled it off. But now, without Ben's prying eyes watching her, she added one more item to the bottom of her list.

THE HARD ONE.

Chapter 15

♥

The next morning, Ben went to work on the countertop for the serving area of the Book & Bean.

Aubrey was two weeks away from her grand-opening party.

Though it would be close, the renovations would be done on time. Ben thought of the coil wire in his pocket. He'd hoped to get at least one more day of driving Aubrey around, even though he was pretty sure he knew exactly what she was up to now.

And it wasn't trouble. In fact, it was the opposite of trouble. She was working at righting her wrongs, and it was tugging at a part of him that didn't want to be tugged.

He hadn't planned on feeling anything for her and was now trying to resign himself to the fact that they had more than just some seriously explosive chemistry. He'd told himself that they could get past that by spending some quality naked time together, but they'd already tried that, and it'd backfired because he'd gotten past exactly nothing. In fact, now all he wanted was more. A lot more.

It was 7:00 a.m. before he heard signs of life from above, and thirty minutes more before the telltale *click, click, click* of her boots alerted him that she was coming down. And, like Pavlov's dog, he started to go hard.

He was ridiculous.

"Ben?"

And just like that, the sound of her husky voice finished the job. He wondered what she'd say to a second round of wild monkey sex, right here, right now. If he just stripped her out of her clothes and sat her on the stack of wood he still had to measure and cut, he could then step between her legs. He'd slide his hands beneath her sexy ass, of course, to prevent splinters. Or they could use her couch. Better yet, he could bend her over the stack of boxes of new stock that'd come in, shove up her dress, and take her from behind.

Yeah. *That* was the ticket.

She came around the corner, and he unbuckled his tool belt, letting it fall to the floor. They were going to do this, and it was going to be good—

"I've got company," Aubrey said. She went to the front door of the store and opened it.

And then one, two, three...*eight* women came in behind her, one of them his own aunt Dee.

Lucky Harbor's resident hell-raisers.

Dee smiled and waved at him, giving him a sweet kiss on the cheek as she passed him.

"What are you doing here?" he asked. Croaked.

"Aubrey's invited my book club to meet at her store," Dee said. She frowned at him. "You sick, honey?"

"No." Dee's book club was a weekly event—"club" being a loose word for a bunch of women who got together, drank too much wine, laughed so loud they could break windows, and talked about everything *but* books. The "club" had been kicked out of the diner, the bar and grill, *and* the senior center. They'd been talking about having to disband.

He glanced at Aubrey.

"I wanted them to have a place to go," she said.

"You're going to need a 'crazy' permit," he said.

Dee smacked him upside the head. "We're trying something new," she said. "Meeting in the early mornings. You know, before people get...feisty."

Ben sent Aubrey a *good luck* look that she ignored. Instead, she walked her guests through the bookstore and sat them in the chairs and on the couch that he'd just made nefarious plans for.

"So," she said, looking to the seniors' ringleader—Lucille, of course. "What do you think?"

"It's perfect," Lucille said. "We're so honored that you'd have us, honey."

Ben shook his head, cleaned up, and left out the back door. Then he stared at Aubrey's car in the lot.

Which was minus its coil wire.

He wrestled with his conscience and lost. Blowing out a sigh, he popped open the hood and began to put it back.

"Whatcha doing?"

He nearly jumped out of his skin, then gave Luke a long look across the engine compartment.

Luke grinned. "Scared ya. You committing a misdemeanor for any reason in particular?"

"I'm not committing anything. And why are you here?"

"Got a call that a suspicious-looking character was lounging around back here and screwing up cars that belong to pretty blondes."

"Bullshit."

"Okay, I didn't get a call," Luke said. "I stopped by Ali's shop to say hey."

No, he'd stopped by the shop to get laid. Because Luke had an unmistakable I-just-got-laid look to him. Ben sighed. He'd like to have that look...

"So want to tell me what you're up to?" Luke asked.

"Hell, no."

Luke grinned. "That's okay. I already figured it out."

"No, you didn't."

"Sure I did. You kissed Aubrey last week, and now you're doing something stupid to fuck it all up."

Ben narrowed his gaze. "Let me guess how you know about the kiss. Facebook?"

"Ali." Luke shrugged. "You were the one stupid enough to do it up against the wall and visible through the window. Rookie mistake," he said, and tsked.

"Don't you have somewhere to be?" Ben asked.

"Nope. So. You and Aubrey, huh? You two going to...?"

Well, at least he didn't know *that* much. Ben didn't answer. Instead he made sure the coil wire was back in place and shut the hood. Then he headed toward his truck.

"Hey," Luke said. "Waiting for the details here."

"Ask your fiancée."

Ben did a morning run with Sam, who, unlike some of his nosy-ass friends, did *not* press him for details on the Aubrey situation.

After their run, Ben headed to Seattle. He found Bob's Auto Shop, parked, and walked to the first open bay. A linebacker-size guy rolled out from beneath a lifted truck, wearing overalls and no shirt. He didn't need one; he had tat sleeves down both arms and over his chest. The patch on his overalls read BIG ED. "Can I help you?" the giant asked.

"I'm looking for Dan Ingalls," Ben said.

Big Ed gave a chin jerk toward the next car over. The guy working on it was built the same as Ed the Linebacker, though he was wearing a shirt. He had tats, too, including a teardrop beneath his eye.

The patch on *his* overalls read BIG BOB.

Ben was sensing a pattern here. "How you doing?" he asked Big Bob.

Big Bob didn't smile, just looked at him as he slowly cracked his knuckles.

A real friendly bunch. Terrific. "Looking for Dan Ingalls," Ben said again.

Big Bob did the same chin jerk Big Ed had done, toward the back of the shop this time. Ben headed back there, very aware that he now had the two guys at his back and most likely yet another one in front of him somewhere. He found a truck, hood up, and indeed there was a guy standing on a step stool, head buried in the engine compartment, torquing something.

"Dan Ingalls?" Ben asked.

Dan didn't stop what he was doing or even look up. "Who wants to know?"

"A friend of your kids."

Dan went still, not even pulling his head out of the compartment. "What?"

He didn't repeat himself. Still keeping track of the big boys, Bob and Ed, at his back, Ben kept his voice low. He wasn't too worried; he'd been in worse spots—far worse—but there was no reason to be stupid.

Dan straightened. He was easily one-third the size of his two co-workers. No muscles. No tats. What he did have was crazy, wild hair, the exact color of a copper penny, flying around his thin, angular face and stark blue eyes. He was skinny as a toothpick and short enough to barely meet Ben's shoulder. "Who are you?" he asked.

"Ben McDaniel. I live in Lucky Harbor, where your girls live in a foster home. A *shitty* foster home," Ben added harshly. "And I wanted to see why they aren't with you."

Dan looked a little shaken. "I don't have kids."

Ben arched a brow.

Dan came down off the stepladder and hitched his chin to indicate Ben should follow him out of the garage. They passed the very large Big Ed, and then the equally large Big Bob, both of whom were watching Ben with stony expressions.

Ben ignored them completely.

"Sorry about that," Dan said when they were outside. "They're…protective of me."

"Why? Are you in some kind of trouble?"

Dan looked away for a moment, then gained a slight measure of Ben's respect when he met Ben's gaze straight on. "I was."

"And your kids?"

Dan shook his head. "I told you, I don't have any."

"Odd, since you have two mini-me's in Lucky Harbor who are your spitting image."

Dan gave a sharp exhale and walked away, going about ten feet before pacing back. "I waived my rights so that they could get adopted."

"Then why are they in a foster home?"

"Because their mom died," Dan said.

"And you didn't feel the need to take them?"

"I couldn't."

"Why?"

"I'm not father material."

"Should have thought about that before you had them," Ben said.

Again Dan paced. "What do you mean, the foster home is shitty?" he finally asked.

"You don't know what 'shitty' means?"

Dan sank to a concrete planter that had nothing it in but dirt and cigarette butts. He shoved his fingers through his hair and studied his knees. "I didn't want this life for them."

"Well, what the hell did you think would happen when their mom died and you didn't step up?"

"I—I don't know. I…I was in jail for a while."

"Yeah, your daughters told me."

He looked sick. "They know?"

"I'm not sure what they know, but they said you're up for, and I quote, 'the big one.'"

"Jesus." Dan rubbed a shaky hand over his mouth. "They're five."

"They're growing up fast."

"Jesus," Dan said again.

"What did you do time for?"

"Being in the wrong place at the wrong time," Dan said.

Ben gave him a *go on* look.

He let out a long breath. "They got me on armed robbery and involuntary manslaughter."

"Christ." Ben shook his head. "Never mind, then. I've got the wrong guy for those girls." He turned to go.

"Wait."

Ben turned back. "What?"

"How are they?"

"What do you care?"

Dan winced but held eye contact. "Listen, you have no reason to believe me, but the whole arrest…it was a mistake, okay? But regardless, I did the time. I paid the price. I'm out. Making myself a life."

"Without them," Ben said harshly.

"I thought they were safe. Happy. Why would I mess with that?"

"Because they need their dad."

"I'm not equipped to handle kids," Dan said. "I wouldn't know what to do with them."

"How about caring about their welfare? You have a job. You're a mechanic, so I assume you have wheels. You could get visitation. Hell, you should have custody."

"I have visitation rights. But I'm not good with kids."

"You're their dad," Ben said again, voice hard. "That means it doesn't matter that you're a pussy—you man up."

"Hey," a low, angry voice said. "You don't talk to him like that."

Ben turned to Big Bob and got sucker punched in the eye.

It was the only punch Bob landed.

Five minutes later, both Bob and Ed were on the ground, Bob holding his ribs and Ed holding his jaw. Ben brushed off his hands. Ed had landed a good blow to the kidney, but Ben was okay. Still, he should probably get back to a gym. Breathing a little hard, he turned to Dan.

Dan, eyes wide, raised his hands. "Hey, I warned you. I told you they were protective of me."

"Yeah." Ben touched his already aching eye. "Thanks."

"You're pretty fucking *badass*," Dan said, impressed. "You were in prison, too?"

"No. I was in hell. Go see your kids."

Chapter 16

♥

Aubrey woke up to a grumpy Gus staring her down. She got up, fed the demanding cat, and then went to work. She unpacked and shelved her new stock. She placed next week's order and spent an hour on hold with her phone company to complain about having Internet only in the western half of the store.

Afterward, a customer came in and spent half an hour walking the aisles and occasionally lifting a book up and looking to Aubrey. "What's this one about?"

Aubrey had ceased to be surprised about the fact that people actually assumed she'd read every book in the store. She'd also learned that the people who browsed the way this woman did almost always left without actually buying a book at all, so she'd started amusing herself by making up plots on the spot. Still on hold with the phone company, she covered the receiver and said, "That one's about an alien who comes to the Wild, Wild West."

The woman nodded and put the book back. One aisle later, she picked up another.

Aubrey searched her brain's database. After half an hour, she was beginning to run out of material. "That one's about a guy who goes a little crazy after a failed marriage and ends up in a dancing contest with another woman."

The woman put that book back, too, and Aubrey told herself she really needed to find a new hobby. But finally the woman came to the front. "Do you have anything like that *Fifty Shades*?" she asked.

"Now, that I do have," Aubrey said, and led her to the romance section.

After the woman left—without buying anything—Aubrey began doing what she'd put off doing all day yesterday: searching for a mechanic. Her selection was limited, as there were only a few in Lucky Harbor, and most likely she couldn't afford any of them. At that thought, she went to her brand-new coffee nook, which she'd already stocked. There was a small flask there for Lucille, who liked brandy in her tea. Aubrey preferred a little tea in her brandy, but she didn't touch either one of them now. No, she went straight for the box of sugar cookies she'd put away for a high-stress day.

Breakfast of champions.

"Hey."

At the sound of Ben's voice behind her, she jumped. "Where did you learn to walk so quietly?"

"Work."

She thought about what that might mean, given that he'd been working in places far more dangerous than she could possibly contemplate. She craned her neck to look at him and gasped. "What happened to you?"

"Nothing."

"*Nothing* gave you a black eye?"

He shrugged.

She went to the freezer beneath the counter and pulled out a small bag of frozen peas.

He looked at the bag. "Why do you have frozen peas in a bookstore?"

"They're for cramps." She placed the bag over his eye, smiling when he sucked in a breath at the cold. "Baby," she said.

His look might have had another man wetting his pants and any woman on the planet licking her lips, but she told herself she was unmoved.

But she wasn't. "What happened?"

"Nothing," he repeated. "What are you doing?"

"I don't answer questions for people who answer a question with another question."

He smiled. "How about we each answer a question?"

She opened her mouth, but he put a finger to her lips. "With a twist," he said.

Her stomach fluttered. "What's the twist?"

"If you don't answer, you get a dare."

Her brain went off the rails at the thought of what a dare might include. But curiosity won over self-preservation. "Deal. Tell me what happened to you."

"I went to talk to Pink and Kendra's dad."

"So…he punched you?"

"Nah. He's just a little guy."

"Then who punched you?"

"Dan and I were having a private little chat and his two linebacker buddies decided they didn't like me much."

"So *they* punched you?"

He shrugged. "One of them got a shot in before."

"Oh, my God, you are the worst storyteller ever," she declared, tossing up her hands and making him smile. "Before *what*?" she demanded.

He watched her, still clearly amused. "Before they decided they were done tangling with me," he finally said.

"Yeah?" she said, eyes narrowing. "And what made them decide that?"

He just kept looking at her.

"You took them *both* down?" she asked, horrified.

"Your turn to talk," he said enigmatically.

"Oh, no," she said. "I had to dig that story out of you. You owe me a dare by default."

"Sure," he agreed too easily in that low, gruff voice that made her nipples harden. "Anything."

She nearly swallowed her tongue. "You can't promise me 'anything,'" she said, annoyed to find she sounded breathless.

He didn't look worried. "Why? Are you going to take advantage of me?"

Her entire body tightened at the thought of all she could do to take advantage of him and the pleasure they could both get out of it.

He took in her expression and laughed softly. "Hold that thought. Now answer my question or face a dare."

"I'm hiring a mechanic."

"Thought you couldn't afford one."

"I can't," she said, trying not to notice that his hair was still wet from a recent shower, and that he smelled really good. Guy good, like soap and deodorant and Ben. She wanted to press her face to his throat. Especially since he'd clearly skipped shaving that morning—and maybe the day before, too—and had the exact right amount of scruff on his face to make him look hot as hell.

He came closer, giving her a better view of the way his broad shoulders stretched the material of his shirt and how his long legs were encased in denim worn to a buttery softness by myriad washings, lovingly cupping certain parts—

He shut the laptop she still had open on the counter.

"Hey," she said.

"Hay is for horses." He hauled her close, making her breath catch in her throat as her gaze drifted to his mouth.

The mouth she'd been dreaming about.

Damn him.

Then she realized that mouth was moving, and the words sank in. "*I* sabotaged your car," he said.

She blinked. "What?"

"Yeah. I removed your coil wire. It's back in now, though. Your car's fine, Aubrey."

When this computed, she went from the good kind of hot to the very bad kind of hot in the blink of an eye. She couldn't even speak. All she did was sputter. A minute ago, she'd wanted to press herself to him like white on rice. She still wanted that. But she wanted to smack him more. She settled on giving him a good shove.

He didn't budge.

"I wanted to see what you were up to," he said. "I wanted to make sure you were okay."

"It was none of your business!"

He shrugged, and that just pissed her off even more. "Why?" she managed. "Why does anything I do even matter to you?"

He scrubbed a hand over his jaw. The sound of his palm scrapping over several days' worth of whisker growth had her belly quivering. *Keep it together.* "*Why,* Ben?"

He shook his head.

"Not good enough," she said. "Tell me why what I do matters to you."

"It shouldn't," he said, meeting her gaze steadily.

She just stared at him. "You're incredible, you know that? You're an insensitive, first-class jerk, and—"

He leaned in. "And what?" he asked, his voice dangerously low.

"And…" Stymied at her ridiculous and invariable reaction to him, she put her hands to his chest to give him another shove, but somehow her wires got crossed and she fisted his shirt instead.

"Dare me," he said softly.

"Dare you to what?"

"Dare me, Aubrey."

Oh, how she hated how well he knew her. "I dare you to kiss me," she whispered, and then to make sure he did, she put her mouth on his first.

He yanked her in hard, so that she fell into him. It was crazy, but she slid her hands up his chest and into his hair to hold him to her. He had one hand up the back of her sweater on bare skin, his fingers spread as if he wanted to touch as much of her as possible. His other hand slid down, cupping her bottom, which made him groan.

"You drive me crazy," he said against her mouth. "You taste so fucking good. You always taste so fucking good."

She might have said *ditto*, but then his tongue stroked hers, and they both moaned. Then he was trailing hot, open-mouthed kisses along her jaw to her ear, which he nipped, and her knees melted. "Damn it," she sighed.

She felt him smile against her skin before he kissed the spot just beneath her lobe. She shivered and knew she was a goner. She was even hearing a ringing in her head—

The store's phone.

She must have missed four rings, because it clicked over to the machine, and they heard her own voice saying, "Book and Bean. Leave a message, and I'll get back to you as soon as possible."

And then came Mr. Wilford's voice.

"Listen, missy. You dug this pumpkin garden; you need to get your skinny ass out here and water it. I'm too old for this. You hear me?"

"Why does everyone call my ass skinny?" Aubrey asked the room.

"It's a good ass," Ben said, hands on it. He squeezed. "*Really* good."

There was a knock at the door, and she pushed free. "Oh, my God. I have work." She poked him with a finger. "Stop distracting me with your mouth!"

"I could distract you with another body part instead. Say the word."

"Oh, no, you don't. You're done distracting me. I don't sleep with guys who sabotage my car. And why did you do it?"

At the second, more persistent knock, he gestured to the door. "You're ignoring a paying customer."

"We're not done with this," she warned him.

"No doubt."

Chapter 17

♥

Mornings were easier these days, thanks to the new routine of hitting the bakery before opening the bookstore.

Aubrey was sitting on Leah's back counter, inhaling powdered doughnut holes left over from the day before. She'd just told them how Ben had pulled her coil wire and had paused, expecting a suitable level of outrage from her friends.

Instead, Leah laughed. She laughed so hard she slid down the cabinet and ended up sitting on the floor.

Ali laughed, too, though she managed to remain upright. "So cute," she said.

"*Cute?*" Aubrey repeated, outraged all over again. "How in the world is that cute?"

"He likes you," Ali said simply, and popped another doughnut hole in her mouth.

"What is this, high school?" Aubrey muttered, reaching for another doughnut hole, too. "And he doesn't like me. And I don't like him. He just did it so he could figure out what I was up to."

Leah nodded. "No doubt. But I bet this entire box of doughnut holes that he also did it because he has a protective streak a mile long regarding people he cares about." She smiled when Aubrey didn't have a ready retort. "And in any case, you could just tell him what you're up to, you know. Or tell us."

Aubrey let out a breath. "I haven't told anyone."

"All the more reason to tell *us*," Leah said. "This"— doughnut hole in hand, she gestured to the kitchen around them—"is the cone of silence. Nothing you say here can be repeated outside this room without permission from the tellee."

"Tellee?" Aubrey said.

"You," Leah said.

Aubrey looked at Ali. Ali nodded and held up two fingers, as though she were making an oath.

"Were you a Girl Scout?" Aubrey asked.

"No," Ali said. "But I totally could've been. I can make all kinds of knots in ropes. And I look pretty good in khaki."

Leah nodded. "This is true."

Aubrey sighed. "Okay, fine. It's my karma. It's...shaky at best. I needed to fix some things from my past, so I made a list."

"A list?" Ali asked.

"Of people I wronged."

"Well, hell, Aubrey," Leah said. "We *all* could make a list."

"Really?" Aubrey asked. "Did either of *you* sleep with your married professor in college? Because he's number seven."

"Okay, that's pretty bad," Ali said after a moment of silence. "But I've made some pretty damn spectacular mistakes myself, so there's no judgment here. Would you like my opinion?"

"Could I stop you?" Aubrey asked drily.

Ali laughed. "Probably not. I told you that I saw you and Ben through the window of your store, right?"

For a beat, Aubrey's heart stopped, until she realized that Ali was referring to the kiss, not the...deed.

"What I saw was really hot," Ali said. "So hot you nearly steamed up the glass. But it was more than just lust. He cupped your head, Aubrey."

"Aw," Leah said on a dreamy sigh. "He did? Really? God, I love that man."

Aubrey shook her head to clear it, but nope, she was still confused. "What does it matter that he cupped my head?"

"It means it wasn't just a kiss," Ali said. "It was more. And we"—she gestured between herself and Leah—"having recently found the loves of our lives, can tell the difference between sex and love."

Leah nodded in agreement.

"When you do it with Ben," Ali went on, "it won't be just sex. It'll be *love*."

Aubrey inhaled wrong and got a bunch of powdered sugar down the wrong pipe.

Leah jumped up to get a glass of water.

Ali helpfully pounded Aubrey's back. When she could breathe without wheezing, both her friends were looking at her rather seriously.

"So you *already* slept with him," Leah guessed.

Aubrey took a moment with that one, because in all

truth, there'd been no actual sleeping involved. "Was it only okay with you when I was just kissing him?"

"No." Leah covered her hand with her own. "No, it's not like that. I think you'll be fantastic for him."

"We're not together," Aubrey said. "Not like that. It was just a one-time thing."

Ali laughed. "Yeah, okay."

"No, really."

"I saw you," Ali said. "I saw the chemistry. Remember when the town hall caught fire, and the entire town was covered in smoke?"

"Yeah."

"Well, I saw more smoke generated between you two than I did at that fire."

At that, Aubrey rolled her eyes.

"I'm serious," Ali said. "Whether you like it or not, you and Ben have something."

For the record, if this was true, she didn't like it. Not one bit.

"Which means you should really tell him about the list," Leah said.

No one was more aware of that than Aubrey. That damn list was starting to eat her alive. "He's seen it. He's guessed about it." She let out a breath. "But he doesn't know that he's on it. I'm *not* telling him that part."

"You could tell us instead," Ali said, fishing.

Aubrey shook her head, and Ali sighed.

"I still think you should tell him," Leah said.

"No," she said firmly.

"That might come back to bite you on the ass," Leah said.

No doubt. "The grudge he earned from me with that

whole coil-wire stunt is currently scheduled to last years," Aubrey said. "So there won't be any more...smoke. And we're done talking about this."

Like good friends, they dropped the conversation and ate some more doughnut holes.

"These are amazing," Ali said. She smelled like roses today, which made sense, since she was looking like she'd rolled in them. They clung to her clothes, as did the scent of the petals.

Aubrey agreed with her friend's assessment of the doughnut holes, but her mouth was too full to talk.

Leah was pulling pies from her oven. "These should go like hotcakes—"

The door out front opened, and the bell rang, signaling a customer. "Damn it," Leah said, and eyed both Ali and Aubrey. "Aubrey. You get it."

"What? Why me?"

"Because you look the most presentable. Just tell whoever it is I'll be right out. Or better yet, serve them."

Ali grinned. "This is why I dress in flower gunk."

Aubrey sighed and jumped off the counter, heading out front. She stopped short at the sight of Ben. She was still mad at him, really mad, but some of that anger faded without her permission at the sight of him standing there with a little girl clinging to each of his hands.

The girls were tiny, a little scrawny, and one of them was dressed in pink from head to toe. The other's hair was falling out of her pigtails, and her dress was smudged and dirty. Also, she had the beginnings of a black eye. It matched Ben's.

His eyebrows went up at the sight of Aubrey. "You take a second job?"

"Yes," she said. "It's called eating doughnut holes." She smiled at the girls, her heart melting a little. They were a little bedraggled and so damn precious. "Hey, there," she said to them. "What'll it be?"

"We don't got any money," the one all in pink said, eyes locked on the display case.

"I'm buying," Ben told her. "Whatever you want."

"Wow," Pink said reverently, nose pressed up against the glass. "Whatever we want? Really? What about those pretty red cupcakes? Oh, wait, no—look at those cookies; they're black and white with little pink dots! Oh, oh! Those pink-and-chocolate thingies! Look at all the pink—"

Ben held up a finger, and she stopped talking. "Whatever you want," he repeated.

"Any of it?" she asked in awe.

"*All* of it, if that's what you want."

The little girl said "Wow" again and very carefully surveyed the displays. "We gotta be sure to get something that won't spill on the car seats you got for us."

"They're borrowed," Ben said. "And they can be washed."

Aubrey stood behind the counter, ostensibly waiting for the kid to make a choice, but really watching Ben with the girls. He wore dark jeans, an untucked button-down shirt, and work boots. His hair was just a little tousled, either from his fingers or the wind, and he looked like a rock star. A really sexy one. He was relaxed, hands in pockets, head tilted down, listening politely to the girls' chatter.

Or the girl. Singular. Because only one of them talked—the one all in pink. She pointed to the cookie section. "Can we pretty please each have one of those big fat chocolate chip cookies?" she asked Aubrey.

"Of course." Aubrey handed one to each twin. The one in pink smiled and said, "Thanks." Her twin didn't smile; she just stared at Aubrey, eyes large and red-rimmed and shimmering, the bruise standing out starkly against her pale skin.

"She says thanks, too," the one in pink said, and hugged her twin.

Her twin nodded and solemnly took a bite of her cookie.

Aubrey gestured to the girl's eye, wondering what had happened to her. "Looks like it hurts."

She nodded again.

"Someone got her with an elbow on the playground," her twin said. "It was mean."

Aubrey's heart squeezed. "Wait here." She ran through the bakery kitchen, past her two startled friends, out the back door, into her bookstore, and to the freezer, where she grabbed her second bag of peas. When she dashed back to the bakery and handed it to the little girl for her eye, Ben smiled.

"Thanks," he said. "Have Leah add the cookies to my tab." He dropped a five into the tip jar. He turned the girls to the door, and then they were gone.

Aubrey was still standing there, staring at the closed door, when Ali and Leah flanked her.

"Isn't he adorable?" Ali asked.

Ben was a lot of things, but Aubrey was pretty sure adorable wasn't one of them.

Chapter 18

♥

With a week and a half left until her grand-opening party, Aubrey stood in the crap-food aisle of the grocery store, trying to decide between cool ranch and salt-and-vinegar potato chips. It was an important decision, and one she took very seriously. Whichever flavor she picked would be keeping her company through tonight's TV session. She went back and forth for a ridiculously long moment before deciding the hell with it and tossing both in her cart. That's when she saw the barbecue-flavored chips as well. Damn. She wasn't supposed to be able to choose between them all, was she? She was reaching for a third bag when she heard her name.

Turning, she came face-to-face with Pastor Mike, smiling his easy smile.

She quickly backed away from the barbecue chips and briefly wished she had fruit and vegetables in her cart. Which was silly. Pastor Mike was a man, not God. He didn't care how many bags of potato chips she consumed.

And probably God didn't care, either. Still, she moved to stand in front of the cart so he couldn't get a good look at its contents, which so far consisted of Advil and the chips.

"How are you?" Pastor Mike asked.

"Great." She wanted that third bag of chips.

Pastor Mike smiled. "Is that why you're chip-loading? Because you're great?"

She sighed and glanced at her cart. "Saw that, did you?"

He smiled. "I love those salt-and-vinegar chips."

"Yeah, me, too."

"So," he said in that calm voice. "How are you really?"

"Well, as you can clearly see, I just loaded about ten thousand calories of chips into my cart, so..." She shrugged.

"I've been hoping you'd come to another meeting."

"Oh, I don't think—"

"There's one tonight." He flashed a charming smile. "Better for you than chip therapy."

"Is there *anything* better than chip therapy?"

"No," he admitted. "But this would be really close. We'd love to see you there. It's at eight thirty."

Well, hell. "Maybe." She paused. "And thanks. You've been so kind—and helpful, too."

He cocked his head, eyes curious. "I haven't done anything."

She thought about the list and how she was working her way down it. And how, in spite of having about a fifty-percent success rate at the moment, it'd felt really good to face those ghosts. "You did a lot," she said. "You motivated me."

He smiled. "Well, then, I'm glad. You've got my number if you need a ride. Otherwise I hope to see you tonight."

She nodded and then went through the checkout. And if she added a candy bar from the evil, *evil* rack right before the cash register, no one but she had to know.

She had one more stop to make before heading home, and suddenly she needed the candy bar to face it. Chocolate courage, she decided. She inhaled it and then headed to the Love Shack. She knew that someone from her list went there every night for a quick nightcap before heading home.

Sue Henderson.

Back when Aubrey had been eighteen, Sue had been an assistant DA. She'd moved up the ranks in the years since. She was a judge now, which only made her all the more intimidating. She was at the bar nursing a white wine when Aubrey approached. The only reaction Sue gave was a simple narrowing of her critical gaze over the rim of her glass.

"Well, that answers the question of whether you remember me," Aubrey said, and gestured for the bartender. She was going to need a drink for this.

"Rumor is you're working your way through town and making apologies," Sue said.

Aubrey stared at her, stunned. "Well, that was quick."

Sue shrugged. "It's Lucky Harbor."

True. Aubrey accepted her wine from the bartender. It was Jax serving tonight. He co-owned the bar with Ford. Jax was handsome and charming—and sharp enough to take one look at Aubrey and Sue sitting together and bring them each a second glass. "On the house," he said, shooting Aubrey a quick wink before moving off.

Sue finished off her first wine and reached for her second. "So."

"So," Aubrey said. Her heart started pounding. This was always the worst part, getting started. But then Sue started for her.

"You put green food coloring in my pool on the day I was hosting a huge, important town hall luncheon," she said. "The luncheon I was hoping would get me from ADA to DA. I spent a fortune decorating my backyard that day, bringing in gorgeous tables and flowers. The caterers had set up around my pool—which, thanks to you, looked like a toilet tank. A really *disgusting* toilet tank."

"Yes," Aubrey said, nodding. "I did that."

"I didn't get to be DA that year."

Aubrey knew that, too. Sue had been her father's neighbor. They were still neighbors, actually. And on the few occasions when Aubrey had been invited to visit, Aubrey had run across Sue, as she and her father had been friends.

Sue hadn't approved of Aubrey's beauty contests and general upbringing. She'd been fond of saying things like "Looks will fade, Aubrey, and you'll find yourself fading along with them" and "I guess your sister really did get all the brains."

Aubrey hadn't really minded hearing the looks-fading thing; she'd known that. But she had minded being held up against her sister and found lacking. Or maybe she'd just been plain tired of all of it by then. Regardless, she'd done Sue wrong. "I shouldn't have put the green food coloring in your pool," she said.

"*And* my pond," Sue added.

"And your pond," Aubrey said in agreement.

Sue stared at her. "That's it? That's my big apology?"

"You did eventually get promoted," Aubrey pointed out. "And you're a judge now. A good one."

Sue looked slightly mollified. "I *am* a good judge. But you stained the pool's finish—did you know that? We had to drain it and redo it. And the pond…you killed my fish."

"I know," Aubrey said. "It was a rotten thing to do." She paused. "You work with troubled teens."

"Yes," Sue said, looking suspicious. "Aren't you a little old to be a troubled teen?"

Aubrey ignored the jab. "You've funded a special program for them at the teen center. You bring in career women once a week to meet with the girls and talk with them about their options. Doctors, lawyers, chefs—"

"I do."

"I thought maybe I could volunteer to do that," Aubrey said casually, even though she felt anything but casual. She felt…nervous. Sick with it, actually. But it was something she wanted to do to help others, especially those who were as emotionally adrift as she had been.

"You want to talk to troubled teen girls," Sue said dubiously.

"Well, who better than a once troubled teen girl?" Aubrey asked quietly.

Sue looked at her for a long moment. "The people I have working with those teens are no longer troubled."

"*I'm* no longer troubled," Aubrey said.

"Just a few months ago, you slept with your boss and lost your job because of it."

When would that stop following her around? "No," she said. "I slept with my *date*, who turned out to be screwing half the town. I quit my job because he also turned out to be slime."

Sue just looked at her.

"Okay, so he was also my boss," she admitted. "But…" Aubrey started to say it wasn't what Sue thought, but the truth was…it'd been exactly as Sue thought. She met the judge's gaze. "You know what? Never mind. It was a ridiculous idea."

Ben had been eating nachos and nursing a beer with Jack and Luke when Aubrey had walked into the Love Shack. She'd gone straight to the bar without seeing him, her gaze locked on someone already there.

At his table, Jack was telling them the story of having to rescue one of the world's dumbest criminals on the job yesterday. Some guy had climbed a tree outside the convenience store to reach the second-story window, where the office was. Presumably the idea was to break in from above, but he got stuck in the window, half in and half out, hanging twenty-five feet above the ground, screaming for help.

Ben laughed at this right along with Luke, but his gaze kept being drawn back to the bar.

And Aubrey, as she'd sat sipping a wine, talking to Judge Sue Henderson.

The two women had looked incredibly cool and calm, but Ben knew Aubrey—knew the telltale signs that revealed the real Aubrey beneath the veneer. Her smile wasn't reaching her eyes. Her legs were crossed, her body still, except for the slight movement of her fingers nudging her glass back and forth. She appeared to be taking a breath every two or three minutes. He supposed that's how she'd survived her rough patches—by going into hibernation mode.

But he'd also seen her looking very much alive and breathing, like she'd just run a marathon, and he much preferred that look to this brittle one.

She seemed to be near a breaking point. How was it that no one but him saw that?

Then the judge had said something, and though Aubrey didn't move, he could tell whatever it'd been, the barb had hit deep. Aubrey nodded, tossed back her wine, and stood. She said something. Sue didn't respond, and Aubrey walked off.

And right out the door.

Ben stood and tossed some bills on the table. "Gotta go."

Luke, gaze also on the door, just nodded thoughtfully.

Jack, having never been particularly thoughtful, said, "Anything to do with the beautiful leggy blonde that just left?"

"No," Ben said.

"Bullshit."

"Leave it alone," Ben told him.

"Did you leave it alone when I was making a fool of myself over Leah?" Jack asked, leaning back lazily in his chair.

"Hell, yeah," Ben said. "I left it plenty. And no one's making a fool of himself here tonight, especially me."

"First of all," Jack said, lifting a finger. "You delivered Leah to my doorstep drunk as a skunk and then left her with me. How was that possibly 'leaving it alone'?"

"Okay, you know the real truth, which is that Leah delivered *herself* to you that night," Ben reminded him. With Aubrey's help, in fact. "I just helped her find you and then made sure neither of you drunk idiots drowned."

"And second of all," Jack went on, as if Ben hadn't spoken, "you are *so* about to make a fool of yourself. I can tell these things." He looked to Luke for confirmation.

Luke lifted his hands. "Don't look at me. I can't tell shit."

"Says the guy who found himself wrapped around Ali's little finger before he could so much as blink," Jack said in disgust. "Never mind him," he said to Ben.

"I'm *not* going to make a fool of myself," Ben said testily.

Jack just grinned. Luke toasted him with his beer.

Ben swore, flipped them both off, and walked out into the night. It was a mild one as far as winter nights went. A little chilly, but dry for a change.

He'd expected Aubrey's car to be long gone, but it was still in the lot. Empty. He walked through the lot to the street and looked both ways.

No tall, willowy, enigmatic blonde in either direction.

He walked to the church, one block away, but tonight the building was dark. Ben stood there, the cold, salty air blowing over him, and suddenly he knew where she'd be.

He crossed the street and hit the pier. Far below, the waves smashed against the pylons and rocks. Everything was closed, but strings of white lights had the entire length of the pier glowing into the dark night. He stilled to listen and heard the soft *click, click, click* of heels. Gotcha, he thought, and followed.

He didn't catch up with her until the very end of the pier. She'd sunk to a bench, pulled her legs up, and had her arms wrapped around her knees. Facing away from him, she was looking out into the inky night.

When he sat next to her, she jumped a little and then glared at him. "I swear I'm going to buy you a bell for your neck."

He didn't smile. Couldn't, because her face was wet, and her mascara was smeared slightly beneath her eyes. The sight made his heart stop. "You're crying."

"No, I'm not."

"Aubrey—"

"Damn it, I told you sometimes I get something in my eyes." She swiped angrily at her face.

Sighing, he slid a little closer and put an arm around her.

She resisted, but he simply held on, and then suddenly she sagged against him. "You really piss me off," she murmured, and turning to him, buried her face in his chest.

He wrapped both arms around her and pressed his head to hers. "I know."

She fisted her hands in his sweater and gripped him tight. "You're still insensitive and a first-class jerk," she said soggily, reminding him of the things she'd said to him when he'd pulled her coil wire.

"I know that, too," he said.

She shuddered and tightened her hold on him.

Something deep in his chest squeezed. It was never easy to watch a woman cry, but when a really strong woman like Aubrey let go, it was even harder. He stroked a hand down her hair. "What's wrong, Aubrey?"

She laughed mirthlessly against him. "You mean you don't already know? You know everything."

He didn't say anything to this, just held her while she cried for a few minutes. Then she sniffed, and if he wasn't mistaken, wiped her nose on his shoulder. "I need to walk," she said, and got up.

He went with her. He could have gone back to Luke and Jack. He could have gone home. He had no reason to stick with Aubrey. No reason except that he wanted to.

They walked off the pier, and she kept going. Past Eat Me, the Love Shack, the post office, the flower shop, the bakery, her own bookstore. They walked the length of Commercial Row and ended up at the rec center.

"You've been working here," Aubrey said. "With the kids."

He nodded.

"I heard you've turned Craft Corner into a huge success," she said. "Leah said more kids show up each time."

He wasn't comfortable with taking the credit. "I've gone twice. And it's all Jack's doing."

Her expression said she wasn't fooled. "You're enjoying it."

What the hell. "Yeah," he said. "I'm enjoying it." He was still surprised at that. But when he'd gone for the second time a few days ago, the director had found out he was certified as an EMT and had asked him to be a staff member. They'd given him a key to the building and a big welcome in lieu of a stipend. Which was fine. His old job—the one that was now going to be his *new* job—would provide a surprisingly decent salary.

"And you took your old job back," Aubrey said, as if reading his mind. "You start soon."

He laughed low in his throat at the power of Lucky Harbor's gossip mill. "Leah?" he asked. "Or Ali?"

She laughed, too, a little guiltily, he thought. "Facebook," she admitted. She paused for a long beat, studying the rec center quietly. "If Hannah were still alive, you'd probably have a bushel of kids enjoying this place by now."

A few years ago, just the thought would've given Ben a stab of pain. But whoever had said that time heals wounds had actually been right. His wounds were healing. Their gazes met. "Most people tiptoe around the subject of my dead wife."

"I don't tiptoe very well."

No, she didn't. It was wrong of him to even try to compare the two women. It was wrong to compare anyone to Hannah. Especially since, with her death, her image had changed in his mind, and her imperfections had faded. He knew that it was simply a coping technique, and that it probably wasn't all that healthy. But Hannah had always been his calm, his eye in the storm, his refuge. She'd had such a quiet, soothing energy, and it'd suited his adventurous soul well.

He hadn't been lying when he told her he'd been with women since Hannah, but his attention wasn't captured. He'd not been tempted to go for another relationship.

Not once in five years.

So the fact that he was suddenly, irrationally tempted by Aubrey made absolutely no sense to him, not a single lick. Aubrey was...not quiet. Not soothing. She was wild and unpredictable.

Hannah's virtual opposite.

Aubrey was watching him now, with those hazel eyes that seemed to see far more than he wanted anyone to.

"Show me what you've done with the kids here," she said.

He grimaced. "It's not all that impressive."

"Show me."

He pulled a set of keys from his pocket and opened the door for her. The place was empty, closed up for the night. Leaving the lights off, he took her hand and led her down the darkened hallway to the room he'd been using. The moonlight slanted into the classroom through the wall of windows, illuminating a series of hanging dream catchers. He'd been taught how to make them by the children on a Native American reservation in Montana when he'd been there several years ago after a devastating flood.

"Pretty," she whispered, standing there in the dark room.

Sadness seemed to come off her in waves. Sadness and…loneliness. God, she was killing him. "Aubrey."

"You give back," she whispered. "You were gone for five years, and still you came home to a place that loves you and you found a way to give back to your town."

"You're trying to give back," he said.

She didn't respond to this, didn't confirm or deny. Or even move. So he moved instead, closer to her, putting a hand low on her back, letting her know he was there. "Tell me what happened tonight."

"It's not important," she said, and shifted to move away, but he caught her.

"It is to me," he said. "Talk to me."

"Sometimes," she murmured quietly into the night, her head turned away from him, resting on his shoulder. "I feel like a really bad person."

He stroked a hand down her back, physically aching for her. He'd like to tell her she was a really *great* person, but she wouldn't believe him. The only thing he could do to coax her out of this mood was to do something he was really good at—which was annoy her. "You're not all *that* bad," he said.

She went still, and then snorted. "And maybe you're not a *total* first-class jerk."

"Oh, I'm still a first-class jerk."

She lifted her head. "No," she whispered.

"*Yes*. Here's why." And he kissed her.

Chapter 19

Aubrey was never prepared for what Ben's kiss did to her. It was like she spent ninety-nine percent of her time walking around in a black-and-white world, and then when he kissed her, colors bled into her vision like a painting.

Not that she needed a man in order to see or feel. No, she had the ability to do those things all on her own, but it was as if being with Ben reminded her of that.

"I love kissing you," he breathed, holding her close against his warm, hard body.

And hell if that didn't melt her bones. "You don't need to work at charming me," she said a little breathlessly.

"No?" His mouth made its way to her ear, giving her a delicious shiver when he licked at the sensitive skin just behind her lobe. "Are you already charmed, then?"

"Just about everything you do charms me," she admitted, goose bumps breaking out all over her body, thanks to his questing mouth. "And we both know I'm a sure thing here tonight. You don't have to work so hard."

He met her gaze, his own filled with amusement. "You're a sure thing? Well, damn, woman, you could've told me."

She laughed, and something about the way joy surged through her, shoving back all the sadness, made her throw herself at him. Literally. She just…jumped him. Fortunately, he had quick reflexes and caught her, though they practically fell to the floor, kissing and groping. Twining her arms around his neck, she pressed her breasts against his broad chest as he kissed her long and deep, with wild, fast abandon. She returned the favor, the both of them panting in the quiet, dark night as they rolled, fighting for the top. She won and straddled him. "This doesn't change anything," she panted.

"Agreed," he said so fast her head spun. Apparently, a small part of her had hoped he'd protest and possibly even say he was rethinking his no-commitment stance. The way *she* was starting to rethink hers…

"We have to hurry," she said, remembering Pastor Mike and tonight's AA meeting.

Ben rolled her beneath him. "I don't like to hurry."

No kidding. She already knew he liked to take his sweet-ass time. He liked to stop and kiss every inch of her skin, tasting her. Licking her. Kissing her…just the memory made her hot. She had no idea what it was about him that flipped her switch every time, but he did it seemingly without trying. She closed her eyes, but she wanted to see his expression, wanted to let his gaze tell her all the things that his mouth never did, so she opened them again.

Yeah, she flipped his switch, too. A relief. "I have an appointment," she said. "We *have* to hurry."

"An appointment?"

Damn Pastor Mike and his charming smile. She checked her watch. Eight o'clock. "I have half an hour," she said. "So no stupid, wussy foreplay. Just fast, hard action." She saw his amusement again. "I mean it, Ben."

"Okay," he said. "We'll table the stupid and…*wussy?*" he asked, seeking clarification.

"Yes," she said impatiently. "Wussy."

"No stupid, wussy foreplay, then," he said. "Just fast, hard action. Got it." He was out-and-out smiling now, but when his gaze settled on her face, he went serious. Intense.

And she went hot, like molten lava. "Now, right?" she asked breathlessly against his mouth.

"Hell, yeah, now." He rose off her, picking her up with him. Reaching out, he hit the lock on the classroom door.

The bolt sliding home was the only sound in the room other than their accelerated breathing. Holding her gaze, Ben then slid his hand around to the nape of her neck and then into her hair, entangling his fingers, pulling her to him. Eyes on hers, he nudged her up against the waist-high row of cabinets lining one wall.

Ben pressed her into the wall and lowered his mouth to hers, almost but not quite touching. Either he expected her to shove free, or he was building the anticipation. Since she had no intention of shoving him away, and the anticipation had already built to an almost painful degree, she wrapped herself around him.

His soft, knowing laugh echoed in her mouth as he

kissed her, and that made her bite his lower lip. Laughing again, he easily took control, holding her still so he could bite her back. Things went a little wild then. She arched into him, trying to make him take action as he ran his hands over her, molding and cupping her to him. Melding them together, the kiss went on and on until she was moaning, helplessly rocking, making him swear and lose some of his tight control. Bunching the hem of her dress in his big palms, he pulled it over her head and tossed it aside.

Her bra went next, and then her panties, leaving her in just her boots.

She went to kick them off, but he stopped her. "Leave them," he said in a rough voice that gave her a rush. Pulling back, he took in the sight of her leaning against the wall, nude except for the boots, and let out a long breath. "You are so fucking beautiful, Aubrey."

"Stop that. I said no foreplay."

"Words are foreplay?"

"When you're the one speaking the words, they are," she said.

He arched a brow.

"Oh, please," she said. "Like you don't know your voice is an aphrodisiac all by itself. Tell me you've got a condom."

He reached into his pocket and came up with one. His shirt was already unbuttoned—her doing. He smelled like the wood he'd been working with in her store. His eyes were dark and heated; his hair was messy from her fingers. A lock of it fell across his forehead.

Just looking at him was foreplay. Damn it. She unzipped him and yanked him into her, kissing him slow and deep. "Remember," she murmured against his mouth. "Don't get attached to me."

He smiled and nipped at her lower lip again. "How about if I just sink into you?"

Her entire body quivered. "That's all I'm asking. Hard, Ben. Hard and fast."

He laughed, but it turned into a rough groan when she rolled the condom down his length. Then he wrestled the control back by whipping her around, bending her over the cabinets, and plunging into her in one deliciously perfect hard stroke. Unable to hold back, she cried out, and he stilled.

"Don't you dare stop," she gasped, already halfway there. She only needed a few more strokes. "Please, Ben. Do it. Do me."

He let out another low laugh, murmuring something that sounded like "You kill me" before giving her what she'd asked for, taking her with an urgency that she knew wasn't Mr. Fast-Isn't-My-Style's usual MO.

But Ben was nothing if not adaptable, not to mention accommodating. She'd said hard, and he gave it to her. Fisting a hand in her hair, he pulled her head back to kiss her, his hand gripping her hip to hold her right where he wanted her.

She melted back into him as he moved inside her, rubbing up against him, making him groan and laugh at the same time. "Killing me," he murmured again.

She could feel the brutal, tempered strength in his every movement, and in response, her body quivered. So damn close… "Ben—"

"I know," he said, brushing her ear with his mouth, whispering things—wonderfully wicked, naughty things that nudged her right to the edge. And then the words that knocked her right over that edge. "Come, Aubrey. I want you to come." And then he slid a hand between her legs to take her there.

She wasn't all the way back to Earth when he growled out, "You are so hot when you let go," and, staggeringly, she came again.

Groaning, he dropped his head to her shoulder, sinking his teeth into her as he tensed and followed her over.

Aubrey never did make it to the AA meeting. Ben trailed her home and then spent the long hours of the night showing her just how important foreplay could be, in slow, torturous detail.

And then he showed her again.

And again.

He took her to places she'd never been, right there in her loft. She liked to think that she'd done the same for him, too, remembering how she'd given in to her desire to kiss every inch of his hard body. Halfway down his torso, he'd sunk his fingers into her hair and whispered hoarsely, "Please tell me I ordered the happy ending."

He'd definitely gotten his happy ending...

She woke up with a start at six thirty the next morning. It wasn't because Ben was leaving; he'd done that an hour ago to go run. Her phone had awakened her. It was buzzing on her nightstand. It was a text from a number she didn't recognize. It read:

Got your number from your father. I thought about what you said and decided you and the teens de-

*serve each other, but you need to work your way up
to them, because—trust me—they'll walk all over
you. You're starting at the Reading Corner with the
youngest terrors we have. Be at the rec center Wed
@ 3:00.*
—Judge Henderson

Aubrey lay back in her bed and smiled. She was so
sated and boneless she wasn't sure she could even get out
of bed. But she gave it the old college try and limped over
to her notebook. There, she carefully crossed off number
six with a satisfied smile on her face.

Except the smile might also be attributed to a certain
sexy Ben McDaniel...

By seven, Ben had run with Sam, showered, and was
standing at Aubrey's car, a coffee in each hand.

She staggered out the door at 7:05, and though she
looked exhausted, she had a smile on her face as she came
to a startled halt at the sight of him.

He didn't attempt to draw her into conversation, just
handed her the coffee. She sipped.

He waited.

She sipped some more. At about the sixty-second
mark, she started to show some signs of life.

"Thanks," she finally said.

"You're welcome. You're also welcome for the
smile."

She choked on her coffee. "For your information, the
smile is because Judge Sue Henderson has *almost* agreed
to let me work with the troubled teen girls at the teen center," she told him.

"And this made you smile?" He shuddered. "That sounds terrifying."

She shrugged and then softened. "And okay, maybe *some* of the smile is because of you."

He felt his own smile slowly crease his face. "Yeah?"

"Yeah." She hip-bumped him. "As you damn well know already. And while we're on this subject, why are you here?"

"Thought you might want a driver again today."

"My car's running fine now," she said, then gave him a wary look. "Right?"

"Right. But since the jig is up and I know what you're up to..."

She didn't take the bait by responding, nor did she volunteer any new information, so he went on. "You might as well let me drive you."

"You only *think* you know what I'm up to," she reminded him.

He shrugged. "Maybe. But I've got a full gas tank and you don't. And even if you won't admit it, you like my company."

"Maybe I just like your body."

"That works, too," he said easily.

"How do you know my tank's on empty?"

"Call it a hunch," he said.

Letting out a breath, she headed toward his truck. He opened the door for her and let her in, then walked around and slid behind the wheel.

"I know what I get out of this," she said. "But what do you get out of it?"

"Your sunny and sweet disposition?"

She laughed, which made his morning.

"Maybe I like your company, too," he said.

She glanced over at him as if searching for sarcasm. He let her look, because for once he wasn't feeling sarcastic.

She pulled out her list. "I need to go to the nursery."

He headed in that direction, neither of them speaking, though the silence was easy. Five minutes later he'd pulled into the nursery parking lot.

Aubrey didn't move to get out of the truck. "Something that has nothing to do with my list—I had a crush on you in high school."

Surprised, he turned in his seat and looked at her. She looked at him right back. It just might have been the most real thing she'd ever said to him, right after what she'd so sweetly whispered in his ear last night—*Please, Ben, please don't stop, you feel so good…*

"I know."

She stared at him for a beat, and then, looking mortified, fumbled with the door handle.

He hit the AUTO LOCK button.

"Damn it. Let me go."

He'd done a lot of that in his life—letting go. He didn't feel like doing it this time.

Aubrey fought the door, but he'd been fast with the locks. When she figured out how to unlock the door, he simply hit AUTO LOCK again. He'd always been damn fast. He gave off that laid-back vibe, but he could move like lightning. His hand slid up her arm to her neck.

"Don't," she whispered. She didn't want him to be nice. She couldn't handle nice.

But of course he didn't listen. Instead he turned her to face him, his expression dialed to confusion.

Stupid male race. They never understood. "I'm embarrassed," she explained.

This appeared to confuse him even more. "Why?" he asked. "You were damn hot in high school. It's just that you were a few years behind me, and I was with Hannah."

She closed her eyes for a beat. "The way you looked at me last night? Back then, I'd have done anything to have you look at me like that."

"Nothing about that time can be changed," he said with a painful gentleness that made her want to run far and wide. "But we're here now."

"We're here now." She stared up at him, because suddenly *she* was the confused one. "What does that mean?"

"We're…" He trailed off.

She waited, but he didn't say more. She knew she should remain quiet and force him to fill the silence, but the suspense was killing her. "We're what? *Together*?" she asked, heart pounding, pounding, pounding.

He rubbed his jaw, and the sound of his stubble seemed loud in the truck interior.

And sexy.

But the movement was a tell, a rare show of uncertainty from a man who always knew his next move. "We're what?" she asked again, needing to know with a shocking desperation.

"We're…" He blew out a breath. "Hell if I know."

Fair enough, she supposed. "Wait here?" she asked, pausing while he hit unlock before sliding out of the truck. She shook the sexy Mr. McDaniel from her thoughts—as if it were that easy—and walked into the nursery, where she asked for Dusty Barren.

"He doesn't work here anymore," the guy at the check-out counter told her.

"Okay," Aubrey said. "Do you know where I could reach him?"

"I'm sorry." The clerk shifted his weight from foot to foot, looking suddenly uncomfortable. "He died last year."

Ben was only halfway through beating Jack's ass on *Words with Friends* when Aubrey came back to the truck, looking solemn.

"I need to go to the cemetery," she said.

This surprised him. He knew this had something to do with someone on her list. Sometimes she was happy when she got through with one, sometimes she would cry—which killed him. He tried to remember who else was on the list from the few brief glimpses he'd gotten, and who might have died.

He had no idea.

So he drove her to the cemetery.

Once there, she again slid out of the truck. Ben watched her vanish over the hill to the right. When she was gone, he got out of the truck, too, and headed to the hill on the left. He walked about a quarter of a mile before he got to the right headstone.

HANNAH WALSH MCDANIEL.

He crouched down and brushed some dirt off the stone. "Hey, babe," he said. "It's been a while." He blew out a sigh and waited for the usual stab of pain.

But it was only an ache. Worse, he had to strain to see her face in his mind.

Her voice had faded a long time ago.

"I'm sorry," he said, and ran his fingers over her headstone again.

He heard the crunch of the frozen ground behind him and knew it was Aubrey. She stayed back a respectful few feet, quiet, which was unlike her.

Quiet had been Hannah's style, but it wasn't Aubrey's. Aubrey was volatile. Passionate.

Hannah had never fought. Never.

And Aubrey fought for everything.

"You had a good marriage," Aubrey said.

She hadn't worded it as a question, but he knew she was asking. And the truth was, he'd always believed he'd had a great marriage. It'd been serene, calm. He'd liked that.

But now…now he wasn't sure whether quiet and calm would do it for him. Since that was a path he didn't want to go down—wondering if he and Hannah would be happy today with the man he'd become—he shrugged off the unsettled feelings the question brought and craned his neck to look at Aubrey. "We were young," he said simply.

Staring at him, she nodded. "Life sucks."

"Sometimes," he agreed, and rose. He searched her face, saw that she'd made peace with whatever she'd set out to do here, which he was glad for. He offered her a hand.

They walked back to the truck in silence.

Chapter 20

Several days later, Aubrey sat at her desk, staring at her open notebook. Number seven on her list was weighing on her mind. She'd worked at the nursery for two weeks in her junior year of high school. The owner had never let her near the plants—he'd claimed to know after one look at someone if he or she had a black thumb, which Aubrey did—so instead, she'd been an all-around grunt, doing whatever had been required: sweeping, answering phones, running errands.

One of the other hired hands had been a special-needs teenager her same age. Dusty Burrows had been big as a horse, so it made sense that he'd been hired as the heavy lifter—bags of cement, manure, trees—whatever'd been needed.

He'd had a crush on Aubrey, which he'd shown by leaving flowers on her car and helping her with chores, all with a sweet smile on his silent face. He'd never spoken to her, not once. He rarely spoke to anyone, only when he had to.

Then one day he *stopped* smiling at her, stopped helping her, stopped leaving her flowers. He stopped being her friend entirely, and she didn't know why.

One year later, she'd been cleaning out her car when she'd found a birthday card, lost and forgotten deep between the seats. It'd been from Dusty, confessing his love for her.

She'd been embarrassed, both for him and for herself, and she'd thrown the card away and not dealt with it.

In hindsight, she'd always known that he most likely thought she'd ignored him or, worse, laughed at him.

She hated herself for that.

The bell over the bookstore's front door rang, and Aubrey prepared a smile. To her surprise, it was Carla. Her sister was in her usual pale blue scrubs, but looking a lot less tired than she had a week ago. "Hey," Aubrey said.

Carla leaned against the checkout counter, her expression impossible to read.

Already becoming a doctor, Aubrey thought wryly. Carla didn't fidget, didn't hedge. She got right to the point. "Do you remember that time you got in trouble at the library?" she asked. "For having sex in the reference section with Anthony, the principal's son?"

"I remember," Aubrey said carefully. "Though I'm surprised you do."

Carla closed her eyes, drew a deep breath, and then met Aubrey's gaze again. "I remember, because it was me."

Aubrey blinked. "Say what?"

"It was me. *I* had sex with Anthony in the reference section of the high school library."

Aubrey stared at her. "One more time."

Carla's smile was tight. "Yeah," she said. "And it gets worse. I knew you got blamed. That you were suspended. I knew you got in big trouble, that Dad jumped all over Mom's shit about how she'd raised you, and in return you then jumped all over Dad for being mean to Mom. It tore up the very tenuous peace between the four of us. But the only thing I felt at the time was this huge, overwhelming relief that it wasn't me who got suspended."

Aubrey was so stunned about the whole confession she could hardly speak. "*Why?*"

Carla looked pained and embarrassed, both new expressions for her. "I had a crush on him. I thought I loved him."

"No: I mean why did you let everyone think it was me?"

"Yeah. Well, that's a lot more complicated." Carla paused. "I'm not proud of it," she said quietly. "But the best I've got is that I really wanted to be brave and strong and independent—like you."

"Me," Aubrey repeated.

"Yes. I wanted to not care what people thought of me," Carla said. "I wanted to be…" She smiled sadly. "Well, *you*, Aubrey. But I wasn't. I wasn't anything close to you. I could only wish I was."

Aubrey stared at her. "Seriously?"

"Hand to heaven," Carla said, and bit her lower lip. "I'm sorry. So sorry. I was rude when you tried to apologize to me, and that was guilt. You're forgiven for that stupid internship thing; *of course* you're forgiven."

Aubrey felt a weight lift. "Yeah?"

"*Yeah*. And thanks for bringing me food and watching out for my plants. You went over and above, and I'm so grateful for you." She drew in a deep breath. "And now…well, I'm sort of hoping *you'd* forgive *me*. For not owning up to my mistake and letting you take the fall."

"It's ancient history," Aubrey said honestly. "And anyway, I did plenty of stuff in that library I shouldn't have. Karma was bound to come around and bite me on the ass at some point."

"You're not mad?" Carla asked softly.

"Trust me. In the grand scheme of my life, that incident was nothing."

"But you were grounded for three months," Carla reminded her. "And Dad…well, he never let you forget it. You took it, though—you took everything he dished out to you, always."

Aubrey shrugged. "I had Mom."

Carla hesitated, and then nodded. "So we're good?"

"We're good," Aubrey promised. And then the two of them shared what might have been their first genuine smile.

The next evening, right after the bookstore closed for the day, Ben went to work on paint touch-up. He'd spent the last few nights painting walls, and the place was looking brand new.

Aubrey came down the stairs from her loft. She was in her coat and boots, her purse over her arm, and he nearly opened his mouth to ask if she'd consider modeling just those boots again. Clearly the paint fumes had gone to his head. "Going out?" he asked.

She faltered briefly. "Yes."

He took in how carefully made up she was, and his stomach clenched. "On a date?" Not that it mattered, he told himself. He *hoped* she was going out on a date, because then it would prove that they weren't anything to each other.

Which is what he wanted.

Totally.

Completely.

Yep—that's what he wanted, all right. To be free…so it made no sense at all that he held his breath for her answer.

"Not a date," she said.

He didn't want to think about the relief that hit him like a Mack truck.

She moved to the door and then hesitated, her hand on the handle, her back to him. "I don't suppose you sabotaged my car again?"

"Nope," he said. "If she doesn't start, it's because she's a piece of shit." He put down his paintbrush and made an executive decision. "How about a ride, Sunshine?"

She glanced back, and he was quite certain she didn't realize that she looked hopeful. "You have more asskicking to do to Jack on your phone?" she asked.

"Always," he said. "Give me a minute to wash up."

"It's okay," she said, in motion again. "I've got this."

He caught up with her. She'd been good with makeup, but he could see the faint smudges of exhaustion beneath her eyes. She hadn't been sleeping. She was worried about something, probably whatever she was going to do tonight. "A minute," he said again, and, to be sure she didn't leave without him, dragged her with him to wash up.

The bathroom was tiny, but he nudged her into it and then crowded her up against the sink as he cleaned up.

"I could've waited out there," she said, sounding a little breathless.

He reached around her for a towel, and she sucked in a breath and then licked her lips. Ben put a hand on either side of her hips and caged her in between his body and the counter.

"What's with the he-man act?" she whispered, her gaze on his mouth.

He smiled. "You think I'm acting…he-man?"

"Yes. What I don't know is why. You trying to impress me, Ben?"

"You're already impressed."

She let out a low, almost reluctant laugh. "You think so?"

"Uh-huh." He leaned in so that they shared their next breath. Her eyes drifted closed, and her lips parted, waiting for a kiss.

But he didn't kiss her.

Her eyes flew open, and he laughed softly.

"You're such an ass," she said with no heat. "And to think I almost admitted that I was going to sabotage my own car so you'd have to give me a ride." When he laughed again, she gave him a push so she could get around him and out of the bathroom. He followed, grinning, enjoying the fact that he'd coaxed her out of her melancholy mood.

It'd started to rain as they dashed out to his truck, and he grabbed her hand to steady her. "Where to?" he asked when they were inside, shaking off the rain.

"Kingsbury."

Kingsbury was a town about twenty miles northeast of Lucky Harbor. She gave him an address in an upscale neighborhood, where the houses were big and bigger and the yards were all cared for by hired hands. "Someone from your list?" he asked.

"There. Park there," she said instead of answering, gesturing to a spot across the street and halfway down the block from the address she'd given him.

It was dusk. In Lucky Harbor, dusk lasted about two minutes, and in those two minutes between light and dark, everything turned a pale blue. When he'd been a kid, he'd always thought it was a magical time, when anything could happen. As an adult, he knew there was no magic.

Aubrey was studying the house intently, not giving much away. But he knew she knew the truth as well—that nothing happened unless you *made* it happen.

In fact, she was working on just that—working hard—and it touched him. Much more than it should have.

As dark settled around them, a car pulled into the driveway of the house. A man got out from behind the wheel and came around to the passenger side. He opened the door and assisted a woman as she got out of the car. For a moment, the man's face and the woman's face were highlighted by the porch lights.

Beside him, Aubrey gasped.

"What?" he asked.

She put a hand to her mouth and shook her head.

"It's something," he insisted.

The couple ducked through the rain together, laughing.

"Who are they?" Ben asked.

"Professor Stephen Bennett," Aubrey said, her voice soft, almost as far away as she seemed from him right now. "He was my English professor."

Ben got a very bad feeling in his gut. "And you came here to what—thank him for teaching you the classics?"

The couple had made it to the covered porch, where Professor Bennett pulled the woman in close to him and was kissing her with considerable heat.

"Time to go," Aubrey said tightly.

Ben glanced at her. She wasn't looking at the couple but rather out into the dark night, her expression pensive. "You okay?" he asked.

"I want to go home."

Ben started the truck and got back on the freeway, but he exited before Lucky Harbor, taking a winding road. When the road ended, he drove a little bit farther on a dirt fire road until he came to a small clearing. Turning off the engine, he got out and came around for Aubrey.

The night was a dark one. It'd stopped raining now, but the ground was soft and wet and smelled earthy. The trees were still laden and heavy with water, and whenever the wind kicked up, more water fell from them. "You warm enough?" he asked.

"Yes. Why?"

"Up for a walk?"

"Here? In the dark?" She looked around. "Where are we?"

"You'll see."

She stared at him for a long moment and then put her hand in his. He led her to what looked like a thirty-foot rock, then pulled his keys from his pocket and flicked on a small penlight he had attached to them. "Watch your step," he told her, but quickly realized that was impossible in her high-heeled boots. "Never mind." Taking her arm, he lifted her and twisted himself around so that he was carrying her piggyback.

"Ben," she gasped, throwing her arms around his neck so she didn't fall. "Put me down."

Ignoring that, he took the steep hill in front of them.

Her breathing hitched. "I'm wearing a skirt!" she said, sounding panicked.

"I know," he said. His fingers were intimately wrapped around her thighs, which were in turn wrapped around his waist. Mmm. He let his hands slide northward until she squeaked.

He laughed, but stopped moving his hands.

"It's not funny," she said. "I'm flashing my goodies to the world back here."

"It's dark, and there's no one out here but us. But if you want me to keep you covered..." Once again his hands went on the move, sliding upward until he squeezed her sweet ass. The only thing between his palms and her skin was her panties, which—God bless them—felt thin and skimpy. His very favorite kind.

"Ben!" She squirmed, nearly climbing over his head. "I'm serious!"

"So am I. Are these lace?"

"Stop it!" She wriggled some more, still trying to climb out of his reach, which only made him crack up again. But he stopped copping a feel. Mostly because he was going straight down the incline now, and concentrating was a good idea.

Worried noises were still sounding in his ear from the anxious Aubrey, who was gripping him for dear life. "Oh, my God," she whispered, dropping her head to his shoulder. "*Oh, my God.*"

"Don't worry," he said. "I hardly ever fall here. Of course I haven't done it while sporting a hard-on before…"

She bit his ear, and he groaned. "I like that," he said. "A lot."

She blew out a breath.

"And that…"

"Oh, for God's sake. You like everything."

"True."

A few minutes later, he let go of her legs, letting her slowly slide down his back.

She quickly straightened her skirt. "You're impossible," she said.

"So I've been told." Taking her hand, he tugged her close, showing her the view in front of them. They stood on the top of the bluffs, on the far east side of the harbor. From here they had a perfect postcard view of the little Washington State beach town, cozily nestled in the rocky cove. The main drag—a quirky, eclectic mix of the old and new—was lit up. Looking at it from here never failed to be a comfort for him.

No matter how far and wide he'd traveled, this was home.

He could see the pier, also lit, jutting out into the water, lined with more shops and outdoor cafés. And the Ferris wheel. He'd loved that damn thing as a kid.

He and Aubrey sat side by side. Eyeing their scenic view of the Pacific Ocean, swirling and pounding the rocky shore three hundred feet below, Aubrey shook her head. "It's so gorgeous. I've never been up here."

"Never?" He found this hard to believe. "You're telling me through all your teenage years here in Lucky Harbor, no guy ever brought you up here to make out?"

She smiled. "I wasn't as easy as I looked."

"I found that a lot with girls back then," he said on a disappointed sigh that made her laugh.

He loved the sound of her laugh. Her eyes lit and her face softened. Not that she wasn't always beautiful, because she was. But when she smiled like that, she relaxed and…let him in.

He knew she wasn't good at it. He got that he was one of the chosen few. He had to admit he liked that and found himself wanting even more.

"How did you ever find this spot?" she asked.

"Luke found it years ago, out of necessity."

"Necessity?"

He smiled. "You were never a teenage boy."

"That is an accurate statement."

He laughed. "As a whole, the breed tends to need a lot of unsupervised time away from authority of any kind. It makes it easier to get in all sorts of trouble, which is incredibly attractive to the breed in general."

She smiled. "What did you all do?"

"Probably best to ask what we *didn't* do. For one thing, we'd steal Luke's sister's stash of pot. Or booze from Jack's dad. We weren't choosy. Whatever we could get our klepto fingers on. Then I'd tell Dee that Jack and I were going to spend the night at Luke's, and Luke would tell his grandma he was going to Jack's."

"Ah," she said. "The switch and bait."

"Yep."

"And then you would…" She arched a brow.

"Hike up here. We'd make a campfire—also illegal—and then get drunk or high and sleep out beneath the stars. We were complete idiots." But those times, just the three of them against the world, were vivid in Ben's mind. They were some of his fondest memories.

"You ever get caught?" she asked.

"Bite your tongue." He smiled. "Nope, we never got caught."

She shook her head, smiling a little bit, too, enjoying the story. "Hard to picture Detective Luke Hanover and Fire Marshal Jack Harper being juvenile delinquents," she said.

"But not hard to imagine me as one?" he asked mildly.

Now she laughed outright. "Benjamin McDaniel, you were born a delinquent."

This was true enough, and he smiled at the sight of her relaxing a little bit, enjoying herself at his expense. "Some things are in the blood, I guess," he said.

Her smile slowly faded. "I didn't mean—"

"I know." He couldn't help the genes he'd come from—he got that. And most of the time he never even thought about it, about his real parents. He'd honestly been kidding. But Aubrey shocked the hell out of him when she put her hands on his jaw and stared fiercely into his eyes. "We're *not* our parents," she said. "We're self-made."

He dropped his forehead to hers. "Is that why you're killing yourself with that list?"

She closed her eyes and laughed softly.

"Tell me about the professor," he said.

Sighing, she pulled back from him and stared out into the water. "I met him when I was in college in Seattle. He taught English there, my favorite subject."

Having hated English, Ben made a face, and she laughed again. "He brought it all to life," she said. "And it dazzled me. He dazzled me."

Ben had a feeling he knew where this was going, and he wasn't going to like it. "Tell me."

"I slept with him," Aubrey admitted out loud for the first time, glad for the dark. "It was against the rules, of course, not that I cared. All I cared about was how this smart, funny, amazing man found me attractive."

"He looks like he has twenty years on you," Ben said.

His voice was low and not nearly as calm as usual. He was mad at the professor on her behalf. But what had happened had been one hundred percent Aubrey's own doing and all her fault. "Forty didn't look so bad," she said. "Not on Professor Bennett." She pulled her knees up and wrapped her arms around them, suddenly a little chilled. "He gave me the attention I'd been seeking, and for one whole, glorious quarter, it was really great."

Ben slid close and rubbed his hand up and down her arm, as if trying to warm and soothe her. "What happened?"

This was the hard part. "One day I heard a couple of the other professors talking about him, how he liked to pick a pretty blonde every semester to be his pet, in spite of the fact that he was a married man. They said someday someone was going to turn him in and he'd lose his job." She paused, remembering the agony and humiliation. "So that's what happened. The college got a tip that he'd been screwing a pretty blonde, and he was fired, a year before he would've gotten tenure."

"Tenure doesn't mean shit when you break the rule and fuck around with an underage minor," Ben said harshly.

"I wasn't underage. I was twenty."

"And he was *forty*," he said. "You were twenty and this guy was forty, and you think this is *your* fault? Hell, no, Aubrey, it doesn't work like that. Jesus. You were just a kid. He took advantage of you."

"You're missing the point," she said. "*I* called in the tip."

He turned her to face him and ducked down a little to look her in the eyes. "You were a *kid*," he repeated.

"I got him fired, Ben."

"Good."

She stared at him. He was sitting there, vibrating tension and being pissed off on her behalf. And then it hit her, why she felt so…moved. No one had ever been pissed off on her behalf before. "I wasn't a kid. I was an adult," she said. "And on top of that, I knew the consequences of sleeping with a professor."

"Did you know he was married?"

"No," she admitted. "Not until I heard those other professors talking about him. I reacted with temper and hurt feelings. I shouldn't have made that call."

"So you went to his place tonight to *apologize*?" he asked incredulously.

"Yes, actually," she said, and then hesitated. "Until I saw him with his wife." She shook her head. "He's still married. Or maybe she's a new wife. It doesn't matter; she was wearing a big fat diamond ring. I'm not going to mess with his life for a second time just to assuage my guilty conscience."

"How about I go mess with his life by rearranging his face?" Ben muttered.

She laughed, but Ben's expression was carved in granite, and her smiled faded. "You aren't serious."

He just looked at her, eyes flat, mouth flat.

He was dead serious.

"No," she said, shaking her head. "No. I want you to forget everything I've told you tonight."

Testosterone pouring off him in waves, he looked away, out at the water, noncommittal. The queen of noncommittal herself, Aubrey cupped his face and pulled him back around. "I mean it," she said. "Put it out of your head."

"How do you suppose I should do that, Aubrey—put it out of my mind?"

Oh, listen to him, all alpha and furious with it. The man who'd made sure she knew that he didn't want a committed relationship with her. She was beginning to suspect he was full of shit about that, but who was she to tell him so? Lots of people hadn't wanted to be with her, including her own father.

But there was a lot of room between nothing and a committed relationship. "We should fill your mind with something else," she suggested, making her voice soft and sultry.

His gaze immediately went all heavy-lidded, and his voice lowered as well, to that sexy drawl that did her in every time. "Such as?"

Her gaze dropped to his mouth. "Well, to be honest, a few things come to mind."

"Tell me," he said huskily.

"Hmm…I'm more into show. Maybe we should go back to my place."

"Or..." He pulled off his jacket and spread it out behind her on the rock.

"Here?" she whispered.

"Yeah." Laying her back, he towered over her, rocking his pelvis to hers, letting her feel how hard he was. "Here."

Already breathless, her body betrayed her by quivering in anticipation. "Someone might come."

"That would be you," he said, and lowered himself down to kiss her.

Chapter 21

At the next Craft Corner, Ben worked to keep his patience but he was quickly losing the battle. Within fifteen minutes, he was already having to resist the urge to bang his head against the wall. He'd made the spectacularly stupid mistake of asking the kids last week what they wanted to make, and they'd voted for a birdhouse, of all things. He'd cheated by buying the materials himself ahead of time and precutting all the plywood, effectively making "birdhouse kits." All the kids had to do was fit the pieces together like a puzzle and then glue and paint. "Right there," he said to Pink, pointing to a spot on her wood. "Glue right there."

"Why?" she asked.

He had twenty-five kids today, and every single one of them had asked him at least a million questions. A billion. Surely they all had sore throats from talking so much. "To hold the roof on the birdhouse," he said for the fifth time.

"Oh, yeah," she said. She'd lost both of her top front

teeth this past week, and she liked to press her tongue into the vacancy. She beamed at him, a toothless grin, and damn if he didn't feel his heart squeeze. Finding himself utterly helpless in the face of her sweetness, he ruffled her hair.

Her smiled widened. "You're awfully good with this stuff, Mr. Teacher."

No matter how many times he reminded her his name was Ben, she still said "mister," and now she'd taken to calling him Mr. Teacher, making him feel about a thousand years old.

"*Real* good," Pink added, clearly impressed. She cocked her head, leveling him with those heartbreaker-in-the-making blue eyes. "Are all dads good with this stuff?" she wanted to know.

Another hard squeeze to his heart. He wasn't sure if he'd survive her. "I don't know." And that was God's truth. He really didn't know jack about dads.

Pink nodded, accepting this with a wisdom that she shouldn't yet have. "I wonder if our dad is," she said softly.

"He is." He could say that much with absolute certainty, happy to be able give her at least something to go on. And then, trying to avoid another barrage of questions, he shifted his attention to her twin. "How's it going, Kendra?"

She shrugged, but her project was pitch-perfect.

"Hey, great job." He crouched down to her eye level, and she smiled the spitting image of Pink's smile—without the missing front teeth, of course. Unlike her sister, however, she didn't say a word, which had his heart rolling over in his chest and exposing its tender underbelly. He ruffled her hair, as he had Pink's. "Maybe you should come to my work and be my assistant," he said.

She nodded vehemently.

"Problem is," he said, unable to believe he was going to say this, "my assistant would have to talk."

Pink leaned in and whispered something in her twin's ear. Kendra listened avidly and then turned her head and said something in Pink's ear.

Pink nodded and looked up at Ben. "She says she wants to be your assistant, but I'd have to come along so I can tell you whatever she needs to say."

Knowing he'd been outsmarted, Ben tossed back his head and laughed. Then he met Kendra's gaze. "Smart girl."

Kendra gave him a thumbs-up.

That night after he dropped them off at their foster home—taking yet a third hard squeeze to his heart as they vanished inside the house—he drove straight to Seattle.

To Bob's Auto Shop.

He walked right past a scowling Bob and Ed. If they wanted another fight, he was perfectly willing to give them one, but neither man stopped him.

He found Dan on his back beneath a Jeep and kicked the cart to get his attention.

Dan rolled himself out and stared up at Ben. "What do you want?"

"You being a dad to your daughters, for starters."

Dan's mouth tightened. "We going to do this again?"

"You're a fucking idiot," Ben said. "You know that, right? You have these two perfect little girls, and you don't even see them. Explain that to me."

"Already did."

"Do it again."

Dan flung the wrench in his hand against the wall with shocking violence.

Ben didn't move a single inch, just arched a brow.

"Fuck," Dan said beneath his breath. He stood up, and though he still barely came to Ben's shoulders, he stepped toe-to-toe with him. "I come from shit."

"So?"

"I went to prison."

"Yeah, I looked that up," Ben said. "You told me it was a bogus charge, but I had to check for myself. The police were feeling pressure from the DA to make an arrest, and you had a juvie record that matched, so the charges stuck. But the rumor is that you really didn't do it."

Dan looked away. "Rumors don't mean dick in a court of law."

"You have a house."

"It's small and needs work," Dan said.

"It's in a good school district," Ben said, and at Dan's look of surprise, he nodded. "Yeah, I checked that, too. You've got a decent job."

"I work for ex-cons."

"Who did their time and turned things around." Ben shrugged at Dan's stare. "I'm good at research. These guys are family men, with kids. They're running this business clean and in the black, and they care about you." He paused, and then dropped the ace in the hole. "And then there's your sister."

Dan's eyes hardened. "Leave her out of this."

Ben liked the protective reaction, but he wasn't going to leave anything out. "You share your house with your twenty-five-year-old sister, who's just graduated college—thanks to you, by the way," Ben added. "She's working as a second-grade teacher. You've got a built-in support system."

Dan looked baffled. "Why do you even give a shit about me?"

"Oh, I *don't* give a shit about you," Ben said. "I give a shit about your daughters—two sweet, adorable five-year-old girls who deserve a whole hell of a lot better than being deserted in a foster home."

Dan stared at him. "I don't even know where to start, man. They must hate me."

"You start by exercising your rights to visitation. You get to know them. You'll see. Neither of them has the capacity to hate."

Ten minutes later, Ben was heading back to Lucky Harbor. Exhausted, he strode through his place, intending to go straight to bed, but there was Jack on his couch, feet up on the coffee table next to an empty bag of chips—Ben's—and two empty beer bottles, also Ben's. Jack's head was back, his mouth open. He was fast asleep. Next to him, equally sprawled out, equally dead to the world, was a snoring Kevin.

Nothing snored louder than a Great Dane.

Except maybe Jack. Ben gave his cousin's leg a nudge. Actually, it was more of a kick.

Jack sat straight up, instantly alert. "Wha—Did I miss the alarm?"

"You're off duty. And you don't fight fires anymore, remember?"

"Oh, yeah." Jack scrubbed his hands over his face. "What the hell time is it?"

"I don't know. Why are you here? Where's Leah?"

"Leah's at book club night. At your girlfriend's book-store, as a matter of fact."

"Aubrey's not my girlfriend. You ate all my chips and drank my beer?"

"Yeah. You'd gone to the grocery store and I hadn't."

Made perfect sense. Ben had certainly done the same to Jack enough times. Living next door to each other made it especially easy.

"I saw the dollhouse in the garage," Jack said.

Well, hell. "So?"

"So you haven't built anything like that since Hannah."

"Don't read anything into it," Ben said. He sure as hell didn't want to. He also didn't want to think about how he'd stalked the bluffs until he'd found the sole house with a dollhouse on the porch. Or how he'd then gone to the hardware store and spent a small fortune buying the materials for the replacement dollhouse he was making Aubrey.

Or why he was making it in the first place.

He plopped down in between Jack and Kevin. Kevin immediately crawled onto Ben's lap for a hug. Obliging, Ben wrapped his arms around the huge dog, giving him a full-body rub that had Kevin groaning in ecstasy. Then he burped in Ben's face.

"Your dog smells like my chips," Ben said.

"He might've had a few."

Ben leaned back and closed his eyes.

"You're not going to talk about what you're building in the garage?" Jack asked.

"No."

"Okay, then I'll talk. At first, I didn't approve of Aubrey for you."

At this, Ben slit open his eyes and looked at Jack. "Didn't approve? What the hell are we, eighteenth-century virgins?"

"I didn't approve," Jack said again, "because I thought she wasn't your type. You're quiet. You're introspective. You don't like flash. You've had a lot of shit in your life, and you came out on top. You're one of the strongest people I know, and whenever I need anything, you're at my back, no questions asked."

"Yeah? Maybe you could learn something from the no-questions-asked thing."

"Don't be an asshole," Jack said. "Hannah was such a great match because she was like you, very much so. I always thought when the day came that you landed yourself in another relationship, you'd need that same quiet strength she possessed, just like yours. But I was wrong. Aubrey is a force. She's not quiet. She's not easy. But in her own way, she's really good for you. She brings you out of your shell. She challenges you. She keeps you on your toes."

"Thanks, Dr. Phil."

Uninsulted, Jack smiled.

Ben didn't. "I'm not getting involved with Aubrey."

Now Jack laughed.

"Shut up. I'm not."

"Okay. But you're involved. Everyone knows it but you. Have you seen Facebook lately? Lucky Harbor's favorite son—you—has a poll up on whether or not you should settle down with Aubrey. Odds aren't in her favor at the moment."

"Jesus." Ben wasn't amused by this. By any of it. "People need to mind their own business. Aubrey could do way better than me. And we have sex," he said bluntly. "That's not the same thing as being involved. Not everyone has the future on their minds, like you and Luke suddenly do."

"I like her," Jack said, no longer amused, either. "A lot. But I'm not saying marry her. I'm saying just relax a little bit and enjoy being back here in Lucky Harbor. Enjoy having a woman who looks at you the way she does. And you look at her, too, you know. I've seen you with those moon eyes."

"Yeah?" Ben asked. "Well, shoot me next time."

Jack ignored this. "I think it's fair to say I know you like no one else does. This thing with Aubrey is different, and you know it."

Ben thought of how she'd been trying to make a difference, giving the seniors a place to go, giving anyone who needed it a place to go. Hell, she was even excited about working with troubled teens. He thought about how she felt in his arms, how she made him feel in hers—like he was the best man she knew and the only one she wanted. She moved him at every turn, without even trying.

And he knew Jack was right. This thing, this… whatever it was that they were doing, it *was* different.

And different was terrifying. And he wasn't ready to fall in love. He'd been there, done that, and it had flattened him. "I've told her, and now I'll tell you," he said. "I'm not looking for a committed relationship. I don't have it in me right now."

"Whatever you say, man." Jack rose and snapped his fingers at Kevin.

Kevin squeezed his eyes tight and pretended to be asleep.

Ben found a laugh after all. "Leave him."

"He ate chili tonight at the firehouse."

"Take him," Ben said.

Kevin sighed and jumped off Ben's lap, farting as he did so.

"Thanks," Ben said, waving the air in front of his face as he rose too.

"Yeah, should've warned you," Jack said. "He's got some serious hang time with those." Jack gave Ben a look that said they weren't closing the file on this subject.

Ben opened the door. "I'm okay, you know. I'm fine on my own."

Jack met his gaze. "Yeah. But you've been on your own a long time. Maybe it's time to try something new."

Chapter 22

♥

Once again Aubrey woke up to a text message that was making her phone vibrate on her nightstand. But this one was from Ben and read:

In the shop.

Odd, she thought. He'd never felt the need to announce his presence to her before. In fact, he seemed to get a kick out of surprising her.

A glance at her clock told her that she had half an hour to get up and get out to water Mr. Wilford's pumpkin patch—which still wasn't growing yet, damn it—and be back here to open on time.

But the text was making her curious. Rolling out of bed, she tiptoed down the stairs to see what he might be doing that he'd found it necessary to warn her about.

He was sitting on the counter in front of the coffee and tea station, sipping from a to-go cup from Leah's bakery.

She could tell by his clothes—slacks and a button-down shirt topped by a jacket—that he was going to his job. His real job. She'd seen him in jeans and a tool belt covered in sawdust, and she liked that look a lot. She'd also seen him in nothing. *That* particular memory gave her a flash of heat, because Ben in nothing was the hottest thing she'd ever seen. That was definitely her favorite look, but seeing him like this, a little dressed up, his broad shoulders stretching his dress shirt to its limits, the top button undone, his tie still loose, as though he weren't quite ready to settle into work for the day, did something serious to her insides.

Get a grip. She tiptoed closer, wanting to catch him unawares, the way he always caught her. Two feet from him, she was grinning widely, like an idiot, her hands outstretched to scare him, when he suddenly twisted and locked eyes on her.

"Damn it," she said.

"The top step creaks."

"I should hire someone to fix that," she said drily.

He didn't answer. He was busy taking in the very skimpy tank top and tiny boy shorts she'd slept in. From the heat in his gaze, she could tell he liked the view. But when he reached for her, she took a step back, out of his range.

"Come here."

Shaking her head, she covered her mouth with her hands. "Morning breath."

"I don't care."

He wasn't scared off by much, she knew. Well, except for a committed relationship, and at that thought, her mood went a little south. "I'm going to shower," she said, and when his eyes darkened with interest, she shook her head. "*Alone.*"

He took another sip of his steaming drink. "I'm really good in the shower."

Her nipples got perky, and she crossed her arms over herself, making him laugh softly.

"Go get dressed," he said. "I've started a new book club."

"What?" That's when she realized she could hear voices. *Little* voices. And then another, not little voice, but a low baritone, and she stared at Ben in horror.

He straightened, set down his drink, and pulled off his jacket, which he wrapped around her. It was warm, and it smelled like him, and it fell to her thighs. Putting a finger to his lips, he took her hand, leading her to the half wall. Then, holding her in front of him, he pressed on her shoulders until she ducked low.

He crouched behind her, cradling her body within his, stroking a hand down her back while she did her best not to notice that he smelled so good she wanted to inhale him.

And/or lick him as though he were a lollipop.

Pressing his jaw to hers, he gestured with his chin to look ahead.

Seated on one of her couches were Pink and Kendra. Their legs were short enough to stick straight out, and they each held a stack of books on their laps. In between them was a man who looked so much like them he could have been their older brother. He was reading out loud from one of Aubrey's favorite children's books, and the girls were enraptured, staring up into his face, hanging on every single word.

"That's their dad," Ben whispered against her ear. "Dan Ingalls. He's got visitation rights."

She craned her neck and looked up at Ben. Once again, he had a several-day-old scruff going on his jaw, and she wanted him to rub it over her body. "Since when?" she whispered, barely staying on topic.

"Since always, apparently. He just didn't exercise them. Until now."

There was something in his voice. Relief, she thought, and reached for his hand. "You did this," she said. "You brought them together."

He shook his head. "It's just a visit. I don't know if he's really into it." He looked at the little girls hanging on every word as their dad read the book.

Her heart squeezed at how important this was to him. The girls had seriously insinuated themselves into his heart. He was invested, whether he wanted to admit it or not.

And as wrong as it was to think it, it gave her hope. Because maybe he could get invested in something else, too. *Someone* else.

Someone like her…

Two days later, Aubrey closed the store, ran her receipts, and realized something shocking. "I broke even today," she said aloud in surprise.

Ben, who'd showed up after work, changed into jeans, and gotten busy on the back shelves, poked his head around the corner. He was covered in a layer of sawdust. "What?"

"I broke even," she marveled.

He flashed her a smile. "Congratulations." He held out a hand. "Come on. I'll buy you a drink."

They went to the Love Shack.

Aubrey was halfway through a tall, cold beer when Pastor Mike walked in the front door and headed to a table. He stopped short at the sight of Aubrey at the bar and then changed direction and headed straight for her.

Crap. She shoved her beer so that it was in front of Ben and lifted her hands the way a basketball player did when he'd just fouled but was trying to pretend he hadn't.

"Aubrey," Pastor Mike said, calm and quiet as ever, but the concern and worry were there in his eyes as he took in the two beers in front of Ben. He glanced at Ben, nodded, and then his attention came back to her. "How are you doing?"

"I'm good. *Really*," she added.

He nodded. "And you know you can call me."

"Yes," she said emphatically. "I know I can call you."

"Anytime."

"Anytime," she repeated, adding what she hoped was a confidence-boosting nod. "Thank you."

When he'd walked way, she blew out a breath, belatedly realizing Ben was looking at her. "What?" she asked.

"Anything you want to tell me?"

"Such as…?"

"Well, either you're having a fling with Pastor Mike or he thinks you're an alcoholic."

Aubrey grimaced. She wasn't sure which excuse to go with. "Maybe I found God."

Ben just looked at her.

She racked her brain, but there really wasn't a good option. "Okay, I didn't know how to tell you, but Pastor Mike and I are madly in love."

Ben shook his head. "Don't ever play poker."

Damn it. "Okay, so he thinks I'm an alcoholic."

"Well, I guess that's better than your sleeping with him," Ben said.

Interesting that *that* would bug him.

"Why would he think you're an alcoholic?" he asked.

"It's…complicated."

A laugh gusted out of him. "That doesn't surprise me."

"Oh, like *you're* a piece of cake," she said, and crossed her arms, insulted. "You know what? I don't want to talk about it."

"Do you ever?"

She rolled her eyes. "You're not exactly Mr. Talkative yourself, you know. You're always sticking your nose in my business about the list and all, but you're holding on to plenty of secrets yourself."

He tossed back his drink and set it down. Then he stood up and held out his hand. "Come on."

She looked at him, suddenly wary. "Where to?"

"Chicken?" he asked quietly.

How was it that he knew all her buttons? "Of course not."

"So then…" He waggled his fingers.

She stared at them and then, with a sigh, let him pull her up.

He brought her to his place. Jack's side of the duplex was dark. So was Ben's, until he unlocked and opened the front door, reached in, and turned on a light.

"What are we doing here?" she asked, hesitating on the front step. Nothing good was going to come of stepping inside.

Okay, scratch that. *Everything* good would come of it, but—

"I want to show you something."

"Oh, boy, I know this game," she said with a lightness she didn't feel.

He smiled. "Something else."

"What?"

He looked at her for a long moment. "Okay, but after I show you, I don't want you to get all weird and try to close yourself off."

"I don't do that."

He gave her a long look.

"Fine," she said, caving. "I totally do that. It's my thing."

"Don't do it to me," he said very seriously, very solemnly.

She stared into his eyes, butterflies bouncing around inside her now. "All right."

"Promise."

"Seriously?" She sighed when he didn't budge. "Okay, I promise not to shut you out. Jeez, I didn't know you had such tender feelings."

He out-and-out laughed at that, and then pulled her through the living room to the kitchen. There, he shoved open a door that led to his garage.

He gave her a look that made an odd feeling begin to course through her. Nerves. Then he flipped on the light, and she gasped at the beautiful handmade wooden doll-house.

Chapter 23

♥

Heart pounding, Aubrey walked to the dollhouse and ran her fingers over the meticulously handcrafted wood. It was beautiful. She wasn't sure how long she stood there before she felt Ben's hand run down her back.

"I don't have any tissues," he said, "but you can use my shirt if you want."

She let out a laugh to hide her sob. "Why? Why did you do this?"

His hand was still on her. He was stroking her as though he just liked the feel of her beneath his hand, but it didn't escape her notice that he didn't answer.

With an unsteady breath, she touched the dollhouse again. It was a three-story Victorian, as hers had been when she was a child. Unlike that one, however, this dollhouse was made entirely of wood—no plastic or cardboard anywhere—and it was of heirloom quality. If she'd been a child, she'd have spent hours having her dolls run up and down the spiral staircase, peek out the numerous windows, and swing open the front door. "Thank you," she whispered. Ali and Leah were right. Her gut was right. She needed to tell him why he was on the list.

But she wasn't ready to lose him.

A little voice deep inside her warned that the longer she waited, the worse the consequences would be, but she told that voice to shut up. She arched a little so that Ben's hand pressed harder against her back. "Ben..."

He stroked her again, slowly this time, more purposefully. She waited for him to speak, but he didn't. His silence was loaded now, weighted with hunger and desire. Her heart kicked into a fast, heavy beat, and everything within her tightened with need.

For him. "*Ben.*"

His hand moved on her again, stroking her hair, then softly sweeping it aside. She felt his mouth against the nape of her neck and was working at drawing in a desperate breath when he turned her around to face him. Cupping her jaw, he kissed her, stealing away the air she'd managed to drag in. His mouth was firm, just like the rest of his hard, warm body, and so male that she melted into him. By the time he finally lifted his head and met her gaze, she'd wrapped herself around him like a pretzel.

"Your choice," he said.

There was no choice. She needed him more than she needed air. And she needed air pretty damn bad. There were a lot of reasons why she should still take the closing-herself-off option, but she knew she wasn't going to. She wanted him to put his hands and his mouth on her. She wanted him to work his magic, and he *was* magic. He was a masterful lover, intuitive and shockingly sensitive. She wanted him to do all the things his eyes were promising, and she wanted that now. "My choice is you," she said.

She'd barely gotten the words out before his mouth was back on hers. He kissed her hard and then pulled back to look at her for a beat before he kissed her again.

And then again.

And then he lifted her up so that her legs wrapped around him. He carried her from the garage to his bedroom, letting her down by his bed, slowly sliding her along his body. Then he stripped her with slow care, groaning as he bared her to his satisfaction. Lowering his head, he splayed his hands on her bare back, drawing her close. Opening his mouth on first one breast, and then the other, he teased her with his tongue, sucking and nibbling.

She moaned—a low, desperately hungry sound—as she slid her fingers into his hair, holding his head to her. She couldn't help it. She was trying to climb his body as though it were a tree when he stepped back and pulled off his own clothes in a few smooth, economical movements.

She just stared at him. His body was incredible, and she didn't think she'd ever get tired of looking at it.

He still hadn't spoken a word.

She might have thought he was entirely unmoved, except he was sporting an impressive erection that made her mouth water. She was still staring at it in awe, thinking *In me now*, when he gave her a nudge and she fell backward onto the bed.

He followed her down, and she moaned again when he kissed her, long and deep. And then he kissed every inch of her, slowly and thoroughly, until she came. Exploded, really.

He put on a condom and entered her, and she came again. Instantly. She cried out in surprise and shock as it went on and on, endless shudders and ripples of pleasure. She was vaguely aware of the sounds she was making and might have been horrified, but she realized she wasn't the only one. When her senses returned, Ben was still over her, muscles quaking, breathing as harshly as she.

After a moment, he rolled off the bed and went into the bathroom.

She told herself to get up and get dressed and then get out. She needed to do so before her heart got any more invested than it already was. Trembling like a leaf, she took a long moment to even sit up, and by then Ben was back. He stood at the side of the bed, voice low, eyes dark and direct. "Stay," he said. And then he slid in beside her, pulling the covers over the top of them, dragging her in against him.

Oh, God. God, he felt so good. But this wasn't real. She needed to remind them both of that and set some boundaries. For his sake. "Ben—"

"Sleep," he said, voice gruff.

"But—"

He tightened his grip. Her cheek was on his chest, her thigh between his. She was breathing in his scent with every breath and couldn't remember ever feeling so content in her life. She didn't close her eyes, she didn't want to miss a second of this, because it wouldn't last. It couldn't. Unable to resist, she let her hand drift over his chest. It was a beautiful chest, broad and sculpted and spattered with light hair from pec to pec. He was warm and hard, and he hummed his pleasure at her touch. "Okay?" he asked quietly in the dark, tightening his grip.

She nodded against him. She was so far more than okay that it was terrifying.

They slept some then, and she woke up in the gray light of dawn, violently aroused. Ben was between her legs, working his magic with his tongue. She came before she had all her faculties working, and then he rose over her and kissed her, slow and unrushed.

Their joining was much more leisurely this time, but no less hot. Maybe it was because they knew each other's bodies now, or maybe it was just sheer animal magnetism, but when he finally slid into her and began a series of driving thrusts, she went out of her mind. And when she climaxed, she nearly burst out of her skin as well.

Afterward, he held her for a long time, and Aubrey reveled in it, afraid of what might happen when full daylight came.

"Shh," he murmured, sounding sleepy.

"I didn't say anything."

"You're thinking so hard you're making me tired." He stroked a big hand down her back to possessively cup her ass, holding her close. "Sleep."

She didn't. Couldn't.

He made a noise like that of a rumbling lion and rolled her beneath him, pinning her to the mattress.

"What are you doing?" she asked, already breathless.

"Wearing you out so you can sleep." He kissed her mouth, her chin, her throat, her shoulder. A nipple. And as he headed further south, she gasped and arched, sliding her fingers into his hair. "Omigod."

"No," he said. "Just Ben."

She started to laugh, but then he got creative with his tongue, and she cried out instead.

He made good on his promise. A long time later, they both flopped to the mattress, breathing raggedly, sated, and completely worn out.

When Aubrey woke again, the sun was shining. She slipped from Ben's arms and stared down at him, still asleep on the bed. He looked relaxed and young. His jaw was rough with stubble, his hair wild from her fingers. And if she wasn't mistaken, he had a bite mark on his shoulder. She'd marked him. Fair enough, she thought, since he'd indelibly marked her. On the inside…

She'd done the unthinkable and started the slippery fall from lust to love.

Or maybe she'd fallen for him a long time ago…

Either way, big mistake. She began scooping up her clothes, but she was still trembling, little aftershocks of great sex. She stilled for a moment to gather herself, and then felt two warm hands settle on her arms and pull her back against an even warmer chest. And then a mouth brushed her shoulder.

"Pastor Mike?" she murmured.

A soft laugh huffed against her skin, and then he bit her. She laughed, too, but her smile fell away, and, unable to keep it inside any longer, she turned to face him. "Ben, what are we doing?"

"About to have some hot morning sex?" He reached for her, but she stepped back, her knees wobbling so badly she sank into a chair.

"But it's *just* sex," she said, meeting his gaze, trying to be as calm as he always was. "Right?"

He held her gaze but dropped his hands from her. "Aubrey—"

"I need to know, Ben. I need to know because I can't be in this all by myself. I can't. I—" God, she was such a hypocrite. She wanted him, like this, just like this. But there was the secret between them, one he didn't even know about. She covered her face.

"Hey," he said gently, kneeling beside her chair, placing his hands on her legs. "I thought you wanted it to stay simple, too."

"I do." But as he'd pointed out several times, nothing was ever simple with her. "Or I thought I did," she added.

He held her gaze, but his own was a little hooded now. "I think of you all the time. And I know an awful lot of it is sex—an awful lot," he said. "But not all."

Her heart did a funny dance. Either hope, or terror, she wasn't sure which.

Both, she decided. Definitely both.

"But," he went on slowly, still holding her gaze prisoner, because he was far braver than she was, "I didn't need this. I didn't want this in my life," he said.

"I know." She rose abruptly. "I've worked hard to keep this just sex—for you, Ben, for *your* comfort level, so you wouldn't think I was trying to drag you into a committed relationship." She turned back and found him standing right there, and she wrapped her arms around his neck. "You're not going to turn into a lapdog, Ben."

His arms closed around her hard. "No?"

"No. And even though I risk breaking my own no-emotions clause, I care about you," she admitted. "More than I wanted to. Much more."

He stared at her as if she'd just told him she was carrying a nuclear bomb.

"It's supposed to be a compliment," she said, and

backed away. "One you aren't expected to return. You know that, right?"

"Goddamn it," he said, and she started at his shocking vehemence, because he never raised his voice. In fact, unless he had his tongue in her mouth, or any of his other body parts entangled with hers, it was difficult to tell what he was feeling.

But she felt his feelings now, loud and clear. Shock. Anger.

Fear.

Sympathy flooded her. He, the guy who was seemingly afraid of nothing, was afraid of her feelings for him. Or maybe he was afraid of what he felt for her.

Not that she blamed him. He'd already given a woman everything he had, and she was gone. "My feelings aren't meant to be a burden," she said softly. "But I won't apologize for them, or take them back."

He closed his eyes. "I care about you, too, Aubrey, but..."

"But you don't want to. I get it." It shouldn't hurt. At all. "Never mind," she said. "Subject change."

"You knew my feelings on this," he said. "From the beginning."

"Yeah. Got them loud and clear," she said.

He studied her for a beat. "Caring about someone means you're open," he finally said.

"What are you saying, that you're not open?"

"I'm open," he said. "I'm an open book." He lifted his hands out to his sides. "What you see is what you get."

Suddenly she knew what he was getting at, and her heart kicked again. "And you don't think that's the case with me."

"You're smoke and mirrors, Aubrey."

Her heart started pounding. He knew. Maybe not the what exactly, but he knew something. "How so?"

"Forget it."

Forget it? Was he serious? She'd pulled on her dress. She had one boot on, the other in her hand. "Tell me or I'll throw this at you."

He shook his head, a small smile playing at the corners of his mouth. "That," he said. "That right there. You dress like you're going to some fancy tea, but underneath the clothes you're ready to brawl for anything you believe in. You want people to think you're tough and that you don't care what anyone thinks, but you do. You care. A lot." He met her gaze. "You care too much."

"Well, I'm not going to apologize for that, either!"

"So why do you keep it your dirty secret?"

"What are you talking about?"

"Your list," he said, and her stomach sank, because here it came. Doomsday. "When are you going to tell me about the list?" he asked quietly.

She looked into his eyes and knew it was a huge risk, but she had to do it or lose him right here and now. "Okay."

"Okay?"

She let out a long, shaky breath. "About a month ago, I kind of wandered into a weekly AA meeting by accident."

"How do you wander into AA by accident?"

"Well, I was—" Running from *him*, in fact. "That's not the important part. The important part is that when I was there, something happened."

"Pastor Mike."

She nodded. "No. Well, yes. Pastor Mike happened.

He thought—" She broke off with a grimace. "He thought I was an alcoholic, so he brought me into that meeting."

He stared at her. "You went to an AA meeting even though you're not an alcoholic."

"Yes. I know. But in the meeting I heard something that struck a chord with me."

"And that was?"

"Make amends with people you've wronged."

He stared at her, and then his eyes softened. "Everyone's made mistakes, Aubrey."

Some more than others... "I know," she said. "I'm just trying to own mine." She was going to have to tell him, and her knees went weak with fear and anxiety.

A frown of concern creased his brow, but just as he stepped toward her, there came the unmistakable sound of Ben's front door opening.

Ben had his jeans on in a wink. Leaving them unfastened, he headed out to the living room, eyes flat and calm, body perfectly relaxed and yet somehow braced for violence at the same time.

"Jesus, Jack," she heard him say.

By the time she finished dressing and fixing her hair, the scent of something delicious was coming from the kitchen. She followed the mouthwatering aroma of bacon and coffee and found Jack at the stove top stirring something, with Ben glaring at him.

Ignoring him, Jack smiled at Aubrey. "Hey," he said. "Sorry for the interruption. Ben here didn't mention that he was having a sleepover."

"Ben didn't mention it," Ben said, "because it's none of your business."

"Testy in the mornings, isn't he?" Jack said to Aubrey,

not looking like he was in a hurry to go anywhere. He grabbed another bowl so that there were three lined up on the counter, and then he began filling them. "Just got off duty and brought a big pot of breakfast casserole to Mr. Sunshine here. There's enough to go around, so have a seat."

"Oh," she said. "No, thanks. I have to—"

"*Sit.*"

"Resistance is futile," Ben said drily. "He'll just wear you down."

"It's true," Jack said.

Ben reached out with his foot and nudged a chair toward her.

She picked a different chair. One that was farther away from him. He arched a brow as he also sat. Kevin, the Great Dane, immediately leaped into his lap. Ben laughed and wrapped his arms around the dog. Kevin snuggled in as though he weighed ten pounds, not 150, and sent Aubrey a look from the security of Ben's arms—*My man, not yours.*

Jack plopped into the chair that Ben had pulled out for Aubrey. "Aw, thanks, man." He blew a kiss in Ben's direction.

In turn, Ben upturned his middle finger in Jack's direction.

Jack grinned. "You're just cranky because you think I'm going to ask Aubrey some awkward questions."

"You're not going to ask a single question," Ben said.

"Seriously," Jack said. "For a guy who just got some, *how* can you still be pissy?"

Aubrey choked on her bite of the breakfast casserole.

Ben shot Jack a fulminating look and leaned over him to pat Aubrey on the back.

"We're just friends," Aubrey said to Jack, smacking Ben's hand away. "And sometimes we're not even that."

Jack grinned. "Do tell."

"Don't," Ben said to her. "Anything you say is just fuel for him. He's Lucille in training."

"Sorry," Jack said, looking anything but. "I just got excited that Ben's got a friend other than me and Luke. He's growing up so fast."

Ben sent him a look that would have had Aubrey peeing in her pants if she had been a man. She stood up and brought her bowl to the sink. She couldn't eat. She couldn't do this. They had so much more to talk about, she and Ben, but she wasn't eager to do that, because then it would be over. She might never be ready for that.

Not that Ben was exactly showing signs of being ready for a relationship either. The most likely scenario was that he wasn't ever going to be ready.

Oh, yes, she knew he wanted her in his bed.

But that wasn't going to ever be enough for her. She knew that now. It hurt, deep down inside, and she didn't know what to do. She'd promised herself she would tell him the truth—she'd very nearly done so only a few moments ago—but now she needed to think. Turning, she looked at Jack. "Thanks for breakfast. I've got to go."

Jack smiled at her. "Anytime."

She didn't look at Ben. She was halfway through the living room before she was aware of him following her, but still she kept going. When she reached for the front door, a bigger hand got there first, holding it closed. She stared at the forearm lined with sinew and strength and let out a breath. "I have to get to the store, Ben."

"You're leaving mad."

"No."

"Now you're leaving mad *and* lying."

She dropped her head to the door. "Ben—"

He put his hands on her and turned her to face him. "There," he said. "Now you can try to lie right to my face."

"I've got to go," she said again. "Please, Ben."

"Shit," he said, staring at her. "You never say 'please'—unless we're having sex."

Behind them, Jack snorted.

When both Ben and Aubrey glanced over at him, he raised his hands in surrender. "I'm going."

"So am I," Aubrey said, and turned to the door.

"We're not done with this," Ben said.

She glanced back to find him standing there in nothing but those low-slung jeans, hands up over his head and braced on the doorjamb, watching her with the expression that never failed to make her body hum. And she could only hope that he was right—that they weren't done with this.

Chapter 24

♥

Aubrey drove past her bookstore and straight to the church. It was early, but the front doors were unlocked. Maybe a church was always unlocked; she had no idea. No doubt the people here were far more trusting than she was. In any case, she let herself in and was grateful to find Pastor Mike in his office, reading.

He looked up with surprise. "Aubrey. I've been thinking about you since you missed the meeting."

Because she'd been in bed with Ben.

And in the shower.

And against the wall…"I'm sorry," she said, hoping she wasn't blushing. "Something came up. But I have"—she looked at her watch—"seventeen minutes, and I've got a problem that's really much bigger than seventeen minutes, but I thought out of everyone I know, you're probably the only one who could help me. I don't know." She blew out a breath. She was rambling. "Can I come in?"

"You already are," he said with a smile. He rose and gestured to a chair. "Tell me the problem."

"It's actually more of a question. About making amends." She hesitated, because now that she was here, she was nervous. Very nervous. What if she'd already screwed up too badly? What if there were no amends that could fix this one last thing on her list, the most important thing on her list?

THE HARD ONE.

"Sixteen minutes," Mike reminded her gently.

"Right." She drew a deep breath. "Okay, so say you have a secret, something you want to apologize for, but by coming out with it, you might hurt the very person you want to make amends to?" She stopped. "You know what? Never mind; I'm not making sense."

"Yes, you are," Pastor Mike said. "It's just a hard thing to say. You've wronged someone. You want to apologize, but in bringing it out into the open, you might hurt the very person you wanted to apologize to. Do I have that right?"

"Yes." She sagged back in her chair. "You're very good at this."

"Don't say that yet." He leaned in and met her gaze. "Aubrey, sometimes you have to go with your heart. The very soul of your heart, where all the goodness is."

"You make it sound easy."

He shook his head. "It's not. That part of your heart is usually protected by pride and stubbornness."

Aubrey let out a half laugh, half groan, and covered her face.

"Sometimes," he said quietly, "you have to do the hard thing, not the easy thing."

She dropped her hands. "But either way feels like the hard thing—on the one hand, telling him, and on the other hand, keeping the knowledge to myself."

"Okay, so what's the *right* thing?"

Aubrey drew in a deep breath and leaned back. The truth was, she'd known deep in her gut for a long time that *not* telling Ben what she'd done all those years ago was *not* the right thing.

Which meant she really did have to tell him.

She had to hurt him.

And then, once she came clean with him, when she freed herself of the burden of the truth, she'd lose him. He wouldn't smile at her anymore. He wouldn't make her day by just being *in* her day.

He wouldn't be in her day at all.

To do the right thing, she had to destroy the best thing that had ever happened to her. "Sometimes," she said miserably, "I wish there was a DELETE button in life."

Pastor Mike smiled sympathetically. "Do you want to tell me what you did?" he asked.

No. No, she wanted to *never* ever tell anyone what she'd done. How she'd broken Ben and Hannah up all those years ago, for a stupid, selfish reason that didn't even matter anymore. Thank God they'd managed to get back together two years later—that they'd had a few years before Hannah had died. But Aubrey knew it wouldn't matter to Ben. All that would matter is that she'd screwed things up for him.

And there was nothing she could do or say to make that up to him.

Nothing.

*   *   *

Aubrey drove back to the bookstore. As she walked through, opening the place for the day, she came to a sudden halt at the sight of the dollhouse set up in the children's section. Weak-kneed, she sat in front of it. Ben, of course. He'd done this—for her.

She spent a few long moments staring at it and then had to reapply her mascara before she greeted any customers.

That night Ben heard a persistent honking from out front of his duplex. When he opened the door to investigate, he found the local senior center dial-a-ride van out front. The door slid open, and a bunch of blue-haired ladies peeked out and waved at him.

The driver was his aunt Dee, though her hair wasn't blue but a bright, shiny platinum blond. He'd long since stopped being surprised by her colorful wigs. He was just happy she was past the worst of the chemo and clearly no longer depressed.

"Get in," Dee said, waving him over. "Tonight's the Winter Festival, remember?"

He remembered, but he shook his head in the negative. Lucky Harbor reveled in its traditions, and Winter Festival was one of them. It involved a lot of beer and wine and dancing on the pier, made possible by stands of portable heaters that kept everyone warm—as though the festivities and alcohol wouldn't do that on their own.

But Ben didn't feel the need to go. Luke and Jack were both working the event, so he figured he'd stay home with Kevin and a movie.

"Ah, come on," Dee coaxed. "We need a designated driver."

"Where's your boyfriend?" he asked. "Why can't he be the DD?"

At that, several male heads popped out, one of them being Ronald, Dee's boyfriend. Another was Edward, Luke's grandfather.

Shit. Everyone was looking at Ben hopefully. He didn't want to do this. He wasn't in a festival kind of mood. He'd worked hard this week, and he was physically exhausted. Mentally, too.

And Aubrey was avoiding him.

And maybe he'd been avoiding her, too, after she'd revealed her feelings. He had feelings, too, and not only wasn't he ready for them, he didn't want them. Fat lot of good that was doing him...

Relenting, he drove them to the festival. "Hey," he said, holding down the door locks before anyone could escape. "This party is over in two hours, you hear me? You must be back at the van in two hours, or you're walking home."

This was met by a chorus of moans and groans. Dee released her seat belt and hugged Ben from behind. "That's only ten o'clock, sweetheart. We aren't pumpkins, you know."

"Don't you all need to get home to take your Metamucil?" he asked desperately, as Dee continued to hug him. There was no rushing a hug from Dee. He'd learned that years ago, when he'd first been dumped on her doorstep. She'd hugged him hello, she'd hugged him good-bye, she'd hugged him whenever she'd passed him in the hallway, and he'd squirmed over every single one. He knew she loved him. Just as he knew that sometimes she hugged him just to torture him and to amuse herself.

That's what family did—fuck with each other. And sweet as she was, she could give as good as she got.

"Midnight," she said now, in her soft but steely voice. "Okay, baby? We'll owe you."

Since he couldn't imagine needing a favor from the seniors of Lucky Harbor, he just disentangled himself and unlocked the doors. "Midnight," he agreed reluctantly. "Be here. I mean it."

As Lucille padded by, she patted his shoulder. "Saw your girl yesterday at the rec center. She was volunteering at Reading Corner."

"Reading Corner?"

"Sure. Craft Corner is Tuesdays and Fridays; Reading Corner is Wednesday. Volunteers come in and read to the kids. She was good, too—did all the voices just right. The kids ate her up."

Ben looked into Lucille's eyes and saw something sly. "What are you up to?" he asked warily.

"Who, me?" she asked innocently.

When the van was empty, Ben stared out at the pier, which was lit up like the Fourth of July. Yeah, the people of Lucky Harbor took their Winter Festival very seriously. The last time he'd been here for the festival, he'd had Hannah with him, and at that thought he braced for the usual stab of agony through his heart. But there was no sharp pain at all, just a sweet ache and the memory of Hannah dragging him out onto the dance floor, which made him smile.

But he still didn't want to go. So he put the van in gear and hit the gas. There was really only one place he wanted to be tonight, and only one person he wanted to be with.

* * *

Alone, Aubrey sat on her bed in a big T-shirt she'd stolen from Ben. Every other item of clothing she owned was either at the dry cleaner or in her laundry basket, waiting for a trip to the Laundromat. Her grand-opening party was only a few days from now, and she was working on the plans. The store calendar had filled up so nicely, with something happening just about every day of the week, that she actually had a shot at making this work.

Too bad she didn't have a shot in hell of making her private life work nearly so neatly. She'd promised herself that the very next time she saw Ben she'd tell him the truth. That he was on her list. She was pretty sure how things would go from there.

South. Fast.

Restless, she rose and started a game of darts. If she got a bull's-eye, she told herself, she'd tell Ben now. She'd get into her car, drive straight to his place, and just spit it out.

Which would effectively ruin the best thing that had ever happened to her...

She got a bull's-eye on the second try. Damn it. "Two out of three," she said out loud, and gathered the darts.

She startled when the single knock sounded at her door. She knew that knock, and even if she hadn't, the way her nipples hardened told her exactly who was on the other side of the door.

He didn't knock again. This was because, as she'd learned, he had the patience of a saint.

Not that there was anything remotely saintly about him.

Still, she glanced through the peephole. Though she hadn't made a noise, Ben looked right at her, brow cocked.

If you open the door, you have to tell him.

On the other side of the door, Ben lifted the bag he held. It was from the Love Shack.

Her head said, *Danger, Will Robinson, danger!* But her stomach growled, and apparently her stomach was the boss. She pulled open the door. "Ben. I—"

He pushed inside as though he owned the place. "Why aren't you at the Winter Festival?"

"I'm...busy."

He glanced at the darts in her hand. "Yes, I can see that." The corners of his mouth quirked but his eyes remained serious. "You up for a game?"

"With me?"

"Three darts," he said. "Highest points combined wins."

"What does the winner get?" she asked.

His gaze ate her up. "Winner's choice."

Her heart took a treacherous leap. Her choice would be to never have to tell him what she'd done, but she knew that was no longer a choice at all. "Are you any good?" she asked.

He shrugged and made himself at home, setting down the bag he'd brought and turning to the dartboard. "Ladies first," he said.

"I stole your T-shirt," she said inanely.

"I can see that." He eyed her from head to toe and back again, lingering, making her very aware of how thin and see-through the shirt was, a fact he was clearly enjoying. "It looks better on you than it ever did on me," he said, voice low and sexy. "Play, Aubrey."

She threw her darts. Two hit the twenty, the last hit the bull's-eye. Trying to hold back her smug smile, she turned to him. "Sixty-five points."

"You're good." He slid his hand around to the nape of her neck and tugged her in for a quick, hard kiss. "But I'm better," he said silkily against her lips.

Every erogenous zone in her body stood up and danced. "Why don't you put your money where your mouth is?"

"Don't tempt me." He kissed her again, and then nipped at her lower lip. Then he pulled the darts from the board, stood at the line, and shot.

For a moment her eyes were on him, on the long, lean, hard lines of his body, and she didn't see his first throw. But his second throw caught her attention.

Triple twenty, just like his first. Uh-oh.

Turning his head, he looked at her, and then threw the third dart. Another triple twenty. He hadn't gone for the bull's-eye. He'd gone for the maximum points on the board. One hundred and eighty, to be exact.

"Hmm," she said. "You're better than good."

"Yeah." He gave her another kiss, this one a little longer, a little deeper, and a whole lot hotter. She was completely melted into him when he pulled back and gave her a light swat on the ass. "Hungry?" he asked. Without waiting for an answer, he grabbed the bag of food and sat on her bed. He pulled out a burrito and un-wrapped the foil, making steam rise. He wafted it in her direction.

Her stomach growled again.

He smiled and patted the bed.

"What about your spoils?" she asked.

"Later."

She crossed her arms. "Now. I want to know what de-vious angle you're working."

"Devious," he repeated. "Wow. I'm wounded."

"Is it going to be sexual?" she asked, unable to keep the hopeful tone out of her voice. "Because I should have specified—if it's something sexual, it can't be from my taboo list."

He laughed. "Sunshine, we obliterated your taboo list the other night."

Oh, yeah. Damn.

"Come eat."

She sat next to him, carefully tucking the shirt around her for modesty, which cracked him up again. "You're full of laughs tonight," she said.

He shrugged. "I like being with you."

Her chest tightened. She'd wanted this, oh, God, how much she wanted this. And now she was going to have to ruin it.

You ruined it a long time ago…

"You were at Reading Corner," he said, halfway through his burrito. "Lucille told me."

"Yes," she said. "Your girls were there. They're so smart, Ben."

"I know. Dan's working on custody."

Her breath caught. "Really? How wonderful for all of them." She paused. "You did that. You brought them together. You gave those girls a real family."

He shrugged.

"It's amazing," she said. "You're amazing."

"No. I just couldn't stand it, them not having anyone. I had my aunt Dee." He ran his thumb over the backs of her knuckles. "Without her and Jack…" He shook his head. "I'd have fallen through the cracks. I probably wouldn't even be here."

Her heart squeezed. "You saved them from falling through the cracks. You gave them so much, Ben."

He busied himself with cleaning up the trash and shoving it back into the bag the food had come in. Then he balled it, aimed for the trash can twenty feet across the room, and shot.

The bag swooshed into the can.

And still he stayed quiet.

"Did I upset you?" she asked.

"No. I like the way you care about stuff," he said. "You aren't quiet about it, and though you're reserved, you aren't shy. When you have your heart and soul in something, you're in it."

Her breath caught. Had anyone ever gotten her the way he did? No. And that's when she knew. Truth was, she'd known for a damn long time. She had her heart and soul in something, all right—*him*. She closed her eyes and gave herself a lecture. *Don't you sleep with him. Don't you dare. Not until you tell him...*

He turned his hand over and entangled his fingers with hers. "I like the way you care," he said again. "I like the way you care about me."

"Is that why you're here?" she asked, heart pounding. "And not at the Winter Festival?"

"I'm the seniors' ride, but wasn't in the mood for a crowd. I have to go back to get them later," he said, and he rose. "I'll take my spoils now."

Oh, God. "We should play another game," she said quickly, and jumped up, heading to the dartboard. "We'll make it the best of two out of three—"

Strong arms wrapped around her from behind, and he turned, effectively caging her in between the hard wall and his harder body. "You reneging?" he asked, mouth against her ear.

"No, but—" She sucked in a breath as his hands roamed over her, molding the shirt to her curves. "I was just thinking it might be more fair if—"

He whipped her around to face him and then backed her to the kitchen counter, lifting her to it.

Her bare ass touched the cold surface, and she yelped.

"I claim *you*," he said, and his lips descended on hers.

She wrapped her arms around his neck and traced her tongue over his lower lip, knowing it drove him wild.

Pinning her with his big body, he let her feel what she did to him. "I've got a question," he said. "A serious one."

Her heart skidded to a stop. Oh, God. "Okay," she whispered tentatively.

"What are you wearing beneath my shirt?"

She stared at him. "Not much," she confessed.

This made him swear roughly, reverently. She laughed again and then realized that whenever she was with him, she was laughing, or smiling.

Or having an orgasm.

It'd been a long time since she'd had someone like him in her life. Maybe since…ever. But even as the warm fuzzies washed over her, so did fear. Because this was all an illusion; he wasn't really hers. And at that thought, her smile faded.

His did, too. "Should I go, Aubrey?"

"You mean…leave? Now?"

"If you want."

"No." She knew she should be embarrassed by how quickly she answered, but she felt only panic at the thought of him leaving. "Don't go."

There. She'd said it. She'd put it out there and couldn't, wouldn't, take it back. Tomorrow would be a different story, and she'd face that then, but for now, right this very minute, she knew what she needed.

Him.

Inside of her.

Ben caught her close and slowly lowered his head to hers, giving her plenty of time to stop him.

Fat chance of that. Not only did she not stop him, she grabbed him and pulled him even closer.

He was smiling when he kissed her, his lips fitting smoothly over hers. Then he straightened and kicked off his shoes and tore his shirt over his head. "It's only fair to even the score," he said.

"So you're being a gentleman by stripping?"

"Exactly."

"I'll help," she said, and unbuttoned and unzipped him so she could slide her hand inside his jeans.

Ben groaned, the sound echoing in the otherwise silent loft, a hotly erotic sound. "Ben?"

He cupped her face and deepened the kiss, and when she was completely lost, he slid his hands beneath the hem of the big T-shirt and cupped her bare bottom. "Mmm," he said, low and husky. Tugging her closer, he continued moving against her so that she could hardly breathe. "Aubrey?"

"Yes?"

"Be sure." Pulling back, he looked deep into her eyes, probably searching for a sign that she was going to regret this. "If I stay tonight," he said, "I'm going to be in your bed in about five seconds. I'm going to make love to you until neither of us can walk."

The words brought a rush of heat. "Was that supposed to scare me off?" she asked.

The faintest of smiles crossed his mouth as he pulled the shirt off her, tossing it behind him, leaving her bare to his gaze. He looked his fill with a groan, and then looked some more.

She was shaking for him. "Ben, I want—"

"Want? Or need?"

He was going to tease her now? "*Need*, damn it. I need—"

"Me." His fingers skimmed up her inner thighs and then in between, making her forget to worry about what exactly he would decide to claim as his spoils, making her forget her stupid list, making her forget just about everything, including her own name. "Say it, Aubrey." He was at her ear, the words hot along her skin. His lips grazed her earlobe, and a rush of heat shot hard and fast southward.

"Yes," she managed as he took her to the bed, pinning her to the mattress beneath his delicious weight. "You. I need you." *Only you...*

"How?" he asked, voice husky as the tip of his tongue played with her nipple before sucking it hard between his hot tongue and the roof of his mouth.

"Th—that," she said on a moan.

"Me kissing you?" He switched to her other breast and gave it the same torturous teasing. "Is that what you want?"

His questing fingers were inching closer and closer to where she needed them, close but not...quite...getting there. "And your fingers!" she gasped, giving up and arching into him.

He rewarded her with both, kissing her hard as his fingers traced their way up her thighs, and then between. The touch nearly levitated her off the bed, would have for certain if she hadn't been anchored by his body. Applying pressure in the exact right spot, his lips—God, those lips, doing diabolical things to her as well—combined the sensations so that her head spun, and she cried out.

"Anything you want," he murmured against a breast. "You want me to touch you? My mouth on you? My hands gripping your hips as I sink in and out of you until we're both screaming each other's name?"

She let her eyes drift closed as her lips parted on a "*God, yes...*" He was still just playing with her, but she was done playing. Fisting her hands in his hair, she pulled his mouth to hers. He let her control the kiss, and another, and another. Finally he lifted his head, gave her a wickedly naughty smile, and took over, shifting down her body, kissing every inch he passed. He didn't stop until he'd made himself at home between her legs, holding them open with his shoulders.

"So beautiful," he whispered, nipping first one inner thigh, and then the other, and then...in between. "Say the magic words, Aubrey. Tell me what you want now."

"Your mouth, I need your mouth."

He gave it to her, and her breathing hitched, and then stopped altogether. Her blood seemed to flow through her veins like liquid fire. White-hot, pulsing need ripped through her as he gave her exactly what she wanted.

When she'd stopped shuddering, he was resting his head on her belly, watching her recover.

"Now you," she said, reaching for him. "I want to feel you inside me. Please, Ben. Inside me now."

He rose up. "Wrap your legs around me." His voice was rough, his hands gentle, as he slid his hand up her legs and directed them around his hips. He sank into her, hard. *Perfect.*

Their groans of pleasure commingled in the air. Leaning over her, he bent low and kissed her—fervent, erotic, rough, and wild.

Her body, already on fire for him, erupted again. Ben's hands slid to her hips, cupped her ass, and, lifting her up against him, he thrust deep. It was enough to have her crying out, arching against him in an attempt to draw him even deeper. "Yes," she moaned, clutching at him. "Like that."

He growled low in his throat as he gave her what she wanted, on his terms. Slow. Purposeful. Taking her to the point of no return and beyond, to a place where she couldn't have said what she wanted next if her life had depended on it.

It didn't matter. Ben seemed to know exactly what she wanted. That was the thing about him. He instinctively knew when to be aggressive, when to be gentle and coaxing, and, best of all, he knew how to drive every last worry right out of her mind.

Chapter 25

♥

A long time later, they collapsed on the bed, gasping, sweaty, breathing like lunatics. Ben threw a hand over his eyes as he tried to catch his breath, because though he could lie smooth as silk when he wanted to, he never lied to himself.

This wasn't just sex between him and Aubrey. This was love.

"I need to talk to you," she said.

"Okay."

She was quiet so long that he dropped his arm from his eyes and turned his head.

She was looking at him, eyes shimmering with a suspicious sheen. "It's about my list," she said softly. "You're on it."

Ben stared at her. "You said I wasn't."

"I...misled you."

He took this in for a full minute, running through his

memories and coming up completely blank. "I don't understand. What did you ever do to me?"

She sat up and reached for his shirt again, pulling it back over her head and down to mid-thigh.

Covering herself from him.

He wasn't liking this much. "Aubrey."

"Don't you want to put something on?" she asked.

"After you answer me."

She ran a hand over her eyes, and he realized her fingers were shaking. "I'm trying," she said. "I've been trying for a while." She shook her head. "No, that's a lie. I didn't know how to tell you. It's been killing me slowly, but I—" She broke off and let out a long breath. "I screwed up."

He pulled her hand from her face. "Just say it."

"Okay." She drew a deep breath. "Do you remember when Hannah broke up with you?"

"Yes." It had been the summer after he'd graduated high school, and he had been night surfing. Alone. It'd been a dangerous, reckless thing to do, but he'd been stupid back then and had often pulled such stunts. It'd been some sort of teenage testosterone-driven dare, a challenge between him and life, and he hadn't been too particular about who might win.

When he'd come back to shore, Hannah had been waiting on the beach for him. She'd stared at his feet and told him she was breaking it off because they were going to college in a few months, and they needed to spread their wings.

He remembered feeling blindsided. He'd told her that he didn't need to spread his fucking wings, and she'd smiled a little bit sadly and said she was setting him free anyway.

He hadn't seen her for two years. He'd finally run into her by sheer accident on spring break, and they'd reconnected. And though she'd never asked and he never told, he'd spent the two years away from her having a damn good time spreading his wings.

"What about it?" he asked Aubrey now.

"I told her you slept around with other girls, one of them being me. It was why she broke up with you."

It took him a moment to find words, and even then he only had one. "What?"

"Yeah." She nodded, chewing on her lower lip. "I caused her to…break up with you."

He shook his head. She was making no sense. "You were two years behind us in school. You didn't even know Hannah."

"We were in after-school tutoring together. I was there for Spanish Two. She was in danger of failing Spanish Four."

"You're lying," he said flatly. "Hannah was a straight-A student."

"She'd always been, yes," she agreed. "But Spanish flattened her. She had to get her grade from an F to a C or lose her upcoming college scholarship. She came to tutoring every day for an hour."

He stared at her as the first inkling of doubt began to creep in. Hannah had been busy every day after school, but she'd told him she was working at the optometrist's office where her mom worked. More than that, the college scholarship thing was setting off alarm bells in his head. Hannah had been all set to go to the University of Washington at Seattle—with him. But after she'd dumped him, she'd gone to a community college instead. He'd always assumed it'd been so that they wouldn't be at the same school. But what if that hadn't been it at all? What if what Aubrey was saying was true—that Hannah hadn't brought her grade up enough and she'd lost her scholarship? "I don't get it," he said. "Why did you tell her we slept together?"

"I'd like to tell you the whole thing," she said, "but the short answer is that I was jealous."

"Jealous."

"Yes." She clasped her hands together and kept her eyes on them. "I'm not proud of that. I'm sorry, Ben."

Was she serious? A "sorry" was supposed to make it all okay? He jerked upright and yanked on his pants.

"Wait," she said, jumping up, too. "Let me tell you the rest—"

"I don't give a shit about the rest." He shoved his feet into his shoes and turned back to her. "Just tell me one thing—why now? Why are you telling me this now?" Then it hit him, and he let out a harsh laugh. "The damn list. You need to clear your conscience. Well, congratulations, Aubrey, you did it. Job well done." He snatched up his shirt and, without putting it on, stormed to the door. Needing to know one more thing, he whipped back. "Wait. Why did she believe you?"

Aubrey stood there before him, pale, eyes filled with regret and other things that he didn't want to see, wearing *his* damn shirt, looking devastated. "I can be very convincing," she said softly.

"Yes," he agreed, staring down at her bowed head. "You can."

She winced as the barb hit, and he told himself he didn't care. "So what was this between us? Amendment?

You fucked me to make up for lying about fucking me?"

"No. *No*," she said. "You saw my list. FUCKING BEN was not on it."

"Well, BEN was on it. Don't tell me you're also fucking the pumpkin man."

"Don't you get it?" she cried. "I didn't plan to sleep with you at all!" She tossed up her hands. "And trust me, this"—she gestured to the bed—"was *not* how I planned to make amends."

"Okay, so out of morbid curiosity, how *were* you going to do that? How were you going to give me back the two years I missed out on with my wife?"

"I didn't know!" she said. "I still don't!"

Suddenly drained, he moved to the door. "You let me know when you figure it out."

When he was gone, Aubrey's legs gave way, and she slid down the wall. Hugging her knees, she dropped her head to her chest and fought the tears.

She remembered that long-ago night as if it were yesterday. She'd been at a party where she hadn't belonged. It'd been for seniors, so she'd been lying low when she saw Hannah and a girlfriend get in Hannah's car to leave. Talking and laughing, Hannah had pulled out into the street without looking and caused a wreck. With the cars still smoking, and horns and alarms going off, Aubrey had watched in disbelief as the two girls had switched spots, crawling past each other in the front seat so that Hannah was no longer behind the wheel.

When the police arrived, Hannah's friend—the sober one—had saved Hannah from getting a DUI.

Aubrey couldn't believe it. As the girl who had always gotten in trouble for every little infraction—and some that weren't even hers—she had been infuriated.

The next day at tutoring, Aubrey had told Hannah that she knew what she'd done. At first, Hannah had pretended not to know what Aubrey was talking about—until Aubrey told her she'd seen it herself. Hannah had paled but rallied quickly, telling Aubrey that no one would ever believe it.

Their tutor had broken up the heated whispered exchange, yelling at them to be quiet and work. Hannah had told him that Aubrey was trying to cheat.

Aubrey had gotten detention.

"You see?" Hannah had whispered. "No one will ever believe you over me. The girl who dresses like a prom queen when she's not. The girl who needs tutoring in all her classes. The girl no one wants. Even your own dad picked your sister over you."

Horrifically wounded by this, her secret and humiliating hot button, Aubrey's mouth had disconnected from her brain, and she'd said, "Ben has no complaints about me every time we meet in the woods." Not about to stop herself—her biggest regret—she'd gone on. "And I'm not the only one he's doing it with, so obviously he's not getting off on *you*."

Hannah had stormed out, earning herself detention right alongside Aubrey. But she'd dumped Ben.

And then eventually fate had stepped in and gotten them back together, though Hannah must not have told Ben about Aubrey's tale.

But he knew now…

* * *

Ben didn't sleep. Every time he closed his eyes he saw Aubrey's face as he'd left. The regret and fear and misery in her expression haunted him, making him want to toss aside his hurt and anger and soothe hers.

So he stopped closing his eyes because he *needed* to hold on to the hurt and anger. He needed that badly, and as to the reason why—well, he didn't want to study that too closely.

When dawn came, he went for a run. He beat Sam to the pier, but not by much. When Sam came up level with him, he stopped and frowned. "You okay?"

Ben grunted in response and took off. Sam caught up with him but didn't ask another question. Ben ran hard and fast, and Sam kept pace, never slowing until Ben did.

Just before they got back to the pier, Sam spoke. "You know where to find me if you need anything."

Ben met Sam's gaze and saw nothing but sincerity. He nodded. "Thanks, man, but I'm good." Actually, he was the opposite of good, and they both knew it, but Sam let the lie go.

Ben skipped the bookstore. The work he had left to do there was minimal. He knew he needed to finish, but hell if he could face her yet. So he went to work and put in twelve straight hours on a subterranean water leak out at the dam, which was threatening the properties below the harbor. That night he stumbled into bed, exhausted, and proceeded to stare at his ceiling for hours.

The next morning he heard a polite knock at his door.

He ignored it.

He ignored the doorbell, too.

But he couldn't ignore whoever the hell was letting himself into his house. He slid out of his bed, prepared to take on the intruder bare-handed and in his boxers, thinking maybe a good old fight would loosen the two-day-old knot in the center of his chest. He was ready when he padded into the living room, but stopped short at the sight of his aunt Dee.

She was in his kitchen, unloading a bag of groceries. She had a carton of eggs in one hand and a gallon of orange juice in her other as she looked up and caught sight of him. "Hey, baby."

There were flowers in a bouquet on his table. "You brought me flowers?" he asked inanely.

"No. They were on your doorstep. I just brought them in. There's a note," Dee added. "It's sealed, or I'd have totally sneaked a peek. Although I can guess."

Ben could, too, but he didn't want to go there. "You going to the senior center today?" he asked Dee.

"Yes. It's bingo lunch."

"Take the flowers with you."

She gave him an assessing look. "Okay. Did you want to go get dressed and eat, or would you rather kick my butt for intruding?"

"I'm still trying to decide."

She smiled. "Go on. Find some clothes. I'll be done here by the time you're back."

"Done with what?" he asked.

"Breakfast, silly."

"Breakfast," he repeated, stunned into stupidity by heartache and lack of sleep.

"Yes." She beamed at him. "Remember all those mornings you got up at the crack of dawn to come make me breakfast after my chemo? Well, I'm returning the favor."

He didn't want breakfast. He wanted…Aubrey. He

wanted her sated and boneless in his bed, with one of those smiles on her face that was just for him, as though he were the best thing she'd ever seen.

At the thought, emotion swamped him. He told himself it was all anger, because she'd ruined it. She'd ruined everything. But the truth was, it felt more like sadness and regret than anger.

Dee's smile faded, and she set down the orange juice and eggs and came to him, wrapping her arms around him. "Rough morning?" she asked quietly.

He shrugged.

Just as he'd done for her all those mornings when she'd been sick and exhausted and scared and hurting, she didn't ask a bunch of questions. She accepted that some days were just shit. "You look like hell," she murmured.

He let out a low laugh. "Thanks." He went to his room to yank on a pair of jeans and then came back to the kitchen.

"Sit." Dee gestured to a chair with her wooden spoon. "You'll eat."

"I'm not hungry."

"Did I ask you if you were hungry? No, I did not." Again she pointed to the chair and when he didn't budge, she shoved him.

"Bully," he said without heat, and let the five-foot-two woman push him down to the chair.

She smiled and patted his shoulder. "I learned from the best, you know."

"I wasn't this mean," he said.

"Oh, please," she said on a laugh and affected his low baritone as she imitated what he'd said to her whenever she'd resisted him. "You will sit there and shut up and eat,

Aunt Dee, and if you don't, I'll force it down your throat."

"I didn't say it like that," he said, but surprised them both by laughing.

She smiled. "Aw, that's better. You probably want to know why I'm here."

"You're here because you're nosy."

"Yes, well, there's that." She came over with a loaded plate and the juice. She set them both down in front of him and hugged him.

"Again?" he asked.

"Hug me back or I'll keep at it."

Because she looked so worried, he let her boss him around. He hugged her back, letting her hold on for as long as she wanted, which was about a year. "I'm getting gray hair here," he finally said.

She pulled back and smacked him upside the head. Then she cupped his face and stared into his eyes. "I'm here because I got the mom feeling that something is wrong. Is it hard being back here?" she asked quietly. "In Lucky Harbor? With us? Is that it? You're going to leave again?"

"No. And it's not hard being back. I like being back," he said, no longer surprised to find that it was absolutely true. He might have started out a true city boy, but he'd also been a lost one, without people who cared. And then he'd landed here in Lucky Harbor, where everyone cared. He liked that—a lot. The place fit him; it always had. "I'm not leaving," he promised.

"Is it Hannah?" she whispered. "The memories of her?"

"No," he said, and when she just kept looking at him, he said, "I miss her. I'll always miss her. But it's not her."

"Then it's Aubrey," Dee said. "Damn. I told you that one was going to be trouble."

"I don't want to talk about it."

Dee paused, still hovering. "Can I just say one thing?"

"Could a freight train stop you?"

She smiled and cupped his face once more. "It was lovely to see you putting yourself out there again. I hope that whatever happened between you two doesn't change that."

He gave her a look. "You're fishing."

"Yes." She paused, and when he didn't fill in the silence, she sighed good-naturedly. "I love you, baby. You know that, right?"

"I know it. I've never doubted it."

Her eyes looked a little damp as she looked him over again, but she nodded firmly. "You'll get through this."

She was right about that; he would get through this. He didn't see much of a choice. Life was funny that way. When it threw him a curveball, sometimes it hit him between the eyes and sometimes it hit him in the gut, but he always kept coming back to bat.

That afternoon, Ben stood bleary-eyed in front of the Craft Corner gang. He was teaching the kids how to make the kite he'd learned to build from some kids in Haiti, when what he really wanted to do was something far more physical.

Like night surf. He was feeling more than a little out of control, but he knew he needed to keep it together, because he still had to go back to work after this. He could have sworn he was keeping his bad mood from the kids, but just as though he'd projected it out there, a fight broke out over a roll of twine between Pink and a scrappy, tough little girl named Dani. "Hey," he said, striding over and breaking it up. "Cool it. There's enough twine to go around."

"That's not what this is about," Pink said, still glaring at Dani. "She's being mean."

"Am not," Dani said.

"Both of you knock it off," Ben said.

But the girls continued to stare each other down, neither one of them speaking.

Jesus, Ben thought. Girls really were aliens. "Kites," Ben said. "Make your kites."

Neither backed down until Ben gave them each a nudge.

Three minutes later the fight was back on.

"Okay," Ben said. "That's it. You have two seconds to tell me what's going on, or we're done here." He looked down at the insistent tugging on the hem of his shirt and found Kendra staring up at him, her eyes filled with anxiety.

"You aren't going to quit, right?" she asked in a small voice.

Ah, shit. Guilt swamped him, and he crouched down to look into the eyes of the little girl who hadn't spoken once in all this time—until now. Apparently her abandonment issues trumped her social anxieties. "I'm not going anywhere," Ben promised. "We're *all* going." He took Kendra's hand in his and rose to his full height, staring at the entire class. "Get your hammers."

Ben had asked Sam for advice on what to do with the kids. Sam built boats by hand and knew his way around tools. On his suggestion, Ben had ordered and bought thirty-five small hammers from the hardware store, along with work aprons and some other tools for the kids. He figured they'd go out to the railroad ties surrounding the yard and hit the shit out of the wood until aggressions were released. It'd always worked for him. "Field trip," he said.

They got halfway down the hall before Ms. Uptight Teacher stuck her head out of the office. "Where are you going?"

"Field trip," the kids yelled excitedly.

The teacher shook her head. "No permission slips."

"We're not leaving the yard," Ben said.

The kids all sighed in disappointment.

The teacher didn't look relieved. "Why are they all carrying hammers?"

"Anger management," Ben said.

Ms. Uptight Teacher was shaking her head before he finished speaking. "No."

He wondered if she practiced saying no to everything, or if it just came to her as naturally as her pinched expression did.

"If you all need a time-out," she said, "there's a basket of kick balls in the yard."

Fine. Ben took the kids to the yard, marching them to the far end. "Okay," he said, lining them up. "New lesson. Anger management."

"What's that?" several kids asked.

"It's when you expel your pent-up negative energy through physical exertion," he said.

They all blinked in collective confusion.

"You know how sometimes you just want to hit someone?" he asked them.

"You mean like when someone tells a *lie about you?*" Pink asked, glaring at Dani.

"Or when they *steal your string for your kite?*" Dani asked, glaring back at Pink.

"Yes," Ben said, stepping between them. "Just like that. But we're *not* going to hit anyone. Instead we're going to hit *something*. Something that won't get you in trouble. In this case, the fence." He set a kick ball in front of each kid, separating them widely enough so that no one could level anyone else, accidentally or otherwise. There he stepped to an empty spot with his own ball. "Go," he said.

Everyone kicked their balls at the fence, which made a very satisfactory sound as it was hit. The balls went flying, and the kids raced after them. They lined up again.

And again.

Ten minutes later each and every one of them was panting in exertion and…smiling.

Except for Ben. He drove Pink and Kendra home and finally found something that did make him smile.

Dan was sitting on the front steps of the house, waiting for his kids.

Chapter 26

Aubrey hadn't had very many shitty days lately, not since Ben had come into her life. But the past few days had been real doozies. It was horrifying, demoralizing, *devastating* to realize how badly she'd messed up. Earlier she'd opened the bookstore determined to hold her head up high. What was done was done. She'd had the best of intentions when she'd confessed her misdeed to Ben, and though she still had to somehow make him understand that, she also had to go on.

She had a lot to look forward to, she reminded herself. For one thing, her store was doing okay. And for another, her grand-opening party was only four days away. She'd do even better after that, or so she hoped.

The bell over the door jangled, and her first customers of the day walked in. Lucille and—oh, crap—Mrs. Cappernackle, the retired librarian.

Mrs. Cappernackle gave Aubrey an indecipherable

look down her long nose. "Lucille informs me you came by my place some time ago."

"Yes," Aubrey said. "I did." She paused. "You don't remember?"

"I've had some health problems," she said, still snooty. "Affects my short-term memory."

Behind her, Lucille swirled her finger by her right ear, making the sign for "crazy."

Mrs. Cappernackle didn't catch this, thankfully. "My long-term memory, however," she went on, eyes eagle sharp and on Aubrey, "remains perfectly intact."

Terrific. Not daring to meet Lucille's gaze, Aubrey bent down to the cabinet beneath the cash register and pulled out the book she'd been saving to give back to the retired librarian.

Mrs. Cappernackle's eyes narrowed. "So you *did* have it."

Aubrey didn't bother to sigh as she handed it over. "It's not the exact same copy. I bought you a new one."

Mrs. Cappernackle opened the book and stared down at a check stuck in the first page. "What's this?"

"Overdue library fees," Aubrey said, hoping it was enough.

Lucille glanced over Mrs. Cappernackle's shoulder, looked at the check, and smiled. "Aw, how sweet. Isn't that sweet, Martha?" she asked Mrs. Cappernackle.

"Hmm," Mrs. Cappernackle said. "I do like it when a person owns up to her mistakes." She narrowed her gaze on Aubrey. "But I still want you to stay out of my library."

Behind her, Lucille made the "crazy" sign again and then nodded, motioning that Aubrey should just agree.

"Done," Aubrey promised.

Mrs. Cappernackle nodded. "I'll wait in the car, Lucille. I'm tired now."

"I'll be right there," Lucille assured her with a gentle pat, and when the door had shut behind Mrs. Cappernackle, she met Aubrey's gaze. "Thanks."

"I have the feeling I should be thanking you," Aubrey said.

"Think nothing of it." She leaned in, eyes unusually solemn. "How are you holding up?"

"Me?" Aubrey asked. "I'm fine." She had no idea what exactly Lucille might be referring to, but best to be "fine" no matter what. Besides, there was no way the world could know about her and Ben yet, or at least she hoped not. "Uh...why do you ask?"

Lucille looked at her for a long moment. "I couldn't help but notice that you're not carrying Ted Marshall's book in here anywhere."

"No." Hell, no.

Lucille nodded. "Wise choice. But you can't keep it hidden forever, honey. Lots of people in town have e-readers now, you know. They're downloading his book regardless."

"My purpose wasn't to keep people from reading it," Aubrey said. "I just didn't want to sell it here. I refuse to help him earn a single penny."

Lucille nodded. "I understand that. So I hope you understand that my book club read it." Aubrey winced. "We didn't tell you, or order the book through your store, because we didn't want to hurt your feelings. But just like with *Fifty Shades*, we were morbidly curious."

"I do understand," Aubrey said. "You don't have to apologize."

"Well, I sort of do." Lucille met her gaze. "It was my idea, you see, and I feel awful about that. Because everyone read the book, all twenty-two of us, and now they're talking about it." She paused as if waiting for a specific reaction from Aubrey.

But Aubrey had no idea what that reaction was supposed to be. "Well, that's good, isn't it?"

"I don't think so, no," Lucille said. "You know Lucky Harbor. Those twenty-two people will tell twenty-two people, and so forth." She shrugged. "People love a scandal. I didn't put it on Facebook, though. I want you to know that."

"Okay," Aubrey said, even more confused now. "What am I missing, Lucille?"

Lucille paused, staring at her. "Honey, have *you* read it?"

"Just the first chapter."

Lucille took this in while moving her lower dentures around some. "Oh, dear."

"You're starting to scare me, Lucille."

Lucille sighed. "He outed you."

"He...outed me," Aubrey repeated. "What do you mean? I thought everyone already knew I was bitchy. That can't be news to anyone."

"It's not just that. He published a picture of you—one of the less revealing pictures you'd posed for, in the grand scheme of things, but still. It's pretty revealing."

"A picture. Of me," Aubrey repeated, aware that she was beginning to sound like a broken record.

"It's the one where you were in the"—she hooked her fingers to signify quotation marks—"Sexy Kitty costume."

Oh, God. *Those* pictures. She staggered back to one of

the big, cozy chairs and fell into it, her mouth open, her heart racing. Crap. *Shit.* She'd thought things couldn't get worse, but this was worse. A part of her past she'd hoped to never revisit was back, biting her on the ass.

She should've been used to it. After all, she'd just spent a month facing her past head-on, and it'd been the hardest thing she'd ever done.

But she'd been fixing her past while concentrating on her future, and that future had just come to a grinding halt. The pictures that Lucile referred to had been taken when she'd been nineteen, during her short "modeling" career. She'd used the money to pay her college tuition. It'd been that or quit school, and she'd never been a quitter. She wasn't going to apologize for that.

But that didn't mean she wanted the pictures from all those years ago to surface now.

Or ever. "I'm going to have to kill him," she murmured.

"Or," Lucille said, "you could hit him where it hurts."

"Hitting him in the nuts might get me arrested," Aubrey said. "And I'm trying to clean up my karma, not make it worse."

Lucille smiled. "I meant his wallet, honey. Sue him."

No—she couldn't. The pictures were on the Internet if someone knew where to look, and since Aubrey hadn't retained the copyright, she doubted she had a leg to stand on.

"Now, mind you," Lucille went on, "the picture he used is nothing to be ashamed of. You have a lovely figure, Aubrey. But the link to the others…"

"He published the website address?" Why, oh, why hadn't she read his entire book?

Because he was slime, that's why.

"He did," Lucille said. "And to be honest, some of *those* pictures...well, they're not quite as...tasteful as the one in his book."

Yeah. She didn't remember a single one in the bunch being...*tasteful*.

Lucille took in Aubrey's expression and frowned with concern. "You really didn't know."

She shook her head. "No."

The older woman sighed. "I'm sorry. Honestly, those pictures, they don't bother me none. I'm a modern woman, you see. But there're *some* people in town who aren't as liberated as I am. They might view this as...well..."

"Porn," Aubrey said flatly.

"Well, only if they haven't read *Fifty Shades*," Lucille said helpfully.

Good God. This was bad. Very bad. While she sat there picturing her reputation's demise, the bell on the store door tinkled. She looked up in time to see her father stride into the store in an elegant suit, his Bluetooth headset on his ear. Clearly he was in work mode.

Aubrey couldn't imagine what had brought him here until his cold gaze met hers. And then she knew.

The pictures. From the frying pan into the fire... "If you'll excuse me, Lucille," she murmured.

"No problem, dear."

"Aubrey," her father said when she'd risen on shaky legs and walked over to him.

"Long time no see," she said lightly. "You missed the last few family dinners."

He didn't buy into the small talk. "You posed nude on the Internet."

She took a moment to try to draw in a deep breath for calm. *Try* being the operative word. "It was a long time ago," she finally said.

"So you're saying there's a statute of limitations on stupid decisions?" he asked.

Ouch. "No," she said carefully. "There's not. Of course not. But at the time—"

"At the time you were in college. What kind of serious college student poses for immoral pictures—"

"It was a legit modeling job, Dad."

"Legit? Please." He stared her down. "I'm bitterly disappointed in you."

"I paid my way through college with those pictures," she said, vibrating with frustration, heartbreak, and now anger. And actually, the anger felt good—damn good. "You were a little busy at the time with the new family, but I paid my *own* way, without asking you for a cent. So I'm sorry if I didn't turn out the way you wanted me to, but you know what, Dad? You didn't turn out the way I wanted you to, either. So consider us even."

Ben worked late. He didn't get home until seven. He'd been texted approximately a million times by both Luke and Jack, demanding his presence for dinner.

They'd clearly sensed a tremor in the force, and now they wanted to drive him crazy. He had missed calls as well, wanting to know where the hell he was.

Ignoring it all, he opened his fridge. Empty. Damn. Figuring he might as well face the music sooner rather than later, he drove to the Love Shack and dropped into a chair at Luke and Jack's table. "You called?" he asked drily.

Luke looked at Jack.

"Me?" Jack asked Luke. "I thought we'd agreed *you'd* do it."

Luke shook his head and pointed at Jack.

Jack sighed and pulled out his phone.

"Forget it," Ben said. "I don't want to see Facebook. Nor do I want to know how the hell Lucille already found out that Aubrey and I broke up."

"Uh…" Luke said, and looked at Jack.

"You and Aubrey broke up?" Jack asked Ben.

"You weren't calling about the breakup?"

Luke shook his head.

Jack tried to pull his phone back, but Ben snatched it, and then went still as a stone.

The picture on the screen was of a woman in a very skimpy kitten costume, which wasn't the problem. The problem was that the woman was hotter than hot.

And she was Aubrey.

She was clearly younger, maybe even not of legal age, posing on her knees, one hand curled like a cat with its claws out, the other holding a whip. She wore cat ears, and her "tail" was curved around her million-dollar bod, which was encased in a snug leather bodice, tiny leather shorts, and stiletto heels.

"It's from an adult costume website," Jack said. "An X-rated costume website. Near as I can tell, there are a small handful of different models, maybe five in total, modeling close to a hundred different costumes that you can order for home delivery—sans the girls, of course."

Luke snorted. "Thorough much?"

"I like to do my research, especially when it involves nearly naked women."

"That's *my* woman," Ben said, and both Luke's and Jack's brows went up.

"Thought you broke up," Luke said lightly.

Ben ignored them and flipped through the site, sucking in a breath because Jack had showed him the most PG-rated costume in the bunch. He found the same younger Aubrey as a "slutty nurse," a "slutty French maid," a "slutty bunny," and a "slutty police officer." Christ. He closed the browser window and handed the phone back. "How the hell did you find this?"

"Lucille came to me with it," Luke said. "Apparently it was in Ted Marshall's book—the one that no one in town read until the seniors got hold of it for their book club."

"Why did Lucille come to you?"

Luke smiled. "She wanted me to arrest Ted for being a 'spineless dickhead.' She's worried about Aubrey because it's already getting around. Someone tweeted about it, and someone else posted some of the pictures on Instagram, and she doesn't want this to affect Aubrey's grand opening on Saturday."

Ben stood up.

"Where are you going?" Jack asked.

"To make sure she's okay."

"Didn't you just say you broke up?" Jack asked.

"He also said she was his woman," Luke said, studying Ben's face. "And speaking of that, maybe we should hear *that* story."

"Maybe we shouldn't," Ben said, and started to walk away.

"Hey," Jack said, managing to block his way. "How come when I'm fucked up, you're all in my face about it, but when you're fucked up, you get to be alone?"

"I'm not fucked up," Ben said firmly.

"You look pretty fucked up to me," Jack said. "I'm with Luke. Let's hear the story. Or should I guess? You decided you were too happy."

"What's that supposed to mean?" Ben asked, his voice very quiet. It was the voice that usually sent men running. But Jack just looked at him, not running anywhere. In fact, he went toe-to-toe with Ben and stared him straight in the eye.

"It means," Jack said, "that ever since you lost Hannah, it's like you don't think you have the right to be happy. She's dead and buried, and you think you have to be, too. That's what running for the past five years was all about."

"It was about helping people," Ben said. "You might recognize the concept, since you've been doing it all these years as a firefighter."

"Bullshit. It was *running*, Ben." Jack punctuated this with a little shove. "I gave you the five years, but it's time to get better. It's time to let yourself have a life." A bigger shove now. "It's okay to do that; there's nothing to feel guilty about."

Ben shook his head. "I get why you think I might feel guilty, and I did feel guilty for a damn long time. But I've moved on."

Jack's gaze said he thought otherwise and that Ben was an asshole.

"You two going to need a referee?" Luke asked, still sprawled out, all relaxed in his chair. "Because if I have to arrest you, Dee's gonna kill me."

Jack didn't look like he cared, and Ben blew out a breath. "This has nothing to do with my happiness," he said. "Aubrey lied to me. So it's over, end of story."

"What was the lie?" Jack asked.

"What does *that* have to do with anything?" Ben asked.

"A lot," Jack said. "If she lied and said, 'Oh baby, that was so good,' when it was only okay, that's not exactly a breakup lie."

"It was an omission," Ben specified.

"Like I-forgot-to-tell-you-I-hate-pizza omission?" Jack asked. "Or, like, I'm-really-a-male-in-chick-clothing kind of omission?"

Ben considered swiping the smirk right off Jack's face with his fist. But then Luke would get all pissed off and call Sawyer, the sheriff, just to make a point. Plus, it was probable that even off-duty Luke was armed. "It was an *omission*, okay?" he said to Jack. "Drop it."

"Well, I would," Jack returned. "Except I'm bad at that."

Luke pulled out his phone and started thumbing through his contacts.

Ben caved. Not because he was afraid of Sawyer but because he didn't have time to be arrested tonight. "Aubrey told Hannah we'd slept together," he said. "That's why Hannah dumped me. Aubrey lied to her and cost me two years with Hannah."

Two years that Hannah deserved…Ben didn't give a shit about himself. But Hannah. She was dead and gone, and she didn't have a voice.

That just about killed him dead and gone, too.

Jack, staring at Ben, dropped the teasing note in his voice. "Well, hell."

"Yeah."

"Wait," Jack said, putting his hand on Ben's shoulder

as he turned to leave. "Wait. Are you telling me that Hannah believed her? And that she never brought it up to you? Ever?"

"So?"

"*So?*" Jack said. "Don't you have to ask why? Or put some of the blame on her?"

"She's dead," Ben said flatly.

"Yeah," Jack said. "And that sucks. Sucks hard. But think about this, Ben. So Aubrey was a bitch in high school. We were dicks. For that matter, Hannah was no angel, either. Whatever. It's old history. Don't let that be an excuse to—"

"If you say *not be happy*, I swear to God—"

"—not be happy," Jack said, the dare in his eyes.

It was an arrow to the chest, because it was the cold, hard truth. He'd done exactly what Jack had said, and he planned to continue onward, thank you very much.

"Okay." Luke stood up. "Look, I should knock both of you knuckleheads into next week myself, but I'd rather go home and be with Ali."

"Tell him he's being stupid, Luke," Jack said, not taking his eyes off Ben. "Maybe he'll listen to the voice of reason."

"I'm not telling him shit," Luke said, and met Ben's gaze, too. "Because he already knows he's being stupid."

Ben shook his head and walked out of the bar, the questions floating in his head. Why had Aubrey done it? Why had she lied to Hannah?

And even more than that, why had Hannah believed her? Why would Hannah buy into the story that he'd cheated on her so readily?

Because she'd been eighteen. Young and foolish, like

him. Of course she'd believed it. This was Lucky Harbor, where gossip was gospel.

And then there was the baseline truth: He'd fully and freely enjoyed the freedom that the two-year breakup had afforded him.

He was going to have to live with that.

He drove for a good thirty minutes before he ended up parking in the alley behind the bookstore. "You are so fucked up," he murmured to himself, and took the stairs to Aubrey's place.

He was only here to make sure she knew about the pictures. He may not have forgiven her, but he didn't want her to be blindsided. That was all. He stared at Aubrey's door for a very long moment before he knocked.

Chapter 27

Aubrey opened her door to Ben and felt the shock reverberate through her. She'd wanted, desperately, to talk to him, to get the chance to explain. There was so much left to say, like how badly she'd felt all these years, and how she'd never meant for them to get into a relationship without telling him the truth, that it'd just happened...

God, it had truly happened. She'd fallen for him, hard.

And she'd blown it, just as hard. He hadn't called or been to the store.

But now here he stood on her doorstep, wearing jeans, scuffed work boots, a gray henley, and an open down jacket, hood up against the rain. Given that she could see only part of his face, and that the part she *could* see was an unshaved jaw, she shouldn't have felt weak in the knees, but she did. She nearly threw herself at him in relief, but before she could move, he said, "Do you know about the pictures?"

She blinked and began to realize that this visit might not be what she hoped. "*You* know about them?"

A muscle ticked in his jaw. "Yeah."

Oh, God. "You read Ted's book?"

"No. But I heard about them and—"

"Heard about them, or saw them?" she asked tightly.

"Saw them."

Damn it. She drew a shuddery breath and tried to figure out what the silver lining might be, but really, there was none. "Do you think a lot of people in town know?" She closed her eyes. "Never mind. This is Lucky Harbor, right? Everyone knows by now. I can't even imagine what they think."

"They think you're hot as hell, that's what they think," he said. "At least the red-blooded males do."

"The pictures are old," she said. "Nearly a decade old. And in some of them I'm in a mask. Maybe people won't recognize me..." Her words faded away at the look on his face.

"You're pretty recognizable, Sunshine."

"I was young," she said softly. "And it was an okay job as far as modeling gigs went. I didn't have to sleep with the photographer, and I made enough money to pay for college."

"Aubrey," he said, and let out a long breath. "I'm not judging you. At all. You've got nothing to be ashamed of. *Nothing*," he repeated, voice like steel, making her eyes sting. "I just wanted to make sure you knew they were out so that you weren't blindsided by them."

He was here because he cared about her, and she decided to take *that* as her silver lining. She stepped back to let him in, but he was already stepping back as well, away from her. "You're…not coming in?" she asked, hating the naked vulnerability in her voice.

He didn't take off his hood, so she couldn't really see his expression, but there was a definite edge to him tonight—and a sense of exhaustion that broke her heart.

"No," he said. "I'm not coming in."

She absorbed the hurt, just one more hurt on a pile of hurts. He gave one curt, barely there nod and started to go. "Ben, I'm so sorry. I—"

"I'm sorry, too."

She stared at him, throat burning. "Why did you come?" she whispered.

"I told you. To make sure you knew."

"*Why?*" she pressed.

He was still a moment, looking at her intently. "It was the right thing to do," he finally said.

An arrow to her heart. Her gut. Her soul. Because the implication was, of course, that *she* wouldn't know the right thing if it bit her on the ass.

"Do you need anything?" he asked.

She nearly laughed, but it would have been a half-hysterical one. And in any case, she had far more pride than sense at this point, so she lifted her chin and looked him right in the eye and shook her head. "I'm fine." She was always fine.

He paused, so she added a smile to prove it. Hell if she'd let him see her sweat. If he didn't want her, she wouldn't beg.

Oh, hell. She *wanted* to beg. Bad.

But after one last long look at her, he turned and walked away.

And she let him.

* * *

Aubrey had thought she was at rock bottom when she'd screwed up with Ben.

She'd underestimated herself.

The next day was a painfully slow day at the store. The day after that was the grand-opening party, and she was beginning to think it might also be her grand closing.

Heartsick, she closed up for the day and then dropped her forehead to the door. *Damn it.* "I'm not going to cry."

"Okay, but just in case, we have reinforcements."

Aubrey whirled around and faced Ali and Leah, who'd come in the back. Ali held a bottle of Scotch and three big red plastic cups. Leah was holding a tray of goodies. "Leftovers from today's baking," she said. "And trust me when I say you don't need anything else when you have this stuff—not even a man."

"That's good," Aubrey said, and swiped at her cheeks. "Because I don't need a man."

Ali set down the cups and poured them each a very liberal dose of Scotch. "A toast," she said, waiting for Aubrey and Leah to pick up their cups. "To us," she said. "And to Aubrey." She toasted Aubrey. "Because you look damn hot in those pictures."

"Yeah," Leah said. "There's going to come a day when you yearn to look like that again." She paused. "And for the record, I've *never* looked that way. Bitch."

Aubrey felt herself laugh for the first time in two days.

They all drank, and Ali refilled their glasses. Leah ordered a pizza. They inhaled it and then raided Leah's bakery for dessert.

"I hate men," Aubrey said much later, out of the blue, and they drank to that, too.

"I can't exactly say I hate men," Ali said. "'Cause I sleep with one of the finest men out there. But I recognize *your* right to hate men." She hiccupped and then paused. "Wait. Why do you hate men again?"

"Because Ben broke up with her," Leah reminded her.

Aubrey nodded. The room was getting a little wobbly. They'd had three double shots each, and the booze had gone straight to her head with exponential power. "He had good reason," she said. "I wronged him."

"That's a chickenshit reason," Leah said. "I love him, I really do, but he's a pussy chickenshit."

Ali snorted Scotch out her nose. "Damn it!"

Aubrey looked at Leah. "You think so?"

"I know so," Leah said, maybe slurring her words a bit. "He's made mistakes, too, you know. Lots of them. He should forgive yours."

"Yes, but it was a doozy of a mistake," Aubrey admitted. "And when it comes right down to it, I did it on purpose, so actually, technically, I don't think that even qualifies as a mistake."

"Hey, love transcends all."

It was Aubrey's turn to inhale the Scotch and snort it out her nose. "Gah," she managed, her throat burning.

Ali was pounding her on the back. She got her breath back, but Ali continued to pound her until, with a weak laugh, Aubrey held up her hands. "I'm okay. But it wasn't love."

Ali and Leah looked at her, then at each other, and then burst out laughing.

"Okay," Aubrey admitted. "So I love him. Damn it. But he doesn't love me."

"Does so," Leah said, refilling her drink. "You just need to fight for him."

Aubrey stared at her. "What?"

"You're a fighter, Aubrey. And I don't mean like this…" Leah put up her own fists and nearly punched herself. "I mean you're not someone who gives up. You go after what you want. Yeah, you screwed up, but you know what? He did, too. He didn't let you talk about it or try to work through it. He just closed himself off."

"Hence the pussy chickenshit moniker," Ali said, and hiccupped again.

"Yes," Leah said. "Because he used what happened as an excuse to run away from what you two had."

Aubrey stared at her. This was true. So true…*why* hadn't he wanted to hear everything? Why hadn't he wanted to understand? And most important, *why had he been so willing to walk away from her*? Thinking about that last question made her stomach hurt, but more than that, it made her really mad.

"Yeah," Leah said, seeing the look on Aubrey's face. "That's what I'm talking about. Hang on, I've got an idea."

"Oh, boy," Ali said. "Those usually involve the police."

"Hush, you," Leah said. She pulled out her phone, hit a number, and put it on speaker.

"Hey, babe," Jack said, a smile in his voice as it filled the room. "More phone sex already? 'Cause I think you wore me out at your last break—"

"No," Leah said quickly, her face red, as she scooped the phone up close to her mouth. "And I'm not alone. Sheesh, I've got Ali and Aubrey here."

"Hey, ladies," he said smoothly. "What're you all doing?"

"Drinking," Ali said cheerfully. "We're commiserating about the penis-carrying race being too slow on the uptake. Present company and your BFF excepted, of course."

"Of course," Jack said. "And Ben, too, right?"

Aubrey growled, and Jack laughed softly. "Yeah, you're right. Our Ben *is* a little slow on the uptake, isn't he?"

"Yeah, *very* slow," Leah said before Aubrey could speak for herself. "And about that—"

"Wait!" Ali interrupted. "I want to hear more about this phone sex during business hours. I'm shocked. *Shocked*, I tell you."

Leah waved a "Shh!" hand at her. "Honey," she said to Jack. "We need a little favor."

"Anything," he said.

"We need a ride. Can you come get us?"

The back door opened, and he strolled in, phone still to his ear. He grinned as he walked up behind Leah, sank his fingers into her hair, and bent over her for a hot kiss.

Ali sighed at the sight. "We'll never get you to Ben's now," she said to Aubrey. "They can go on like this forever. They never run out of air."

It was true, apparently, because they kept kissing.

"See?" Ali said, and then shoved her way in between the smooching couple.

Jack lifted his head and smiled into Leah's dazed eyes. "Your wish is my command, babe."

Leah smiled up at him dopily. "Wow."

Ali sighed. "Damn it, now I miss Luke."

"Didn't you just see him at lunch?" Aubrey asked her.

"That was hours ago."

Jack grinned. "You ladies are all looking a little schnockered. Where do you need to go?"

"Ben's." Leah pointed to Aubrey. "She needs to tell him something *muy importante*."

Aubrey nodded grimly. "*Muy importante.*"

Jack's grin widened. "This is going to be fun."

Aubrey understood the sentiment from his point of view. After all, it hadn't been all that long ago that Ben and Aubrey had delivered an inebriated Leah to Jack. That the situation was now reversed clearly pleased Jack to no end.

Of course that had turned out great, and this didn't have a chance in hell of ending anywhere close to great.

Still grinning, Jack offered Aubrey his arm. She took it because she was more than a little off her axis, and not just from the alcohol. Jack loaded her into his car, and Ali and Leah piled in behind her.

"We're your courage," Leah said.

"She doesn't need courage," Ali said. "She's kick-ass. She's *made* of courage."

Aubrey felt her heart swell. "Don't," she said quickly. "Don't make me cry. I'm mad, and I need to stay mad."

"This'll help," Jack said, and powered all the windows down.

"Hey!" they all protested immediately as freezing air hit them in the face.

"Fresh air will keep you ladies from tossing your cookies in my car," Jack said. "I hope," he added under his breath.

Aubrey didn't say anything, because her buzz was starting to wear off and a case of nerves was setting in.

Leah squeezed her hand. "Screw the nerves. This situation isn't all your fault."

Aubrey nodded. It *was* all her fault, but she was going to go with pretending that it wasn't, because Leah was right about one thing. The nerves didn't belong here. She needed to find her mad. After all, she'd honestly been trying to do the right thing by facing her past. Maybe she failed in the delivery, but her heart had been in the right place. She'd *needed* to do the right thing, because the only way she could be the kind of person she wanted to be now was to acknowledge the person she'd been.

Ben didn't have that excuse. He was using her screw-up as a reason to hide behind his fears of getting attached again. "I'm a fighter," she said.

"That's right," Ali said.

"I'm going to fight for him."

"Yeah, you are," Leah said, and put up her fists, once again nearly hitting herself in the face.

"Careful, Tiger," Jack said into the rearview mirror. "How much did you all drink?"

"Not enough," Aubrey said as he parked in front of the duplex. Ben's truck was in the driveway, and her heart kicked up a notch at the sight of it.

"*No* eavesdropping," she said to her posse, and got out of the car.

There in the dark, she stood on the sidewalk a moment, gathering her scattered thoughts. In her peripheral vision, she saw Ali, Leah, and Jack tiptoe into Jack's house, and she breathed a sigh of relief, grateful there'd be no witnesses for this.

Chin up, she strode to Ben's front door and knocked.

No response; nothing but a gaping silence.

Aubrey knocked again, with a fist this time, matching the rhythm of her pounding heart.

More silence.

She backed up, to the grass yard. Picking up a small rock, she aimed it at Ben's upstairs bedroom window, and then heard the little *tink* that told her she'd hit her mark.

The window opened, and Ben stuck his head out. "What the hell?"

"I want to talk to you," Aubrey said.

He took this in for a beat. "There's this newfangled thing called a phone..."

Good point. Why hadn't she just called him? Her thoughts scattered on the wind. Damn that Scotch, slowing her thought process. "I know it's late," she said, craning her neck to try to see him. "But you should know something."

"That you've got a good arm?"

She wished she could see his expression. "I wanted to say that the only way I can be the kind of person I want to be is to acknowledge the person I was." Her tenuous balance gave way then, and she stumbled back a few steps, nearly toppling over. The damn boots. They didn't go with Scotch. By the time she looked up to Ben's window again, he was gone.

"Fine," she said and crouched low to look for another rock. Not a large one to bean him over the head with—though that had a *lot* of appeal—but another small one for his window. She wanted to get his attention, not get arrested.

Then, behind her, Ben's front door opened, and she nearly fell onto her butt. He was wearing a pair of low-slung black knit boxers and nothing else but sheer male perfection. His hair was mussed, his eyes heavy-lidded, and he had a way-past-five-o'clock shadow. Unable to stop herself, she let her gaze run south, over the ripples of his abs, the ridge of his obliques, which were bisected by a trail of dark silky hair that disappeared beneath those deliciously indecent low shorts.

In spite of the frigid air, she felt herself begin to heat from the inside out. She had to swallow hard to keep her heart from jumping right out of her throat. When she finally managed to look into his face again, he arched a dark brow.

And just like that, her temper kicked back in. "I have more to say to you," she said.

"You've been drinking."

She pointed at him. "Yes." She paused and tried to gather more of her wayward thoughts. "But that has no bearing on this."

He said nothing, just leaned against the doorway. He had a scar she'd never noticed before over one pec—one really great pec—and she wondered where he'd gotten it, and if it'd hurt. And if she could kiss it—

"Aubrey," he said.

She met his gaze. Right. She had things to say. "Okay, first of all, I didn't sleep with you to make amends. I slept with you because I wanted to."

He still didn't say anything, and she pointed at him again. "And you know what? It was your own damn fault. It was those jeans you wear, and the tool belt. It was the size of your hammer!"

From off to the side came a few commingled gasps of shocked laughter, and both Ben and Aubrey turned to look.

Jack's front window was open, and three faces were pressed up to the screen.

Ali, Leah, and Jack. The Three Stooges, though only two of them were drunk as skunks.

Aubrey narrowed her eyes and shooed them, but no one shooed. "I said no eavesdropping!"

"Jack's window just happened to be open," Leah said. "So really, that's not eavesdropping. At least not technically. Because technically—"

Jack put his hand over her mouth and shut the window, though none of them moved away.

Ben gave them a single hard look, and Jack grinned. But he did lower the shade on the window, leaving them alone.

Ben turned back to Aubrey. "The size of my hammer?"

Yeah…she couldn't believe she'd said that, either. She opted to try to find the moral high ground and lifted her chin. "You're missing my point."

He crossed his arms over the chest that she wanted to lick from the sternum to the edge of his boxers and beyond.

Focus, she ordered herself. "I couldn't help myself," she said. "Being with you. I knew it was a bad idea. Hell, *you* knew it was a bad idea. And yet we did it. We *both* did it, Ben."

He continued to just look at her, and this reminded her that she was mad. "Look," she said. "I'm tired of you not saying anything. So stop being quiet and speak up."

"I'm used to quiet."

"Well, that's just great," she said, tossing up her hands. "Because I'm so not good at quiet."

"No kidding."

She refused to let him get her off track with his pissiness, even if he had good reason for it. "Ben," she said, stepping closer. "I'm so sorry I hurt you. And I'm sorrier than I can say about what I told Hannah. I was a horrible bitch back then. But I'm not that person anymore. I have no excuse except that I was miserable and Hannah had everything I wanted, including you. But that's not who I am now."

He still didn't say anything, but she could tell he was processing what she'd said. She should just shut the hell up, but she had this chance to talk to him. She didn't know if she'd get another, so she needed to put everything out on the table. "And I never meant to keep the truth from you," she said. "I honestly didn't know how to tell you, much less fix it."

"It can't be fixed," he said.

There was another gasp from Jack's duplex. At this, Ben swore under his breath and yanked Aubrey inside. He slammed the door and faced her, hands on hips.

"It can't be fixed?" she repeated shakily.

"Well, what did you think, Aubrey? You stole two years of my life with Hannah. How did you expect me to react? And you slept with me before you told me. And you kept sleeping with me." He paused, and she wondered if he was remembering how little sleeping had actually been involved.

And how good it had been between them...

"I can't get past that part," he said quietly. "I was on your list so that you could make amends, not mess up further."

"I wasn't with you because of her," she said. "Or the list. That part...just happened."

He closed his eyes and swiped a hand over them.

Not exactly the reaction she'd been hoping for. "We have something, Ben. You know it, and I know it. Here, in the present, we have something. I don't want to walk away from that, or go quietly into the night. That's not who I am."

"No," he murmured, meeting her gaze, his unfathomable. "You're the one who waits until midnight, decides she has something to say, and can't contain it."

She was pretty sure that wasn't exactly a compliment, so she ignored it. "I'm in this, Ben. You're important to me. It's why you were on my list."

"You and that list." He inhaled, long and slow, and then shook his head. "I just want to forget it. Get over it."

She was standing there, helplessly struggling to overcome her past, fix her present, *and* secure her future all in one fell swoop. But she was watching Ben's face, and it told her the truth, the terrible truth. "I'm willing to fight for you, for us," she said slowly, taking in the devastating realization. "But you're not." She staggered back a step, feeling like she'd been hit by a train. "You're not," she repeated to herself softly, trying to make it sink in.

It didn't want to sink in. "You're not willing to fight for us at all," she said. "You're really going to use this as an excuse to get out."

"There's nothing to get out of," he said. "There was no us."

Rubbing her chest, she stared up into his eyes, which were wiped of emotion, just completely blank. And that hurt the most, she thought dazedly, in shock that he could do this, just walk away. She couldn't fight that. She didn't know how. And though she hated it, she had no choice.

She had too much pride to be the only one in this, the only one fighting.

"I'll be by to finish the wood trim," he said.

He didn't finish the rest of that sentence, which was clearly "and that's it." He didn't have to.

"Forget it," she said.

"It was a gift," he told her. "And I finish what I start."

She had to laugh. It was better than crying. And she'd cried her last tear over him, she promised herself. "Are we seriously having some stupid conversation about the trim after you just dumped me?" she asked in disbelief.

"I didn't dump you," he said. "We were never exclusive."

And the hits kept coming, even if it was the utter truth. "You're right," she said. "This was never a relationship—which we were both perfectly clear about from the get-go." She really hadn't meant to get involved, but she had, and the damage was done. He'd been it for her, the only man she wanted to be with. Not that she'd ever fully allowed herself to believe...

Okay, she had. She'd let herself believe. Her mistake. But she'd been there; she *knew* she wasn't the only one who'd fallen, damn it. He'd done it, too. He'd shown it in every look, every touch. Every kiss. "You can pretend this is about the past, but it isn't," she said. "I think you fell for me, too. And I think it scared you. I get that you've been hurt. But that's life, Ben. Life is one big fat gamble, and the odds are *never* in your favor. So you either go for it anyway and toss the dice or you don't play. But not playing?" She jabbed him in the bare chest with her finger. "That's the coward's way out. And I hadn't pegged you for a coward. Figure your shit out."

Chapter 28

Ben was still standing there in the butt-ass-cold door-way of his place in nothing but his boxers when Jack opened his own door. "You're an idiot," he said, and then ran down the sidewalk after Aubrey. Grabbing her, he redirected her 180 degrees and poured her into his car.

Ali and Leah came out of Jack's house, both taking the time to glare at Ben as well.

"What he said," Leah told him, gesturing her head toward Jack.

And then they were gone, leaving Ben alone to wonder when the hell everyone had gone from wanting him to steer clear of Aubrey to wanting them to be together.

The next morning, Ben got up early to head into work. It was a Saturday, which was perfect. He could catch up a little bit. He swung by to pick up Pink and Kendra and give them a lift to their rec ball soccer practice.

Because five-year-olds didn't judge. Things were

black and white for them. They didn't give a shit that maybe he was afraid to be happy.

The girls were in their yard playing with…Dani. Proof positive that the logic of women was far beyond him.

At the school field, he stopped and put the truck into park. He unbuckled the girls and held on to the back of Pink's jacket when she went to slide out of the vehicle. "Hold on a sec," he said. Christ—he was going to do it; he was really going to ask. "I thought we didn't like Dani."

Pink shrugged. "She said she was sorry for being mean."

Kendra nodded, her pigtails flying.

Just like that, just that easy. Ben looked into their sweet, innocent faces and felt something shift within him. They were so damn resilient. So easy to please. So completely full of life.

And so full of forgiveness.

He wished like hell he could be five again, when a "sorry" fixed everything. But it couldn't now. Nothing could.

The girls hopped out of the truck, but not before pressing sloppy wet kisses on his jaw in thanks.

Bemused, Ben sat there for a long moment, absorbing the fact that he'd just been schooled on life and forgiveness by a couple of five-year-olds. God, he was tired. So fucking tired. But every time he closed his eyes, he could see the pain in Aubrey's gaze. It haunted him.

He'd hurt her. She'd finally opened up to someone—him—and he'd tossed it right back in her face.

She was trying to right her wrongs, trying to be a person she could live with, and he'd used her past against her. Which meant this wasn't about Aubrey at all. It was about him and his own fears of letting someone in as far as he'd let Hannah—which hadn't worked out so well for him.

But what had happened to Hannah hadn't been his fault, and Aubrey was right. Life was a risk. He could hide from that or...live it.

The choice was his.

Figure your shit out. That's what Aubrey had told him, and at the time that had just pissed him off because he'd thought she'd been the one who needed to figure things out.

But he'd been wrong about that, too.

The news of what Aubrey had done to Lucky Harbor's beloved Ben McDaniel spread like wildfire. That on top of the nudie pictures pretty much did her in.

Foot traffic to the store on the day of her grand-opening party was practically nonexistent, and Aubrey knew in her gut she was sunk. "No one's going to come to the opening tonight," she told Ali and Leah as they arrived to help her set up.

"That's okay," Leah said. "We'll eat the cupcakes ourselves."

"Not exactly the point," Ali murmured.

Leah took in Aubrey's obviously devastated face. "Right," she said quickly. "We'll buy a bunch of books, too."

The bell above the door pinged, and they all turned in renewed hope as Carla walked in. She wasn't in scrubs today but was wearing a dress, and at the sight of her, Aubrey's anxiety ratcheted up a couple of notches.

"Wow," Ali whispered. "You have a look-alike."

Aubrey ignored her. "Hey," she said to her sister.

"Am I early for the grand-opening party?" Carla asked, looking around.

Aubrey found her voice through her surprise. "No. We're it. We're the party."

Leah held out a tray of cupcakes as Carla looked around in confusion.

"Long story," Aubrey said.

"Cupcake?" Leah asked.

Carla took one and moaned. "Oh, my God."

Leah beamed. "Better than an orgasm, right?"

"I don't remember what an orgasm feels like," Carla admitted, and they all laughed.

Aubrey poured her a hot tea. "Thanks for coming and supporting me."

Carla met her gaze. "Well, we are sisters."

Aubrey felt some of her anxiety drain away as she nodded, unable to speak. But though her anger had drained as well, she was still flatlined by an unbearable sadness. She'd handled things wrong—all of it. "The party wasn't my smartest idea. Who really opens a bookstore these days?" She shook her head. "No one, that's who."

"Well, that's a piss-poor attitude, missy," Lucille said, coming into the store, carrying a stack of papers. "I'm surprised at you. You're supposed to be all kick-ass— Wonder Woman. Did you ever see Wonder Woman give up?"

"Lucille," Aubrey said. "You know how much people loved Hannah. You know I can't compete with that. Not after what I did."

"What you did," Lucille said, "was human. All of us have stuff we're ashamed of. Every single one of us. And if people don't remember that, well, shame on them."

Carla looked at Aubrey. "What happened?"

"She was human," Lucille repeated, and patted Carla's hand. "And nice to see you here, honey."

Aubrey shook her head at Carla's questioning gaze. "Later," she said.

Or never…

"What is all that?" Ali asked Lucille, gesturing to the things she'd brought.

"I made flyers to help bring people in for the party." Lucille held them up. It was a cartoon of a blond Wonder Woman. Her hair was drawn to resemble Aubrey's own smooth mane and was held back by a gold crown with a star in the middle. She was standing among stacks and stacks of books, hands on hips, looking pretty kick-ass. In the background were brownies, a teakettle, a laptop, and a tool belt.

"A tool belt?" Aubrey asked.

Lucille smiled. "I see Ben in here pretty regularly, so I wanted to make sure people knew that this is a hot-guy magnet. Nothing says 'hot guy' like a tool belt, you know." She pulled three automatic staplers from her huge purse and handed them out. "Okay, girls, time to get busy."

"Me, too?" Carla asked, holding a stapler, staring down at it.

Aubrey shook her head. "No, you don't have to—"

"Sisters," she said to Aubrey. Lucille handed Carla a stack of flyers, and Carla took them.

Aubrey smiled past the lump in her throat. "Thanks."

Lucille had grabbed a cupcake in each hand and was

sinking into a couch. "Hustle, ladies," she said around a full mouth. She licked chocolate off her lips. "Go on, now." She waved a cupcake. "No time to waste. I'd planned to put up a notice on Facebook, but as it turns out, I'm grounded from my account."

"How do you get grounded from your own Facebook page?" Carla asked.

Lucille shrugged unrepentantly. "One too many pictures of hot guys not wearing enough clothes. But I started an Instagram account, so it's all good."

Ben sat at his desk. Because it was a Saturday, employees who happened to be in the building kept to themselves, making it quiet. Usually his favorite state.

I'm used to quiet, he'd told Aubrey, and he'd meant that. But today it haunted him. Because he also liked Aubrey just the way she was: fiery, passionate, tough. It was bothering him that he'd let her think he didn't like those things about her.

There was a lot bothering him. He was a first-class asshole, as Jack had made clear. Jack was a lot of things, but as much as Ben hated to admit it, one of the things Jack almost always was was *right*.

Yes, Aubrey had taken away two years of time that Ben might have had with Hannah. Might. Because the truth was, he'd made the most of those two years. He'd enjoyed the hell out of himself, and an even bigger truth was that he wouldn't want to take that time back. He'd been too young for a serious relationship with Hannah back then, and only in hindsight could he see that. If they'd stayed together, he'd have blown it anyway.

All on his own.

And then there was Hannah herself. Ben had loved her—he'd loved her with everything he had, and she'd loved him. But she'd never have come to his house in the middle of the night and thrown rocks at his window to demand his attention. She'd never have yelled at him or made a scene. And she sure as hell wouldn't have fought for him. She *hadn't* fought for him, when it had come right down to it.

Instead she'd let him go without so much as the truth. Or any words at all. She'd tossed him away.

As he'd done to Aubrey.

He dropped his head and thunked it on his desk a few times.

"Careful, you'll shake something loose."

Ben lifted his head and found Lucille standing there watching him. "What are you doing here?"

She showed him a flyer for Aubrey's grand opening, and he had to smile at the image of Aubrey as Wonder Woman.

It fit.

"I'm making sure people remember to go to her grand-opening party," Lucille said.

Ben nodded. "You're a good person, Lucille."

"I am," she said. "And I thought you were."

"What does that mean?"

She just looked at him with her rheumy, knowing eyes.

"You're going to have to give me a hint," he said.

"How about a couple of hints?" Lucille said. "Such as since when do *you* judge someone for making a mistake? You've made plenty yourself, Benjamin McDaniel. Remember when you and Jack and Luke broke into the Ferris wheel's machine room and set it running in the middle of the night? Or how about when your aunt had the entire search and rescue team looking for you when you'd gone night surfing? Everyone thought you'd drowned, but there you were on the harbor, right on the beach, sleeping through your own rescue."

He winced. "I was young and stupid."

She gave him a baleful stare.

"I'm not going to discuss Aubrey with you," he said flatly.

"No, of course not. We're discussing your stupidity. Your assness. Your—"

"I got it," Ben said tightly.

"Yeah? Then do something about it, big guy."

"For the record," he said, "I was just getting ready to handle this situation."

"Well, could you speed things up a little bit?" she asked. "Our girl doesn't have all damn day. Right now she's all alone in her shop surrounded by nothing but books and cupcakes that no one's eating."

He didn't like that image. "No one came?"

"Her friends Ali and Leah came," she said, with an emphasis on *friends*, as though he should be ashamed of himself for not being one of them. "Her sister showed up, too," Lucille added. "But no one else. Lucky Harbor thinks it needs to be mad on your behalf."

Hell. That was not what he wanted. "It's none of anyone's business. What happened is between me and her."

Lucille crossed her arms. "Are you referring to way back, when she got mad at Hannah and told her a lie about the two of you? Are you seriously going to tell me that when you heard *why* Aubrey did it that it didn't make a difference to you?"

Ben went still, thoughts spinning in his head so fast he felt whiplashed.

Lucille was staring at him. "You didn't even ask Aubrey why she told Hannah that lie, did you?"

"I asked," he said. But she hadn't answered.

And he hadn't pushed.

"Oh, for Peter, Joseph, and Mary's sake!" Lucille said, exasperated. "I need to be paid for this job."

"What job?"

"Matchmaking. You young people don't even know how to communicate. Listen to me very carefully. Aubrey caught Hannah in a lie—a big one—that caused someone else a lot of problems. It pissed Aubrey off, because at that time she wasn't getting away with diddly-squat."

Ben shook his head. "What lie could Hannah have possibly told that would have upset Aubrey? They weren't even friends."

Lucille was clearly over this. "Remember that car accident she was in?"

Ben did remember. Hannah had been in the passenger seat when her best friend had gotten in an accident. Later that friend had been sued by someone in one of the other two cars involved. Thankfully, Hannah had been unhurt, but she was devastated over her friend's troubles from the fallout. "Yes. I remember."

Lucille's expression softened. "Honey, this isn't easy to say. I don't like to speak ill of the dead. *Hannah* was driving that night. The two girls switched places before the police came because Hannah had been drinking. She'd had a scholarship to lose and a father she was terrified of. A DUI couldn't happen for her."

Ben stared at her. "That's crazy. Hannah would never have let someone else take the blame."

"But that's exactly what she did," Lucille said quietly. "And Aubrey saw it."

"How do you know this?"

"Because that someone else is my granddaughter." Lucille patted him on the arm. "She said that Aubrey confronted Hannah about the accident, and Hannah denied it." She gave Ben a long look. "Hannah used Aubrey's bad reputation against her, to discount anything Aubrey might say. And then Aubrey let her mouth run off with her good sense when her temper got the best of her."

Ben didn't know what to make of any of this, and he wasn't at all sure that the details mattered at this point. It was in the past, and it would stay there. It didn't matter—none of it mattered; he knew that now. Standing, he headed to the door, but then he stopped to go back for the flyers. Lucille plowed into the back of him. Her hands came up, and because she was scarcely five feet tall they ended up on his ass. He craned his neck and looked down at her.

"Sorry," she said, but didn't remove her hands. In fact, if he wasn't mistaken, she gave him a little squeeze.

"Lucille," he said ominously.

"I know." She pulled her hands away—rather reluctantly, he thought—and sighed. "It's just been a long time since I had my hands on buns that firm."

Shaking his head, he grabbed the flyers and strode out of his office. He stopped at every person he saw, thrust out a flyer, and demanded that person's presence at the bookstore. "There's going to be stuff to eat," he said, and glanced at Lucille for confirmation.

She nodded. "Goodies from the bakery. And also hotties with buns of steel."

After Ben got everybody to leave their desks and head down the street, he took a picture of the flyer with his phone and attached it to a text message, which he sent to everyone in his contacts list who lived in Lucky Harbor—and to a few who were close enough to get their asses in a car and drive here. Then he hit up the fire station, not surprised to find that Jack had already sent everyone down to the bookstore.

Then Ben headed that way as well, stopping at every place in between. He even hit up Sam, who was working alone in his harbor warehouse, sanding away on a gorgeous boat.

"You want me to go to a party?" Sam asked in disbelief, straightening. He was covered from head to toe in sawdust.

"Yeah," Ben said.

Sam stared at him, and then let out a slow smile. "So the rumors *are* true. You've fallen for the bookstore chick."

"Shut up and get your ass to the party."

By the time Ben walked into the Book & Bean, it was filled, the crowd noisy and happy. The best sound of all was the sound of the register steadily ringing.

He was stopped by Mr. Wilford, who was shocked to report that he actually had pumpkin plants growing—in late winter.

Dee was there, too, and gave him a big hug. Just about everyone he knew was there, except the one person he wanted to see. He strode quickly through the store, completely ignoring anyone else who tried to talk to him.

He finally found Aubrey behind the coffee and tea station, serving a line of customers. She was flushed, looking relieved to be serving at all. She wore a pretty dress, her hair was up, and she was smiling.

She hadn't fallen apart. She'd picked herself up and carried on. He loved that about her.

He loved *her*.

Chapter 29

♥

At the hush in the crowd around her, Aubrey looked up, her smile slipped, and all the air vacated her lungs.

"Hey," Ben said, eyes calm and on hers, his voice quiet. "I'm looking for a book recommendation."

"A book recommendation," she repeated, heart pounding so loudly she couldn't hear herself think. Their rapt audience didn't help much. "You want a book recommendation."

"Yes. I need one on male groveling. I thought maybe there might be a *Relationships for Dummies* or something."

She wasn't sure what to make of this, so she lowered her voice. "Listen, about the other night. I wanted to apologize—"

He shook his head. "You already apologized. Several times, in fact."

"But—"

"It's enough," he said, and lithely vaulted over the

counter. "And now it's my turn." He stepped closer and put his hands on her hips. I'm sorry, Aubrey." His fingers tightened on her. "I'm sorry I was such an ass that I couldn't see past my own insecurities and fears."

Around them, their audience gave a collective "Aww," but Aubrey ignored them, not taking her eyes off Ben. "Go on," she said cautiously.

"You said you fell for me."

She flushed, thinking about everything she'd flung at him that night, including rocks. "Ben—"

"You also said *I* fell for *you*. I blew that off, but you were right, Aubrey. I did fall, hard and fast, and"—his mouth twisted wryly—"a little bit against my will."

She tried to pull free, but he held tight. "I liked it," he said. "Too much, to be honest. So when you told me about your list, I used it to back away from you. You were right about that, too. Probably we should start a new list now, of all your rights."

Thoughts rolling in her head like tumbleweeds, heart aching, she shook her head, afraid to hope. "Where are you going with this, Ben?"

"I want you," he said. "I've wanted you every single minute of this entire winter. I also need you. From the bottom of my flawed heart."

Their audience "aw'd" again, but Ben paid them no more mind than Aubrey did, his gaze still on her. "I can remember every single smile you've given me," he said, "every word you've ever said to me."

She melted a little at the sweetness of his words, but shook her head, unable to give up the doubt, the fear that this wasn't going where she so desperately hoped it would.

Unperturbed, he smiled. "I also remember every eye roll. And every single time you went toe-to-toe with me and drove me crazy."

A few people tittered and giggled.

Aubrey tried to free herself again, but he held on to her with shocking ease, even laughing softly, the bastard. He gestured to the store around them. "Hell, Aubrey, I dragged this job out to twice as long as it should have taken," he said, "just so I could keep seeing you."

"Well, that's good to know," Lucille whispered to someone. "I was beginning to think the boy didn't know what he was doing."

Ben slid Lucille a look before turning back to Aubrey. "I loved watching you work. It might've been the pretty dresses that promised a softer side to you, a side only I got to see, but I loved watching you run this world—your world. I loved watching you find your place. I loved watching you take me on and calling me on all my shit." He ran a finger along her temple and gently tucked a loose strand of hair behind her ear. "I love your spirit, your passion. I love everything about you. I love *you*, Aubrey."

The crowd sighed in unison, and as if they were watching a tennis match, their heads all turned toward Aubrey for her reaction.

She had plenty of reactions, the biggest being the fact that her heart suddenly didn't fit inside her rib cage. But she wasn't one hundred percent ready to believe. "You said you liked quiet," she said. "I'm not quiet."

"I said I was used to quiet. But I've learned something about myself. I also like *not* quiet." He smiled. "A lot."

And just like that, the little kernel of hope she'd so ruthlessly tamped down finally found room to breathe and grow. "Yeah?"

There was a smile in his eyes now. And relief. "Yeah."

Lucille leaned over the counter toward Ben and stage-whispered, "I don't think you need a book recommendation at all. You're doing pretty darn good."

"Thanks," he said.

"But the two years I stole," Aubrey said. It hurt her to even say it, but she had to get it out, all of it. There could be no more secrets. "What about them?"

He shook his head. "I mentioned I was an ass, right? I never should've blamed you for that—"

"But I—"

"Yeah, you did," he said. "And then I went on to make the most of those two years. It's over and done, Aubrey," he promised. "And anyway, I'm hoping if I play my cards right, you're going to give me a lifetime."

This cause a huge gasp from the crowd, and Aubrey matched it with one of her own. "What?" she whispered, certain she'd heard wrong.

He dropped to a knee.

"Oh, my God." She put her hands to her mouth and stared down at him.

"You're everything I need," he said. "Everything I'll ever need. And I've needed you, Aubrey, for a long time. Every single second since you threw that drink in my face."

She choked out a half laugh, half sob. "You never said—"

"I should have. Another mistake," he said, his expression serious. "The good news is that I learn from my mistakes, always. Marry me, Aubrey. Marry me and give me forever."

She felt her eyes go wide. Felt her heart kick hard. From her peripheral vision she was aware that the entire crowd had surged forward to peek over the counter in order to get a look at Ben McDaniel on one knee.

"Are you going to reject me in front of at least one hundred of our closest friends and family?" he asked lightly.

She looked into his eyes and realized he wasn't nearly as calm, cool, and unruffled as he was pretending to be, and it squeezed her heart. "No," she said.

His expression grew very serious, and there was absolute silence in the room. "No," he repeated, clearly trying to figure out what exactly she was saying no to—the proposal or rejecting him.

Letting out a laugh, Aubrey dropped to her knees in front of him, eyes burning as she met his gaze. "I mean yes."

"So…yes you'll marry me, or yes you're rejecting me?"

"Yeah, honey," Lucille piped up, leaning over the counter. "There's a pretty big difference there."

"Yes, I'll marry you." Leaning into him, Aubrey wrapped her arms around Ben's neck as their audience broke out in applause.

"Shh!" Lucille snapped above them. "I can't hear; I want to hear!"

"There's nothing more to hear," Aubrey said, eyes on Ben. "It's all been said."

Ben's eyes smiled first, and then the smile spread to

his mouth. And then he lowered that smiling mouth and kissed hers.

"You've given me so much," she said against him. "What do *you* get?"

His eyes soaked her up, as though maybe he'd never get enough of her. "You."

It's in His Kiss

Chapter 1

♥

Oh, yeah," Becca Thorpe murmured with a sigh of pleasure as she wriggled her toes in the wet sand. The sensation was better than splurging on a rare pedicure. Better than finding the perfect dress on sale. Better than...well, she'd say orgasms, but it'd been a while and she couldn't remember for sure.

"You're perfect," she said to the Pacific Ocean, munching on the ranch-flavored popcorn she'd bought from the pier. "So perfect that I'd marry you and have your babies, if I hadn't just promised myself to this popcorn."

"Not even going to ask."

At the sound of the deep male voice behind her, Becca squeaked and whipped around.

She'd thought she was alone on the rocky beach. Alone with her thoughts, her hopes, her fears, and all her worldly possessions stuffed into her car parked in the lot behind her.

But she wasn't alone at all, because not ten feet away,

between her and the pier, stood a man. He wore a rash-guard T-shirt and loose board shorts, both dripping wet and clinging to his very hot bod. He had a surfboard tucked under a biceps, and just looking at him had her pulse doing a little tap dance.

Maybe it was his unruly sun-kissed brown hair, the strands more than a little wild and blowing in his face. Maybe it was the face itself, which was striking for the features carved in granite and a set of mossy-green eyes that held her prisoner. Or maybe it was that he carried himself like he knew he was at the top of the food chain.

She took a few steps back because the wary city girl in her didn't trust anyone, not even a sexy-looking surfer dude.

The man didn't seem bothered by her retreat at all. He just gave her a short nod and left her alone.

Becca watched him stride up the pier steps. Or more correctly, she watched his very fine backside and long legs stride up the pier steps, carrying that board like it weighed nothing.

Then he vanished from sight before she turned her attention back to the ocean.

Whitecaps flashed from the last of the day's sun, and a salty breeze blew over her as the waves crashed onto the shore. Big waves. And Sexy Surfer had just been out in that. Crazy.

Actually, *she* was the crazy one, and she let out a long, purposeful breath, and with it a lot of her tension.

But not all…

She wriggled her toes some more, waiting for the next wave. There were a million things running through her mind, most of them floating like dust motes through an open, sun-filled window, never quite landing. Still, a few managed to hit with surprising emphasis—such as the realization that she'd done it. She'd packed up and left home.

Her destination had been the Pacific Ocean. She'd always wanted to see it, and she could now say with one hundred percent certainty it met her expectations. The knowledge that she'd fulfilled one of her dreams felt good, even if there were worries clouding her mind. The mess she'd left behind, for one. Staying out of the rut she'd just climbed out of, for another. And a life. She wanted—*needed*—a life. Employment would be good, too, since she was fond of eating.

But standing in this little Washington State town she'd yet to explore, those worries receded slightly. She'd get through this; she always did. After all, the name of this place nearly guaranteed it.

Lucky Harbor.

She was determined to find some *good* luck for a change.

A few minutes later, the sun finally gently touched down on the water, sending a chill through the early-July evening. Becca took one last look and turned to head back to her car. Sliding behind the wheel, she pulled out her phone and accessed the ad she'd found on Craigslist.

Cheap waterfront warehouse converted into three separate living spaces. Cheap. Furnished (sort of). Cheap. Month to month. Cheap.

It worked for Becca on all levels, especially the cheap part. She had the first month's rent check in her pocket, and she was meeting the landlord at the building. All she had to do was locate it. Her GPS led her from the pier to the other end of the harbor, down a narrow street lined with maybe ten warehouse buildings.

Problem number one.

None of them had numbers indicating its address. After cruising up and down the street three times, she admitted defeat and parked. She called the landlord, but she only had his office phone, and it went right to voice mail.

Problem number two. She was going to have to ask someone for help, which wasn't exactly her strong suit.

It wasn't even a suit of hers at all. She hummed a little to herself as she looked around, a nervous tic for sure, but it soothed her. Unfortunately, the only person in sight was a kid on a bike, in homeboy shorts about ten sizes too big and a knit cap, coming straight at her on the narrow sidewalk.

"Watch it, lady!" he yelled.

A city girl through and through, Becca held her ground. "*You* watch it."

The kid narrowly missed her and kept going.

"Hey, which building is Two-Oh-Three?"

"Dunno, ask Sam!" he called back over his shoulder. "He'll know, he knows everything."

Okay, perfect. She cupped her hands around her mouth so he'd hear her. "Where's Sam?"

The kid didn't answer, but he did point toward the building off to her right.

It was a warehouse like the others, industrial, old, the siding battered by the elements and the salty air. It was built like an A-frame barn, with both of the huge front and back sliding doors open. The sign posted did give her a moment's pause.

WARNING: PRIVATE DOCK
TRESPASSERS WILL BE USED AS BAIT

She bit her lower lip and decided that, after driving all day for days on end, her need to find her place outweighed the threat. Hopefully…

The last of the sunlight slanted through the warehouse, highlighting everything in gold, including the guy using some sort of planer along the wood. The air itself was throbbing with the beat of the loud indie rock blaring from some unseen speakers.

From the outside, the warehouse hadn't looked like much, but as she stepped into the vast doorway, she realized the inside was a wide-open space with floor-to-rafters windows nearly three stories high. It was lined with ladders and racks of stacked wood planks and tools. Centered in the space was a wood hull, looking like a piece of art.

As did the guy working on it. His shirt was damp and clinging to his every muscle as it bunched and flexed with his movements. It was all so beautiful and intriguing—the boat, the music, the man himself, right down to the corded veins on his forearms—that it was like being at the movies during the montage of scenes that always played to a sound track.

Then she realized she recognized the board shorts, or more accurately the really excellent butt, as she'd only moments before watched it walk away from her.

Sexy Surfer.

Though he couldn't possibly have heard her over the hum of his power tool and the loud music, he turned to face her. And as she already knew, the view of him from the front was just as heart-stopping as it was from the back.

He didn't move a single muscle other than one flick of his thumb, which turned off the planer. His other hand went into his pocket and extracted a remote. With another flick, the music stopped.

"You shouldn't be in here," he said. "It's dangerous."

And just like that, the pretty montage sound track playing in her head came to a screeching halt. "Okay, sorry. I'm just—"

Just nothing, apparently, because he turned back to his work, and with another flick of his thumb the planer came back to life. And then the music.

"—Looking for someone," she finished. Not that he was listening.

On the wall right next to her, a telephone began ringing, and the bright red light attached to it began blinking in sync, clearly designed just in case the phone couldn't be heard over the tools. She could hear it, but she doubted he could. One ring, then two. Three. The guy didn't make a move toward it.

On the fourth ring, the call went to a machine, where a recorded male voice said, "Lucky Harbor Charters. We're in high gear for the summer season. Coastal tours, deep-sea fishing, scuba, name your pleasure. Leave a message at the tone, or find us at the harbor, north side."

A click indicated the caller disconnected, but the phone immediately rang again.

Sexy Surfer ignored all of this.

Becca had a hard time doing the same, and she glanced around for someone, *anyone*, but there was no one in sight. Used to having to be resourceful, she let her gaze follow the cord of the planer to an electric outlet in the floor. She walked over to it and pulled it out of the wall.

The planer stopped.

So did her heart when Sexy Surfer turned his head her way. Yep, Sexy Surfer was an apt description for him. Maybe Drop-Dead Sexy. Either way, he took in the fact that she was still there and that she was holding the cord to his planer and a single brow arched. Whether it was displeasure or disbelief was hard to tell. Probably, with that bad 'tude, not many messed with him. But she was exhausted, hungry, out of her element, and a little bit pissed off. Which made her just enough of a loose cannon to forget to be afraid.

"I'm trying to find Sam," she said, moving closer to him so he could hear her over his music. "Do you know him?"

"Who's asking?"

Having come from a family of entertainers, most of them innate charmers to boot, Becca knew how to make the most of what she'd been given, so she smiled. "I'm Becca Thorpe, and I'm trying to find Two-Oh-Three Harbor Street. My GPS says I'm on Harbor Street, but the buildings don't have numbers on them."

"You're looking for the building directly to the north."

She nodded, and then shook her head with a laugh. She could get lost trying to find her way out of a paper bag. "And north would be which way exactly?"

He let the planer slowly slide to the floor by its cord before letting go and heading toward her.

He was six-foot-plus of lean, hard muscle, with a lot of sawdust clinging to him, as rugged and tough as the boat he was working on—though only the man was exuding testosterone, a bunch of it.

Becca didn't have a lot of great experience with an overabundance of testosterone, so she found herself automatically taking a few steps back from him, until she stood in the doorway.

He slowed but didn't stop, not until he was crowded in that doorway right along with her, taking up an awful lot of space.

Actually, *all* of the space.

And though she was braced to feel threatened, the opposite happened. She felt...suddenly warm, and her heart began to pound. And not in a terrified way, either.

He took in her reaction, held her gaze for a moment, then pointed to the right. "The front of the building you're looking for is around the corner," he said, his voice a little softer now, like maybe he knew she was torn between an unwelcome fear and an equally unwelcome heat.

She really hoped the heat was mutual, because it would be embarrassing to be caught in Lustville by herself. "Around the corner," she repeated. Did he know he smelled good, like fresh wood and something citrusy, and also heated male? She wondered if she smelled good, too, or if all she was giving off was the scent of confused female and ranch-flavored popcorn.

"What do you need with that place?" he asked.

"I'm the new tenant there. Or one of them anyway."

His expression was unfathomable. "I take it you haven't seen it yet."

"Not in person," she said. "Why? Is it that bad?"

"Depends on how long you're staying," he said. "More than five minutes?"

Oh, boy. "I don't actually know," she said. "It's a month-to-month rental. Lucky Harbor is sort of a pit stop for me at the moment."

His gaze searched hers. Then he nodded and moved back to his work. He plugged the planer in and flicked it on again.

Guess their conversation was over. She was on her own. And if that thought caused a little pang of loneliness inside her still-hurting heart, she shoved it deep and ignored it, because now wasn't the time to give in to the magnitude of what she'd done. Leaving the warehouse, she turned right.

To her new place.

To a new beginning.

Chapter 2

Sam Brody lifted his head from the boat he was building and let his gaze drift to the north-facing window. The sky was a kaleidoscope of colors as the sun vanished, but he could still see the quiet, industrial street, and the backside of Tough Girl as she walked off.

And walking off was just as he wanted her, too. He turned his concentration back to the hull. He was good at concentrating. If his childhood hadn't drilled it into him, then working on an oil rig for seven years—where paying attention meant the difference between life and death—had certainly done so.

But damn if not two seconds later his gaze flickered to the window again.

Yep, she and her sweet bod were gone. She had a backbone, but she also had those warm, soulful brown eyes, and one of those smiles that could draw a man right in.

And a sassiness that could hold him there...

And she was going to be right next door. Not good news. The warehouse she'd rented was a complete piece of shit, cold in the winter, hot in the summer, not easily secured or safe. Not his call, of course, but he didn't like that the landlord had put her in there, alone. Lyons should've known better. The place had been up for sale for years now, but no one in Lucky Harbor was stupid enough to sink any equity into that money pit. Still, Sam should've bought the thing himself just to keep it empty.

Empty, and quiet.

The phone rang again, and the accompanying red lights gave him an eye twitch. He'd been ignoring the calls while trying to work, figuring one of the guys would get the hint and pick up. But neither Cole nor Tanner was good at hints. No, for his two partners to get something, they had to be hit over the head with it. Besides, Sam knew damn well it amused the hell out of them to make him answer the phone.

Finally he snatched the phone just to shut it up and snarled, "Lucky Harbor Charters."

There was a brief pause, a hesitation that made him feel like a jackass as his gaze skimmed the big sign that Cole had taped above the phone for Sam's benefit alone. It read:

Smile.
Be friendly.
Ask "Can I help you?" in a tone that suggests you actually mean it, and not that you'd like to rip the head off whoever's interrupting you.
(You smiling yet?)

Refusing to smile on principle, Sam did make the effort to sound friendly as he spoke into the silence. "Can I help you?"

"Sammy? That you?"

Sam closed his eyes. "Yeah, Dad. It's me."

"Oh, good." Mark Brody laughed a little sheepishly. "I remembered the number right this time. So…how's it going?"

This wasn't the question his dad really wanted to ask, but at least the guy had become self-aware enough to feign interest. In the past, his dad would've gotten right to it. *Got a little extra for your good old dad? Thanks, love ya.*

"Sammy? You there?"

Sam scrubbed a hand down his face. Yeah. He was here. He was always here, from all those crazy years when Mark hadn't had it together enough to keep Sam from landing in foster care, to now, when Mark still didn't have it together. "How much you need?" Sam asked.

"Uh…" His dad laughed again, guilt heavy in the sound. He'd spent a total of maybe ten minutes being a dad, so he'd never really gotten the hang of it. "That's not why I called."

Yeah, it was. Of course it was. They had a routine. Sam would call his dad to check in every week, never getting a return call until Mark ran out of money, which happened every few months or so. "It's okay, Dad. Just tell me."

"A grand."

Sam opened his eyes and stared at the sign.

Smile.

Be friendly.

"A grand," he repeated.

"Carrie needs to buy stuff for the baby, and—"

"Got it," Sam said, not wanting to hear about the demands of Mark's latest woman. Or the baby that'd be Sam's half sister when it arrived in a few months.

A baby sister.

It didn't defy the odds any more than picturing his dad trying to be a real dad…"Did you ask for the paternity test like we talked about?"

"Well…"

"Dad—"

"She'd kill me, son. You have no idea how touchy pregnant women are."

Sam bit back anything he might have said because there was no point. His father had made a career out of getting ripped off by women. "You need to find a way to try," Sam said.

"I will."

Sam blew out a breath. He wouldn't try. "So a grand, then. To the usual bank account?"

"Uh, no," Mark said, back to sheepish. "I closed that one out."

More likely, the bank had kicked him out for repeatedly overdrawing his funds.

"I'll email you the new info," his dad said. "Thanks, son. Love ya."

The *love ya* was so rote that Sam wondered if Mark even realized he was saying it. Not that it mattered. Nor did his response, as his dad had already disconnected.

The phone immediately rang again. Resisting the urge to throw it out the window, he yanked it back up, wondering what his dad could have possibly forgotten. "Yeah?"

"Hi, um…is this Lucky Harbor Charters?" a female voice asked, sounding uncertain.

Shit. Sam glanced at the sign. He still didn't have a smile in him so once again he attempted friendly. "Yes, you've reached LHC."

"Oh, good. I'd like to book a deep-sea fishing trip for a family reunion. It's our first big reunion in five years and we're all so excited. There's going to be my dad, my grandfather, my two brothers, my uncle—"

"Okay, great. Hold please," Sam said, and punched the HOLD button. He took a deep breath and strode out of the warehouse and to their "yard." This led to the waterfront. There they had a dock, where their fifty-foot Wright Sport was moored.

Hours ago, Tanner—their scuba diving instructor and communications expert—had texted Sam that he was working on their radio system.

"Hey," Sam called out to him. "How about answering a damn phone call once in a while?"

"You're the one inside," Tanner said, not stopping what he was doing, which didn't look to be work so much as sunbathing. Not that he needed it with the mocha skin he'd inherited from his mother's Brazilian roots. He'd stripped to a pair of board shorts, a backward baseball cap, and reflective aviator sunglasses, and was sprawled out on his back, face tilted up to the sun.

"Busy, are you?" Sam asked drily.

"Cole and I chartered the midnight cruise last night and didn't moor until three a.m."

"And you slept until two p.m., so what's your point?"

Tanner lifted a middle finger.

Sam gave up and strode up to the smaller building—a

hut really—that they used as their front office and greeting area. The rolling door was up when they were open for business and shut when they weren't.

It was up now, and Cole was sitting behind the front counter. He was their captain, chief navigator, and mechanic, and was currently hunt-and-pecking at the keyboard of his laptop. The fingers stopped when Sam reached into the bucket beside the counter and pulled out one of their water guns. The thing had been touted as a squirt gun, but the more apt term would have been *cannon*. Sam weighed it in his hands, decided it was loaded enough, and turned back to the door.

"What the hell are you doing?" Cole asked.

"Going to spray the hell out of Tanner."

"Nice," Cole said, fingers already back to hunt-and-pecking. "Carry on."

Sam stopped in the doorway and stared at him in surprise. Cole was their resident techno-geek. He wore cargo pants with handy pockets and could fix just about anything at any time with the ingenuity of a modern-day MacGyver. And he always, *always*, objected to fighting among their ranks. "What's up?" Sam asked him.

"Trying to work. Go away."

"If you're working so damn hard, why aren't *you* answering the phones?"

Cole lifted his head and blinked innocently. "Phones? What phones? I didn't hear any phones."

Sam shook his head. "We need to get that damn ad in the paper."

Cole's fingers clicked one last key with dramatic flair. "Done," he declared. "Ad placed."

"What does it say?" Sam asked.

Cole hit a few more keys. "Looking for self-motivated admin to answer phones, work a schedule, greet customers with a friendly attitude, and be able to handle grumpy-ass bosses named Sam."

Sam arched a brow. "You'd push the buttons of a guy holding a loaded water cannon?"

Not looking worried in the slightest, Cole smiled and reached down beneath the counter, coming up with his own loaded cannon, which he casually aimed at Sam. "You forget who bought these."

"Shit." He turned to go.

"You're forgetting something else," Cole said.

Sam looked back.

"Tanner's ex-profession as a Navy SEAL."

"Shit," Sam said again, lowering the cannon. He was pissed, not stupid.

"Good choice."

"Line one's for you," Sam said.

Becca wasn't much for regrets so she decided not to stress over the fact that she'd rented a third of a dilapidated warehouse sight unseen. Thanks to Sexy *Grumpy* Surfer's warning—*I take it you haven't seen it yet*—she'd been braced.

But not braced enough.

The building was similar to Sam's in that they were both converted warehouses, and had the same floor-to-rafter windows. But that's where the similarities ended. Her warehouse hadn't been nearly so well taken care of. According to the landlord—an old guy named Lyons— the place had once been a cannery. Then an arcade. Then a saltwater taffy manufacturer with a gift shop. And finally a boardinghouse, which had last been used for a bunch of carnies in town for a long-ago summer, and they hadn't been kind.

At the moment the entire warehouse was a wide-open space divided into three units by questionably thin walls. Each apartment had a rudimentary galley kitchen and bathroom and was filled with a variety of leftover dust and crap from the previous renters—hence the *furnished (sort of)* part of the ad. In addition to beds and tables, this included some odd-looking carnival equipment and a saltwater taffy pull.

Or possibly a torture device…

Becca and Mr. Lyons walked through each of the apartments. The first unit was cheapest since it was the smallest, and also the coldest, as it got the least sun exposure.

Since cheap was right up her alley, and she didn't have to worry about cold for another six months, she'd handed over her check.

"If you need anything," Mr. Lyons said, "yell for the guys across the alley. Tanner's almost always on the dock or their boat, but he's a real tough nut to crack. Cole's good for fixing just about anything. But Sam knows all there's to know about these old warehouses. He's your man if you need anything."

Sam again. But she decided she'd need his help *never*. "Got it, thanks."

"He's not exactly shy, so don't you be," Lyons said. "Just don't try to date any of them. They're pretty much ex-hell-raisers these days, but still heartbreakers, each and every one of them."

"I'll keep that in mind," Becca said, knowing she could

and had handled just about anything a woman could face. She absolutely wouldn't be needing help.

Not an hour later, she was in the bathroom washing her hands when she found a huge, black, hairy spider in her sink staring at her with eight beady eyes. She went screaming into the alley, jumping up and down, shaking out her hair, and jerking her limbs like a complete moron.

"You lost again?"

She let out another scream and whirled around to face—oh, perfect—Sexy Grumpy Surfer. He was in faded jeans, a white T-shirt, and mirrored glasses, looking movie-star cool and sexy hot.

He arched a single brow.

"There's a spider in my bathroom sink," she said, still gasping for breath.

"That explains the dance moves."

Ignoring this *and* him, she checked herself over again, still not convinced she was spider-free.

"Need help?" he asked.

"No."

He shrugged and turned to walk away.

"Okay, yes," she admitted. Damn it. "I need help." She pointed to the offending building. "First apartment, door's wide open. The evil culprit is in the bathroom sink."

With a salute, he vanished inside her building.

She did not follow. She couldn't follow; her feet had turned into two concrete blocks. And if he came out without having caught the spider, she was going to have to move out. Immediately.

Two minutes later, Sexy Grumpy Surfer reappeared, the smirk still in place. She wasn't going to ask. She refused to ask. But her brain didn't get the message to her mouth. "You get it?" she demanded, and was rattled enough not to care that her voice shook a little bit.

"Got it," he said.

"Sure?"

He gave her a head tilt. "Do you want me to swear on a stack of Bibles, or my mother's grave?"

His mother was in a grave. That was sad and tragic, and she knew later she'd think about it and mourn for them. But for right now, she wanted assurances. "Your word will do."

"I'm sure I got the spider."

Whew. She sagged in relief. "Okay, then. Thank you."

"I don't suppose you'd do those moves again."

Was he laughing at her? She narrowed her eyes at him because yeah, he was laughing at her. "I don't suppose."

"Shame," he said, and then he was gone.

Becca went cautiously back inside. She glared at her bathroom mirror for a few minutes and told herself she was fine, move on.

She was really good at that, moving on. She stood in the center of the drafty space with her two suitcases, her portable piano keyboard, and her pride. There were a few other things, too. Fear. Nerves. Worry. But she'd done it, she'd made the move to reclaim her life, and at the realization a new feeling settled into her chest, pushing out some of the anxiety.

Hope.

Nightfall hit in earnest, and she had nothing to do with herself. No WiFi, no cable. Just her imagination. When it kicked in gear, picturing the relatives of the doomed spider creeping out of the woodwork to stalk her, she hurriedly pulled out her e-reader to distract herself. It was an older model, and she had to hold up a flashlight to read by. She could've left an overhead light on, but then she'd have to get out of bed later to turn it off. This wasn't a new problem. She couldn't have said how many times in the past she'd dropped the flashlight and e-reader on her face while trying to read in bed, and sure enough, twenty minutes in, she dropped the flashlight and e-reader on her face.

Giving up, she drove into town, found a local bar and grill named, of all things, the Love Shack. She ordered a pizza, took it back to her place, and ate alone staring out the huge windows.

The view was an inky black sky, a slice of equally inky black ocean, and the alley that ran perpendicular from the street between the other warehouses.

Three guys were carrying what looked like scuba gear into Sexy Grumpy Surfer's warehouse. Three *hot* guys, one of them Sexy Grumpy Surfer himself. They were laughing and talking as they made several trips.

Interesting. Sexy Grumpy Surfer could laugh…

She watched while eating her pizza and thought maybe she didn't need cable after all.

It was quiet when, an hour later, she walked outside with the empty pizza box, down the dark alley to the Dumpster. Real dark. There was no sign of a single soul now, and Becca hummed a little tune to herself to keep from freaking out, one of her own.

Not that it helped. A sound startled her, and she nearly jumped right out of her skin.

About five feet ahead, three sets of glowing eyes turned her way.

Raccoons.

They were sitting on the Dumpster, having a feast. She laughed at herself, but swallowed her amusement when the six eyes narrowed on her, all accusatory-like. "Sorry," she said. "But I'm pretty sure you're not supposed to be foraging around back here."

The raccoon closest to her growled.

Yikes. Becca lifted her hands. "You know what? None of my business. Carry on." Whirling to leave, she had taken one step when she suddenly found herself pinned against the wall by a big, hard, sculpted, warm body, two big hands at either side of her face. She gasped in shock, and at the sound, her captor went still as well. Then his thumbs were at her jaw, forcing her to look up at him.

"It's you," he said, and she recognized his voice. Sexy Grumpy Surfer. As fast as she'd been pinned, she was unpinned. "What are you doing?" he wanted to know.

Her mouth dropped open. "What am *I* doing? How about what are *you* doing? You scared me half to death."

"I thought you were following me."

"No." But okay, she *had* been watching him earlier—two entirely different things, she told herself. "I was just talking to the raccoons—" She gestured to where they'd been rifling through the trash, but they were long gone, the traitors. Shakily she started to bend to pick up her fallen pizza box, but he retrieved it for her, tossing it into the Dumpster.

"You need to be careful," he said.

She gaped at him, her fear turning to temper. "The only danger I was in came from you!"

"Lucky Harbor might be a small town," he said, "but bad shit can happen anywhere."

"I know that," she said. And she did. She knew far more than she should.

He was in a pair of loose black sweats, battered athletic shoes, and a T-shirt that was plastered to his flat abs and broad chest with perspiration. She realized he'd been running, hard by the look of him, though he wasn't breathing all that heavily. If she hadn't been feeling so defensive, she might have thought about how sexy he looked. But she *was* feeling defensive, so she refused to notice.

Much.

"You okay?" he asked.

Well, now was a fine time for him to ask, *after* he'd nearly given her a heart attack. "Yeah, I'm okay," she said. "I'm totally okay." Because saying it twice made it so.

"It's late," he said. "You should go inside."

Becca wasn't real good at following nicely uttered requests, much less an out-and-out order. "Maybe I was going somewhere," she said.

He crossed his arms over his chest. "Were you?"

He wasn't going to intimidate her. She no longer let herself get intimidated. But it wasn't really intimidation she was feeling, not with the interesting heat churning in her belly from his nearness. Then he stepped even closer, and she forgot how to breathe, even more so when he cupped her face and tilted it up so he could study her. With a gentleness that surprised her, he stroked the pad of his thumb beneath her left eye.

"You've got a bruise on your face," he said.

She pushed his hand away. "No, I don't."

"You do." Those intensely green eyes held hers prisoner. "What happened?"

She reached up and touched the tender spot. "I was reading in bed and smacked myself with my flashlight and e-reader."

He stared at her. "Is that your version of *I ran into a door*?"

She let out a mirthless laugh, which made his frown deepen. Apparently laughing in the face of an overprotective alpha wasn't the right move. "Seriously," she said. "I did this one all on my own."

"This one?"

Well, shit. An overprotective, *sharp* alpha. "Have you ever tried to read in bed?" she asked, feeling contrary. "You hold the flashlight and e-reader above your head and if you start to fall asleep or relax, it's *smack*."

He gave one slow blink. "Maybe you should sit up when you read."

"Maybe." But she wouldn't. She loved to read while lying down in bed. Which meant that she'd be hitting herself in the face again real soon.

Sexy Grumpy Surfer didn't move, nary an inch. Then he told her why. "I'm not going anywhere until you go back inside," he said.

"Why?"

He just looked at her, and she realized that he was still in protective mode.

"Fine," she said. "Be all silent and mysterious. I'm going in." She pointed at him. "But *not* because you told me to."

His mouth twitched, but he said nothing.

"Has anyone ever told you that you have a strange sense of humor?" she asked.

"Yeah," he said. "I've heard."

Chapter 3

There was still the night's chill on the air when Becca woke up the next morning. Early sun rays were doing their best to beat back the dark shadows of the night, stabbing through the cloud layer with hints of soft yellow and orange.

She rolled the kink out of her neck from sleeping on the floor. Today was the day she further depleted her savings by buying furniture.

And other essentials, such as food.

Today was also the day that she got her act together. She stared at the portable piano keyboard leaning so deceptively casual-like against one of her suitcases.

As a jingle writer, all she had to do was write a catchy tune for a given product. That was it. Write a jingle, sell it to the ad agency that had her on retainer, and accept their thanks in the form of a check.

Except she'd been having trouble for a year now. Her muse had shriveled up on her, and she was eking out only the barest minimum to keep her agency interested. Her latest assignment was simple—come up with something catchy for Cushy toilet paper. A relatively easy and insignificant enough assignment, right?

Right.

With a sigh, she grabbed a roll of the toilet paper that the company had sent her, shoved it in her tote bag, and headed out. The first person she came across was the same boy on the bike who'd nearly hit her the other day. "Hey," she said, flagging him down.

He slowed. "Sam's probably in his warehouse—"

"No, this question's for you." She pulled out the roll of toilet paper. "Feel this. What does it make you think of?"

He blinked.

"I'm writing a commercial for it," she told him.

"That's weird," he said, but he reached out and took it. Considered. "I guess it feels nice to squeeze," he finally said.

"Good, but unfortunately, that commercial's already been done," she said. "Give me something else."

"Okay…" The kid scratched his head. "It's…soft?"

"Soft," she said.

"Yeah. You know, cushy."

She blew out a breath. "Thanks."

"I wasn't any help at all, was I?" the kid asked.

"You were great," she told him, and waved as he rode off.

She walked to the pier for more ranch-flavored popcorn, which she'd bought at the ice cream stand. The same twenty-something-year-old guy was there today.

"You're back," he said.

"Yep. You give good popcorn."

He smiled. "I know. I'm Lance, by the way."

"Becca," she said. "I'm new to town." Lance was small, painfully thin, and had an odd sound to his voice, like his chest was hollow. She glanced at the jar on the counter, with a DONATE TO CYSTIC FIBROSIS RESEARCH poster taped to it, and felt a pang of worry and empathy for him.

"So what'll it be, Becca New to Town?" he asked.

She smiled. "Ranch-flavored popcorn." She paused. "And a single chocolate scoop."

"Living large," he said. "I like it."

When he brought the popcorn and ice cream to her, she held up the roll of toilet paper. "Question," she said. "What does this make you think of?"

He laughed. "That's going to cost you a double scoop, at least." But he squeezed the roll of toilet paper. "Tell me why I'm humoring the crazy lady?"

"Because she writes the songs for commercials," Becca said. *Sometimes. If she's very lucky*. "And I need one for Cushy toilet paper. Only I'm stuck."

"So your brain's...plugged?" he asked playfully. "Your brain's got a big...load?"

She laughed. "Don't quit your day job."

He squeezed the roll again. "You know," he said casually. "I get sick a lot."

Her heart pinched. "I'm sorry."

"It's okay. But I use this brand for blowing my nose. It's softer and more gentle than tissues."

She smiled and handed back the ice cream cone she hadn't yet licked. "Okay, now *that's* worth a double."

He made it a triple.

A million calories later, she was back in her place,

and she managed to come up with a little—emphasis on little—jingle for Cushy. She sent it off to her agency, fingers crossed.

Standing up, she moved to the window and took in a most mesmerizing sight.

Not the ocean, though that was pretty damn fine, too.

But Sexy Grumpy Surfer—SGS for short, she'd decided—side by side with one of the other guys from last night, the two of them doing pull-ups on some metal bar. Given their easy, economical speed and the way they kept turning to eyeball each other, they were competing and not for the first time. They were shirtless, their toned bodies gleaming with sweat in the early-morning sun, definitely outshining the Pacific Ocean.

"Wow," she whispered. She had no idea how long she stood there, or how many impossibly difficult pull-ups the two men did before they both dropped lithely to the ground, straightened, and gave each other a shove.

Their laughter drifted to her ears and she found herself smiling along with them. A sweaty tie then, she decided, and realized she was a little hot herself.

Hot *and* bothered.

Sexy Grumpy Surfer looked damn good laughing. The other guy moved off, back toward the small building between the street and beach, but SGS remained. Turning only his head, he unerringly met Becca's gaze.

Crap. She dropped like a stone to the floor and lay flat. He hadn't seen her, she thought. He totally hadn't. The glare on the window had blocked his view. Yeah, for sure he'd missed her...

Slowly, she rose up on her knees to take a quick peek and winced.

He was still there, hands on hips, looking right at her.

He'd missed exactly *nothing*, and she suspected he rarely did.

Then the clouds shifted, and suddenly the sun was shining right on him, like he was the best of God's glory. Since the sun was also bright, making seeing details difficult, it was probably—hopefully—her imagination that his mouth quirked in a barely there smile as he shook his head at her.

Her stomach quivering, she ducked again.

And then from her position prone on the floor, she forbid herself from looking out the window ever again.

Ever.

Crawling to her suitcases in the center of the loft, she sat cross-legged, pulled out her list of Must-Buys, and added curtains. Curtains would keep her from being distracted by her view. Curtains would keep her on task.

And away from further embarrassment.

She showered, dressed, and left the warehouse, sending a cautious look down the alley.

Empty.

Relieved, she left. Several hours later she was back, followed by Eddie, the kid on the bike, whom she'd paid to help lug her loot. Thankfully he came with an older brother who had a truck, and equally thankfully, Lucky Harbor had a "vintage" shop, a really great one. She'd found everything she'd needed there, including gently used sheets that she bought for curtains.

In far less time than it'd taken to shop, she had curtains up and the bed made, and she was sitting on it, staring at an email from her ad agency.

Becca,

  The Cushy jingle works. I've sent accounting a request to get you payment. Next up is Diaxsis, the new erectile dysfunction medicine. Details and deadline info attached, if you're interested.

Not *Great job, Becca.* Not *You're back, Becca.* Not *We've put you back on our top tier, Becca.*

But neither was it *You're fired, Becca,* so she'd take it. But Diaxsis? She blew out a breath and hit REPLY:

I'm interested.

The next morning, Becca opened her eyes and let out a happy breath. She'd actually slept, and if there'd been bad dreams, she didn't remember them. Turning her head, she stared at the curtains where a weak daylight poked in around the edges.

The insulation in her building was either poor or nonexistent. She could hear every single time the back door of the building next to hers opened.

It opened now.

Don't do it, she told herself. *Don't go look. You're stronger than this. You don't need the distraction...*

But like Pavlov's dog, she got up and peeked through the curtains.

It was foggy out, but the bigger news was that Sexy Grumpy Surfer was back. It looked chilly, and yet he was in another pair of board shorts and a T-shirt that hugged the width of his shoulders as they flexed enticingly while he dumped the contents of a shop vac into the trash bin.

Sex on a stick.

He didn't look up this time, and Becca forced herself away from the window. She showered, ate the leftover ranch-flavored popcorn—breakfast of champions—and gave her keyboard a long, hard look. "Today," she told it. "Today, you give me something better than *It works*."

Sitting on the bed, leaning back against the wall, she pulled the keyboard onto her lap.

A year. A year since she'd composed jingles for the best national brands, and the reasons why were complicated. She'd lost her muse, and her footing. On life. That had to change. Hence the across-the-country move. A new venue, a new beginning. But she still needed to prove herself, if only to the woman in the mirror.

Her parents wouldn't ask her to prove herself, she knew this. Growing up, they'd never asked anything of her, other than to take care of her brother while they worked crazy hours in the jazz clubs of New Orleans. *Watch Jase*, that's all they'd ever expected her to do.

Though only two years separated her and her brother, Becca felt far older, always had. She'd done her best to take care of him, succeeding better at some moments than others. But at least the promise of his talent had been fulfilled. He was a wonderful concert pianist.

Now she wanted, *needed*, to be wonderful at something, too.

And yeah, yeah, being worthy shouldn't be tied up in financial success—or lack thereof—blah blah. But whoever had said that had clearly never had to pay their rent on time.

Her cell phone vibrated. The screen said *Jase calling*.

Until recently, they'd been close, and had talked frequently. Except, just like her early—and short-lived—success with jingle writing, this too had turned out to be an illusion. A glossy veneer shown to the world, while the truth was hidden deep inside them both.

She stared at the phone until it went to voice mail.

Two seconds later came a text. *You okay?*

Completely okay, she texted back. Liar, liar, pants on fire…

But hell if she'd give anyone she cared about more stress to deal with. She turned her phone off, ignored the guilt, and spent the rest of the day alternating between nesting in her new place and trying to work a jingle about the male erection.

And maybe, also, looking out her windows a little bit. She told herself it was the ocean that drew her, but mostly her gaze was drawn to the alley. In addition to the pull-ups, she'd now seen Sexy Grumpy Surfer carrying a large duffel bag to the boat moored at the dock, washing down said boat with the same two other guys she'd seen before, and taking a hard, brutally fast run along the beach with yet a third guy.

Seemed like maybe Lucky Harbor was a hot-guy magnet.

By the end of the day, Becca needed sustenance and a change of scenery, so she headed into town. She could've gone to the diner Eat Me, but instead she walked a block farther, past the pier, to go back to the Love Shack.

She told herself it was the atmosphere. The place was done up like an Old West saloon, with walls lined with old mining tools, tables made from antique wood doors. Lanterns hung from the exposed beam ceiling, and the air was filled with laughter, talking, and music from the jukebox in the corner.

She ordered a burger and sat by herself to eyeball the *real* reason she'd come back here—the baby grand piano in the far corner. It was old, and had clearly been around the block decades ago, but it called to her. She stared at it, torn between wanting to stroke it, and wanting to run like hell.

Jase might the real talent of the Thorpe family, but there'd been a time when the two of them had been a duo. Maybe she'd never been quite as good as he was—not that her parents had ever said so, they didn't have to—but she'd been good enough to boost Jase's talent. The press latched on to them early, and they'd even become pseudo-celebrities.

Things had been good, until she'd turned seventeen. With that age had come some self-awareness, and a serious case of the awkwards. Besides the headaches and bone aches that had come with a late, fast growth spurt, she'd lost all coordination, including her fingertips. Practically overnight she'd turned into the Graceless Ugly Duckling, exemplified.

The following month, their manager had gotten them invited to compete at the prestigious Walt Disney Concert Hall in Los Angeles. The place had been filled with people—more than two thousand—and all Becca remembered was being struck by sheer, heart-stopping panic.

She'd tanked, and the press had ripped them to shreds.

Shaking off the memory, Becca paid for her food at the bar and took in the sign at the register that said: HELP WANTED. She glanced at the piano and gnawed her lower lip. Then she gestured for the bartender. "Who do I talk to about the job?"

"Me," he said with a smile as he set aside the glass he'd

been drying to shake her hand. "I'm Jax Cullen, one of the owners."

"Is it a hostess position?" she asked hopefully.

"Waitressing," he said. "You interested?"

Was she? She glanced at the piano and *ached*. And she knew she was *very* interested, skills or not. And there were no skills. None. "I am if you are," she said.

Jax lost his smile. "Shit. You don't have any experience."

"No," she admitted. "But I'm a real quick learner."

He studied her, and Becca did her best to look like someone who was one hundred percent capable of doing anything—except, of course, handling her own life. She flashed him her most charming smile, her "showtime" smile, and hoped for the best.

Jax chuckled. "You're spunky," he said. "I'll give you that."

"I'm more than spunky," she promised. "I bet you by the end of my first night, you'll want to keep me."

He held her gaze a moment, considering. "All right, I'll take that bet. How about a trial by fire starting now?"

She eyed the room. Not full. Not even close. "Who else is working?"

"Usually on a night like this, two others. But both my girls are out sick tonight and I'm on my own, so you're looking like good timing to me. If you're any good."

The piano in the far corner was still calling to her, making her braver than usual. "I'm in," she said.

Jax gave her an apron and a quick rundown of what was expected. He told her that here in Lucky Harbor, familiarity was key. Everyone knew everyone, and the trick to good service—and good tips—was friendliness.

Then he threw her to the wolves.

The first half hour remained thankfully slow, but every time she walked by the baby grand, she faltered.

Play me, Becca...

At about the twentieth pass, she paused and glanced around. Not a soul was looking at her. She eyed the piano again, sitting there so innocuously, looking gorgeous. Damn. She'd played on her keyboard, but not a piano. Not since two years ago when she'd quit. She'd had a near miss with going back to playing a year ago, but then things had gone to all sorts of hell, reinforcing her stage fright and giving her a wicked case of claustrophobia to boot.

Play me, Becca...

Fine. Since fighting the urge was like trying not to need air, she sat. Her heart sped up, but she was still breathing. So far so good. She set her fingertips on the cool keys.

Still good.

And almost before she realized it, she'd begun playing a little piece she'd written for Jase years ago. It flowed out of her with shocking ease, and when she finished, she blinked like she was waking from a trance. Then she looked around.

Jax was smiling at her from behind the bar and when he caught her eye, he gave her a thumbs-up. Oh, God. Breaking out in a sweat, she jumped up and raced into the bathroom to stare at herself in the mirror. Flushed. Shaky. She thought about throwing up, but then someone came in to use the facilities and she decided she couldn't throw up with an audience. So she splashed cold water on her hot face, told herself she was totally fine, and then got back to work to prove it.

Luckily, the dinner crowd hit and she got too busy to think. She worked the friendliness as best she could. But she quickly discovered it wasn't a substitute for talent. In the first hour, she spilled a pitcher of beer down herself, mixed up two orders—and in doing so nearly poisoned someone when she gave the cashew-allergic customer a cashew chicken salad—and then undercharged a large group by thirty bucks.

Jax stepped in to help her, but by then she was frazzled beyond repair. "Listen," he said very kindly, considering, "maybe you should stick with playing. You're amazing on the piano. Can you sing?"

"No," she said, and grimaced. "Well, yes." But she *couldn't* stick with playing, because she couldn't play in front of an audience without having heart failure. "I really can do this waitressing thing," she said.

Jax shook his head but kept his voice very gentle. "You're not cut out for this job, Becca. And there's nothing wrong with that."

She was beginning to think she wasn't cut out for her life, but she met his gaze evenly, her own determined. "I bet you, remember? By the end of the night, you'll see. Please? One more try?"

He looked at her for a long moment and then sighed. "Okay, then. One more try."

A group of three guys walked in the door and took a table. Fortifying her courage, Becca gathered menus and strode over there with a ready-made smile, which congealed when she saw who it was.

Sexy Grumpy Surfer and his two cohorts.

Bolstering herself, she set the menus on the table. "Welcome, gentlemen."

SGS was sprawled back in his chair, long legs stretched out in front of him crossed at the ankles, his sun-streaked hair unruly as ever, looking like sin personified as he took her in. She did her best to smile, ignoring the butterflies suddenly fluttering low in her belly. "What can I get you to start?"

"Pitcher of beer. And you're new," one of them said, the one with the sweetest smile and the bluest eyes she'd ever seen. He had short brown hair he'd forgotten to comb, some scruff on a square jaw, and was wearing cargo pants and a polo shirt with a small screwdriver sticking out of the breast pocket. "I'm Cole," he told her, "and this big lug here…" He gestured to the dark-haired, dark-eyed, darkly dangerously good-looking guy next to him. "Tanner." Then he jerked his chin toward SGS. "You apparently already know this one."

"Yes," Becca said. "SGS."

They all just looked at her.

"Sexy Grumpy Surfer," she clarified.

Cole and Tanner burst out laughing.

SGS just gave her a long, steady, paybacks-are-a-bitch smile.

"Or Grandpa," Cole offered. "That's what we call him because he always seems to know the weirdest shit."

"And Grandma works, too," Tanner said. "When he's being a chick. No offense."

Sam sent them each a look that would've had Becca peeing her pants, but neither man looked particularly worried.

"And your name?" Cole asked Becca.

She opened her mouth, but before she could answer Sam spoke for her. "Peeper," he said. "Her name is Peeper."

His steely but amused gaze held hers as he said this, which is how Becca finally saw him smile. It transformed his face, softening it, and though he was already ridiculously attractive, the smile—trouble-filled as it was—only made him all the more so. It gave her a little quiver in her tummy, which, as she couldn't attribute it to either hunger or nerves, was not a good sign.

"Peeper," Tanner repeated slowly, testing it on his tongue. "That's unusual."

Still holding Becca's gaze, Sam said, "It's a nickname, because she—"

"It's my big eyes," Becca broke in with before he could tell his friends that she'd been caught red-handed watching them like a...well, peeper. "Yeah," she said. "I've bowled him over with my...peepers."

Sam startled her by laughing, and the sound did something odd and wonderful and horrifying deep inside her, all at the same time. Unbelievably, she could feel herself standing on the precipice of a crush on this guy. She'd been attracted before, of course, plenty of times, but it'd been a while since she'd taken the plunge.

A long while.

She hoped the water was nice, because she could feel the pull of it and knew she was going in.

Chapter 4

♥

When Becca was called to the bar, Sam watched her go, sass in every step. She was in one of those flimsy, gauzy skirts that flirted with a woman's thighs, and a stretchy white top. Her hair was piled on top of her head, but strands had escaped, flying around her flushed face and clinging to her neck. She'd clearly had a rough night because she appeared to be wearing both beer and barbecue sauce.

"Cute," Tanner said, also watching.

"She's off limits," Sam said, and when they both looked at him in surprise, he shrugged. "We're concentrating on business right now."

Tanner coughed and said "bullshit" at the same time.

"It does feel like Grandma here's holding out on us," Cole said, still watching Sam.

Sam didn't want to get into the real reason, which he told himself was that clearly Becca was trying to get her footing, and yeah, she put off a tough, I've-got-this vibe, but there was something about her that told him it was a facade. "She's new to town," he said. "Let her settle before you start sniffing around her."

"I will if you will," Tanner said with a smile. It faded when he caught Sam's long look. "Kidding," he said. "Jesus. Hands off your Peeper, got it."

The nickname of course had jackshit to do with her eyes—though they were indeed big and luminous. They were also a warm, melted milk chocolate, and filled with more than a little trouble.

Sam wasn't opposed to trouble. In fact, he was absolutely all for it.

When *he* was the one causing it.

But this woman was trouble in her own right. He'd been amused at catching her watching him from her window—several times—but it wasn't amusement he felt now. Because this was the second time he'd been within touching distance, and it was now two for two that she'd sucked him in. It wasn't her looks, though she was pretty in a girl-next-door way. Nor was it her feistiness and ability to laugh at herself.

Instead it was something else, something he suspected had to do with the singular flash of vulnerability he'd caught in her eyes.

She wasn't quite as tough as she wanted the world to believe.

And hell. *That* drew him. Because Sam knew all too well what it was like to not be nearly as tough as you needed to be. Something he didn't like to think about. "We doing this or what?" he asked the guys. "We have shit to decide."

"Anyone ever tell you that you're a fun sucker?" Tanner asked.

Sam slid him a look, and Tanner blew out a breath. "Shit. Yeah, we're doing this."

Cole lifted a shoulder and nodded.

Neither of them liked these weekly business meetings, but if they didn't have them, then all the hard decisions were left to Sam. He was good at making hard decisions in his life—he'd had to be—but this was about the three of them, equal partners. "So we agree," he said. "We're hiring someone to take over the crap none of us wants to do."

"Told you," Cole said. "Ad's in the paper."

"You get any calls yet?"

"Yes," Cole said. "Lucille."

Lucille was a thousand years old and the local gossip queen. She had a heart of gold, but a nose made for butting into other people's business. "No," Sam said. Hell no.

"Way ahead of you," Cole told him. "Especially after she said she couldn't wait to sit on the beach and take pics of us on and off the boat for her Pinterest Sexy Guys page. She thought she could manage our phones and scheduling in between her photography. She said something about hoping we go shirtless, and us signing something that allows her to use our images for—and I'm quoting here—the good of women's mental health everywhere."

"Christ," Tanner muttered.

"I told her we had an age requirement," Cole said, "and that our new admin had to be under the age of seventy."

"How did she take that?" Sam asked.

"She was bummed, said even her fake ID showed seventy-five, but that she understood."

Becca arrived with their pitcher of beer, except it wasn't beer at all; it looked like…strawberry margaritas.

"You all decide on your order?" she asked, setting down three glasses.

"New Orleans," Cole said, watching Tanner pour himself a strawberry margarita.

Becca looked startled. "What?"

"You're originally from New Orleans," Cole said.

She stared at him. "How did you know that?"

"You're good, but I'm better," Cole said. "I can hear it real faint in your voice."

"Ignore him," Tanner said, toasting her with his glass. "He's a freak."

"A freak who knows we didn't order a chick drink," Cole said as Tanner sipped at his strawberry margarita.

Becca gasped. "Oh, crap. This isn't yours." She nabbed the glass right out of Tanner's hand. "I'm sorry. Don't move."

She snatched the pitcher as well and vanished.

"She *is* cute," Cole said. "Not much of a waitress, though."

"She's not as bad as Tanya," Tanner said. "She stole from you."

"Borrowed," Cole corrected. "I let her *borrow* some money for her mom, who was going to lose her home in Atlanta."

"Did you ever get your money back?" Tanner asked mildly.

Cole pulled out his phone and eyed the dark screen as if wishing for a call.

Tanner rolled his eyes. "You didn't. You let her walk with three grand of your hard-earned money. Oh, and by the way, I've got some land to sell you. Swamp land. It's on sale, just for you."

Sam shoved his iPad under their noses before a fight could break out. He didn't mind a good fight now and then, but Jax and Ford, the owners of the Love Shack, frowned on it happening inside their bar. "If you two idiots are done, we're in the middle of a financial meeting here."

"You're right," Tanner said, and straightened in his seat. "Give it to us, Grandma."

Sam gave him a long look. "It's a good thing I'm too hungry to kick your ass."

He'd been in charge of their money since their rig days. Back then, there'd been four of them: himself, Tanner, Cole, and Gil, the lot of them pretty much penniless. But thanks to his dad's unique ability to squander his every last penny, Sam had learned to handle money by the age of ten. He'd been tight-fisted with their earnings, squirreling them away—earning him that *Grandma* moniker. He'd shut his friends up when, at the end of the first year, he'd shown them their savings balance.

They'd had a goal, their dream—the charter company, and their seven years at sea had been extremely profitable.

And deadly.

They'd lost Gil. Just the thought brought the low, dull ache of his passing back as a fresh knife stab, and Sam drew a breath until it passed.

They'd nearly lost Tanner in that rig fire as well. Tanner still limped and was damn lucky to have his leg at all, something Sam tried not to think about. "We talked about expanding," he said, "hiring on more people and buying a new boat."

"When we have the money for it," Tanner said. He was their resident pessimist. Never met a situation he liked. "We said we'd revisit the issue when we were ready. No loan payments."

Sam hadn't been the only one to grow up on the wrong side of the poverty line. "No loans," he said.

Cole hadn't taken his eyes off Sam. "You already spend all your time bitching and moaning about not having enough hours in the day to make your boats," he reminded him. "You'd have heart failure if we expanded our business right now. Have you updated your will? You left everything to me, right?"

"We start with more staff," Sam said, ignoring him. "Office help first, then hire on an additional crew." He pointed at both Cole and Tanner. "You guys are in charge of that."

"Why us?" Tanner asked.

"Because I'm busy making you rich," Sam said.

Becca was back, with a pitcher of beer this time, and a huge plate of nachos, chicken wings, and pesto chips. "Your order," she said.

The guys all looked at each other, and Becca paused. "What?" she asked.

"We didn't order yet," Sam said.

"Oh for the love of—" She slapped Tanner's hand before he could snatch a nacho, picked up the platter *and* the beers, and once again vanished.

She was back a breathless moment later, looking flushed as she held her order pad. "Okay, let's start over. I'm Becca, your server for tonight."

"You sure?" Sam asked.

She let out a theatrical sigh. "Listen, I'm not exactly in

my natural habitat here." Suddenly she straightened and gave them a dazzling smile as she spoke out of the corner of her mouth. "Quick, everyone look happy with your service. My hopefully new boss is watching. I made a bet with him that I could handle this job and I have tonight to prove it."

Sam craned his neck and saw Jax at the bar, watching Becca. "It'd help if you were actually serving," he said.

"Working on that," she said, and vanished.

The three of them watched her go for a moment. She went straight to the bar, smiled at Jax, grabbed a tray of drinks, and then brought them to a table. That she had to take drinks right out of a few people's hand and switch them to someone else's made Cole and Tanner chuckle.

"She can't serve worth shit," Tanner said. "But she does have a great smile. And those eyes. Man, it's like when she looks at you, you're the only one she sees."

Sam watched her take an order from the table. One of the customers said something and she tossed her head back and laughed. Not a fake I-want-your-tips laugh, but a genuine, contagious one that made everyone at the table join her.

Cole and Tanner were right. She *was* cute. And as he already knew from catching her staring at him several times now, she absolutely had a way of making a guy feel like he was the only one she saw.

She left the table and vanished into the back, coming out a moment later with a tray laden with plates of food. The muscles in her shoulders and arms strained as she moved, and Sam found himself holding his breath. Maybe she did suck as a waitress, but no one could deny that she was working her tail off. She got all the way to the back table before she dumped the tray.

Down the front of herself.

The man closest to her must have gotten sprayed because he flew to his feet and held his shirt out from his body, jaw tight. He said something low and undoubtedly harsh given the look on Becca's face as she bent to clean up the mess. Grabbing her elbow, he gave her a little shake, and before Sam gave it a second thought, he was on his feet and at Becca's back.

"You're the worst waitress I've ever seen," the guy was yelling. "You are nowhere near good enough for this job."

The barb hit. Sam could tell by the way Becca took a step back as if slapped, bumping right into him.

"You're going to pay for the dry cleaning of this shirt, do you hear me?" the guy went on.

"Hard not to," Sam said, steadying Becca. "Since you're braying like a jackass."

Becca slid Sam a look that said she could handle this. When he didn't budge, she made a sound of annoyance and turned back to the pissed-off customer. "I'm sorry," she said. "And of course I'll pay for your dry cleaning." Then she bent again to clean up.

Sam crouched down to help her scoop the fallen plates onto the tray, but she pushed at him. "I've got this," she whispered. But she was trembling, and her breath hitched. "Stop, Sam. I don't need you to help," she insisted when he kept doing just that.

He'd disagree with her, but that would only back her into a corner. So he continued on in silence, and then when she vanished into the kitchen, he went back to his table.

Tanner and Cole were grinning at him.

"What?"

"You tell us what," Cole said.

"I was just helping."

"No, helping would be going into the kitchen and wrangling us up some burgers," Tanner said, rubbing his belly. "I'm starving."

Sam shook his head and turned on his iPad again. "Where were we?"

"You were playing hero," Tanner said.

Sam ignored this. "Our boat fund will hit its projected mark this year," he said.

Both Cole and Tanner blinked at him.

"You're serious," Tanner finally said. "You really did manage to pay us and save a mint while you were at it."

"Do I ever joke about money?" Sam asked.

"Holy shit," Cole said. "Just how much are we making anyway?"

Sam thumbed through the iPad, brought up their receivables, and shoved the screen across the table.

They all stared at the numbers and Tanner let out a low whistle.

"Why the hell are you so surprised?" Sam asked, starting to get insulted. "I send you both weekly updates. Between all the chartering and the profits from the boats I've been building, we're doing good."

Both Cole and Tanner still just stared at him, and Sam shook his head in disgust. "I could be ripping you guys off, you ever think of that?"

"Yeah," Cole said. "Except you're a terrible liar and you're not nearly greedy enough."

Needing the beer Becca had taken away, Sam went to

the bar for a pitcher. The bar was crazier than usual, and Sam realized he saw only a hungry crowd and no sign of Becca at all. He took the pitcher back to his table and poured.

"To Gil," Cole said, and as they always did, they drank to Gil's memory.

A few minutes later, wondering if maybe Becca had gotten her sweet ass fired, Sam stepped into the hall and found her standing there with her back to him, hugging herself with one arm, the other hand holding her cell phone to her ear.

"No, I can't come play at your concert," she was saying. "I'm— They're paying *how* much?" She paused. "Wow, but no. I can't— Yeah, I'm fine. In fact, I've got my toes in the sand right this very minute, so you just concentrate on you, okay?" She paused. "The noise? Uh…it's the waves. It's high tide."

This was when she turned and caught sight of Sam standing there. Flushing a deep red, she held his gaze. "Gotta go, Jase. The whitecaps are kicking up and it's making my muse kick into gear." She lowered her voice and covered her mouth and the phone, but Sam heard her whisper, "And *don't* come out here. Okay? I'm good. Really, really good. So just stay where you are." She disconnected and made herself busy stuffing the phone into her pocket before flashing Sam her waitress smile. "I think your order's almost up."

"How would you know? You've got your toes in the sand."

She drooped a little. "Yeah. I'm probably going to hell for that one."

"Jase?" he asked.

"My brother." She sighed. "You know families."

Yeah, Sam knew families. He knew families weren't necessarily worth shit, at least not blood families. He wondered what her story was, but before he could ask, she sent him one last shaky smile and walked away.

Chapter 5

It was two thirty in the morning when the bar finally got quiet. Becca was cleaning up, or supposed to be, but really she was staring at the piano again.

It was always like this. She'd be drawn by the scent of the gleaming wood, the keys, the beauty of losing herself in the music.

And then she'd sit and the anxiety would nearly suffocate her.

It'd taken her ten years of playing, from age seventeen to twenty-seven, ten years of needing anxiety meds to get on stage, before she'd admitted she didn't have the heart for that life. She might have said so sooner but her brother had needed her, and her parents had depended on her being there for him. A painful crush on their manager Nathan had only added to the pressure. The crush had eventually evolved into a relationship, but when that had failed, she'd walked away from the life.

That had been two years ago.

She'd been working at an ad agency ever since, writing jingles for commercials. Behind the scenes really worked for her, though about a year ago, Jase had hit rock bottom and Nathan had come to her, pressuring her to give their world another go.

She'd refused, but the aftermath from that confrontation had killed off her muse but good.

Becca had promised herself that she'd never again duet in any capacity. Especially relationships.

Now, at age twenty-nine, she decided she was all the wiser for that decision, and not missing anything.

Play me, Becca...

Once again she looked around, and when she saw no one watching, she allowed herself to sit. Before she knew it, her fingers were moving, this time playing one of the first songs she'd ever learned, "Für Elise" by Beethoven. She'd been twelve and had eavesdropped on Jase's lessons. He'd hated practicing, but not Becca. She'd been happy practicing for hours.

When she finished, she sat there a moment, alone in the bar, and smiled. No urge to throw up! Progress! Getting up, she grabbed her things from the back, turned to go, and found Jax standing there.

"You going to freak out again if I tell you that you're really good?" he asked quietly.

"At waitressing?" she asked hopefully.

"No, you suck at that."

She sighed.

He smiled and handed her an envelope. "The night's pay."

She looked down at it, then back at his face. "I'm not invited back, am I?"

He gave her a small smile. "Did you really want to be?"

She blew out a breath. "No."

His smile widened, and he gently tugged at a loose strand of her hair. "Come play piano anytime you want. You'll make bank in tips." He looked at her. "Breathe, Becca."

She sucked in a few breaths. "I'm not ready for that."

His eyes were warm and understanding. "When you are then."

She laughed softly, unable to imagine when that might be. "Thanks, Jax."

"You going to be okay?" he asked.

A lot of people asked that question, but few really wanted to hear an honest answer. She could tell Jax genuinely did. But being okay was her motto, so she mustered a smile. "Always," she said.

She walked home, let herself into her building, and then stopped short when she realized that the middle apartment, the one next to hers, was open. The front door was thrown wide, and from inside came a bunch of colorful swearing in a frustrated female voice.

Becca tiptoed past her own door and peeked inside the middle unit. There were lights blaring, boxes stacked everywhere, and in the center of the mess stood a young woman about her own age, hands on hips, surveying the chaos.

"Hi," Becca said, knocking on the doorjamb. "You okay?"

The woman whipped around to face Becca, a baseball bat in her hands before Becca could so much as blink. She took one look at Becca, let out a short breath, and lowered the bat. "Who are you?" she demanded.

Becca let out her own shaky breath. She was good with a bat, too, but it was one thing to have it in your hands, say at a softball game. It was another thing entirely to be in danger of having it wielded at your head. "I'm Becca Thorpe," she said. "Your neighbor. And I recognize you. You were working at the vintage store where I spent a fortune the other day."

"Oh. Yeah." The woman grimaced and set the bat aside. She was petite, with dark hair and dark eyes. Caucasian features but she looked somehow exotic as well. Beautiful. And wary. She was wearing low-slung jeans, a halter top, and a bad attitude as she dropped the bat. "Sorry if I woke you."

"You didn't," Becca said. "I'm just getting home from being fired from my first day on the job at the bar." She smiled, thinking that she would get one in return, but she didn't.

"Olivia Bentley," the woman said. "Sorry about the job, I'll try to keep it down in here."

"It's okay. I just moved in, too. Need some help?"

"No."

"You sure?" Becca asked. "Because I—"

"*No*," Olivia repeated, and then sighed. "But thank you," she added as she moved toward the door in a not-so-subtle invite for Becca to leave.

"Okay then." Becca took one step backward, out of the doorway and into the hall. "Well, good—"

The door shut on her face.

"—Night," she finished. Apparently, she wasn't the only one having a rough day.

Sam told himself he was too busy to be curious about Becca over the next few days. He and the guys took a client for an overnight deep-sea fishing trip. They also

had two scuba trips. They were running ragged, but that was the nature of the beast for the summer season.

Not much of a sleeper, he tended to stay up late, which is when he did the paperwork required for the business, and his boatbuilding. He liked to do both alone. In fact, he liked to *be* alone.

He'd noticed that there were now curtains on the lower windows of the building kitty-corner to his. And that sometimes, he could hear the strains of a piano playing. The classical music wasn't something he'd have thought was his type, but he found himself keeping his own music off in order to hear more of it.

He also noted that when he ate at the bar and grill, there were no pretty, curvy, charismatic brunette waitresses spilling beer and mixing up orders.

Telling himself to stop noticing such things at all, he was in the office of his shop working on his laptop on finances. His own, and the few others he took care of. One of those very people walked in about an hour later.

Amelia Donovan had her latest investment statements in hand.

"I need an English translation," she said, and tossed the statements onto his desk.

Amelia was Cole's mom. And in some ways, maybe the best of ways, she was also Sam's. He'd landed with her one of the times that his dad had screwed up enough that social services had stepped in. Once Amelia had gotten him, she'd made sure she was his only foster care after that, which meant that for most of Sam's trouble-filled teenage years, he'd seesawed between his dad's place and Cole's.

Sam hadn't been easy.

Actually, he'd been the opposite of easy.

But Amelia had accepted him in her house without fuss up until age seventeen, when he'd left to go work on the rigs in the Gulf. She'd even forgiven him when Cole had given up a promising college baseball career to follow him. She was a born caretaker, handling her large family with the perfect mixture of drill-sergeant and mama-bear instincts. She easily kept track of everyone, from their birthdays, to their coming and goings, to whom they were dating. She always knew if her little chicks were bored, happy, upset, or hurting.

What she couldn't ever seem to do was balance her own checkbook.

Cole's dad had passed away the previous year from a heart attack, and Sam had been doing the banking for Amelia, handling all her other finances as well. But the reality was, he'd been doing that for years anyway. She'd retired from her high school teaching job and was still doing okay, a feat she attributed entirely to Sam, always saying that she owed him.

She didn't owe him shit.

Sam didn't care how much money he'd made her in investments, he could never repay the debt of having her watch out for him and keep him on the straight and narrow.

Or at least as straight and narrow as he got…

He picked up the statements and looked at her. "It's late. You okay?"

"Yes. I just got held up watching *The Voice*." A natural beauty, Amelia had turned fifty last year, but looked a decade younger. Cole had gotten all of his charm and easy charisma from her. She was barely five feet tall, of Irish descent, and had the temperament to go with it.

And a backbone of pure steel.

Sam handed her back the statements. "The English version is that you made a shitload of money this quarter, so no worries."

She nodded, but didn't smile as he'd intended.

"What?" he asked.

"Nothing." But she was clearly biting her tongue about something.

He knew her well and braced himself, because that look meant she had something on her mind and there'd be no peace until it came out. "Just say it," he said.

"I heard that your father called you." Her sweet blue gaze was filled with worry. "Is it true?"

Well, shit. There was no love lost between Amelia and Mark, mostly because Amelia had always had to clean up Mark's mess—that mess being Sam. It didn't matter that he and his dad had lived in Seattle. She'd made the two-hour drive and claimed him whenever he'd needed her.

"Sam," she said. "Is it true? Did Mark call you?"

"Listen, it's late," he said, trying to head off a discussion he didn't want to have. "Let me walk you out—"

"It's a simple enough question, Samuel."

He grimaced at his full name, the one only *she* used. Pulling in the big guns. "Yeah, he called. I call him, too, you know that."

Her eyes went from worried mom to very serious mom. "Honey, I need you to tell me you weren't stupid enough to give him another penny."

"You know, it lowers a person's self-esteem to call them stupid," he said with mock seriousness.

"Damn it!" Amelia stalked to the door that led to a hallway and into the small kitchen.

Against his better judgment, Sam followed, watching as she bypassed the fridge, going straight for the freezer, exclaiming wordlessly when she found it empty.

"You used to always keep vodka around," she muttered. "Where's the vodka?" She turned to him, hands on hips. "Sometimes a woman needs a damn vodka, Sam."

He knew that. He also knew that sometimes a man needed a damn vodka. For a long time after Gil's death, vodka had soothed his pain. Too much. When he'd realized that, he'd cut it off cold turkey. It'd sucked.

These days, he stuck with the occasional beer and did his best not to think too much. "I've got soda," he said. "Chips. Cookies. Name your poison."

"*Vodka*."

He sighed and strode over to her, shutting the freezer, pulling her from it and enveloping her in his arms. "I'm okay. You know that, right?"

She tipped her head back to look up into his face. "Does it happen often?"

"Me being okay? Yes."

She smacked him on the chest. "I meant your dad. Does he call you often then?"

"I call him every week," Sam said.

Her gaze said she got the distinction, and the fact that Sam was usually the instigator didn't make her any happier. "And do you give him money?" she asked.

"When he needs it."

She gave a troubled sigh. "Oh, Sam."

"Look, he's getting older and he's feeling his mortality," he said. "He's got a silly, frivolous woman, and a baby coming—"

"Which is ridiculous—"

"—And he realizes he fucked up with his first kid."

"You think?" She cupped his face. "Sam, I don't like this. I don't like him taking from you. He's done nothing but take from you, and I know damn well it affects your relationships. Because of him, you let women in your life here and there, but you don't let yourself fully rely on anyone, ever. That isn't healthy, Sam. Is Becca any different?"

He thought of the only woman who'd caught his eye lately. Becca. She certainly wasn't the type of woman to rely on anyone. "I think she might be," he said.

"But will you be able to rely on her? That's what a woman will want, Sam. For you to do the same."

He gave a short laugh. "You're way ahead of yourself."

"Well, I worry about you," she said. "All of you."

"Marry off all those crazy daughters of yours, and then we'll talk," Sam told her.

"You're changing the subject on me."

"Trying." He sighed at the dark look she shot him. "Look, I don't like that he's getting older and feeling regrets. Or that he doesn't have enough money to support that kid. He's my dad. What would you have me do?"

Amelia sighed and shook her head. Then she went up on tiptoe and kissed his cheek. "I know better than to argue with you. I'd do better bashing my head up against the wall."

He smiled, as this was true. "So you'll leave me alone about it?"

"No." She kissed his other cheek. "But I'll give you some peace. For now."

It was nearly midnight when she left, with one last long hug that Sam endured. When he was alone, he shut the laptop and hit the lights. Bed was the smart decision but he was far from tired. Thinking about his dad had dredged up some shit he didn't want dredged.

He needed to expel his pent-up energy. Usually he did this by running with Ben, a longtime friend from town. Like Sam, Ben appreciated the art of not talking much, which meant they were well suited as running partners, but Ben wasn't sleeping alone these days, and it was too late to call. So, restless and edgy, Sam hit the beach by himself, pushing himself hard. He tried to clear his mind, but things kept popping into his head.

Love ya, son.

It drove him crazy how his dad threw around the words like they meant nothing. Love, real love, would have protected him from being taken from their home due to neglect. Real love would have forgotten the stupid get-rich-quick schemes that never came through and attempted to keep a job so they had a roof over their heads and food in their kitchen.

Sam shook off the bleak memories and kept running. The past didn't matter. The here and now mattered. Building boats. Running the charter business. Coming through for Cole and Tanner the way they'd always come through for him.

But the past was a sneaky bitch, and for some reason, tonight he couldn't escape her. Not even an hour later when he was back where he started, standing on the sand in front of their hut, breathing heavily.

A sliver of a moon cast the beach in a blue glow, allowing him to see the small shadow sitting on the sand a few feet away.

Becca.

Chapter 6

Sam stood still for a beat, thinking that if he was smart, he'd turn and get the hell off the beach without saying a word. Not when he was this wild on the inside, this edgy.

But apparently he wasn't smart at all because his feet didn't budge.

She wore an oversized sweatshirt and flannel PJ bottoms, her arms wrapped around her legs, a tiny little gold ring encircling one of her bare toes. Under her tough-girl exterior, she was soft and sweet, and had a smile that moved him.

Her body moved him, too, and again he told himself to keep going and not look back.

And again, he didn't budge. She looked like a quiet, calm, sexy-as-hell oasis, and she was drawing him in without even trying. "Thought Lucky Harbor was just a pit stop," he said over the sound of the surf hitting the sand. "But you're still here."

Becca tilted her head back and leveled him with those melting dark eyes. "Appears that way."

"In your PJs," he noted.

She looked down at herself. "It's my Man-Repellent. Guaranteed to deflect a guy's interest with a single glance."

The PJs were baggy, but there was a breeze plastering the material to her body, which was a complete show-stopper. He laughed softly, and she narrowed her eyes. "What?" she asked.

"Let's just say they're not as bad as you think."

She blinked, then lowered her gaze, taking the time to carefully brush some sand from her feet.

It occurred to him that he was making her nervous by looming over her, so he shifted back a foot or so and crouched low to make himself nonthreatening. He added a smile.

She visibly relaxed. "You probably shouldn't flash that smile at me too often," she said.

"Why?"

"It's…attractive," she admitted. "You're attractive. Which you damn well know."

"But I'm wearing my woman-repellent gear," he said, and she laughed. It was a really great laugh.

He'd felt the pull of their chemistry from the very beginning, and had wondered if she did as well. No need to wonder now; it was all over her, however reluctantly she felt it. He needed to walk away now, before this got any more out of hand.

Instead, he spoke. "Is there a reason you want me to be repelled?" he asked.

"You mean am I crazy, or in a relationship?"

"Yeah," he said. "Either of those."

"Not in a relationship." She smiled a little thinly. "Jury's still out on the crazy thing, though. You?"

He gave a slow shake of his head. "Negative on both."

She dropped the eye contact first, instead taking in his body in a way that revved his engines. "Do you always run that hard?" she asked, her voice barely carrying over the sound of the surf hitting the sand.

He shrugged.

"I see you sometimes in the mornings," she said. "And you do. You always run that hard."

He smiled. "Peeper to the bone."

"Can't seem to help myself," she admitted.

He dropped to the sand beside her and didn't miss the fact that she stiffened up at his quick motion. To give her a minute, he stretched out his tired legs. "I worked at sea for seven years. I missed running. I promised myself when I got off the rig, I'd get back to it."

She took her gaze off his body to look into his eyes. "What was the job?"

"I worked for a consulting firm monitoring the deep drilling rigs. We'd go out for months at a time, no land in sight."

"We?"

"I had a crew," he said.

"You were out at sea with a bunch of guys for months at a time?"

"There were a few women too," he said. Three, to be exact, one of whom had neatly sliced Cole's heart in two.

"What was your job out there?" Becca asked.

"OIM. Offshore installation manager." He shrugged again. "Basically just a fancy title for babysitting the operation."

"All of it?"

"I handled the business side of things," he said, "the shifts, the tasks, everything."

"*Sam knows everything*," she said softly. "That's what people keep telling me."

He didn't know everything. He didn't know, for example, why he was so drawn to her. Or what made her so wary.

"Must have been a tough job," she said.

"The job was hard as hell," he agreed. He had few good memories of those years, working his way up from grunt worker to manager. After they'd lost Gil, he and Tanner had come back to Lucky Harbor with Cole, who'd wanted to be here to take care of his mom and three sisters. Tanner had needed recovery time. And it'd been as good a place as any to start their charter company.

"So you retired from the rigs and now you run, surf, take people out on charters, and handcraft boats," she said.

He slid her a look.

"Peeper, remember?" she said. She bit her lip but a sweet, low laugh escaped. "Plus, I looked you up."

Now it was his turn to narrow his eyes. "Why?"

She squirmed a little, which he found fascinating. Actually he found *her* fascinating. "I've spent the past three mornings at the diner for the free WiFi," she said. "I've been…researching."

"Me?"

"Not *just* you. But I was curious," she admitted.

"Yeah? You didn't get enough information from watching me out the window?"

"Hey," she said on another laugh. "I can't help it that you're pretty to look at."

At this, he went brows-up. "You said attractive. You didn't say pretty."

"*Pretty*," she repeated, still smiling.

He loved her smile. "I'm not pretty." But he was smiling now, too.

"Okay," she said. "You're right. *Pretty* is far too girlie a word for what you are."

They looked at each other. The air seemed to get all used up then, and his heart beat in tune to the pulsing waves. "What else did you learn about me, in your...*research*?" he asked softly.

Her gaze dropped to his mouth. "That you guys take people deep-sea fishing, scuba diving, that sort of thing. Also, your charter company's got four and a half stars on Yelp—although I'm pretty sure some of those reviews were written by women who want to date you because there's lots of mentions of the three hot guys who run the company."

He winced, making her laugh again.

"Might as well own it," she said. "Also, did you know that the town of Lucky Harbor has a Pinterest account? The woman who updates it has a board there for her favorite things."

"Lucille," he muttered.

"And one of her favorite things," Becca said, "is *you*."

He grimaced. "Lucille's a nut."

"She seems very sincere."

"Okay, so she's a *nice* nut," he said. "A nut's a nut."

"People around here seem to look to you as a leader, as someone to turn to," she said. "If there's a question, people say *Sam'll know*, but I've noticed something." She waited until he met her gaze. "No one seems to really know *you* except for maybe Cole and Tanner."

That was just close enough to the dead truth to make him uncomfortable.

"I think it's because you come off as a lone wolf," she said, head cocked as she studied him. "And then there's your approach-at-your-own-risk vibe."

Hard to deny the truth, so he didn't bother.

"I mean you're really good on the fly," she said quietly, as if talking to herself, trying to figure him out. "And you're good at helping people, but you're not readily available to get to know."

It was a shockingly accurate insight, but he went with humor. "Not seeing the problem," he said.

"Well, it's *interesting*, is all."

"Interesting?"

"Yeah." Again she looked at his mouth. "Because your distance is perversely making me curious to know more. And I haven't been…curious in a long time."

There was another surge of that something between them. Heat. Hunger. At least on his part. Testing, he shifted a little closer, moving slowly because he was learning that fast tripped a switch for her, and not in a good way. As he came in, she dragged her teeth over her lower lip and her eyes went heavy-lidded in invite. Their mouths nearly touched before she suddenly pulled back, jerking to her feet. "Sorry," she said breathlessly. "I thought I heard something."

They both listened. Nothing but the waves hitting the rocky sand, and her accelerated breathing.

She grimaced. "I guess not."

He stood as well and kept things light by giving her some space. "You didn't keep the waitressing job."

"Turns out I'm not much of a waitress."

"What are you?" he asked.

"Well, I'm supposed to be a jingle writer, but that's not working out so well, either."

"A jingle writer?"

"I write songs for commercials," she said. "Nothing nearly as difficult as risking limb and life at sea for seven years, I know, but it presents its own challenges."

"Would I recognize any of your jingles?" he asked.

"Maybe, but nothing recent. The one I just turned in was for Cushy toilet paper."

He grinned. "Nice. What are you working on now?"

She hesitated, nibbling on her lower lip again. "Di-axsis."

"Which is…?"

She blew out a sigh. "An erectile dysfunction med."

He laughed. "And you're having a…*hard* time?"

"Funny," she said. "It's all fun and games—unless you have to write the jingle. At the moment, I'm wishing I had a job serving ranch-flavored popcorn on the pier instead. Or *anything*."

"I used to want to be a rock star," he told her.

"Yeah?" she asked. "What stopped you?"

"I'm completely tone-deaf and can't sing worth shit."

She laughed, and he smiled at the sweet sound of it.

"Is that why your music's so loud that the windows rattle?" she asked. "You're in there pretending to be a rock star?"

"I work to it," he said. "Or I did. The past few days I've been listening to whatever it is you're listening to."

She froze. "You can hear me messing around on my keyboard?" she asked, sounding horrified.

He paused. "That's you? You're fantastic."

She immediately shook her head. "No."

"Actually, yeah."

"No, I mean you can't listen." There was a new edge to her voice, and she took a step back. "I can't play if I have an audience."

"Why not?"

"Because I choke," she said, sounding genuinely upset.

"Okay," he said quietly, taking in the fact that she was now pale by moonlight. "I'll pretend not to listen. How's that?"

"No." She didn't relax or smile. "Because I'll know you're only *pretending* not to listen."

She wasn't being coy here, or searching for compliments the way women sometimes did. She was truly unable to bear the thought of him hearing her play. "I could wear earplugs," he said.

She stared at him, then looked away, to the water. "I sound crazy, I know. But I don't play for audiences anymore. I'm only playing for myself now, while trying to come up with my next jingle."

"You used to play for an audience?"

"Oh, God, Becca," she muttered, "just shut up." She pressed the heels of her hands to her eyes. "I really need a subject change."

"Is that why you left New Orleans?"

"How is that a subject change?" She dropped her hands and sighed. "I left New Orleans because I needed a break from…things. Family, to be honest. It's hard to explain."

"Maybe that's the problem," he said. "Maybe you're too focused on the past instead of the here and now."

She stared at him.

He stared back.

"Maybe," she finally said softly. "You don't ever do that? Get stuck in the past?"

Sam didn't like to think about the past at all, much less try to get back to it. "Hell no."

"So…you're a little broken, too?" she asked hopefully, her eyes locked on his with great interest.

"I'm not broken."

She sighed. "Of course not, since you have a penis."

"What does that mean?"

"Guys don't admit to being broken," she said.

He laughed, and she stared at him. "Okay," she said, "you've really got to stop doing that, laugh all sexy-like, Mr. Broken Sexy Grumpy Surfer."

"I'm not broken," he said again. *Much.*

"Well, if you were, I should let you know, I've heard of this remedy…"

"Yeah?"

Again she dragged her teeth over her lower lip. "Maybe it's not a remedy so much as a…temporary fix. Like a Band-Aid," she said, tipping her face to his.

There was an intimacy that came with the dark night, and with it came an ache. An ache for a woman. This woman. It'd been a while since he'd held someone, gotten lost in someone. The truth was that no one had tempted him in a while.

Becca did. Becca with the dark, warm eyes, the sweet smile, and the pulse racing at the base of her throat. He wanted to put his mouth there. He wanted to put his mouth to every inch of her, and he reached for her hand, slowly pulling her in so they stood toe-to-toe. "What's the Band-Aid?"

"Seeing as you're not broken," she said, "it doesn't matter."

Sam ran a finger along her temple, tucked a stray strand of hair behind her ear, and took in the quick tremble that racked her body at his touch. "What matters to me is how *you* got broken," he said.

She closed her eyes, and his smile faded. "Someone hurt you," he said.

"No." She turned away. "It was a long time ago."

Yeah. Someone had hurt her. He turned her to face him and waited for her to open those soulful eyes. Whatever had happened to her had cut deep, but she wasn't down for the count.

He could relate to that.

"I don't talk about it," she said.

"Instead, you put a Band-Aid on it."

"Yes." She hesitated, and then set her hand on his chest, slowly, lightly dragging her fingers from one pec to the other as if testing herself out for a reaction. He hoped she was getting one because the simple touch stirred anything but simple reactions within him.

"It's been a while," she murmured, "but I remember this as a proven effective method for healing all."

He loved that she wasn't too shy to speak her mind. And frankly, he also loved that she'd made the first move, hesitant as it was. He'd make the second. And the third. Hell, he'd make whatever moves she was receptive to, and hopefully chase away her demons while he was at it. But when she leaned into him, he slid his hands down her arms, capturing her wrists to stop her. "I need to take care of something first," he said.

"Oh." Some of the light died from her. "I get it."

"No." He held on to her when she would have pulled away. "This isn't a rejection, Becca. I want you." He dipped down a little to look right into her eyes, wanting to make sure she really got him. "I want you bad, but I'm all sweaty from my run. I need a shower, a quick one, I promise. But my shop doesn't have one, and my house is ten minutes away, so I need you to be patient while I—"

"I've got a shower," she said. Her gaze dropped to his mouth, her tongue darting out to wet her lips. He groaned and gave in, kissing her.

Fucking perfect.

That was how she tasted. She made a little mewling sound and pressed closer, like she thought maybe he was going to vanish.

Fat chance.

He slanted his head and kissed her the way he liked it, open-mouthed, wet, and deep. He let go of her wrists and things got a whole lot hotter real fast. Their hands bumped into each other as they moved, grappling for purchase, hers running over his chest and arms, his gliding up her sides, inside the bulky sweatshirt she wore.

She moaned into his mouth.

He lost his head a little bit then. Or maybe he'd lost it the moment he'd first laid eyes on her, he didn't know. She made him so dizzy he couldn't think straight. "Becca," he said, and from somewhere, he had no idea where, he found the strength to pull her back.

Their gazes met, and at the heat—and uncertainty—in hers, he kissed her again, soft this time. When she let out a shaky breath and slid her arms around his neck, he held her off again. "Shower first," he said.

"And then?"

The hopefulness in her voice went straight through him, and he kissed her again, until she moaned into his mouth, her reaction taking away his ability to think clearly. "And then," he promised, "whatever you want."

Chapter 7

♥

It wasn't often Becca acted recklessly, or with abandon. In fact, it was almost never.

But Sam of the beautiful eyes and sexy voice and surprisingly sharp wit was bringing it out in her. She deserved this, she reminded herself. A night of no strings, a night lost in a man's arms.

This man's arms.

She led the way to her front door. She had the very hot and sexy Sam Brody standing at her back, and she was wondering if she was really going to do this.

Could she?

Then Sam leaned in and kissed her neck, and she quivered in arousal.

Oh, God. Yes. Despite her trepidations and unease and the fact that her lady bits might have rusted up and withered from disuse, she was going to do this.

And she was not going to let anything intrude.

She was going to get naked, and she was going to have a good time while she was at it.

Olivia entered the building just then, walking fast, head down. When she looked up, she nearly tripped over her own feet at the sight of Becca and Sam standing there. "Oh," she said in clear surprise.

Sam nodded at her. "Olivia."

They knew each other, Becca realized, with an odd pang of something. Jealousy? Nah, that couldn't be.

Could it?

Olivia nodded back at Sam and started to walk past them, but then she stopped and turned back to Becca. "I know I owe you an apology for the other night."

"For what?" Becca asked.

Olivia was in another pair of jeans, very cute high-heeled wedges, and a gauzy top that showed off her enviable figure. She was beautiful and aloof, and her expression was hooded as it had been the other night, but she had the good grace to grimace. "Slamming my door on your nose," she said. "I'm not really a people person."

"Duly noted," Becca said drily.

Olivia grimaced again. "I know you were trying to be a nice neighbor, and I was a jerk. I'd like to make it up to you. Seriously," she said at Becca's look of surprise. "Food fixes all, right? I make the best homemade pizza out there. So dinner, on me." She slid Sam a glance. "When you're not busy."

Becca swiveled her gaze to Sam, wondering how he stacked up against homemade pizza.

He arched a brow at her.

Olivia shocked Becca by laughing. "Another night," she said, and vanished inside her place.

"You wanted to give me up for pizza," Sam said.

"*Homemade* pizza," Becca corrected, and put her key in the lock, jerking at the feel of his hot mouth on the back of her neck.

"I'm going to make you forget about the pizza," he whispered against her skin.

She shivered, having underestimated the power of a man's kiss on her neck. "Are you sure you want to make a promise you might not be able to keep?" she managed.

"I always keep my promises."

She hoped so. God, she hoped so.

Five minutes later, Becca stood outside her bathroom, hands and forehead on the door, body thrumming with emotions she almost didn't recognize.

Desire.

Need.

From the other side came the sound of her shower running.

She had a man in her shower.

Good Lord, she had a man in her shower. Picturing Sam in there all hot and naked, using her soap, rubbing his hands over his body, was making her good parts tingle. And she had a lot of good parts, many more than she remembered...

She smiled in relief, then shook her head at herself. Why was she fantasizing about the naked man in her shower instead of being *in* the shower with the naked man?

She chewed on her thumbnail another moment, giving brief thought to being shy, but then quickly discarded that as it hadn't gotten her anywhere all year.

Open the door, Becca.

She opened the door.

Steam rolled over her as the water beat against the tile floor. Taking a deep breath, she fixed her eyes on the sight before her. The glass door was fogged over but she could see the faint outline of Sam's body. She had a side view, and it was a good one. He had one hand braced on the wall in front of him, his head hanging low as he let the water pound between his shoulder blades.

Becca's gaze followed the trail of water down his sleek back, over the perfect, succulent curve of his ass, and down the backs of his legs to his feet.

He was gorgeous.

Sweating now, she had to strip off her bulky sweatshirt. At the movement, he glanced over. Seeing her there, his gaze went fiery and suggestive. Teeming with raw passion, he reached for the soap, running his hands with perfunctory speed and precision over himself.

Becca stared. She started to say something, but then he wrapped his hand around himself. Eyes locked on hers, he held on but didn't stroke, and she got all hot and bothered from wishing he would. "You didn't lock the door," she managed. "So I, um…"

He smiled a very dangerous, alluring smile.

She stood there, her entire body vibrating with need, but trying desperately to be cool, like having a man in her shower was no big deal. In truth, it was a big deal. A *huge* big deal. Her heart was just about racing right out of her chest.

Her terms, she reminded herself. This was on her terms and she was in control. She could stop this at any time.

But she already knew she wasn't going to want to stop.

Sam lifted his hands and shoved his hair back from his face.

Her body tingled. And though he was the one in the shower, she was the one getting damp. Reaching over to a drawer, she pulled out the sole condom she had. She'd gotten it as a party favor a few years back, and because it was blue, and blueberry-flavored to boot, *and* an "extra, extra" large, she'd kept it for laughs. It'd been a while since she'd had use for a condom, and she sort of wished it wasn't blue, but it was better than nothing.

Water and suds continued to sluice down Sam's body, and, even hotter now, Becca pulled off another item of clothing—her long-sleeved tee.

Sam swiped at the fogged-up glass on the shower, presumably to better see her, and smiled. "You've got a lot of layers on."

She flushed. "I was cold earlier."

"I'll keep you warm."

She utterly believed him. She pushed off her flannel PJ bottoms next, which left her in a thin cotton cami and an equally thin pair of cotton panties.

Given the fire in Sam's eyes, he approved, but she hesitated, because whatever came off next was going to reveal more of her than had been seen by another human being in a while.

"Keep going," he said, voice husky.

Erotic.

When she didn't move, he gave her a come-here finger crook.

Her legs took her the last few steps, and then she was in the shower, the water plastering her cami and panties to her body.

Sam groaned at the sight and hooked an arm around her, settling a hand low on her back, pulling her into him. He did this slowly, giving her plenty of time to stop him.

She didn't.

Not only didn't she stop him, she reached up and slid her fingers into his wet hair and pulled him down, hoping for a mindless kiss.

"You're shaking," he murmured. "Still cold?"

"No."

He met her gaze. "You're nervous."

"Aren't you?"

He gave her a heart-melting smile. "It's going to be good, Becca, I promise."

Another promise. She could have told him she didn't believe in them, but there was something so absolute about his voice, something so sure in his eyes. "Okay," she whispered.

He smiled against her lips, and then brought his other hand up, tilting her face to suit him as he kissed her. Soft at first, then serious and demanding, and though she'd hoped he'd take her out of her own head for a while. He did even better than that, and an utterly unexpected wave of desire washed over her. She sank her fingers into his thick, unruly hair and held on.

He was right so far. It was good.

So good she lost herself in the sensations of being held, the barrage of heat and need, and a hunger so strong it made her weak in the knees.

When was the last time a man had made her weak in the knees?

A long time.

Too long.

His tongue swept along hers, and she moaned into his mouth. At the sound, Sam pulled back and gave her a very hot look. She tugged him in again because he was a good kisser. The *best* kisser. In fact, he was the king of all kissers, so much so that when he ended the next kiss, she'd have slithered to the shower floor in a boneless heap of arousal if he wasn't holding her up with a strong arm around her back. The fingers of his other hand unpeeled hers to see what she still held fisted. When he caught sight of the extra-large blueberry condom, he smiled.

"I was planning ahead," she whispered.

"Love a woman who plans ahead." He set the condom on the soap rack, and then nudged a wet cami strap off her shoulder. Lowering his head, his lips grazed her jaw, her throat, across her collarbone. "Mmm," he murmured against her skin, then pulled back a fraction of an inch to meet her gaze, his own hot as fire and intense. "Tell me this is what you want, Becca."

She opened her mouth but nothing came out. Why was nothing coming out?

"If I stay," he said very gently but with utter steel, "I'm going to take you to your bed and make you feel so good that you forget whatever is putting that hollow look in your eyes. I promise you that."

Another promise, but this one seemed as irresistible as the last one, so in answer to his very alpha-man statement, she mustered up some courage and pressed up against him, running her hands over sleek, hot, wet, male skin. God. God, he felt good.

His hands went to her hair, releasing it from her ponytail so that his fingers could run through the wavy, wet mess. "Becca?"

He wanted the words. "Stay," she said.

He peeled her out of her cami and panties and groaned at the sight of her bared before him, kissing her long and hard and wet and deep. He grabbed the soap, and with a dark, heavy-lidded smile, started with her arms. Her stomach and chest were next. Slowly and deliberately, his hands stroked upward, teasing the heavy undersides of her breasts until she sighed with pleasure, her head falling back to thunk against the tile. "Sam."

"Learning what you like," he said, and then kept teasing her until she said his name again, not so soft, and finally, oh God finally, his thumbs brushed over her nipples.

She sucked in a breath and trembled from head to toe. So long. So long since she'd felt this way.

He let his fingers come into play then, meeting up with his thumbs, gently rolling. "Well, you like that."

She couldn't talk, but if she could have, she'd have said she *loved* it. Luckily he didn't seem to need words because he dropped to his knees and soaped up her legs next, running his hands up the backs of them, cupping her ass, squeezing, before stroking back down. Then he began again with the front of her, up her shins, her thighs. And then between.

She gasped. "Sam—"

"Open, babe."

"Um—" she started, thinking she was in *way* over her head, but he took over, his hands urging her to spread her feet. She did, and found herself wide open in every possible way, but there wasn't any space in the shower or her head for self-consciousness, not with his hands on her.

And his mouth. And God, his mouth...

He took his sweet time about it, too, stroking, touching, kissing, licking every single inch of her so that she was breathing like a lunatic, worked up into a near frenzy. "Sam," she gasped again. "Sam, I'm going to—"

"Do it," he said, mouth still on her. "Come."

She flew apart, but he was right there to put her back together again, holding her, slowly bringing her back. When she could, she blinked her eyes open and caught his slow, sexy-as-hell smile.

He'd watched her lose it, and she realized she badly wanted to do the same for him. Pulling him upright, she admired his gorgeous, tough, hard-muscled body with her hands first, and that was so good that she had to taste, too. She slid to her knees to do just that.

Pressing her mouth low on a very sexy spot just beneath his hip, she watched in pleasure and fascination as the muscles in his abs jerked. She wasn't too sure of her skills in this arena, but he looked good enough to lick. So she did. And then again.

And then she took him into her mouth.

He made a low, rough noise, and she looked up at him through her lashes. His head was tipped back, eyes closed, the water flowing over his face and down his chest. His fingers slid in her hair and held on. She tensed, but his hold remained gentle, not guiding or pushing her. It was more like he needed the grip just to hold on, which actually made her feel powerful, and sexy. So sexy...

All good signs, she figured, and continued on, absorbing the groan that came from above her and echoed against the tiled walls when she experimented a little bit.

"Sweet Jesus," he muttered, his body as tense as a

tightly coiled spring ready to snap. After a few moments, he swore and roughly hauled her up.

"What's wrong?" she asked.

Nuzzling his face in her neck, he shook his head. "Gotta slow down or I'm gonna come."

"Wouldn't that be only fair?"

He groaned again, kissed her, and then said against her lips as he hoisted her up, "I want to be inside you when I come, when we *both* come."

The words nearly sent her up in flames, but she needed to tell him—

"Hold on to me," he said. Leaning her into the tile wall, he slapped a hand out for the condom. "Magnum blueberry," he read with a lip twitch.

She'd had her hands around him. And her lips. So she was speaking on good authority. "At least the size is right."

He snorted and, holding her pinned against the wall, seared his mouth to hers. She parted her lips for him and garnered herself a low, sexy growl from the back of Sam's throat as their tongues touched. She'd been doing her best to stay lost in his gaze, in his kisses and touches, and not let Real Life intercede, but she still had to tell him. "Sam."

He sucked at the sweet spot right beneath her ear and her eyes nearly crossed in ecstasy. "Sam," she said again, but he wasn't listening. She tapped his chest. "Sam, I need to—"

"Anything," he murmured and kept kissing her, his hot mouth robbing her of cognitive thought.

"I—" She blinked. "Anything? You can't offer me anything."

"Why not?"

She paused and appeared to process this question very seriously. "Well...I could take advantage for one."

"Go for it," he said hotly, letting out a slow, absolutely wicked bad-boy smile. "Just remember, paybacks are a bitch."

She shivered, not in fear but in arousal. Good Lord, he was potent. "I'm trying to tell you something."

"Okay, babe," he murmured, and kissed his way along her jaw toward her mouth. "You tell me whatever you want while I—"

"Sam!"

At the seriousness in her voice, he again lifted his head, giving her his full attention. Which she'd totally and completely underestimated, because Sam's full attention made it difficult if not impossible to think. "I don't want to disappoint you, but—"

"Becca." His features immediately softened. "You won't. You couldn't—"

"I won't come with you inside me," she blurted out.

He went still for a beat. "No?"

"I...can't." Oh, God, this was embarrassing. Why had she thought this a good idea? She should have faked it. But she wasn't good at faking it. "I want to, I try to, but it just doesn't happen for me. And sometimes that can be...upsetting for a guy, I know, and I just really don't want you to be upset."

Something passed across his eyes, and it wasn't pity or she'd have shriveled into a tiny ball and died. She couldn't put her finger on it because he kissed her, softly at first, then not so softly, and before she knew it she was panting for air and whimpering with need, gripping him like he was her lifeline.

"Becca."

"Huh?" she asked dimly.

"Open your eyes."

She did with difficulty and met his very intense gaze.

"You couldn't disappoint me if you tried," he said, and with that, he turned off the water, grabbed a towel, and dried her.

She was so lost in the pleasure of him running the towel over her body, and the way he then tossed aside the towel to use his hands—and mouth—deliciously rough, demanding, and thorough, that she didn't even realize they were moving until they fell together on her bed.

There he began all over again from the beginning, with long drugging kisses and teasing touches that had her rocking into him, desperate for release. He made her come twice like that, once with his fingers, and then again with his mouth, so that she was still thrumming with adrenaline and shuddering with it when he finally rolled on the blue condom and pushed inside her. His hands slid beneath her bottom and pulled her into him, grinding the two of them together with every stroke. Her eyes drifted shut but he nipped at her lower lip until she opened them again.

His gaze was intently fierce, so much so that she quivered. "Stay with me," he said. He had one arm wrapped around her; the other slid down the back of her thigh, further opening her up for him as he thrust long and hard and deep, holding her gaze captive in his the entire time. The muscles in his arms and shoulders strained with the effort of holding himself back, keeping the pace slow.

Heaven.

She was close, so shockingly, desperately close, her

nerves were screaming. "Please," she gasped, unable to say more. Luckily for her Sam didn't need additional instruction. It took only a few more of those hard, masterful strokes for him to bring her to the very edge of sanity, and then his arms pulled her in even closer, so that they touched in every way possible, skin on skin, and the exquisite slow sliding of friction sending her flying. As the surprise orgasm rippled through her, she clenched tight around him, absorbing his low, rough groan. With one more thrust, he came right along with her.

It was a long few moments before she regained control of her limbs and could loosen the arms she had in a death grip around his neck. "Sorry," she murmured and tried to pull back.

But Sam was having none of it. "Stay with me," he said again, and then brushed a kiss over her damp temple. Lifting his head, he studied her. "You okay?"

"I— You—" Words failed.

He huffed a soft laugh and kissed her. "Yeah, you're okay," he said, and slid out of her. She made a sound of helpless regret at the loss, and he kissed her again. "Don't move," he commanded, and vanished into her bathroom.

He was back in less than two minutes, sliding beneath her covers and hauling her in tight against him. He'd made good on his promises, proving that when he warned her about something, it was best to listen. It'd been good, and he'd indeed made her forget about the pizza.

He held her for a while, certainly long beyond what she'd have deemed the polite amount of cuddle time, his cheek resting lightly on top of her head, his arms around her. She had her face plastered to his bare chest and was listening to his steady heartbeat beneath her, waiting for him to extract himself.

He never did.

Finally, exhausted, she fell into a coma-like sleep and woke with a smile on her face to the sun streaming in her windows.

And an empty bed.

Chapter 8

Sam might have left Becca's bed as surprisingly as he'd arrived in it, but the bigger surprise had been what had happened in it.

She smiled every time she thought about it, which was often enough to prompt Olivia to stop in the hallway the next day and ask Becca what was so damn wonderful.

Becca had laughed but shaken her head. She wasn't going to share, but it turned out that despite Sam's silent departure, having crazy hot sex was good for a person's frame of mind.

Real good.

Becca didn't come up with a jingle for Diaxsis over the next few days, but she felt infinitely relaxed about it. She felt infinitely relaxed about everything, including the fact that it was time to supplement her jingle income. The only thing that could have improved her mood was a Sexy Grumpy Surfer sighting.

But she didn't get that. Not from her window, not on the beach, not from his boat, not anywhere Sam I am...

She did get pizza with Olivia. And as promised, it was homemade, and out of this world. Becca learned that Olivia not only ran the vintage store but owned it, which explained her fabulous clothes. She also made a mean chocolate chip cookie, and if Sam hadn't already rocked her world, Becca might have said the cookies were better than orgasms. As it was, the cookies were a close second.

But though they'd spent several hours together, Olivia didn't open up much, and her eyes stayed hooded.

Olivia had secrets.

As Becca had her own, she hadn't pushed.

She spent a few days perusing the want ads and cleaning up her space, making it a home. She realized that said a lot about Lucky Harbor being more than a so-called pit stop, but she wasn't going to feel bad for loving it here.

Three days after her night with Sam, she'd unwrapped a new—to her—lamp and couch she'd bought from Olivia's shop and was lugging the paper the lamp had been wrapped in to the Dumpster when she realized Sam was there with his shop vac. He was emptying the bag when he caught her staring. He stared right back like maybe he liked what he saw. He did that, she'd noticed, showed his appreciation in nonverbal ways. With his eyes. His slow, sexy smile. The sound he made deep in his throat when he—

"Hey," he said.

Wherever he'd been, he'd gotten some sun and, as usual, looked good enough to eat. "Hey yourself." She turned to go.

"About the other night," he said to her back. "I didn't

mean to vanish on you. I got called out on a job that took me away for a few days. And out of cell range."

She had to admit that she'd wondered if he'd disappeared to distance himself from what had proven to be an explosive chemistry between them. At the realization that this wasn't what had happened, something loosened in her chest. *Relief.* She hadn't scared him off. "You're covered in sawdust," she said inanely.

He looked down. "Got home late last night and went right to work on a boat I'm building for another client." He shifted closer and stroked a thumb over her jaw. "You okay?"

Something about his proximity made her a little speechless, so she nodded.

His eyes never left hers as he appeared to search for the truth in this statement. He sifted his fingers through her hair, gently gliding his thumb beneath her eye. "Your bruise is gone."

"Yes, and I've grounded myself from reading my e-reader at night."

He flashed that dangerous smile, which faded some when his cell buzzed. "Talk," he said into it, and then listened a moment. "Cole already left? Shit. Did you flush out the engine? Check the water pump? Yeah? It's got good water flow? The water hot or warm?" He listened some more. "Sounds like something's stuck in the outflow tube. Shut it down, I'll be there in ten." He ended the call.

"Problem?" she asked.

"There always is."

"And you're the go-to guy?"

"At the moment," he said, master of short sentences.

He looked at her then. Like really looked at her, in a way no one else ever seemed to. "How's the jingle writing going?"

She mimed hanging herself with a rope.

He smiled. "Need another Band-Aid?"

The words were like a hot caress, and she felt her nipples react hopefully. "You have an engine problem requiring your attention," she reminded him.

"There's always time for a break."

She laughed. Spoken like a man. "I'd have my mind on work," she said.

He flashed her a very bad-boy smile. "Becca, I can promise you, your mind wouldn't be on work."

Her pulse took a hard leap at yet another promise. "I suppose everyone's entitled to a little bit of a break now and again," she said softly. "Right?"

His eyes darkened, and he stepped closer, just as a car tore into the lot. A woman leapt out, slammed her door, and went hands on curvy hips as she tossed back her long blond hair. "So you *are* alive," she said, glaring at Sam.

"Selena." His voice was so carefully neutral that Becca took a second look at him. His expression, fun and sexy only a moment before, was now closed off.

The woman standing in front of them was tall, leggy, and built like Barbie. Beachy Barbie. She wore a red-and-white sundress that looked so good she might have walked right off the runway and gave Becca a hard, speculative look before turning to Sam. "That was fast."

Becca knew she should've been insulted, but actually she was secretly tickled pink if this beautiful creature was jealous of her.

"I've called you like twenty-five times and left you a

bunch of texts," Selena said to Sam. "Your phone broken?"

"No," he said.

Becca waited for him to explain. He'd been gone for a few days, out of range, yet he didn't say a word in his defense.

Steam practically flew out Selena's ears. "So you're what," she asked in disbelief, going up in volume with each word, "*ignoring* me?"

"It's been a month," he said. "I thought there was nothing left to say."

"I've got plenty left to say!" Selena screeched. "And if you'd answered even a single call, you'd know it!"

Sam looked pained. "My office then."

"Oh, *hell* no," Selena said. "This shit's going public now. You took me to Cottonwoods. Cottonwoods is a *serious* place, Sam. It says we're in a relationship."

"We went to Cottonwoods because you *asked* to go there," Sam said. "It was our second date, and over appetizers you informed me you were researching sperm donors so you could get inseminated."

Selena's crazy eyes narrowed. "And?"

"*Sperm donors*," he repeated, as if this explained all.

"You saying I scared you off?" Selena asked. "You're not afraid of anything, Sam, and you damn well know it."

Becca swiveled to get Sam's reaction. She might not have dated him twice, or gone to Cottonwoods—wherever that was—but even she already knew Sam Brody wouldn't admit to be scared off by a single thing.

When Sam didn't respond, Selena whirled to storm off, giving Becca a not-so-accidental shoulder shove. "He's dead inside, you know," she snapped. "He's magic in the sack, but trust me, he's not worth it."

Becca didn't respond, and Selena shook her head. "Don't say I didn't warn you."

A moment later, her tires squealed as she left the lot.

There was an awkward silence as Becca and Sam watched her go. Well, *Becca* was feeling awkward. Hard to say what Sam was feeling. He kept his own counsel. "Okay, yeah," she finally said, "I can see why you might not like to live in the past."

Two days later, Sam stood in the hut at the front counter. He had notes on three different napkins, one scratched in ink on his forearm, and another on a piece of wood from his shop in his back pocket.

And the phone was still ringing.

He was at the end of his rope, for lots of reasons. He hadn't managed to break away from work long enough to get any time alone with Becca. And he wanted to be alone with her. Not just to get her naked again, though he wanted that, badly. But he also wanted to get inside her head and learn more about her.

Cole came in from the boat. He and Tanner had taken out a group of twelve before the crack of dawn for a deep-sea fishing trip.

Sam had stayed behind to catch up on paperwork—which he hadn't gotten to thanks to the phones. "This place is insane," he said. "No one writes shit down."

"You're the one who won't use the schedule," Cole said.

Tanner trailed in behind Cole, dripping water everywhere as he limped in, carrying some of the gear. "He doesn't use the schedule to prove a point."

"Not true," Sam said.

Okay, it was totally true.

"I'm trying to work." He jabbed a thumb in the direction of the warehouse behind them. "But the fucking phones keep ringing, and no one's answering them. Why isn't anyone answering?"

"You know why," Cole said. "We haven't hired anyone yet. Were any of the calls from prospective applicants?"

"Yeah," Sam said. "Which is why I'm in here. I made appointments with three people. One didn't show."

"And the other two?"

"One was Lucille," Sam said. "Again. She showed up in a bikini to prove she was—" He used air quotes. "Beach-savvy."

They all shuddered.

"I reminded her that we'd discussed this, that there were age limitations to this job," Sam said. "And then she accused me of being a geriatric bigot. She said I should be expecting to hear from her lawyer."

Tanner grinned. "And the third?"

Sam looked at Cole. "Your sister."

"Aw, Christ," Cole muttered, scrubbing a hand over his face. "Which one?"

"Does it matter?" Tanner asked. "They're all crazy."

Cole held out a palm to Tanner. "Pay up."

"What?" Tanner said, still dripping water everywhere.

"You swore you wouldn't make fun of my family anymore, remember?" Cole asked. "And I said that you couldn't stop yourself, and you said you could, too, and then I said I bet you, and you said no sweat, and I said put your money where your mouth is, and you said fifty bucks. So…" He wriggled his fingers. "Fifty bucks, man. Right now."

Tanner shrugged. "Can't. I'm holding all this wet gear. I can't reach my wallet."

"Turn around, I'll get it."

This made Tanner grin and shake his head. "It's in my front pocket."

Cole yanked his hand back like he'd been bitten. "No way am I touching your front pocket. Sam, *you* do it."

"Why me?"

"You get me my money, and I'll hire someone today so you can stop bitching."

Sam sighed and shoved his hand down Tanner's front pocket.

The door opened behind them. Becca walked in and stopped short at the sight of Sam with his hand down the front of Tanner's pants.

"Am I interrupting something?" she asked.

Cole was grinning like a Cheshire cat. "Yes."

"*No*," Sam said, and pulled out Tanner's wallet. He flipped it open, pocketed all the cash, then shoved the wallet back at Tanner.

"Hey," Cole said.

"*Hey*," Tanner said.

Ignoring them both, Sam turned to Becca.

She waved an ad that he recognized from the local paper. *Their* ad. He met her gaze and saw the truth—she was going to apply for the job. "No," he said. He couldn't hire someone he'd slept with. No matter how good a time he'd had. And he'd had a *great* time.

"Too late," Becca said. "I already applied online as the ad suggested. And I don't want to toot my own horn or anything, but I'm pretty perfect for this job."

"Still no," Sam said.

She gave him a long look. "Afraid I'll scream at you about you being dead inside like your ex did?"

Cole and Tanner cackled at this like two annoying hens while Becca tapped the ad. "—It says right here that you need someone strong on phones and with good people skills." She lifted her gaze and looked at all three of them. "I'm both, by the way. I worked as an admin in a New Orleans ad agency all last year while I was writing jingles."

"Jingles?" Cole asked.

"I write jingles for commercials and stuff," she said. "It's all in the application. You'll see."

"No shit," Cole said, looking impressed. "You any good?"

"At jingles?" She shrugged. "I did a big soup campaign. Oh, and you know the commercial for Indie Burgers?" She began to sing, "...tell me how you like it, tell me how you want it—"

Cole joined in for the finish, "I want it smokin', I wanna feel the heat..." He grinned. "That was a good one. What else did you do?"

Her smile went a little stiff. "Well, nothing for a while after that. But I just finished up one for Cushy toilet paper. Now I'm stuck on my latest project."

"What's it for?" Cole asked.

She paused. Sighed. "Diaxsis."

Cole shook his head, looking clueless. "What's that?"

Tanner grinned. "I know."

"Probably shouldn't be proud of that, man," Sam said, laughing when Tanner gave him a shove.

"What the hell is it?" Cole asked.

Tanner held up a limp finger and then straightened it. He accompanied this with a brow waggle.

Becca sighed. "Back to my application," she said. "The good news is that if I could keep a staff of twenty-five organized, most of them angry women, the three of you'll be a piece of cake."

"You think men are easier than women?" Cole asked.

Becca laughed.

"Yeah," Cole said, smiling at her. "You're probably right."

Okay, Sam thought, so there was more to cute, sweet Becca than met the eye. She had brains, and she wasn't a pushover.

But neither was he. "You'd need references," he said.

"You can call mine," Becca said, but then her easy smile faded some. "But as I already noted on my app, I'd appreciate it if you wouldn't say exactly where your business is located, or where I am."

There was a beat of silence as this request was absorbed, and Sam felt something tighten in his chest. "You in any sort of trouble that we should know about?" he asked, just as serious now as she.

"Nope," Becca said quickly. *Too* quickly.

Damn.

Sam exchanged a look with Cole and Tanner. Not a one of them didn't recognize a problem when they saw one.

Becca lifted the ad again. "You need someone to start ASAP. Luckily, that happens to be exactly when I'm available." Her smile was back. "ASAP."

"I gotta ask," Tanner said. "You any better at phones than you are at waitressing?"

Cole gave him a dirty look, but Tanner shrugged.

"Yes," Becca said, not looking insulted in the least. "I'm much better at phones than waitressing."

As if on cue, the phone rang. Cole, Tanner, and Sam groaned in unison.

Becca gestured to it. "May I?"

Cole waved at her, like *Please*.

She leaned over Sam, teasing him with her scent and a brush of her arm against his as she grabbed the phone. "Lucky Harbor Charters," she answered. "How can I help you?" She paused, listened politely, and then said, "I'm sorry, Sam no longer works here. No, there's no forwarding address. Thank you for calling." She disconnected.

"What the hell?" Sam said.

"It was Selena."

Cole grinned. "You're hired."

Tanner nodded. "And keep that snooty tone in your voice. Sounds authoritative and sexy. I like it."

"No," Sam said.

"Two to one," Tanner said.

Sam gave him a look.

"What?" Tanner said. "She's prettier than you *and* friendlier than you."

"Plus, I just promised you I'd hire someone today," Cole said. "Voilà, *done*."

Sam ushered Becca to one of the stools in front of the counter. "Give us a minute," he said.

Then he manhandled Cole and Tanner out the front. The three of them stood on the beach. "No," he said firmly, arms crossed.

"Give me one good reason," Cole said.

Sam searched his brain. He couldn't come up with one *good* reason. But he had lots of *bad* reasons, starting with the fact that he'd slept with her.

Except there'd been no sleeping.

And every night since, he'd dreamed of her. Really hot dreams about how she'd felt writhing beneath him. She had this way of helplessly whispering his name over and over again—Christ. He had to stop thinking about it. "This isn't a good idea," he repeated.

"She wants the job," Cole said. "And we need her." He paused. "Unless there's a reason working with her would be a problem? Like, say, she's an ex who's a nut job? But usually, that's Tanner's area of expertise."

"Hey," Tanner said.

Cole gave him a long look, and Tanner sighed. "Fine," he said. "That's definitely my area of expertise. But Sam doesn't go for nut jobs. He keeps his entire life compartmentalized. He wouldn't work with someone he likes."

Cole's face changed. "Shit, that's it." He turned back to Sam. "That's why you said she was off limits. You *like* her."

"What is this, high school?" Sam asked.

"No," Cole said. "Because you didn't like anyone in high school. You loved them and left them."

Definitely not going there, Sam decided. "We're not doing this, and before you whine about it, you both owe me. You," he said, pointing at Tanner.

"Me, what?"

"The night you went skinny-dipping with some chick. She stole your clothes and you had to walk home butt-ass naked."

Tanner winced. "That was a million years ago, man."

"You came knocking on my window for clothes," Sam said, "which I handed over without giving you shit. Well, not too much shit anyway. And you." He turned to Cole.

Cole opened his mouth, but Sam plowed ahead. "Remember the night you were grounded and not supposed to go out? Except you did, and you got drunk, and I had to drag your trashed ass home, and when your mom caught us at the door I let you pretend it was me who was plastered, that it was me who'd needed saving so that you didn't get grounded for the rest of your life."

"Why do you remember this shit?" Cole asked, mystified.

"For days just like this."

Chapter 9

Becca knelt on the stool beneath the open window, shamelessly eavesdropping on the guys. She'd spent several days now searching for a viable, short-term job that would fit her criteria. One, she wanted to stay in Lucky Harbor for at least the summer. Two, she didn't want anything too demanding, as after a day of work she'd then be putting in long hours writing her jingles. And three, it had to be something she was good at.

She was good at being in control, good at being in charge.

She could really see herself doing this job. What she hadn't seen was Sam's reticence, though she should have. Of course he didn't want to work with the woman he'd so spontaneously boinked almost a week ago.

Except it'd felt like a lot more than just a quickie.

And really, there'd been nothing "quick" about it, or Sam. He'd taken his time with her, touching, kissing...*everything*. And she'd responded to him. Fully. That'd been the most shocking. She'd more than merely responded to him. She'd gone up in flames for him.

But that didn't mean he wanted a repeat.

Or that he'd want to hire her to work for him.

Damn it. She leaned in toward the window, trying to see better. The three of them stood close, and though they looked like laid-back surfers, there was clearly a lot more to them than that. Cole was the most approachable of the bunch, but he wasn't a pushover. Tanner had a look to him that said he'd been around the block and it hadn't been an easy ride.

And then there was the tough, impenetrable, guarded, hard-to-crack Sam.

At the moment, they were talking, shades locked onto shades. She wasn't quite close enough to hear what they were saying, but their body language fascinated her. Damn, she wished she could catch their words. She got down, scooted the stool closer to the window, climbed back up, and pressed her ear to the screen.

"If you're having trouble hearing, maybe you should just stick your head out the door."

At the unbearably familiar voice behind her—*Sam's*—she squeaked in surprise and fell off the stool.

"A peeper to the end," he said, sounding not surprised at all. His arms easily lifted her up, straightened her out, and released her.

A little frazzled by the way his hands on her reminded her of their night together, she blinked him into focus and flashed a charming smile.

He didn't return it. "You need this job," he said flatly.

This wasn't worded as a question, but she knew he was asking nevertheless. "Yes," she said.

He didn't look happy. "You realize that you're totally overqualified. Why here?"

"I like the beach."

He stepped closer. "Why else?"

"I—" It was hard to think now, with him in her space. "I need the money to supplement the jingle income, at least until I get back onto a higher tier of products."

"You could play the piano," he said. "You're amazing. I bet you could get a job—"

"Not an option," she said flatly.

Sam studied her for a moment, during which she did her best to look like a woman with no secrets.

He clearly didn't buy it. "I've got a couple of problems," he said. "You lied to your brother about your job. And you don't want anyone from your reference list to know where you are." He stepped into her, his hands cupping her face, tilting it up to him. "Are you in some kind of trouble, Becca? Do you need help?"

Her throat tightened at the concern in his eyes, but she shook her head. "No."

"Then why?"

"I don't want to talk about it," she whispered.

His thumbs glided over her jaw. "I'm pretty sure I'm missing pieces to your puzzle," he finally said.

Yes, he was, but those pieces were for her only. Besides, *she* couldn't put herself back together again, so she didn't expect others to be able to do so. "Look, I'm no big mystery," she said. "Just a girl who could use a job."

When he spoke, his voice was surprisingly gentle, and nearly broke her. "If that's true, why not tell me what's going on? Maybe I can help."

She closed her eyes. He'd already helped and didn't

even know it. "I just want to go back to being successful at something on my own."

He was quiet for a moment. "There's more to this story," he finally said.

Fed up, she tossed up her hands. "Well, of course there is. Isn't there more to you than being a sexy, grumpy surfer? Are you going to tell me why *you're* all tough and guarded?"

"No," he said. "But I'm not asking you for work, either."

She let out a breath. "I'm going to do a great job for you," she said, the one thing she was utterly confident about. "Isn't that enough?"

He just looked at her, and she sighed. "Look, if I suck," she said, "you can let me go. No hard feelings, I promise."

"And what about our other feelings?"

This stopped her. "Aren't we done with those feelings?"

He considered this, and then set her heart to racing when he slowly shook his head. He then stepped even closer and pulled her into him. Their thighs brushed. Other things touched, too, her soft abs to his deliciously concrete ones, for example, as he slowly lifted her to the counter. He splayed his big, callused hands on her thighs and spread them so he could step in close.

He was hard, deliciously so.

Her breath caught. Her heart kicked.

Lowering his head, he ran the tip of his nose along her jaw, and then his mouth was there, too, on the sweet spot beneath her ear.

Her entire body gave a hard tremble, and she tried to

close her legs but he was still between them. His index finger lifted her chin, and their eyes held as he let his lips touch hers. Then he threaded his hand through her hair, tilted her head farther back, and kissed her again, parting her lips, slowly stroking her tongue with his own.

When he finally released her, she realized she was gripping him tight. She let go and blinked as she struggled to regulate her air intake. "Okay, so we're not done with those feelings," she admitted.

He just looked at her, all dangerous and alluring. "You wouldn't like working for me," he said.

He had no way of knowing that she could handle just about anything. "I can handle you," she said, "even if you can be a little bit badass and hard."

"Sometimes harder than other times," he said, and she blushed.

His eyes heated.

"You know what I think?" she asked. "I think you're all hard-crusted on the outside, but you don't scare me because I know the truth."

"And what's that?"

"That on the inside, you're soft and gooey," she said.

"You're wrong about the soft."

She gave a slow shake of her head. "It's a compliment. There's nothing wrong with soft. I'm soft."

"On the outside," he agreed. "And I love it. But you're pure steel on the inside. I love that, too."

"Are you going to hire me?" she asked.

"The girls are insisting."

"The girls?" she asked.

"Cole and Tanner."

She smiled.

A faint one curved his lips as well, but his eyes remained steady. Solemn. "There are conditions, Becca."

"Oh, boy," she said.

His smile met his eyes at that, but it faded and she got Serious Sam again. "If we work together," he said, "we're not sleeping together."

"Because you'll be my boss?"

"Because working with someone and sleeping with that same someone is a bad decision."

"And…you don't make bad decisions?" she asked. "Ever?"

"I try very hard not to."

Well, good for him. But she didn't happen to have his self-restraint or discipline. She'd made a lot of bad decisions, and apparently that wasn't going to change anytime soon. "Are you saying I need to pick between the job and sleeping with you again?"

"*Again?*" Cole asked.

Becca turned to the door where, yep, Cole stood, looking fascinated by their conversation.

"Shit," Sam said. He strode to the door and shut it in Cole's face. Turning back to Becca, he went hands-on-hips, looking ticked off.

But Becca was annoyed, too. And a little insulted to boot. He thought she couldn't separate out their physical heat from the job. Or even worse, he was worried she'd get attached to him and yell at him about being dead inside…"You know there's a difference between having sex with someone and having a white picket fence with that someone, right?" she asked.

He just looked at her.

Okay, so it wasn't playtime. And she wasn't feeling

playful anyway. "Seriously, Sam? You want me to choose?" Her lips were still tingling from the kiss he'd laid on her, and if she was being honest, so were other parts of her body—such as every erogenous zone she owned. This was because she now knew *exactly* what he could do to her. Which was more than any man in far too long. If ever.

And he, apparently, could take it or leave it.

Take or leave *her*.

"I pick the job," she said. Look at that, it was an easy decision after all.

He didn't react. He just studied her for a long beat. "The hours are five to two," he finally said, giving her no clue as to how he felt about her decision.

"Five…*a.m.*?" she asked in disbelief.

His lips twitched. "You want to change your mind?"

Oh, hell, no. Even if she loved to sleep.

"You could get better hours playing at the Love Shack for their dinner crowd," he said.

"I want *this* job."

"And your brother," he said. "Didn't he offer you a good-paying job?"

"Not interested."

Again she received a long look. And again she got a little tummy quiver. He was good at evoking that.

"The early start is because we're almost always booked for an asscrack-of-dawn deep-sea trek or a sunrise scuba tour. We need someone to open up shop, start the coffee, greet the customers, and answer the phones."

"What about the later part of the day?" she asked. "Don't you take people out for sunset or whatever?"

"Yeah, but it's the mornings and midday when we get

the most traffic. We can handle the evening stuff our-selves for now."

Five. In the morning...

"Think about it," he said.

She looked out the window. Tanner and Cole were stripping off what looked like scuba gear. They'd both lost their shirts, leaving them in just board shorts.

Holy hotness, Batman.

"In New Orleans, my office view was the brick wall of the building right next to me," she said. "This view is better."

She didn't hear Sam move, but suddenly she felt him at her back, warm and strong and stoic as ever. Her eyes drifted shut as he stroked a finger down the side of her throat, making her body tremble yet again.

Yeah, he was real good at that.

He was good at a lot of things, she was discovering.

"Think about it," he said again softly.

And then he was gone.

Chapter 10

♥

Becca knocked on Olivia's door and waited. After a moment, she felt movement behind the peephole and knew she was being studied. She hoisted the bag of sandwiches she'd just bought from the diner. "Hot pastrami on rye," she said, waving the bag enticingly. "And fries."

The door opened. Olivia's gorgeous dark hair was piled up on top of her head, held there with a fabulous silver-and-pearl clip that Becca knew had to be vintage. Olivia looked her usual beautiful and remote, but there was something new.

She was covered in paint.

"What are you doing?" Becca asked.

"You can't hear my paintbrush as I paint my bathroom?" Olivia asked. "Because the insulation is so nonexistent, I can hear you breathing when you're not playing your keyboard."

Well, crap. "How do you know it's not my radio?"

"The radio doesn't have the musician swearing *Oh shit, that sucks* after each song."

Good point, Becca thought. She sighed. "I'll keep it down."

"I like it," Olivia said.

"You like my playing, but not necessarily me?"

Olivia shrugged. "I made you pizza," she said. "Which I don't do for anyone else. So I must like you a little. What's with the food?"

"Funny you should ask. I'm actually trying to bribe you into liking me more." She waved the food again. "Is it working?"

"Maybe." Olivia peered at the bag and inhaled deeply. "Did you say fries?"

"Yep. And brownies."

Olivia narrowed her eyes. "*Store*-bought brownies?"

"Yes," Becca said, "but give me a break here; I need a friend. And trust me, store-bought is way better than my homemade."

Olivia didn't look impressed.

"They're from the bakery," Becca said, which was a little piece of heaven and everyone in town knew it.

Including, it seemed, Olivia. "Yeah, okay," she relented, and let Becca in.

Olivia's place had been transformed. The open, empty warehouse was now filled with warm, comfy furniture, floor lamps, and throw rugs. "Wow," Becca said. "It looks like a real home now."

"That's the idea." Olivia dug into the food like she hadn't eaten all day.

"What's behind there?" Becca asked, gesturing to an

antique screen that blocked off a good third of the open space.

"Overflow stock for my store. Now you. You're doing the hot surfer."

Becca choked on a bite of her sandwich.

"Sam," Olivia clarified.

"I know who you mean," Becca said on a laugh. "I'm just not sure my question and your question are on equal measure."

Olivia smiled. "Yeah. You're totally doing him. You going to eat your brownie?"

Becca sighed and handed it over. "I want points for that."

"You get points for the hot surfer."

Sam punched in the phone number for Becca's first reference. He was leaning against their front counter. Tanner was sitting on it, absently rubbing his aching leg, watching him. They'd just come in from a scuba excursion with a bunch of college students, which had been a little bit like herding wild horses.

"You trust her," Tanner said, reading her application on his tablet. "Or you wouldn't have slept with her."

Jesus. "Cole has a big mouth," Sam said in disgust.

Tanner flashed a grin. "Cole didn't tell me shit. You just did."

Sam considered putting his fist through that grin.

"You won't," Tanner said, reading his mind.

"Only because I wouldn't want to mess up your pretty face."

Tanner couldn't be deterred. "So," he went on. "You trust Becca, which means you're calling those references for something else. It's about *her*, not you. You're wondering about her."

Wondering. Worrying...

"You could do this the old-fashioned way, you know," Tanner said, "and just ask her what you want to know."

"Calling her references is the smart thing to do," Sam pointed out. But Tanner was right, he *did* trust her. At least as much as he trusted anyone. What he didn't trust was the flashes of unease he sometimes saw in her pretty brown eyes, or her claims that she wasn't in trouble.

He wanted to know her story.

Her first reference was her boss at the ad agency.

"Excellent employee," the guy said when he came on the line. "Hard worker, loyal, compulsively organized. A great office manager, not so great at the jingles. We were sorry she had to leave town so suddenly. I'd hire her back in an instant as an admin, but she said she wouldn't be coming back to New Orleans for a while. Shame. Still, she's on contract for the jingles, and I'll take what I can get from her."

Next up was a co-worker. "Becca Thorpe?" the woman asked. "Loved her. Very hard to see her go. She struggled with jingle writing, I know, but she didn't struggle to keep us organized. Such a sweet thing, too. She'd give a stranger the very shirt off her back. Certainly gave much of her life over to her family. Her brother mostly. That was a rough situation, but she's resilient. You'd be lucky to have her."

Sam didn't believe in luck. Sam believed in good, old-fashioned determination and making one's own path. He knew what his path was.

But now he wanted to know about Becca's.

*   *   *

Not in the mood to put together a meal for herself, Becca went back to the Eat Me diner for dinner. She was half-way through bacon and eggs—nothing said comfort food like a hot breakfast for dinner—when an old woman slid into the booth across from her and smiled.

"Hi," she said to Becca. "You don't know me, but I know you. And I just wanted to say that you play the piano like an angel."

"Um," Becca said. "Thanks."

The old woman just kept smiling at her.

Where Becca had come from, if a stranger slid into your booth, you had your cell phone in hand, your thumb hovering over 911. Especially if that stranger knew something about you, like, say, the fact that you played the piano—which you'd told no one.

But the thing was, this stranger was barely five feet tall, had blue-gray bristle for hair, matching blue-gray eyes gone filmy from age, and wore bright red lipstick. She also had more wrinkles than an uncooked chicken, and a harmless-looking smile that Becca didn't buy for a minute.

"I'm Lucille," she said. "I kinda run this place."

Becca looked around. "The diner?"

"No, Lucky Harbor."

"So you're the mayor or something?" Becca asked.

Lucille smiled. "Not the mayor, but actually, that's a great idea. I'm more of a...social organizer."

"Oh," Becca said, having no idea what a social organizer might do for an entire town, but impressed that a woman of her age had a job at all.

"I was at the bar the other night, late," Lucille said. "I

got my hormone meds mixed up and couldn't sleep. Jax makes a mean hot toddy."

Becca went still. Late the other night she'd walked to the Love Shack, and when the bar had emptied out, she'd played. "I didn't see you."

"I know," Lucile said, smiling. "I'm geriatric stealth. You're an amazing piano player, anyone ever tell you that?"

Becca felt nauseous. "Maybe once or twice."

"You playing tonight?"

"No." Maybe.

"I'd sure like to hear you again," Lucille said.

"Sorry, but I don't play for an audience." Anymore. "I write jingles now."

"Yeah? Like what?"

"Like for soup, and toilet paper." She grimaced, thinking of her latest assignment, which she still hadn't figured out. "I'm currently a little bit stuck."

"Really?" Lucille brightened. "I'm real good at making stuff up. What product?"

Crap. "Diaxsistheerectiledysfunctionmed."

"What's that?" Lucille cupped hand around her ear. "Speak up, hon, I'm old as dirt."

Becca sighed. "It's Diaxsis."

"Shut the front door," Lucille said on a wide grin.

"It's an erectile dysfunction med—"

"I know what it is." Lucille cackled and rubbed her hands together in delight. "And now you're speaking my language. What are you stuck on exactly? You oughta write a song that someone of an age could sing to her man! Like how he shouldn't be embarrassed to need the pill, 'cause us women need *it*, and by *it* I mean—"

"I know what you mean!"

"I'm just saying, those commercials all miss my age demographic. We're not dead yet, you know."

"I'll take that into consideration," Becca said. "Soon as my muse comes back."

"Maybe your muse needs a distraction. Something to fuel your creativity. You ever teach music?"

Becca actually found a laugh at that. She'd played music, dreamed music, worked for and about music, ate and slept music, then run like hell from music, but she'd never taught. "No."

"Could you?"

"Well, probably," she said slowly. "But…"

"But it'd be better if it was, say, younger?" Lucille asked, reading her mind. "Like, young, eager-to-learn school-aged kids?"

"Well, maybe," Becca said, failing to see where this was going.

Lucille grinned. "I was hoping you'd say that. The rec center needs someone to teach kids for Music Hour on Monday, Wednesday, and Friday afternoons. I'm on the board, and you have no idea how happy everyone'll be that I found you."

"Wow," Becca said, impressed. "You tricked me."

"Only a little. We'd pay you."

Becca had already been shaking her head, but she stopped at the pay part. "You would?"

"You bet. We'll need references, of course, someone who could vouch for you not being a felon or anything of that nature." Lucille slid her a card. It said ORACLE OF LUCKY HARBOR and gave a cell number, website, and a physical address. "The website is my Pinterest," Lucille said.

Becca stared down at it. "I've been to your boards."

Lucille smiled. "Yeah, they're good, right? I used to be on Facebook, but got kicked off. The addy's for my art gallery. Email me your résumé and references today, okay? We can get you going by tomorrow. The kids'll be so excited."

By the time Becca got back home, she was excited, too. Maybe she couldn't play in front of people, but she could sure as hell teach kids to do so. She sat on her bed and played around on the keyboard, determined to come up with something for Diaxsis and get it off her plate. After a few hours, she had a jingle. She hadn't been able to give Lucille her wish about aiming the song at the eighty-ish crowd, but hopefully they'd appreciate it anyway. She sent it off and then crawled beneath her covers, her thoughts on the fact she now had *three* jobs.

She could only hope at least one of them worked out...

When Becca's alarm went off the next morning at the obscene hour of zero dark thirty, she spent a moment revisiting the pros of the charter job. Or, more accurately, the cons. But in the end, she rolled out of bed, showered, dressed, and made her commute into work, which was the short walk across the alley.

Cole was already there. "You look like you could use some coffee," he said. "Maybe the new girl could do it."

Becca laughed and headed to the coffeemaker. She went through the motions while yawning, and then realized nothing was happening. The coffeemaker was playing possum. She waited another moment, yawning again. Outside, the sky was dark. This was because the sun hadn't risen yet, since it was five oh five.

In the morning.

She actually wasn't even sure that she'd ever seen this time before.

And still no caffeine emerged from the coffeemaker. "I'm counting on you," she said to it. "I need you, bad."

"Sometimes you gotta give it a good whack," Cole said, looking more awake than anyone should ever look at this ungodly hour. He was in loose board shorts and a T-shirt advertising some dive shop in the Caicos.

Unlike her, who in deference to the early chill was in jeans, boots, a tank, a tee, *and* a sweatshirt, complete with hoodie, hat, scarf, and gloves. Yes, it was summer, but this was Washington State. At this time of morning, it was forty degrees, and she believed in comfort over style.

"Here," he said, nudging her over. "I've got it. If Sam shows up before there's coffee, he'll bitch like a little girl."

Becca had seen Sam grumpy, but he was more of a silent grump. She couldn't imagine him actually bitching about anything, and at her expression, Cole laughed. "You ever catch him early in the morning?" he asked.

"Nope." He'd been long gone from her bed by daylight.

"Well, he's a bear," Cole said. "We usually just toss him some caffeine and then stay out of arm's reach until it sinks in." Cole hit the side of the coffeemaker.

Nothing happened.

He went to hit it again, but the door opened and in came the bear himself. He was dressed almost identically to Cole, with the addition of a backward baseball cap, his mirrored aviator shades—even though the sun still wasn't up—and a scowl. He met her gaze, and despite that scowl, something shimmered between them.

Becca knew she wasn't going to survive this without caffeine, so she smacked the side of the coffeemaker like Cole had.

"What are you doing?" Sam asked.

"Working."

"No, I meant why are you beating the shit out of the coffeemaker?" he asked, his voice still morning-gruff, like he hadn't used it yet.

She had no idea why she found that so incredibly sexy. "Cole said I have to beat the thing up to get it to work."

Sam gave Cole a head shake and came up behind Becca, reaching an arm around her to stroke the machine. "Come on, baby," he murmured. "You know what I want."

Cole snorted.

Becca melted.

And the coffee machine purred to life.

"Show-off," Cole said, and headed to the door.

"Hey," Sam said. "Where are you going?"

"Tanner's on the boat. We've got a group of eight."

"Yeah, I know," Sam said. "Because *I'm* taking them out with him."

"Uh, no. I am," Cole said.

"Uh, no," Sam said, imitating Cole's voice. "*You're* training the new girl."

The "new girl" grimaced.

Cole shook his head. "*I'm* with Tanner today. It's on the schedule."

"No, it's not," Sam said.

Cole pulled out his phone and began to thumb the screen furiously.

Becca raised her hand. "Yeah, hi. If one of you would

just train me already, I'd be able to straighten out this very sort of thing."

Cole looked up from his phone. "No one can *ever* straighten this shit out."

"I can," she said, doing her best to look confident in that fact. Scheduling was a piece of cake. It was writing jingles that was killing her. "I'll bet you."

"Competitive little thing," Cole said to Sam. "I like her."

Sam looked at Becca. "You lost your last bet," he reminded her.

And the one before that, but who was counting. "I won't lose this one," she said, determined. *Desperate*. She had to get something right. This was it, she could feel it.

She felt Sam's gaze linger on her, felt the weight of his consideration. "Is everything a competition with you?" he asked.

She met his green eyes, and like it always seemed to between them, the air shimmered.

"Ha! It finally loaded." Cole waved his phone beneath Sam's nose. "See? I *am* the one scheduled for this morning."

"You changed it," Sam accused.

Cole's expression went innocent. Far too innocent. "Why would I do that?"

"So I'd have to stay and train the newbie."

"Oh, for God's sake!" Becca exclaimed. "Standing right here!"

"He didn't mean it," Cole told her.

"Yes, he did," Sam said.

Cole rolled his eyes. "I'm heading out," he said to Becca. "We're on radio. Our Float Plan's behind the counter. We'll check in. Have fun." He paused and sent Sam a quick look. "And whatever you do, don't let him intimidate you. He's all bark, no bite."

"I'm not worried," Becca said. She was sure she could handle Sam. She took a peek at him. His expression was cool, irritated, and not in any way as friendly as he'd been while buried deep inside her body. She amended her earlier thought to *possibly* she could handle him.

"You'll be great," Cole said, patting her shoulder. He took one last look at Sam's face. Whatever he saw there made him smile. "But maybe you should go a little easy on him; he's had it rough."

She looked at Sam's face, too. "Rough as in dating gorgeous blondes named Selena who yell at you in the alley, or rough as in getting to go boating all day long for a living?"

Cole tossed back his head and laughed. "You get a raise for that. I'll tell our accountant." He turned to Sam again. "Give her a raise."

"Sam's the accountant?" Becca asked.

Cole was full-out grinning at Sam now. "Yeah."

Sam narrowed his eyes and Cole sidled to the door just as Tanner stuck his head inside. "Come on, man, paying customers waiting."

"We were just discussing who gets to train the new girl," Cole said.

"I'll do it," Tanner said, flashing a smile at Becca. "I'd be happy to."

Sam jabbed a finger in the direction of his partners. "You. And you. Outside," he said, shoving his glasses to the top of his head. "Now."

Once again, the three alphas moved outside.

Becca moved to the window and watched their shadows have a huddle in the predawn light. This time, unfortunately for her, the window was closed. Still, their body language was fascinating. They stood close—no avoiding eye contact. Clearly they knew each other well enough to get in each other's faces without worrying about the niceties.

Becca's inner circle consisted of family, her mom, dad, and brother, and they were pretty laid-back, go-with-the-flow kind of people. They'd rather pull their own teeth than have a confrontation or hurt anyone's feelings.

Especially Jase's. Her brother was the desperately yearned-for son, the prodigy, the wonder child. He had to be protected and coddled and taken care of, at any cost. Always and forever. Becca had been tasked with this, and she'd done her best, even through his stress and anxiety and ultimate pain pill addiction. She'd done everything she could for him, until it had cost her.

Big time.

She'd left to save herself, and there'd been no fight about it. No discussion at all, really.

Unbelievably, the silhouettes of the three big tough guys didn't fight, either. They stepped back from each other and…began a game of…rock paper scissors?

Less than a minute later Sam strode back in.

"You won," Becca said, surprised.

He gave her a long look. Nope, he hadn't won.

He'd lost.

Chapter 11

I called your references," Sam said.

Becca sucked in a breath. She'd known he would, because no matter what their appearances, he and his partners were not just three fun-loving guys. They were also sharp businessmen and smart as hell. "And?" she asked.

"You were widely beloved at your last job, and everyone was sorry to see you go." He paused and gave her a long, speculative look. "In such a hurry."

Her heart skipped a beat.

"Care to explain the hurry?" he asked.

"No."

"There was a rough situation with your brother."

She felt herself go still. "What?"

"One of your references mentioned it. Said you were resilient, though, and that I'd be lucky to have you."

Becca closed her eyes.

"Is he the one who hurt you?"

She opened her eyes and met his, and the concern in them. "I never said anyone hurt me."

"But someone did."

"Jase wouldn't hurt a fly," she said.

Sam didn't point out that she'd just given him a non-answer, but it was in his gaze as he poured a mug of coffee, then surprised her by handing it over.

She took it, then began to add creamer and sugar. Sam poured another mug and leaned back to watch her add more sugar to hers. "So you take a little coffee with your sugar then?"

Grateful for the subject change, she shrugged. "I like it sweet."

He drank from his steaming mug. "I like it hot."

She got all tingly, damn it. No more tingling for him! Feeling very warm suddenly, she unwrapped the scarf from her neck.

Sam remained silent, but his lips tipped at the corners.

She tugged off her gloves as well.

"Déjà vu," he said.

At the mention of her striptease in her bathroom, she felt herself blush. "It's cold here in the mornings. Very cold."

"Bird bones," he said.

She opened her mouth and then shut it. "Okay, I'm trying to drum up some outrage at being compared to a bird," she finally said. "But I have to admit, it's better than some other things I've been told about myself."

"Such as?"

"I once had a date mention something about a Butter-ball turkey."

Sam went still. "Did you kill him?"

Becca knew she wasn't heavy, but she was curvy. She used it to her advantage when she dressed. It was only in her…undressed activities that sometimes her insecurities came out. "No."

"Want *me* to kill him?"

"No!" she said on a laugh. "It can be true, from certain angles."

"Bullshit." He didn't make a move toward her, didn't touch her with anything but his eyes, which were flashing temper now. "You're perfect."

She laughed again, and he smiled. "Your body," he clarified. "Your *body's* perfect."

"But the rest drives you crazy," she reminded him.

"*Everything* about you drives me crazy." He drank his coffee and set down the mug. "So. You've made a choice."

"Actually, that was you," she reminded him. "I'm not on board with the whole having-to-choose thing. At all." Deciding to let him digest that, she took a moment to look around.

The hut had a front counter, several stools in front of it, a love seat, and a small refrigerated drink display and snack shelf. One entire wall was taken up with a display: scuba gear, snorkel gear, a paddleboard, a kayak, paddles, and more. "So what's the routine?" she asked.

"No routine, every day's different." He walked with her behind the counter. "But this is where you'll be most of the time." He unlocked a drawer and pulled out a laptop. "The schedule's here, but there's a problem. It's never up to date because we end up just scratching stuff down whenever and wherever we answer the phones."

She looked at the stack of notes on napkins, scribbled on paper bits, and even on a piece of wood.

"Yeah," he said to her unspoken question. "Asinine, we get that. But the Internet is painfully slow—Cole's working on that—and in the meantime, this is our way of dealing with it."

"Because you're guys?"

He lifted a broad shoulder. "What can I say, we're messy and unorganized."

"Which is how both you and Cole showed up for the same job this morning," she said, boggled at the chaos.

"Actually, no. Cole's a cheat, and can be bought by a pretty face."

"A pretty face?"

"The client's an LA print-ad model whose parents live here in Lucky Harbor. She's home for a short visit, and as she always does, she's taking her brothers and dad out fishing."

She narrowed her eyes. "Which is why you and Cole were fighting for the job."

"Actually," he said, "all three of us fought for it, but Tanner won."

"*Fought?*"

"We raced to the end of the harbor and back for it."

"Tanner's the fastest runner?"

"Swimmer."

Her eyes bugged out. "You guys *swam* from here to the end of the harbor and back?"

Sam shrugged. "Even with his bad leg, Tanner's a fish; no one can catch him. But then the client added four friends, so Tanner needed an assist."

"And you wouldn't have minded...*assisting.*"

He shrugged again, which translated—in guy speak—to no, he wouldn't have minded assisting.

"Men are annoying," she said.

He didn't look bothered by this blanket assessment of his species. "We don't do the clientele."

"Or the employees," she said.

"Or the employees." He pointed to the phone. "That's going to ring all day. People call for information. They ask questions or want to see about booking a trip. We've been trying to build a mailing list, so when the calls come in, we've been gathering contact info for a database."

He was standing close. He didn't have much of a choice; the space behind the counter was tight, and he was big. Normally, she really liked her own space bubble, and in fact got claustrophobic without one, but with his hair still damp and curling around his ears from a recent shower, and his warm, strong bod so close they kept brushing together, claustrophobia was the last thing she was feeling.

"The gist is this," he said, either ignoring their chemistry or no longer feeling it. "We have a fifty-foot Wright Sport boat. We're available for hire for just about anything. Cruises, deep-sea fishing, whale-watching, snorkeling, scuba diving—novice or expert. Tanner handles most of the planning and charting of the scuba, snorkeling, and fishing expeditions. He's lucky as hell and can always find the sweet spot. Cole's the captain of the boat, and our mechanic."

"And you?" she asked. "What is it you bring to the table?"

He met her gaze. "I'm the people person."

She laughed, and he actually flashed a smile at her. "Okay," he said. "That might be a little bit of a stretch."

"You do okay," she said softly.

Their gazes locked, and then his dropped to her mouth. "I have my moments."

His voice gave her a rush of warmth, but before she could say anything else, the phone rang. Sam gestured for her to sit at the stool and answer. As she picked up the receiver and said "Good morning, Lucky Harbor Charters," Sam pulled over the second stool. Their thighs brushed, his hard and muscled.

The space behind the counter seemed to shrink even farther.

"Hi," the caller said in her ear. "I heard you guys might have a big summer bash, complete with fireworks. Is that true?"

Becca looked at Sam.

Sam shook his head.

Becca put the call on hold.

"It's something we talked about," Sam said. "A sort of customer-appreciation thing. But no one has time to even think about it."

"I can do it for us," she said.

He went brows up at the *us*, but he shook his head again. "It's too much work, the organization of the party, and fireworks and—"

"What do you have against fireworks?"

His look said he realized she wasn't referring to actual pyrotechnics, but the hot sparks between the two of them. "*No* fireworks," he said. "Besides, none of us is certified to do a fireworks show."

"I thought all males knew how to blow stuff up."

"I didn't say we don't know how. I said we're not certified."

"So we hire someone." She tapped the computer. "Show me your schedule for August."

Sam leaned in, and his fingers worked the keyboard. Their thighs were still touching, and so were their upper arms. He was big and toasty warm, and he smelled good enough to lick, but she controlled herself.

He'd chosen.

And then she'd chosen.

Sam showed her the screen and then didn't move back, which she found interesting.

And arousing.

Their August schedule was indeed already busy. Plus, she had to take into account all the trips that hadn't made it onto the calendar yet because they were still floating around as scribbled notes, but there was still room. "You have the beachfront, right?" she asked.

"Yeah."

"So let's throw that customer-appreciation bash," she said.

He just looked at her.

"You have me now," she said, and felt herself blush again. Why was everything sounding sexual? "I can help with the planning and the work."

He just looked at her some more.

"Okay, I'll plan *all* of it," she said. "Your clients will love it."

"Are you always this relentless?"

"Yep. Stubborn as hell, too. Sorry, I forgot to put that on my job application." And then, sensing his acquiescence, she leaned in and kissed his firm, hard mouth.

She'd meant it to be just a quick peck to soften him up, but that's not what happened. In fact, it was the opposite of what happened, because he hauled her off her stool and onto his lap.

One of his warm, hard arms banded around her hips, the other hand cupping the back of her head, tilting it to the angle he wanted. And then he claimed her mouth like he meant it. In less than two heartbeats, he'd made her forget her own name, that she had a caller on hold, and what day of the week it was. When he was done—and he took his sweet-ass time about it, too—he lifted his head and surveyed her expression, his own a lot more mellow, his eyes heavy-lidded and sexy.

Clue one that she wasn't the only one affected. Clue two was currently poking her in the butt. She had one arm tight around his neck and the other hand fisted in his hair, holding on. That was all she could ever do when he got up in her space like this—hold on for dear life.

With one last indiscernible look, he dropped her back into her chair.

"We having fireworks or what?" she managed.

"Shit," he said, and scrubbed a hand over his face. "Yeah. We're having fireworks. More than I realized, apparently."

With a smile, she picked up the phone. "Yes," she said to the waiting customer. "We're having a bash complete with fireworks. If you leave your information, I can make sure you're in our system, and that way you'll get our invite."

Sam shook his head when she'd hung up. "Hope you can pull this off," he said.

"I can." With her eyes closed. She was good at organizing and planning. Really good. "What else do I do?" she asked.

Sam showed her a list of services and prices so that the next time someone called, she'd be prepared to book a trip. "Stick to what we've got listed here," he said. "Don't add anything new unless you check with one of us. If anyone needs something you can't answer, Cole or Tanner are on radio."

"But not you?"

"I don't typically spend a lot of time in here," he said.

"Because using your people skills is really hard on you?"

"Yeah," he said drily, "and because if I'm not out on the water, then I'm in the shop working on the financials, or building a boat." He stood up. "Another thing you'll do is check out our rental equipment. Snorkel gear, paddleboards, kayaks…" He moved to a door behind her and opened it up to a back room.

Sam led her in there and flicked on the light. There were no windows here. The place was tight quarters and filled to the gills with gear and equipment on racks that looked well taken care of and perfectly organized. One wall was lined with a huge industrial sink.

"The cleaning tank," he said. "We bleach the rental gear between uses to hotel standard code."

She nodded but took in the dark, closed-in feel of the room. The claustrophobia was relatively new, as far as her neuroses went, and even as she thought it and remembered what had caused it, the air was sucked from her lungs. "You need a bigger hut," she whispered.

"Undoubtedly," he said, his back to her as he eyed the shelves. "You ever snorkel? Paddleboard? Kayak?"

She swallowed hard. "Not a lot of that where I came from."

He laughed quietly, and she might have reveled in the deep, masculine sound, but she was starting to sweat. The walls were closing in on her; she could feel them. "Um, I need to…" She gestured to the door, and practically leapt back to the front room.

She thought she'd covered her tracks pretty well as she leaned casually against the front counter and managed to stay still while sucking in big gulps of air, but when she looked up, Sam was standing close watching her.

He didn't try to touch her, for which she was grateful. Touching her in the midst of a burgeoning anxiety attack only made it worse. "Whew," she said with a fake smile. "It's hot back there, right?"

He walked to the glass-fronted fridge and pulled out a bottle of water, which he uncapped and then handed to her.

She gulped it down, grateful he was going to let her have her little freak-out. "I'll learn all this stuff real fast," she promised.

He met her gaze. "You have nothing to prove here, you know that, right?"

Uncomfortable with the straightforward, brutally honest words that conflicted with his oddly gentle voice, she just nodded. "I know."

"But if the guys and I are out on the boat and you get a customer, you've got to be able to go in there," he said quietly.

"I know. I get it. I'll be fine." She held her breath, thinking he was either going to fire her on the spot, or push for details.

He did neither. "All right," he said, apparently trusting her. He could have no idea how much that meant to her, and it took her a moment to swallow the lump in her throat.

He didn't miss that, either. He simply gave her the moment she needed, watching her closely but not interfering as she got her shit together. "Hang on a second," he said, and vanished into the equipment room for a moment. He came back with a tote slung over one broad shoulder.

He held out a hand, which she took without even thinking, and let him lead her down to the dock. The boat was gone, but he opened the tote and spread out some gear. "Consider this lesson number one," he said.

"For what?"

"Life."

She laughed. "What does snorkeling have to do with real life?"

"Teaches you how to live in the here and now, for one thing." He looked up at her in the early dawn light to see if she got him.

She got him.

"Plus you need to know how this stuff works," he said. "If you stick, we'll have more lessons."

"I'm sticking."

He didn't respond to this. Instead, he stripped out of his ball cap and T-shirt, rendering her mute.

He slid into the water and showed her how to work the snorkel gear.

She nodded a lot, and said "uh-huh" a lot, and tried not to drool. When he was done, he effortlessly hoisted himself out of the water and back onto the dock. He shook like a big, shaggy dog, spraying her with water.

"Hey," she said.

He surprised her with a quick grin that short-circuited a few brain cells. Then he gathered the gear and carried it back to the hut and into the equipment room, dumping it into the sink to be cleaned. She watched from the doorway while he returned everything to its place and then moved aside for him to pass.

Instead, he stopped with her in the small space. "You okay?"

"Yes." Even with him near, she was okay. Actually, she was more okay than usual—and she had no idea what to make of that.

His mouth smiled, but his eyes remained serious. And possibly a little bit sympathetic, which she didn't want to see, so she moved into the front room. And because her knees were a little weak, she sank to the couch.

"Is it tight spaces?" he asked quietly, "or being in tight spaces with a man?"

She stilled, hating that she'd been so transparent. She studied her feet, and then picked at a nonexistent piece of lint on her sweatshirt.

"I see," he said.

But he didn't see. He couldn't possibly see...

He pulled on his shirt again, and then his hat, and crouched in front of her, balancing with ease on the balls of his feet. "Customers aren't allowed back there, period," he said. "Now that you're on board, none of the three of us needs to get into it, either. It's all your domain during the hours you're here. Got me?"

He was saying that she had no reason to feel anxious here. A warm feeling filled her stomach and started to spread. She smiled, and this time it was real again. "Got you."

He studied her for a moment, and his mouth quirked. "You're going to be good for us," he said. "You smile like that at any of our customers, and they'll be lining up for our services. Ready for more training?"

"Ready."

Once again he moved behind the counter with her. They stood close and remained that way while he showed her how to check the equipment in and out. In doing so, they kept brushing against each other, and she began to heat up again. She pulled off yet another of her layers, leaving her in just the tank top that was now sticking to her like a second skin.

Sam closed his eyes, took off his baseball cap, shoved his fingers through his hair, and then replaced the cap. Everything about him said big, bad, frustrated testosterone overload. She met his gaze.

"You're right," he said. "We need a bigger hut."

Chapter 12

♥

That day Becca went to the rec center after work. Lucille had called and said they'd be waiting for her. Assuming she was going in for an interview, she changed into a cute sundress from Olivia's store, added a denim jacket and wedge sandals, and made her way over there.

She was met by a really great-looking guy in navy-blue cargoes and a polo shirt with a firehouse insignia on the pec.

"Jack Harper," he said, offering her a hand. "Fire marshal. How you doing?"

"Great." She pulled her résumé from her bag. She'd doctored it up some. Okay, a lot. "I know I don't have teaching experience, Mr. Harper, but I do have a four-year degree in music and—"

"Jack," he said, and took her résumé, which he promptly scanned and then rolled up and shoved in his back pocket. "And you're hired." He gently nudged her down the hall and to a classroom, filled with at least twenty kids, all in the neighborhood of…young. "You've got an hour and a half with them. Good luck."

"Wait." She grabbed his arm. "Are you telling me I start now?"

"Actually," he said, looking at his watch. "Five minutes ago. And between you and me, I wouldn't dally. They're good kids—until they get bored."

Indeed, the natives were restless. She could see two girls, twins by the look of their matching wild red hair and toothless grins, climbing up on their desks to do God knew what. A couple of boys were throwing balled-up paper at each other. Two more were crawling beneath the desks on some mysterious errand.

Jack swore beneath his breath, leaned into the classroom, and gave a sharp whistle.

Everyone froze.

"Good," Jack told them. "More of that. Pink and Kendra, get down. Alex, Tray, Jose, and Carlos, don't make me come in there." He paused while everyone got into their seats like little angels. "Now stay just like that," he commanded, "until Ms. Thorpe says otherwise. She's the boss, and what the boss says goes."

"Impressive," Becca muttered to him.

"Trust me, that'll only work for a minute tops," Jack said. "If all else fails, there's a bag of candy in the teacher's desk. Use sparingly. Sugar's their crack."

"But…" She stared at the kids. "I didn't realize I'd be starting today. I don't have a curriculum. Or instruments. Or—"

"We have some stuff that was donated." He fished a key out of his pocket and set it in her palm. "In the storage closet." He gave her a quick heart-fluttering smile. "Good luck."

He'd handled the kids with a few quiet, authoritative words, no problem, and she hoped to do the same. Heart pounding, she walked into the room. "Hey, kids. So who likes music?"

Everyone's hands shot straight up into the air like rockets.

Becca smiled in relief, walked over to the storage closet, and unlocked it. There was a pile of flutes and a string bass that had seen better days. There was also some percussion—and by that she meant two beat-up snare drums, a set of crash cymbals, and a xylophone. It all gave her a bad flashback to middle school band practice.

Turning from the closet, she pulled her iPad mini from her purse and brought up her keyboard app.

Immediately six of the twenty kids were able to do the same on their phones. "Look at that," she said. "We're halfway to a band already."

The kids cheered. Laughing, Becca pushed her desk back, sat on the floor, gathered everyone around her, and did the only thing she knew how to do.

Plowed her way through.

The next day, Sam was at work in his warehouse. He'd sheathed the wood hull with a layer of fiberglass cloth for durability, both topsides and bottom. Now he was applying resin, making the weave of the cloth virtually transparent, bringing out the wood's natural tone. The result was a stiff, strong, stable, watertight composite wood/epoxy/fiberglass hull that was virtually impervious to the effects of moisture. He was concentrating, his every muscle aching from the strain, so that he almost didn't hear the door open and close.

Almost. Because here, in his shop, he heard and saw everything. He never invited anyone in here. Even Cole and Tanner rarely ventured in.

It was his place, his zone.

He didn't turn to look at the door; he didn't have to. He recognized the footsteps as Becca's. Soft but not hesitant, her spontaneity and easy joy showing in every step despite whatever life had handed her—which clearly hadn't been all rainbows and kittens. Boggling, And a little bit scary.

"Hey," she said, coming up behind him. "Is it okay for me to enter the Man Cave or do I need to perform the secret handshake or something?"

He laughed. "Smart-ass."

"Sorry," she said, not looking sorry at all. "My mouth's always been a problem."

Yeah, a *big* problem. He remembered that mouth, and exactly what it felt like traveling the length of his body. Even now, in the light of day, her lips were full and shiny with gloss, and he had a hard time looking away from them. And then there was the fact that she smelled like peaches and cream.

He wanted to eat her alive.

"I've got a few messages for you." She stepped to his side, taking in his work. "Pretty," she said. "Is there a good profit in making boats?"

"Not really."

She ran a hand over the sleek wood. "So you do it because...you're good at it?"

"No."

She looked up at him. "Okay, man of mystery. If not for the profit, or to show it off, then why do you build boats?"

"For myself."

"For yourself?"

"Yeah," he said, and because a slight frown had formed between her brows, he reached out and stroked a finger there to ease the tension. "You should try it sometime," he suggested. "Doing something for yourself."

"I moved across the country for myself."

"That's not why you moved," he said.

Something flashed in her eyes and was gone. "You think you know why I moved?" she asked.

"You needed to get away from something," he said.

She made a noncommittal kind of noise, not giving a thing away. Then she paused. "So what do you think I should do for myself then?"

"Whatever feels right."

She stared at him for the longest beat, and then she surprised him. She stepped close, so close they were toe-to-toe and everything in between, and his only thought was Oh, Christ, *this* feels right. He let his hands go to her hips.

"Something for myself," she murmured.

"Yeah."

"Hmm." Her hands rested on his chest, her fingers gripping the material of his shirt over his pecs. He wasn't sure if she was holding on for courage or because she wanted to touch him.

"I haven't been able to think of something to do for myself for a long time," she said.

"And now?"

She stared at her hands on him. "I still might need help in that area."

He tipped her face up to his and looked into her eyes, and he saw that she had courage in spades. "Several things come to mind," he said.

"Are these things…good for me?" she asked.

"Not a single one."

She both laughed and trembled against him, and damn but that shouldn't send lust rocketing through his veins, and yet it totally did.

"Good's overrated anyway," she whispered.

He couldn't believe how much he wanted her. Wanted to press her up against the boat. Or bend her over it. Both ways, he decided. All ways. "We said we weren't doing this anymore," he said, more than a little shocked at how gruff his own voice was and at the need coursing through him. "Not while you work for me." And he'd meant it. He fucking one hundred percent had.

"No, *you* said that," she reminded him. "*I* didn't sign on for the not-doing-it program. And besides—" She made a big show of looking at the time on her phone. "I'm off the clock." She smiled at him guilelessly. "Lunch break. And last I checked, it wasn't an employer's business what his or her employee does on their lunch break."

Closing his eyes, Sam let out a long, admittedly shaky breath. He was in trouble here. Big trouble. "Becca—"

"Shh," she said. "Or the boss'll fire me. We have to be really quiet. Really, *really* quiet." And then she rocked her hips into him.

And rocked his world. Because just like that, he was a dead man. He tightened his grip and groaned at the feel of her, and she murmured "Shh" again, softly, sexily.

Using the hand he had tangled in her hair, he drew her in closer. Meeting him halfway, she went up on her tiptoes and snagged an arm around his neck. He already knew she kissed like she appeared to do everything else: with her entire heart and soul.

In other words, amazing.

He was halfway to heaven, his tongue buried in her mouth, his hands full of warm, soft, curvy Becca, when a throat clearing had her jerking away from him.

Sam was much slower to lift his head, to let go of her sweet, hot body and register that Amelia stood there, smile in place, brows arched in that way mothers the planet over had nailed down.

"I brought you cookies," she said, "but you look like you're already having your dessert."

Sam bit back his sigh. "Amelia—"

Amelia arched her brow further.

Years ago, maybe the second or third time he'd landed in her house, she'd tried bossing him into a curfew. He'd been a smart-ass and had called her Mom. He'd been joking, but she'd liked it, preferred it, and to this day she made him call her that. "*Mom*," he corrected.

"Better. Now, don't mind me," she said, coming into his shop the way no one else ever did.

Well, except the woman who'd been in his arms only a few seconds ago, the woman now staring at Amelia, gaze confused, probably wondering at the "Mom" thing.

Amelia smiled a warm welcome at Becca as if she was the hostess at a tea party. "And you are…?"

"Becca."

"Ah," Amelia said, offering a hand. "The new hire." She sent Sam a long, hard glare that wasn't all that hard to interpret. It said: *Why are you tangling tonsils with the new girl?*

Sam scrubbed a hand over his face and took the container of cookies from Amelia. "Becca, Amelia is Cole's mom and—"

"Just Cole's mom?" Amelia interrupted, eyes flashing.

Well, shit, here we go, Sam thought. "And okay," he said. "Also a sort-of mom to me."

Amelia snatched the container of cookies back, making Sam grimace.

"You know what I mean," he said.

"No," she said. "You'd best clarify. Immediately, if you want these cookies. And let me just tell you right now, they're your favorite—double fudge with chocolate chips—and they're my best batch yet. And also, keep in mind that what I just saw going on in here is blackmail material, so make it good, sweetheart. *Real* good. *Sort-of* mom?"

There were few people who'd ever gone out on a limb for Sam, and he didn't even need the fingers of one hand to count them. Amelia was one. "How about you were the only mom I ever had?" he asked.

"Oh." Her beautiful blue eyes filled, and she sniffed as she stepped toward him, her arms outstretched. "Oh, Sam, you're so sweet."

Sam endured her hug and a kiss to each of his cheeks, and then she was gone. "Sorry about that," he said to Becca, who was nibbling her lower lip, her thoughts seemingly far away. "You okay?"

"She was like a mama bear with you," she said, sounding a little bit awed. "She'd probably fight to the end for you."

"Would, and has."

When she just looked at him, he let out a breath. "My mom died when I was five. My dad was never real great at being a dad. I landed in foster care. A lot."

Her eyes softened. "Oh, Sam."

"Amelia used to take in the occasional foster kid, and the minute I ended up at her place, she…claimed me." He gave a small smile. "She's protective."

"That's where you met Cole."

"Yeah."

"He claimed you, too," she said.

"The apple didn't fall far from the tree there," he agreed. "But we claimed each other."

"That's incredibly sweet." Her eyes were suspiciously shiny, but before he could get a good look, she turned to the door. "I gotta get back to work."

And then she was gone, too, leaving him to wonder at the sadness he'd seen in her gaze. Had no one ever been willing to fight for *her*?

Chapter 13

Becca tossed and turned, one odd and uncomfortable dream chasing another. Her parents were there, only they weren't her parents. They were her employers, asking her to take care of Jase.

"I already do," she said.

"You left him. You walked away," they accused.

And then Jase was standing there with him. "You did," he said. "You left me."

"No, I—" But she broke off when Jase turned into Sam.

She reached for Sam but he took a step back and was flanked on either side by Cole and Amelia.

"We've got him," they said.

She stared at them, seeing the bond, and turned back to her family.

Her parents and Jase had vanished.

She was alone. Feeling an odd sensation in her chest, she looked down and saw her heart crack in half. With a gasp, she sat straight up in bed.

She looked down at her heart. Still in her chest. That was good. As to whether or not it was cracked in half, that was another question entirely.

It was four thirty. Since there would be no more sleep, she checked email and saw that she had one from the ad agency.

Her Diaxsis jingle had been accepted, and she'd been sent her next assignment. Eagerly, she'd loaded the doc and read.

The assignment was for a line of personal hygiene products.

She flopped on her back and stared at the ceiling, allowing a few moments of self-pity. When she was over herself, she sat up and stared at the email for another moment. Then she hit REPLY, responding with what she thought was calm grace, explaining that she realized she had to earn her way back into good graces after her yearlong slow spell, but that she felt she'd come through twice in a row now and wanted a better product to write about.

Like, say, something, anything, that wasn't mortifying to put on her résumé.

It was hours later before she got a reply.

This is what we have. Take it or leave it.

She took it.

The day was a hot one. Sam went for a predawn run with Ben and then found himself trapped in his warehouse office hunched over the books for hours, sweat running down his back.

Or maybe he was hot because he'd headed to the hut

earlier to check on Becca and had found her running his world with an ease and charm he'd never managed, wearing a snug white tee and bubblegum-pink shorts, looking heart-stoppingly amazing.

At the memory, he reached into his fridge to grab a badly needed soda and discovered it empty. Tanner, of course. The guy would walk all the way over here to steal Sam's last soda rather than hit the store.

Sam rose to go himself, when someone knocked on the open doorjamb.

His dad.

And behind him, Becca.

"Hey, son." Mark said this tentatively, and he had good reason. He rarely made an in-person visit, preferring the telephone to suck Sam dry.

"Dad," Sam said. "What're you doing here?"

Mark set a lopsided-looking snowman on Sam's desk.

"Found this in your mom's storage," Mark said. "You made it for me, remember?"

Sam remembered. He'd been seven and looking forward to a promised fishing trip. Sam had made the clay snowman with the lady who babysat him while waiting for his dad.

And waiting.

Mark had never shown.

"I know you don't like company in here," Mark said, "but your cutie-pie admin here told me where to find you. She said it'd be okay."

Sam gave his "cutie-pie" admin a long look.

Becca met his gaze, her eyes filled with sympathy.

Which, for the record, Sam hated.

"He wanted to see you," she said apologetically. "I

know you don't like unannounced company in the Man Cave, but it's your dad, right? So I locked the hut and put up a sign saying I'd be right back."

Mark beamed at her. "You're great. Isn't she great, son?"

Sam thought about bashing his head against his desk. "Yeah. Great. What's up, Dad?"

Mark shrugged. "Nothing. Just came to see you."

"You never come to see me," Sam said.

Instead of responding, Mark turned his head and looked out into the open area of the warehouse, eyeing the boat Sam was building. "Impressive."

"I already put money into your account," Sam said, crossing his arms.

"Yeah." Mark didn't meet Sam's eyes, but kept them on the boat. "Thanks."

"Christ," Sam said. "It wasn't enough."

"No, it was enough," Mark said. "It was great. It's just that…" He trailed off.

"What?" Sam said. "It's just that what?"

"She kicked me out. Changed the locks and everything."

Sam stared at him. "Let me guess. She also wiped out your account."

Mark lifted a shoulder.

"Are you fucking kidding me?" Sam asked.

No longer smiling, Becca stirred. "Sam—"

"*Again?*" Sam asked Mark. "Seriously?"

Mark sighed with clear misery.

Sam wasn't moved. At all. They'd done this dance too many times. Hell, all Sam's life. His dad never learned. Nor, apparently, did Sam. "Why can't you do what you did last time and grovel?" he asked. "Or whatever it is you do that reels them in."

"Sam, he's got nowhere to go," Becca said softly. "And—"

"Already told her your sob story, I take it," Sam said over her head to his dad.

Mark looked guilty as hell and Sam shook his head, working on not grinding his back teeth into powder.

"I thought maybe I could stay here," Mark said. "I'll stay out of your way."

Sam's gut tightened. Having his dad here would kill him. Or drive him to kill his dad.

One or the other.

"Mark," Becca said softly. "Can you give us a minute?"

"Sure, darlin'," Mark said, and with one last look at Sam he stepped out of the office.

"He said he's had some problems," Becca said quietly.

"Yeah," Sam said. "Lots of them. He gambles, he drinks, he lies. Pick one. You shouldn't have brought him here, Becca."

"Not her fault," Mark said firmly, back in the doorway. "She tried to tell me that no one comes in here without permission, so don't you blame her."

"And yet you came anyway," Sam said. "You took advantage of her sweetness and pushed your way through with one of your bullshit emergencies."

"It *is* an emergency," Mark said.

"Sam," Becca said with soft reproach. "He's—"

"No, darlin'," Mark said. "Don't defend me. It's okay. I deserve his mistrust, believe me." He met Sam's gaze. "I'm sick."

Sam felt this news reverberate through him. He searched his dad's expression. The truth was there, and his gut tightened painfully. "How sick?"

Mark grimaced.

"Cancer?" Sam asked. "Your heart?"

"No." Mark paused. "Liver stuff."

Sam drew in a long, unsteady breath, unable to reconcile all the years-old resentments with the new and terrifying fear for his dad's health. "I've got a spare bedroom at the house," he said. He spent the majority of his time here. This was his *real* home, his *first* real home that he'd gotten for himself, and he wasn't sure he could share it with his dad.

"Thank you," Mark said, with genuine humility. "I won't be a bother."

Feeling like a first-class dick, Sam reached into the desk, pulled out a key, and tossed it to his dad.

Mark pocketed it with a nod of his head. "See you later then. Love ya, son."

Sam closed his eyes, and when he opened them Mark was gone. Not quite trusting himself to speak, he stayed still. After a moment, he felt a gentle hand slide up his back.

"You okay?" Becca asked.

He was a lot of things. Gut sick. Angry. Furious, even. And afraid. One thing he was not was okay. Shoving free of the desk, he dislodged her hand, picked up the snowman on his desk, and chucked it across the room.

It shattered on the far wall.

Becca leapt back, inadvertently slamming herself into his desk. At the impact, she jumped away and then tripped over his trash can, hitting the floor on all fours.

"Jesus." Sam crouched down and reached for her. "You okay?"

It was her turn to shove free of him, and he discovered

he didn't like the feeling very much as she got to her feet on her own.

He got slowly to his as well. "I'm sorry. I didn't mean to scare you."

She shook her head. "You didn't. I...saw a spider. It's gone now."

Shit. He really was an asshole. "Becca—"

"I'm...fine. Totally fine."

"You said it twice."

"So?" she asked.

"Saying it twice implies that you're not fine at all."

"No. Saying it twice makes it true," she said.

Sam let it go because she was desperately trying to calm her breathing while not meeting his gaze. He watched her hand shake as she lifted it to push her hair from her face.

"Becca," he said softly.

"I'm sorry, I shouldn't have brought him back here without asking—"

"It's not your fault. Becca—"

"Is he really sick?" she asked, clearly not wanting to discuss her reaction.

"I have no idea, but I'm going to find out."

She stared at him. "And if he is?"

"I'll take care of him."

She eyed the snowman on the floor in a thousand pieces. "My break's over," she said, moving to the door.

As gently as he could, he caught her by the wrist and slowly reeled her back in. Her breathing was still a little off, and her eyes were far too bright, but she met his gaze. "What?" she asked.

There were lots of *whats* going through his mind, but

he settled on one. "You're safe here," he said. "You know that, right?"

"Of course I know it."

"I was just pissed off because—"

"He drives you crazy. But he's your dad. I get it."

He could see that she did, but they were going to have to circle back to that fascinating subject because it wasn't what he wanted to cover right now. "You thought I was going to hurt you."

"No," she said. "Of course not."

Chest tight, he bent his knees to look into her eyes as he slowly slid his hands up her arms to cup her face.

"My break's over," she said again.

He shook his head and pulled her into him.

She remained frozen for one beat, then relaxed against his chest, pressing her face into his throat. They stood like that for a long moment. "I didn't think you were going to hurt me," she said. "I just…you surprised me."

"I lost my temper." He pulled back and met her gaze. "It doesn't happen very often, but I can lose my temper and not hurt you."

She nodded. "I know."

He wanted to believe that. He pulled her in again but the phone started ringing, accompanied by that stupid red light Cole had put in to be funny, and Becca backed away. "Later," she said.

Sam tried to go back to the books, but after an hour he gave up. He pulled out his cell and called his dad. "Define liver problem."

There was a long pause. "I don't know medical shit."

"Dad." Sam rubbed his temple. "Be straight with me. For once."

"It's a liver problem," he repeated.

Sam drew in a deep breath and let it out slowly. "What's the plan?"

"My insurance's crap."

Of course it was. "What's the plan," Sam repeated.

"I don't know yet. I'll fill you in when I do." Mark paused. "Your woman's a real catch, you know. You should hold on to her."

"She's not my woman, dad. She's my employee."

"Son, if that's true, then you're not as smart as I've always thought. She gave me a sandwich."

"Becca gave you a sandwich."

"Yeah, and she put chips on it. The girl's brilliant, I tell you."

"When did she feed you?"

"After I left your shop, I sat on the beach for a while, then wandered back to the hut. Becca asked if I needed anything, and I said not unless she had a sandwich, and she said she *did* have a sandwich, and yeah. It was amazing."

"You realize that you probably ate *her* lunch."

"She said she didn't want it."

Sam rubbed his temples again but it didn't help. The headache was upon him. "She was just being nice," he said. "Next time, if you're hungry, come to me. Got it? Not her, never her."

"Why not?"

"Because she'd give you the shirt off her back, Dad." *And you'd take it...*

"She said it was okay," Mark said stubbornly. "She said I could go see her any time I wanted."

Sam could actually feel his blood pressure rising. Before he had a stroke, he said, "I've got to go."

"You coming home soon?"

The thought of going home to his dad didn't help the blood pressure levels one little bit. "I don't know."

"Can't work the remote."

Sam closed his eyes. "I'll text you directions." He disconnected and considered throwing his phone, but then he spotted the pieces of the snowman still on the floor. *Shit.* He headed out and down to the hut, telling himself it was to get a soda.

He found his newest employee working the phones, the computer—hell, everything around her—with quick order.

When she saw him watching her, she tossed him the key to the back room. "Need two kayaks for these gents," she said, nudging her chin in the direction of two college kids waiting off to the side.

Sam caught the key but kept walking toward her until she was forced to tip her head up to meet his gaze. "You gave my dad your lunch?" he asked quietly.

Something flickered in her gaze. "Working here, Sam."

"You gave my dad your lunch."

"He was hungry."

"He's a fucking mooch, Becca."

"He's still your dad, Sam."

He dropped his head and studied his feet for a moment, then lifted his head. "Are you hungry?"

"No."

She wouldn't tell him if she was. He knew that damn well. Her picture was in the dictionary under Stubborn.

"The kayaks," she said, clearly not wanting to discuss this. Or anything. Not that he blamed her. He hadn't wanted to talk to her earlier, and she'd been right the other day when she'd told him she was a quick learner. She'd learned from him how to be emotionally unavailable.

Sam watched the clock and tried to catch Becca after work, but he got caught handling the boat with Cole because Tanner had a previous commitment. By the time they finished mooring it, the hut was closed up and Becca was gone.

No strains of a haunting piano came from her windows, and she didn't answer her door. With no reason to stand there in the hallway and wait for her like a stalker, he went back to his shop to work. He had the table saw on when a sound penetrated.

A piano?

He snapped off the saw and the music, and lifted his head.

Nothing.

He was losing it. He went back to work, but five minutes later he hit the switch again when he was sure he heard a piano.

It stopped immediately.

And then he got it. She was only playing when she thought he couldn't, or wouldn't, hear her. Goddamn it. Dropping everything, he strode out the door. Night had long ago fallen. He had no idea what time it was. Late.

Becca's place was dark, but he was on to her now. He moved across the alley and knocked. She didn't answer, but he'd expected that. He pulled out his phone and called her.

No answer.

He texted: *Open your door.*

Her response was immediate: *Not home.*

Bullshit. He could *feel* her. He didn't care how crazy that made him, it was true. He knocked again, just once, softly. "Not going away, Becca."

There was a huge hesitation from the other side of that door; he could feel that, too.

Then it slowly swung open.

Chapter 14

♥

Becca had answered the door against her better judgment, and at the sight of Sam standing there, a little bit edgy and a whole lot hot, she cursed herself for being weak. "You should be at home with your dad," she said, and started to close the door.

He caught it and held it open. "I have questions," he said.

"I'm busy."

He looked around at the apartment. "Doing…?"

"Writing a jingle. A very important one." She crossed her arms. She'd admit she was writing for a line of feminine products…never.

"I'll start with an easy one," he said, apparently not caring. "Ben told me he saw a Snapchat of you teaching at the rec center."

"Snapchat?"

"It's an app where you send a picture, but whoever you sent it to can only see it for a few seconds—"

"I know what Snapchat is," she said. "What was I doing on it?"

"That's what I'm asking."

She stared at him. "One of the kids," she muttered. "My money's on Pink."

"So it's true?" he asked. "You're teaching music to kids?"

"Apparently."

He took that in for a moment and nodded. "It suits you. Moving on to the next question."

She leaned on the doorjamb, all casual-like, as if she wasn't aching at the sight of him so at ease in his own skin—which, by the way, was dusted with wood shavings. "You miss the I'm-busy part?" she asked.

His eyes softened. Warmed. "I'll make it worth your while."

Her knees wobbled. Stupid knees. "No, you won't," she said. "You've gone all prim and proper and stodgy on me."

"Stodgy?"

She shrugged.

He stared at her, then let out a sound that might have been a laugh as he hauled her in close and personal, and kissed her right there in the doorway. It was a really great kiss, too, all slow and long and deep and hot.

Finally, when she was good and speechless, he pulled back and looked into her eyes. "Why do you play the piano when you think I can't hear you?" he asked.

Still not the question she expected, but not exactly one she wanted to answer, either, so she dropped her gaze from his beautiful, piercing eyes and looked at his throat. But this only reminded her that she liked to press her face there and inhale him because he always smelled amazing, like the ocean, like the beach, like one hundred percent *yummy* man. "That's ridiculous," she finally said.

He put a hand on her stomach and nudged her clear of the doorway, then stepped inside her apartment.

"Hey," she said.

He eyed the portable piano keyboard on her bed and the blankets wrinkled like she'd just been sitting right there playing—which, of course, she had.

He turned back to her, brow raised.

She crossed her arms. "I—" But she broke off because he got right in her precious space bubble. Like he'd forgotten he'd made her choose between him and the job. She'd been trying to maintain some distance, but it wasn't easy because…well, because she still wanted him, damn it. And she especially couldn't maintain any distance with the taste of him still on her tongue.

Then he cupped her face and made her look at him, and she couldn't remember her name much less why she didn't want him to cup her face like she was the most precious thing in his life.

As if.

"Why do you play the piano only when you think I'm not listening?" he asked again, his eyes unwavering, telling her that her answer really meant something to him.

She closed her eyes.

He merely shifted closer. "And why," he whispered against her lips, "are you giving me attitude when you used to give me sweet, like maybe you *want* to piss me off so I'll go away and leave you alone."

"Because I want you to go away and leave me alone," she whispered back.

"Because you don't want to talk about things," he said, calling her on it. Didn't he know that wasn't the polite thing to do? The polite thing to do was let her hide, damn it.

"You prefer to live in your head instead of the here and now," he said.

"Correct," she said back, and gave him a long look from beneath her lashes. "And anyway, you've asked your questions. Where's my *worthwhile*?"

His gaze heated about a gazillion degrees as he leaned in and kissed first one corner of her mouth, and then the other.

She tightened her grip on him, closed her eyes, then moaned and dropped her head to his shoulder when he stopped.

"You still work for me?" he asked, voice gruff.

Great. They were back to that. "Unless I'm fired."

"If I fired you, would you go get a job that better suits your abilities?" he asked.

"Like?"

"Like…being a full-time music teacher. Or writing more jingles."

"Because I just love writing about feminine products." Damn it, she hadn't meant to let that slip. "If you laugh," she warned, "our friendship—or whatever this is—is over."

He paused, as if doing his best to bite back his amusement. "How about doing whatever floats your boat?"

"Why do you care about what floats my boat?" she asked.

He didn't have an answer for that, apparently, since he said nothing, just looked at her with those eyes that seemed to see far more than she wanted him to.

"Stop worrying about me," she finally said. "It's not your problem. *I'm* not your problem."

"I don't know what kind of men you've had in your life, Becca, but that's not how I work."

"What are you saying? You're in my life?"

"Yes."

She didn't know what to make of that, so it was her turn to say nothing, but she couldn't help but stay a little too close. It was his warmth, she told herself. In any case, she wasn't the only one feeling…things. She could feel him still hard against her. "Your body doesn't agree with the not-sleeping-with-your-employee decree."

"You know I still want you," he said. "That's not exactly a secret. But I want to know what happened today in my office more."

She pulled back, but he caught her. "It was nothing," she said.

"Becca." His eyes were still on hers, his voice low but oddly gentle, as if he knew she'd just told a big, fat whopper.

And then, oh God and then, he cupped her face yet again and lowered his head, brushing his lips across hers. "It was a lot more than nothing," he said with another soft, devastatingly gentle kiss.

She sighed and pressed her face into his neck.

"I get that you don't know this about me yet," he said. "But you can trust me."

She lifted her head. "I do trust you."

"Not yet, you don't." He let his thumb glide over her lower lip, the one tingling for more of his mouth. "But you can," he repeated.

"Sam—"

"You'll tell me when. I won't push, Becca." And then with one last soul-warming kiss, he was gone.

Over the next few days, the guys were busy nonstop and nearly always gone. During that time, Becca had plenty to keep her occupied. Her mind was something else entirely. She wondered what Sam would do if she said *When*.

She wondered if she even could say *When*.

Lucille stopped by to visit.

"Thought I'd see about trying paddleboarding," the older woman said.

Becca tried to picture Lucille on a paddleboard in the harbor, but mostly all she could see was the Coast Guard trying to rescue her. "Um…"

"You don't think I'm too old, right?" Lucille asked.

"Well…"

"Because I keep in great shape." Lucille pointed to a biceps. "I've been hauling cans of prunes to the senior center all morning—"

"It's just that the guys are out of town," Becca said. "And first-timers need instruction."

"Oh." Lucille sighed. "Damn. That's a shame."

"A big shame," Becca agreed.

"I'll just come back another time." But she didn't leave. Instead, she made herself comfy on a stool. "So how's the jingles going? What are you working on?"

Becca sighed. "Feminine products."

Lucille grinned. "Sorry, honey, can't help you with that one. I don't need 'em anymore. Why don't you get something good to write about, like denture glue? I need a new brand and could use a suggestion."

Once Lucille finally left, Becca took a lunch break and

went to work on a curriculum for the kids at music hour. She needed to keep them busy, she discovered, or tiffs broke out among their ranks over who got to play what. So in addition to teaching them basic chords, they were working on how to respect other people's space bubble. The latter was a far more difficult lesson, but it would come along.

Everything would come along.

Or so she told herself in the deep, dark of the night when her insecurities beat the crap out of her.

After another homemade meal with Olivia—to-die-for lasagna this time—Becca finally wrote a passable jingle for the feminine products and sent it off.

And late at night, when she couldn't sleep, she played. Afterwards she'd walk home from the Love Shack at two thirty in the morning, alone with the salty ocean breeze and the moonbeams and her own troubled thoughts. A few nights back, on her first night playing, she'd heard something, someone, and she'd run the half mile to the warehouse, slammed into her loft, and with the lights still off plastered herself to the side of one of her windows.

Just in time to watch Sam vanish into the shadows.

The second night, she'd felt him as well, but when she'd stopped in the middle of the street and spun a circle to confront him, she'd been alone.

The next morning, when he'd come in for coffee, she'd searched his calm, even, handsome features for some sign that he was walking her home every night, but he gave her nothing.

So she kept it to herself. Because she knew what he was doing. He was just trying to give her back something he thought she was missing—her music. She appreciated that, even as she resented the fact that she was also missing something else.

Him in her bed.

You'll tell me when.

The man confused the hell out of her. But denial had always been her friend, and that hadn't changed. Early one morning, she unlocked and opened up the hut. She might have been hired to answer phones and greet customers, but she'd taken over handling their website, too. And then there was the ongoing planning for the upcoming Summer Bash, which had taken on a life of its own.

She started the coffee, brought up the schedule, handled all the charter's online email and site correspondence, and then got to the Summer Bash stuff. Sam had reluctantly signed off on the pyrotechnics contract, the band, and the promos on Facebook and Twitter.

Becca was still planning out the logistics, hiring high school kids from the rec center for the setup on that day, renting tables and chairs and awnings. She was figuring out the decorations, too, some of which she'd found in the back storage room. She'd hauled out a big duffel bag filled with strings of white lights, wanting to use them along the dock and to decorate the boat. Problem was, the lights were literally in a huge ball, a tangled mess.

She'd been working on that here and there, and was at it again, sitting cross-legged on the floor, when Sam came in. He strode straight for the coffee. Saying nothing, he brought his mug up to his delectable mouth and eyed her over the rim as he drank. When the caffeine sank in about two minutes later, he finally spoke. "Mornin'."

"Morning." She paused, wondering which direction to

take this conversation. Were they mad at each other? Still circling each other? Ignoring each other?

She gestured to the stack of paper, napkins, and whatever else they'd been writing email addresses on for months. "I realize you all had a system going here with this lovely pile, but I have good news—my system's better. I've got you all caught up."

He smiled. "Glad to hear that. You've been busy."

"More than you know. Right now I'm working on the decorations." She gestured to the big mess of lights in front of her. Stuck on yet another knot, she swore beneath her breath. "And by the way, this is a really stupid way to store your lights."

"Yeah, and if Tanner sees that mess, he'll kill Cole. Tanner's pretty fanatical about the equipment." Sam hunkered in front of her, took the ball, shoved it back into the duffel, and rose, slinging it over his shoulder.

"What are you doing?" she asked.

"Taking care of it."

"You're going to untangle that mess?" she asked.

"I'm going to take care of it," he repeated.

Okay then. So she rose, too. "How's your dad?"

"Sprawled out on my couch watching movies and eating me out of house and home."

"So he's...okay?"

"I don't know," he said. "I'm seeing his doctor later today."

Sam didn't give off a whole lot of "tells," but neither did he hide much. If he was feeling something—anger, amusement, arousal, whatever—he didn't seem to have much of a problem showing it. When his gaze met hers, she saw hints of worry mixed with irritation.

He didn't yet know what to think, and he was withholding judgment until he knew.

Which made him a whole lot smarter than her.

She tended to react first and think later. Hence the dreaming about him. The yearning for him. The kissing him the other night…In order to not repeat that mistake, she tore her eyes off his fine-ass self and instead looked at the walls.

There were a bunch of pictures, and she'd had a lot of time to study them. Most were of clients, some holding up large fish, others in scuba gear or just mugging for the camera on the boat and dock. There was one of a younger Sam, along with Cole and Tanner and another guy, the four of them on what appeared to be an oil rig, looking pretty badass. The next picture was in the same locale, but just Sam, Cole, and Tanner, with Tanner on crutches. "Seems like it must have been a real rough job," she said. "And dangerous."

Sam nodded, though to which she couldn't say. Maybe both.

"Did Tanner get hurt out there?" she asked.

"Yeah." He came to stand next to her, his gaze on the picture. "We nearly lost him along with Gil in a rig fire."

"Oh, my God." She turned back to the pic of the four men. She looked at Gil, so young, so full of life, and felt a pang for what they'd been through. "I can't imagine how awful it must have been."

"It sucked."

Sam didn't use a lot of words. He didn't need to. The few he chose were effective. She imagined *It sucked* covered it all. She took in the rest of the pictures, one with the three of them on a smaller boat than the one currently moored outside. "You've upgraded," she said. She turned to face him. He was wearing black board shorts today and a plain gray T-shirt. No ball cap this morning, but his sunglasses were in place. "You've given yourself a great life here," she said, realizing she was more than a little envious. "Working with your closest friends. All the adventures…"

A customer walked in. Actually, four customers, college buddies who wanted to rent surfboards along with Sam's expertise to tutor them. Becca logged the equipment rental, and Sam headed out with them.

On the beach, all of them stripped out of their shirts, but Becca had eyes for only Sam. She tried not to look but she honestly couldn't help herself.

Then he turned back, and caught her staring.

She considered dropping to the floor like she'd done when she'd gotten caught staring at him before, from her apartment, but it was far too late for that.

"Hey, Peeper," he called, and crooked his finger at her.

Damn. She met him halfway on the dock.

"You got a suit?" he asked.

She tore her gaze off his chest. "Suit?"

"A bathing suit," he said, looking amused. "Are you wearing a bathing suit under all those layers you're so fond of?"

"Yes," she said. "But I don't know how to surf."

"Lesson number two, in five minutes."

Oh, my God. "I don't—"

"You're still living in your head," he said. "Can't live in your head when you're surfing. On the water, you live for the here and now. Log yourself out a wet suit so you don't get cold. Five minutes," he repeated. "Give yourself an adventure." And, as it turned out, he gave her the adventure. She wasn't ever going to become a pro surfer, but she'd had the time of her life.

Late that afternoon Sam walked into the town medical building for a meeting with his dad's doctor.

Dr. Josh Scott had been ahead of Sam in school by about five years, but they'd gone rock climbing together a bunch of times, so Sam expected to spend a few minutes bullshitting before getting to the nitty-gritty of his dad's health problems.

What he didn't expect was to find his dad in the waiting room.

With Becca.

"Hey," she said, coming to him. "Your dad asked for a ride."

Mark nodded but didn't rise. It was hard to tell if his small smile was the usual *I'm up to shenanigans*, or an apology. "Next time," Sam said, looking into Becca's eyes. "Call me. You don't need to spend your time driving him around."

"I don't mind."

"I do," he said.

Her eyes narrowed a little bit, but she said nothing. She turned to his dad. "You take care of yourself," she said. "And if you need another ride, or anything, you know how to get me."

Mark gave her a real smile. She leaned in and kissed his cheek, and then, without another look at Sam, headed to the exit.

"Becca," he said.

Her response was to shut the door, with her on the other side of it. Great. Sam turned his head and met his dad's gaze.

"Son, seriously," Mark said. "I really believed you had all the brains in the family."

A nurse brought them to an exam room, and Josh came in wearing a white doctor jacket with a stethoscope around his neck and a ready smile. "Mark. Sam," he said. "Good to see you both. Sorry about the circumstances."

"And what exactly are the circumstances?" Sam asked.

Josh looked at Mark.

Mark looked guilty.

"You didn't tell him?" Josh asked.

"You do it so well," Mark said.

Josh gave him a pained look and turned to Sam. "Liver's failing. Slow, long deterioration, most likely caused by alcohol abuse. It's not acute. I've put him on meds and requested a diet that includes no alcohol and a moderate exercise plan. A lot of the time, the meds work and slow the deterioration down, but sometimes they don't."

Sam sat heavily. "And if they don't?"

"We'll see. Maybe a transplant if there's a serious life-style change," Josh said, and paused. He didn't say it, but Sam heard it—*if he's lucky*. Sam looked at his dad.

Mark met his gaze, the usual flash of guilt in his eyes.

Shit. "It's going to be okay," Sam said.

Mark nodded.

"It is," he reiterated, because like Becca said, saying it twice would make it so.

Chapter 15

Sweet baby Jesus," Olivia whispered.

Becca hummed her agreement but didn't take her eyes off front and center, which was a pack of three surfers out in the water. Cole, lean and rangy. Tanner, with more bulk to his muscle.

Sam, of the broad shoulders and ripped abs.

Becca stared at them and took a lick of her ice cream.

Olivia stared at them, too, and took a lick of her ice cream.

It was Sunday afternoon, and they were both off work. They'd made a pit stop at Lance's ice cream stand on the pier, where Becca had also bought a bag of ranch-flavored popcorn for herself for later, and then they'd planted themselves on the sand to watch the show.

"I'd have paid money for this," Olivia said. "Who's the deliciously mocha-skinned one?"

"Tanner," Becca said.

"Tanner's pretty damn fine," Olivia said.

"They're *all* fine."

Olivia snorted. "Like you're looking at anyone besides Sam."

This was true. Still, Becca tore her gaze off the guys to look at her cohort. "How do you know Sam but not Cole or Tanner?"

"Sam stopped one night on the highway when I had a flat tire and helped me fix it. Until I moved into the warehouse, I'd never seen the other two; they're not exactly my shop's usual clientele."

Becca smiled at the thought of any of the three guys shopping at the very lovely but very feminine store Olivia had created. "You could probably easily go out with either of them, if you're interested."

"I'm not," Olivia said. "At all." But she kept looking.

So did Becca.

That night, Becca FaceTimed with Jase, who was at her parents' house. He asked her again to come to Seattle for his upcoming concert.

And though Seattle was only two hours from Lucky Harbor, she once again declined.

Her mom and dad tried to pressure her into saying yes. They were worried about Jase, and for good reason. But Becca couldn't carry that burden alone again, not even for Jase.

"He can't continue without your support," her mom said.

Becca wanted to say, *And what about me? Who's giving me support?* But it was far too late for that question.

Jase had nudged their mom out of the way and rolled his eyes at Becca. A we're-in-this-together gesture that was so familiar, Becca *ached*. He looked good, she thought. Great actually. Rested. He'd gained some of his weight back, but the telltale signs were there, and she knew why her mom and dad were worried. He talked too fast, too scattered, and his eyes were way too bright.

He didn't ask her about herself. He didn't dare, because he knew. And when Becca came right out and asked him if he was using, their connection was suddenly lost.

She tried calling him back but he'd gone radio silent.

And a radio-silent Jase was never a good thing. Anxiety kept her up all night, watching the moonbeams dance across her walls. At dawn, she forced her concerns out of her head and went to work. Since she was early, she started the coffee and used her phone to search for cheap sheet music for the kids.

A minute later, Sam walked in. As he did every morning, he went straight for the coffeepot. He was in his usual uniform of loose, low-slung board shorts and a tight rash-guard T-shirt that clung to his mouthwatering body, complete with the cool sunglasses that made him look like the perfect combination of delicious and trouble. "Good weekend?" she asked.

"I worked on a boat."

"You did?" she asked. "I never saw you."

He eyed her over the rim of his mug. "Yes, you did. You and Olivia watched us surf."

"Oh." She felt the blush creep up her face. "Saw that, did you?"

"Little bit," he said, obviously amused. "So did Lucille, by the way. She posted a pic of you on Pinterest, and you both look like you might be drooling."

"It was really good ice cream," she said weakly, and

desperately sought a subject change. "So, how's your dad?"

"He's facing liver failure, but there's meds, and his doctor is hopeful."

"And you?"

"I'm going to kick his ass if he screws this up," Sam said simply. "He's not acting like a guy who got some really bad news. He's acting like he was awarded a trip to Disney World."

"That's because he's living with you. It's a dream come true for him."

Sam didn't say anything to this. Instead, he gestured to her phone screen. "What's that?"

Clearly, he'd made his own subject change. "I'm trying to find music for the kids."

"You get a budget, or you spending your own dough?" he asked.

"No budget." She shrugged. "It's not too expensive, and I want to do this right with them. What's going on with the lights?" she asked, pointing to the duffel bag on his shoulder.

He set it at her feet.

She bent down and unzipped it, and then stared at the neatly stacked lights, still in their packaging. "You bought new ones," she accused.

"Yeah, so?"

"So that's cheating."

"You had a problem, it's solved," he said simply.

She stared at him. Wasn't that just like a guy. "I could have untangled them," she said. "Eventually. I'd have saved you money."

"Now you don't have to."

Maybe she should have been annoyed. Instead, she felt that frisson of awareness skitter up her spine. His gaze met hers, his heated, and she had to remind herself to breathe. Not just awareness, she admitted, but hunger.

Need.

Damn. He was potent.

Luckily the phone rang, and she shook off the lust and answered, "Lucky Harbor Charters, how can I help you?"

Unluckily, she sounded breathless and...aroused.

Sam drank more coffee, but he had a definite smugness to him, cocky bastard.

"The grouch in yet?" Mark asked in her ear.

Becca watched Sam mainline the coffee and wondered if he was ready to face his dad this early. "Uh..." Sam's laser beam eyes were still on her. She smiled reassuringly.

He didn't return it.

"Darlin', I know he's there. If you're there, he's always nearby somewhere."

Was that true?

"How about you just hand him the phone."

Her gaze was still locked on Sam's. "Maybe I should take a message."

"Darlin', you're sweet. Way too sweet for the likes of him. And if I wasn't dying of liver failure, I'd prove it to you myself."

Sam took the phone from Becca's hand. "Stop trying to protect me," he told her. "And stop flirting with my employee," he said into the phone.

"Just showing you how it's done," came Mark's tinny voice, loud and clear, making Becca realize that Sam had heard everything his dad had said.

"You okay?" Sam asked.

"Never better. Except for the fact that I'm on my deathbed. But you, you're not okay."

"What are you talking about?" Sam asked.

"You've got a good couple of decades left before you've got old-man problems and need a blue pill to get it up, and you're ignoring that pretty young thing right in front of you."

Sam looked at Becca.

Becca busied herself by racing her fingers over the keyboard of the computer.

Sam leaned over her and booted up the dark screen.

Becca bit her lip and met Sam's amused gaze. With a blush, she turned away.

"What do you need, Dad?" Sam asked. "I left you breakfast on the stove."

"Oatmeal's disgusting," came Mark's answer.

"Oatmeal's good for you."

"Sheila called," Mark said. "She wanted to remind me I promised to pay for the crib."

"Didn't she already steal all your money?" Sam asked.

Mark sighed.

"You ask for that paternity test yet?"

"Only an asshole would do that right now," Mark said.

"A *smart* asshole," Sam countered.

"It's not an expensive crib," Mark said. "I told her to go cheap with all this shit."

Sam rubbed the spot between his eyes. "You can't go cheap, Dad. Not with a baby."

"It's just a loan," Mark said.

"Uh-huh," Sam said.

"So…you've got enough to cover it?"

"Yeah, Dad," Sam said. "I've got enough."

"You're not going to have to steal it, are ya?"

"Dad—"

"Kiddin'," Mark said. "Sheesh. This kinda reminds me of when we needed rent money, and you nearly got the shit beat out of you for—"

"Yeah, great times," Sam interrupted. "Gotta go. Check your account later on today."

"Love ya, Sam."

Instead of responding, Sam reached past Becca and hung up the phone.

"That was nice of you," Becca said into the heavy silence. "To loan him money."

"It won't be a loan."

She figured. "It's sweet he always says he loves you," she said. "Really sweet."

Sam looked like maybe he wanted to say something, but he didn't.

"What?" she asked.

"They're just words."

"Well, yes," she agreed. "But it'd be nice to hear them."

He looked at her for a moment. "So your parents, they never—"

"They're not…demonstrative." How the hell did they get on this? Oh, yeah. Her own big mouth. "I want to hear how you nearly got beat up."

"The rent was past due, and there was no food. We needed money." He shrugged. "So I found some."

"Found?"

"The apartment next door was a grow house," he said. "The lady who ran the place liked me. She used to feed me sandwiches sometimes. I was in her kitchen when she was called to another part of the house. I went to her utensil drawer—which was where she kept her cash hidden—and borrowed some. Then I went to a house down the street where there was always a pool game. I doubled my start-up money in an hour. Where I got caught was trying to return the original amount to the utensil drawer."

She stared at him. "How old were you?"

"Thirteen."

"Holy crap."

He shrugged. "I was an old thirteen."

She imagined that to be true.

"My dad took a lot of shit from the neighborhood for it," he said. "We eventually had to move. It was really stupid of me."

"How was any of that your fault?" she asked indignantly.

He laughed. "I stole the money, Becca."

"You had no choice!"

"There's always a choice," he said.

She shook her head. "You were a kid. Practically a baby. You were stuck in a bad spot and didn't know better."

"The pool house where I played, those guys weren't exactly Boy Scouts. I brought some real trouble down on my dad's head."

She wondered if he always did that, took everything on his shoulders, but she already knew that he did. She rose out of her chair and moved toward him. And then, as he so often did to her, she got in his space and cupped his face. "Not your fault," she said.

He flashed a small smile that shifted his stubbled jaw against her palms and gave her a shiver of pure lust.

This seemed inappropriate given the conversation, so she let him go and stepped back. "So how many times did that happen, you nearly getting killed trying to keep you and your dad together?"

He made a noncommittal sound and turned to the counter to set down his empty mug, rolling his shoulders like his neck hurt. "You ask a lot of questions."

It occurred to her that he'd probably watered down the story, and hadn't even told her the worst of it. She moved close and set her hands on his shoulders.

His muscles were vibrating with tension.

"Shh a sec," she said, and dug into him, pressing her thumbs into the strained muscles.

He held himself still for a long moment under her ministrations, but finally she felt his shoulders drop and relax, and he let out a low, very male sound that seemed to have a direct line to her nipples.

"Seems like you do have a weakness," she murmured.

Reaching back, he grabbed her hand, bringing it to his mouth and kissing her palm. "More than one."

Her stomach fluttered. "So, tell me. Did you stay out of trouble after that?"

"Oh, hell no. There was the time I threw the football through the window of a different neighbor—"

"Ha," she said, laughing. "I did that, too. Only it was a softball. I had to work for a month on the yard, and my brother still teases me about it." She met his gaze and saw that he was smiling, but there was something else there. "Did you have to work on the yard to make up for the cost of the glass, too?" she asked.

"Not exactly. The ball sailed through the window and beaned the neighbor on the head, and gave him a concussion. Which wouldn't have been a problem, except he happened to be having sex with the woman who lived on the other side of him. While her husband was at work."

She gaped. "Serious?"

"Serious as the heart attack she claimed to have. The guy came after my dad with a tire iron."

"Oh, my God."

"Luckily my dad's tire iron was bigger," he said.

She blinked. "Holy cow. What happened?"

"My dad got arrested, and child services got involved."

"Oh, Sam," she breathed. "I'm so sorry."

He shook his head. "Don't be. That, and a whole host of other shit, landed me here, in Lucky Harbor. With Cole's family."

"And you don't blame yourself for any of it, right?"

He laughed, but the sound was mirthless.

She reached for his hand and entangled their fingers. "Okay, so you do blame yourself. I know you must feel pretty stupid about that, seeing as what I said before is still true—none of what happened was your fault."

He choked out another low laugh, but she could see how uncomfortable he was that he'd told her the story. She wasn't uncomfortable; she was the opposite. She was getting a real peek inside the tough, impenetrable Sam Brody, and she liked that peek. She liked the man. But she knew saying so wouldn't be welcome at the moment, just as she knew she had to lighten the mood or he'd leave. "You probably get a different reaction when you tell a woman that story, right?" she asked in a teasing tone. "You probably get all hugged up on and then taken to bed to be mothered."

His green eyes gave her a look that said he was on to

her but that he'd play. "You want to take me to bed and mother me?"

"Well, mothering you isn't the *first* thing that comes to mind..."

He smiled. His arm slid around her waist, and he brought her up against his hard body. "That's good to hear," he said, "but I've never told a woman that story before."

"Why not?"

"You really do ask a *lot* of questions."

This was true. "It's the writer in me," she said. "Even if I'm just a jingle writer."

He laughed. "It's not the writer in you. It's the *nosy* in you."

"Maybe," she admitted.

"Once a peeper...," he said, and kissed her neck.

She shivered. "It's hereditary," she claimed. "My parents, they're nosy about everything. Where's Jase's itinerary, what's Jase doing right now, why isn't he answering his cell, who's he seeing? Blah blah." She caught the look on his face and shut up.

"Does everything they're nosy about have to do with Jase?" he asked.

From day one..."They don't really have to be nosy about me," she said. "I'm usually the together one. Terrifying as that is to imagine." She flashed a smile.

He didn't return it. Instead, he was looking at her like she was starting to make sense for him, and she didn't like the way that felt. "Jase has some...issues," she said. "He was born premature and almost died a bunch of times. He was small and weak, and played the piano like an angel. He wasn't exactly a popular kid. It didn't matter when we were traveling and playing together, but after I stopped, it was hard for him. I still protected him the best I could, but as it turns out, out I wasn't all that good at it." She paused. "He says he's been sober for a few months now, and I have high hopes he's being honest about it." Hope, but not a lot of faith.

"He's an addict?"

"Yes, but he's not a bad guy." And damn it, there she went defending him again. That was a hard habit to break.

"If he's a good guy, then why weren't you honest with him on the phone at the Love Shack?" Sam asked.

"Wow." She gave a little laugh, uncomfortable at the direction the conversation had taken. Clearly, he believed Jase was a threat to her, but that wasn't the case. At all. "You have a long memory. I just don't want him worrying about me, that's all," she said. "He's got a lot on his plate with his upcoming tour. There's so much pressure there. He's got this huge musical gift, but he's not good at concentrating."

Sam looked into her eyes. Something intense there made her feel both good and just a little bit off her axis. "And what about you?" he asked quietly.

"What about me? I walked away from that life."

"Why?"

"I screwed it up. And *now* who's asking too many questions?" she asked. "Anyway, I went into jingle writing, and that's that."

"Everyone screws up, Becca," he said. "Some more than others." He raised his own hand in the air and waved it.

She laughed despite herself. "I'm not cut out of the same cloth as my family," she said. "I'm not nearly as talented. Jase is amazing. He's just not all that good about harnessing it. We're a dysfunctional family, I know, but I'm pretty sure that's the definition of family."

He nodded, clearly knowing all about dysfunction. "It's time."

"Time?"

"For lesson number three," he said.

The quick subject change threw her. As did how fast her body tightened at the thought of what that lesson might entail. At what she *wanted* it to entail.

"Boating," he said.

She sighed.

He laughed.

She gave him a little shove, or she went to, but he caught her up and surprised her by pulling her in for a hug that made her blow out another breath. "You know what you are, Sam Brody?" she whispered, wrapping her arms around his neck. "A big, fat tease."

They both knew there wasn't an ounce of fat on him. They also both knew exactly what she meant. She wanted him again. Still. And she knew she wasn't alone in that wanting. But she found she was alone in the falling. And she *was* falling, for him. She was falling for a guy who didn't intend to fall back. She got it, she really did. In Sam's head, love meant people relying heavily on you, and you couldn't necessarily rely on them back.

If she pursued a relationship with him, it'd be an uphill battle all the way, but that wasn't what held her back from saying *When*. It was far simpler than that.

Just the one night with him had nearly ruined her for all other men. Another night would do her in for sure. "Boating sounds good," she said.

Chapter 16

♥

Much later that night, Becca was sitting on her bed with her keyboard, staring down at her notebook where she'd scrawled some lyrics. She was playing her fingers over the keys, looking for a melody, when a knock came at the door.

She knew Olivia was working in her shop late tonight, so it couldn't be her. The third apartment was still vacant. Becca hadn't ordered a pizza, and she knew Sam was avoiding her at night because he was smarter than she was. Especially after he'd taught her how to operate their boat today, a venture that had ended up being more a lesson on self-control and restraint.

She'd never been good at either.

But now she could at least passably assist on any excursion if needed, and that ability, along with all the other new skills she'd picked up this summer, made her feel good.

Really good.

Setting the keyboard aside, she rose and made her way to the door. "Who's there?"

No one answered.

Going up on tiptoe, she peeked through the peephole.

No one. Odd. She backed away and sat back on her bed, but didn't reach for the keyboard. She glanced out the windows. Night had fallen, and she hadn't pulled the sheets over them. Which meant she was basically sitting in a fishbowl.

She heard a sound from the hallway.

Her stomach clenched as fear slid into it. She'd read somewhere that a brain recognized fear in less than one second and prepared itself by flooding the body with adrenaline. Turned out that was absolutely true.

You left the fear behind, she reminded herself. Long behind. Gone were the days of jumping at every noise outside her New Orleans apartment.

Besides, she was in Lucky Harbor. Nothing to be afraid of here. But she reached out and turned off her lamp. This made her slightly less visible, but it also put her in the dark. She moved to the windows and yanked the sheets across them. Halfway back to the lamp, she heard another sound from the hallway.

Fear stole her breath, and she backed up until she ran herself into the countertop of the kitchen. She could hear her own breathing, harsh and panicked, and it brought her back to last year. Angry at herself, she grabbed her purse and rifled through it for her phone. She stared at the dark screen. She didn't have a lot of options here. Calling her first choice was going to make her look weak and vulnerable, and oh, she hated both with a passion.

She called anyway.

* * *

Sam had closed up the warehouse and was halfway home when his cell vibrated from an incoming call. Not his dad telling him yet again why his crook of a girlfriend thought she needed a five-hundred-dollar stroller, though the name that flashed on his screen didn't ease his tension any.

Becca.

There was only one reason for a woman to call this late at night. And though he'd never been adverse to a booty call, he hesitated. A booty call was light. Casual.

But nothing was ever casual with Becca. They'd gone there once, and he now knew that she had the potential of getting to him, *really* getting to him, in a very big way.

The biggest.

And still, he answered. "Hey," he said. "What's up?"

"I don't know." Her voice was a soft whisper. A scared soft whisper. "You're not by any chance outside my door, are you?"

"No, but I can be." In the middle of the deserted highway, he whipped a U-turn.

In his ear, Becca let out a breath. "No. It's fine. I'm sure it's nothing. Never mind." And she disconnected.

Sam pounded out her number again and waited through three tense rings before she picked up.

"I'm sorry," she said. "I'm being ridiculous. Ignore me."

"Not gonna happen, babe. Tell me what's wrong."

"I heard a sound." She was still whispering and still sounding terrified, which just about killed him. "Thought I heard footsteps outside my door, and then a knock. But no one was there."

"Cole's still on the boat," he said. "I'm going to hang up and call him. Keep your phone in your hand. Ten seconds, Becca. I'll call you right back—"

"I don't want to bother—"

"Ten seconds." He disconnected and called Cole, waiting with impatience for him to answer, hating that Becca was scared and alone.

Cole finally answered with a "Yo, Grandma."

"You on the boat?" Sam asked.

"Yeah, I'm calibrating the—"

"Run over to Becca's. She heard someone outside her door and is terrified."

"On it," Cole said, good humor gone.

Sam disconnected and called Becca back.

"Are you here?" she asked breathlessly.

"Not yet, but Cole is," he said. "Any second now. I'm going to stay on the phone with you until he's got you."

"You don't have to—"

"I'm staying on the phone," he said firmly, grinding his teeth when he got caught at the train tracks just outside of town and had to wait for a train. "Is Olivia home?"

"No, she's working late," Becca said.

"You expecting anyone?"

"No." She blew out a breath. "God, it sounds so dumb now. I shouldn't have watched *Criminal Minds* earlier. I'm okay. I'm okay."

Hearing it twice, knowing she was trying to make it true, almost had him smiling as he downshifted for a light. "You locked in?"

"Yes, but seriously, I'm sure it's nothing. Someone was lost, probably…"

"Make sure you're back from the windows so you're

not highlighted to anyone outside," he said. "Sit tight, I'll be there in five."

"You don't have to—"

"Becca. I'm already almost there. And Cole should be there any second."

Even as he said it, through the line he could hear three short knocks on the door, and then Cole's voice. "Becca. Honey, it's me."

"He's here," Becca said to Sam, her voice filled with relief.

"Peek first, Becca."

"I see him."

"Okay, babe. I'll be right there."

It took him three more very long moments to get back to the harbor. He ran up to Becca's door, and Cole answered.

"She's spooked," he said in a low-pitched voice. "But she won't let me get close enough to touch her. I don't know what's up. I don't think it's good, bro."

Sam's gaze searched out the loft and found Becca in the club chair by her bed. She had her arms wrapped around her legs, her forehead to her knees, looking like a ball of misery. He strode directly to her and crouched beside the chair. "Hey," he said softly.

"I'm sorry," she said to her knees. "I totally overreacted. I'm fine, really."

Anyone could see plain as day she was just about as far from fine as she could get. He set a hand on her bare foot, and she nearly leapt out of her skin. "Just me," he said softly, keeping his hand on her.

Her skin was icy, but she curled her foot trustingly into his big hand.

Sam glanced back at Cole, who gave him a small shake of his head as he filled a glass of water and brought it over.

Sam took it from Cole and handed it to Becca. "Drink this."

While she did, Cole quietly said, "I ran the exterior to get here. Didn't see anyone. The door to the building was closed but not locked. Her door was locked. No cars in the lot but mine." Cole squatted beside Sam and looked into Becca's pale face. "How you doing, honey?"

"I'm sorry," she said. "I really appreciate—"

"Never be sorry for wanting to be safe," Cole told her. He glanced at the hand she'd allowed Sam to set on her and gave her a small but warm smile. "Anytime. Okay?"

"Okay," she whispered.

He nodded. "You're safe with Sam. You know that, right?"

She met Sam's gaze and gave her own small but warm smile, if a bit wobbly. "I do know it."

Cole nodded once more and left. Two minutes later, he called Sam. "There's a UPS package on her neighbor's doorstep. That's probably what she heard."

Sam hung up and told Becca.

Becca grimaced. "Way to overreact, right?"

"No worries," he said.

She nodded. "Thanks for coming, but you don't have to stay—"

"You're shaking." He pulled off his sweatshirt and tugged it over her head.

"I'm cold."

"I'm thinking shock," he said. "This, tonight, was a flashback for you, wasn't it?"

She busied herself getting wrapped up in his sweatshirt and didn't speak.

"Come home with me tonight, Becca."

She stared at him for a long beat. "You don't like people in your space."

"I don't," he said. "But you're not people."

For the first time since he'd arrived, her eyes lost their guard, and she laughed softly. "I'm fine here."

"Yeah. And you'll be even more fine at my house."

"I'm not sleeping at your house, I'm sleeping here."

"Who says there'll be sleeping?" he asked, attempting to lighten her mood.

She rolled her eyes. "You don't mean it," she said so glumly that he laughed. "You're just being suggestive because you want me to get over being freaked out."

He rose and scooped her up out of the chair, smiling when she squeaked and threw her arms around his neck to catch her balance. "Maybe I just wanted an excuse to kiss you."

"But—"

He stopped her protests with his mouth and then selfishly kept kissing her because the taste of her was like a drug. When he finally pulled back, he set his forehead to hers.

She took a long, unsteady breath. "Thanks for being here for me," she whispered.

He started to answer flippantly, but stopped when he realized how much it meant to him as well, that he could be there for her. "Anytime, babe."

And for the first time in his life, he actually meant it.

Chapter 17

♥

Becca strained to get a look at Sam's neighborhood as he drove. She knew enough about Lucky Harbor to know this was a very nice part of town, with big houses on bigger lots, overlooking the bluffs where a hundred feet below the Pacific Ocean churned against the rocky shore.

Sam's house was a beautiful older Craftsman style, white with blue trim, and too many windows to count.

Every light was blazing.

Sam swore beneath his breath as he opened his front door to a blast of Marvin Gaye wailing "Let's Get It On." "I'm going to have to kill him," he said.

Becca had wondered what Sam's place would look like, whether it'd be neat or messy, filled with guy crap or empty and sterile.

It was none of the above. The living room was large and airy and had windows facing the bluffs. There were big, comfy couches in the living room and an even bigger TV, in front of which were a few stacks of CDs and

DVDs. There were various things strewn about, athletic shoes, a sweatshirt, a kayak leaning against a wall. No personal pictures, though, and nothing that said *hot single guy*, either. Definitely lived in, but not necessarily claimed.

Sam moved to the coffee table, grabbed a remote, and hit a button.

The music stopped.

Then he strode out of the room. Not ready to be left alone, Becca followed. The kitchen was gorgeous. Granite countertops, wood floors, high beamed ceilings. It was also a mess. The island was littered with the remains of what looked to have been a pizza-and-beer dinner. Clothing was haphazardly dropped across every surface; a man's pair of jeans, a woman's bra. A red lace thong…

"Definitely going to kill him," Sam muttered. The double French doors were cracked and led to a deck.

There was a hot tub there, from which came the whoosh of the jets and the unmistakable sounds of a man's voice and a woman giggling.

Sam stepped out the French doors, and again Becca followed, figuring that by the steam coming out his ears, father and son might need a referee.

"You've got to be fuckin' kidding me," Sam said.

Mark was indeed in the hot tub with a woman, and as the undies had indicated, they were buck naked.

Becca immediately whirled back to the doors, but unfortunately she'd let them shut behind her when she'd come out, and naturally they'd locked. "Crap," she said, rattling the doors for good measure.

Behind her, Mark and the woman were making noises over the sound of the jet bubbles that were going to haunt her for the rest of her life. Sam, too, if the growl from deep in his throat meant anything. *"Dad,"* he clipped out, sounding like he was forcing the word past cut glass.

There was the sound of water sloshing, and she imagined the couple breaking apart. "Oh, hey," Mark called, and against her better judgment, Becca took a peek.

Thankfully, both the nudists were now in the water up to their necks.

"Didn't expect you so early, son," Mark said. "Next time I'll hang a tie on the door or something for notice, yeah?"

Sam shoved his hand into his pocket and came up with his keys, which he handed to Becca so she could unlock the doors and get inside, but, working on sheer nerves now, she promptly dropped them.

"Hi, Sam!" the female called cheerfully, her hands over her ample breasts. "It's lovely to meet you. I've heard a lot about you." She grinned. "I'd shake your hand, but…"

Sam let out an inarticulate sound, and she peeked at him as he squeezed his eyes shut and pressed the heels of his hands to them.

"Sorry, son," Mark said. "After the stroller fight, I asked Sheila for a paternity test like you've been suggesting. She came clean—I'm not the daddy." He smiled at the naked woman. "So then I went out to celebrate, and met Brandy here at that bar out on Highway Forty-two."

Brandy giggled and waved, like there could be any guessing about which one of them was Brandy.

"You're not supposed to be drinking," Sam said. "And pizza's out, too. I took you to the dietitian, and she gave you the recommended list."

"I don't like salad or fish."

Sam's mouth tightened grimly. "Do you like living?"

"I was liking it a whole hell of a lot more about four minutes ago," Mark said.

"You're supposed to be taking it easy," Sam said tightly.

"Oh, he was," Brandy piped up. "I was doing all the work."

Mark beamed at her. "And you're good at it, honey."

Sam let out a breath. "Gonna have to empty the tub and bleach it."

Becca had picked up the keys and was trying to find the right one.

"You two want to join us?" Mark asked. "The water's great."

"Fuck it," Sam muttered. "I'm gonna sell it. The whole house." He snatched the keys from Becca's hands and unlocked the door. He gave her a little shove inside, followed her in, and slammed the door behind them hard enough that the glass rattled.

"Sam—"

He leveled her with a dark look that for some inexplicable reason didn't scare her anymore. He evoked a lot of feelings within her, but fear wasn't one of them. "He's trying to be something to you," she said.

"Well, he succeeded. He's a pain in my ass." He hustled her out the front door and back to his truck, where he whipped away from the curb with a squeal of tires. Not all four. Just two.

Becca grabbed the dash. "If you'd just give him some of your attention, your time—"

"We're over this conversation," he said firmly.

She waited until they were on the highway. "Listen," she said gently. "I know he screwed up a lot while you were growing up, but I think he genuinely regrets—"

"*Over it*, Becca."

"Really?" she asked, feeling her own temper rise. Whenever *she* was over a conversation, he still pushed.

He must have heard the annoyance in her tone because he slid her a look that had male bafflement all over it, like she'd just asked him if she looked fat in these jeans or what he liked about her.

Somehow that was worse, that he truly didn't get it, the clueless man. "Why do you get to push me to talk, and I can't push you?"

"That's different," he said immediately.

"How?" she asked. "How's it different?"

He downshifted into a turn and said nothing.

"Yeah," she said, crossing her arms. "Thought so."

"Get off your soapbox, Becca," he said, apparently just as annoyed with her as he was with his dad. "It's not like you've ever really told me shit about you."

Okay, that was possibly true.

Five tense minutes later, he slid into a parking spot outside of the Love Shack and turned to her.

She made a point of looking out the passenger window.

Sam sighed, the sound filled with frustration and regret. "Look," he said, "he drives me crazy, okay? And I'm a total ass. I'm sorry."

So foreign was the notion of a guy apologizing to her for something that she jerked around to stare at him.

"You look confused," he said.

"One of us is supposed to be pissed off," she said softly. "Maybe both of us. But you're not mad at me. And

I don't feel mad at you." She shook her head. "I don't know what to do with that. Or you, for that matter."

He slid his fingers along her jaw and into her hair, then pulled her close enough to press his mouth to hers. "If you weren't my employee, I'd show you what to do with me." He kissed her again and then whispered against her lips, suggestions on exactly what she might do with him, each hotter than the last.

She felt herself quiver and then get wet, and she stared at his mouth, having some trouble with her thought process.

"We straight?" he asked.

"Um…"

His eyes were heated, but they lit with a little humor now as he ran the pad of his thumb over her lower lip. "Yeah," he said. "We're straight." He pulled back. "I could use a drink. You?"

"*Yes.*"

He pulled her from the truck and into him, giving her a really tight, really hard, really great hug. "You're so damn sweet," he said into her hair.

She tipped her face up. "Because I interfere?"

He smiled. "Because you care enough to interfere."

"Yeah? You have your sweet moments, too, you know," she said. "Not a lot, mind you, but a few here and there."

He tossed his head back and laughed.

"What?"

"That's the first time anyone's ever said I was sweet," he said, still grinning.

"You apologized to me. And that was sweet."

"I apologized because I was an ass. That's what you do when you've been an ass."

"Not everyone who acts like an ass apologizes," she said.

His smile faded, and he hooked an arm around her neck, drawing her into him again, pressing his mouth to her temple. "They should," he said against her skin.

Cole and Tanner were at a table inside, and Sam and Becca joined them.

Cole smiled at Becca. "How you doing?"

"Better," she said. "Thanks again. I'm so sorry—"

"No apologies for that," Cole said. "Ever." He gestured to Jax behind the bar, who brought two more longnecks, one each for Sam and Becca.

Cole lifted his in a toast. "To Gil."

"To Gil," they all said, and Becca was moved by their low, serious voices that rang out together. They ordered sliders and fries and another round.

Sam made the next toast. "To my dad's health," he said.

This surprised and pleased Becca. "See?" she said to him. "*Sweet*. But your dad looked fine to me."

"Yeah," Sam said, "but I plan to kill him later, so—"

"Sam," she said on a surprised laugh. "You're not."

"Okay, maybe not kill him," he said. "Not all the way."

"What'd he do now?" Cole wanted to know.

"Doesn't matter," Tanner said. "You're not going to kill him because I'm not using our boat fund to bail you out again, not when we're getting so close to another boat."

"Again?" Becca asked Sam.

Sam gave Tanner a long look.

Tanner took a long pull on his beer and didn't look concerned. "Did we forget to tell you that you work for an international felon?" he asked Becca.

Her mouth fell open, and she stared at Sam, who flipped Tanner the bird.

Tanner flashed a grin.

"Yeah, it's true," Cole told her. "The last time we had to bail him out, I almost had to try and sell Tanner here for a night just to have enough."

"You *did* try and sell me for a night," Tanner said.

Becca choked out a laugh, and Sam rolled his eyes. "Why does that story change the more you drink?" he asked Tanner.

Tanner pointed his beer at Sam. "*You* weren't there. You were cooling off in a Mexican prison. We could've just left you there, you know. But did we? No."

"Instead you got yourself arrested as well," Sam reminded him.

"Hey, that was Cole's fault," Tanner said. "He told me to kiss the wrong woman."

"Okay," Becca said, setting down her beer. "I'm going to need to hear this story. The real story."

Cole grinned. "I'll tell it."

Tanner groaned but Cole ignored him. "We'd just left the rig job," he told her. "We'd bought our first boat, a real piece of shit to be honest, but she was all ours. Well, ours and the bank's. We were on the water, and our GPS went down. Tanner here insisted he could navigate without it. We were in the southwest Gulf, and he turned us a little too far south, where we came across some Mexican pirates—"

Becca gasped. "Oh, my God, pirates? Really?"

"Oh, yeah," Cole said. "They boarded us, too. Said they were the..." He used air quotes here. "Authorities. And genius here"—he jabbed a thumb at Sam—"decided that they were full of shit and told them so."

"Okay, yes, I did that," Sam said. "But in my defense, they were wearing a combo of outdated U.S. and British military gear. They looked suspicious."

"They hauled his big mouth off to the clink," Tanner said.

"Which left me," Cole said, gesturing to himself, "the brains of the operation, to figure out how to spring him."

"Hey," Tanner said. "I did my part. You told me to sleep with the town mayor's daughter." He smiled at Becca. "She was in the bar we stumbled into to come up with a plan." He grimaced. "Except—"

"Except it turns out that she was the *wife*, not the daughter," Cole said. "Which left me bailing out the *two* of them."

"Did you have enough to bail them both out?" she asked.

"He sure as hell didn't," Sam said. "Because he'd used his month's pay on being stupid."

Becca looked at Cole, who shook his head. "That's another story altogether."

"So how did you bail them out?" Becca asked.

"He sold our fuckin' boat," Tanner said on a huge, sad sigh. "The *Sweet Sally*, gone forever."

"It was that," Sam said, "or leave you to become Big Bubba's jail-mate bitch. And afterward, we bought a better boat."

"He didn't care then," Cole said, and turned to Tanner. "You were still recovering and supposed to be taking it easy, but instead you were on this walk on the stupid and wild side, remember? Gil had just—"

"Hey," Tanner said, no longer smiling. "Don't go there."

"—died," Cole said.

"I mean it," Tanner said. "Shut up."

"What, we just toasted to his memory," Cole said, "but we can't toast to your trip to Crazy-Town?"

Tanner shoved free of the table. "I'm out."

"Aw, come on," Cole said. "Don't get like that—"

But Tanner was gone, striding out the door and into the night.

Sam set down his beer. "Really?" he asked Cole.

Cole sighed and got to his feet. "I suppose I should go after Mr. Sensitive."

"Maybe you want to give him a few minutes first," Sam suggested. "So he doesn't rearrange your face again."

"Yeah." Cole straightened his shoulders like he was bracing for battle. "Hey, if I don't show up for work tomorrow, call out a search party, okay? I'll be the one in concrete shoes at the bottom of the harbor, waiting on a rescue." He paused, and when Sam only shrugged, he sighed. "Nice knowing ya," he said to Becca, and headed out after Tanner.

"Is he really in danger?" Becca asked, worried.

"From his own big, fat mouth, maybe." Sam stood up and pulled her with him. "Want to play?" he asked, gesturing to the piano.

Her heart gave a little kick, and she looked around. The bar was still full. "No, but thank you for asking."

The night was dark and quiet. Becca looked up at her big, silent, gorgeous escort. "At least this time I can thank you for walking me."

He arched a brow.

"You usually vanish into the night," she said. "Like Batman."

He looked at her but didn't say anything, neither confirming nor denying.

At Becca's apartment building, Olivia came out of her door with a duffel bag. "Hey," she said. "There was a spider in my bathroom. I need to sleep on your couch." Without waiting for a response, she walked into Becca's apartment and left Sam and Becca alone in the doorway.

Becca looked at Sam. "You got in touch with her somehow."

He kissed her. "Night. Sleep tight."

"See?" she said. "Sweet." Then she caught his hand, went up on tiptoe, and gave him a good-night kiss.

Chapter 18

♥

After work the next day, Becca was walking across the alley toward her apartment when someone called her name. Turning, she came face-to-face with Mark.

"Hey there," he said with a smile. "I was just heading in, looking for Sam."

"The guys are gone," she said. "Out on the water with clients."

"Ah, gotcha." His smile was still in place, but he looked worried. Really worried.

"You okay?" she asked.

"Well…I had a little car mishap."

"An accident?" She put her hand on his arm, looking him over.

He took her hand in his and squeezed it. "I see why he's into you, darlin'; you're really something special. But no, I didn't have an accident. I'm fine."

"Oh. Good," she said relieved. "And Sam and I aren't—"

"Because he's an idiot. I know," Mark said. He rubbed his jaw ruefully. "He might've gotten that from me."

"Actually," she said, "*I* might be the idiot."

Mark smiled. "See? Special. Because now you're protecting the idiot."

Becca laughed. "Tell me about your car mishap."

He went back to looking rueful. "I got my ride repo'd."

"Oh, Mark."

"I know, I know. I need to grow up. But right now, I need to get to the doctor, I have an appointment."

"You can borrow my car, if you'd like," she said. "Fair warning, though, it's a piece of shit."

"Pieces of shit are my specialty," Mark said. "You wouldn't by any chance have another of those amazing sandwiches with chips on it lying around, would you?" He flashed her a smile that was so similar to Sam's, she smiled back helplessly.

"No," she said, "but I can make you one."

"Yeah," he said with a smile. "Definitely special."

That night Becca sat in Olivia's apartment sharing Chinese takeout and some wine.

And woes.

They started with work woes. Olivia's were physical. She'd been in Lucky Harbor for a year now and was outgrowing her store. It was why she'd moved into the warehouse apartment. She'd been living above the store, but that space was now needed for stock storage.

Becca's work woes were mental. She was trying to teach music to a group of kids who'd never played an instrument in their lives, and it didn't take a shrink to know that she needed this more than they did.

And then there was the fact that she was falling for her stoic, sexy boss. But as Olivia pointed out while refilling their glasses for the second or third or maybe fourth time, "If you put those two things aside, things are good for you."

This was actually true, of sorts. Work was going pretty well. She had the Summer Bash plans under control, and she'd finished updating the charter website. The guys had been doing double the work, taking calls for reservations and then having to enter everything into the system. But now the site was fully operational, and people could book themselves.

"I bet you're worth your weight in gold," Olivia said. "Come work for me; it'll be better for you."

"How's that?" Becca asked. "You have three hot guys in board shorts, shirts optional, working at your shop to look at all day?"

Olivia snorted. "No, but if you work for me, then you can sleep with Sam."

Which brought them to the next subject—man woes.

"I'm not sure we're going there," Becca said. "And anyway, I'm not in a hurry to have him as an ex."

"Yeah," Olivia said. "Exes suck."

She looked at Olivia with interest. "Tell me an ex story."

"I once had a boyfriend who was an FBI agent."

"Wow."

"Wait for it," Olivia said, not nearly as impressed as Becca.

"Uh-oh."

"Yeah," Olivia said. "He said being an agent was why he had to come and go without warning, and why he didn't have to call."

"Well, that sucks," Becca said.

"Gets worse. One night I had a break-in, and he happened to be with me. He ran out the front door screaming into the night like a little girl, without so much as looking back for me." Olivia shook her head. "FBI agent my ass."

They both laughed. Some of the hilarity had to be attributed to the wine, but mostly it was Olivia's delivery. She knew how to spin a tale, and she knew how to be kick-ass, and not just the pretend, fake-it-till-you-make-it kind.

Becca needed to learn that particular skill.

"So…," Olivia said, making the word about fifty syllables.

"So what?"

"So now it's your turn to regale *me* with an ex story," Olivia said.

Becca became suddenly extremely engrossed with finishing her wine. "I don't really have all that many," she finally said.

"Come on. Be serious."

"I am serious," Becca said.

Olivia had been lying flat on the couch, her head hanging over the side, while Becca—sitting on the floor—braided the long mass. But at this statement, Olivia lifted her head, pulling her hair from Becca's hands.

"Unlikely from a woman who looks like you," Olivia said slowly, taking Becca in, "with that gorgeous hair and those big, warm eyes, not to mention your amazing skin, which probably came from a rosy-cheeked baby with unicorn wings who poops golden fairy dust."

Becca laughed. "You should be the writer."

Olivia's smile reminded Becca that her new friend still

had lots of secrets. "So no ex at *all*?" Olivia said, heavy on the disbelief.

"Well, sure," Becca said, busying herself with picking out a fortune cookie. "A few here and there."

"Name 'em," Olivia said.

"Taylor Bennett," Becca said. "He dumped me because I couldn't name the jazz songs he played."

"Uh-huh," Olivia said. "And how old were you?"

"Seventeen."

"That's the best you got?" Olivia asked.

She racked her brain. The problem was, during those years, she'd been traveling with Jase, and it hadn't exactly been a normal coming-of-age situation. She'd dated, but hadn't really sunk her teeth into any real relationships other than with Nathan. "There were others, just no one memorable."

"Come on, there's got to be a story to tell."

"Maybe." Becca nudged the fortune cookies around with her fingers. "But I don't like to revisit the only other one I've got."

Olivia was quiet a moment. "This have anything to do with our impromptu sleepover?"

Becca shrugged. She didn't want to go there sober, much less half-baked.

"Men are bastards," Olivia said with feeling.

Becca made a noncommittal response to this and opened her fortune cookie.

Your future is your own, it said.

"Damn it," Becca said. "This one's defective."

Olivia peered over the edge of the couch and read it. "Hey, it sounds good to me. I like making my own future."

Becca shook her head. "I'd rather hear something like:

Your future is prosperity-filled, or *You'll spin money from your ass*, or…"

"Or," Olivia said, "*There's a hot guy waiting for you if you only open your eyes?*"

"Yeah. That's a good one."

Olivia rolled her eyes. "It's a *true* one."

"That's ridiculous. My eyes are open."

Olivia laughed and came up on an elbow, eyes slowly going serious. "How do you not realize that you actually, really do have a hot guy waiting for you?"

"I don't."

"You *do*."

"Don't."

Olivia sighed. "You're an annoying drunk."

This was undoubtedly true. "I chose the job, remember?" she asked.

"Sam doesn't care about the job. That's not what's holding him back."

"How do you know?" Becca asked. "You've holed up in here, laid so low no one even hardly knows you're here."

Olivia shrugged. "I've got windows, don't I? And I've been around longer than you. I know that he looks amazeballs on a surfboard, that he looks amazeballs on a boat, that he looks amazeballs—"

"Okay, okay," Becca said, and she did laugh then. "I get it. He looks amazing *all* the damn time."

"Yes, but it's more than that. It's how he looks at you."

Becca sighed. "Listen, I pretty much forced him into giving me the job."

"Honey, no one forces Sam Brody to do anything."

Also true…But he'd known she needed the money, and that had been that. He cared about her. He cared about all the people in his life. Cole and Tanner, for example. He'd do anything for them, and had. The same went for his dad, and Cole's mom. Sam was a man who was careful with his emotions, he'd been brought up to be, and yet he could still give and care with every ounce of his body.

Unlike her.

Oh, she cared, but not deep. Going deep hurt. She'd learned that once and had never looked back. She loved her parents because they were her parents, but she couldn't count on them.

And then there was Jase. When that situation had gotten to be too much for her to handle, she hadn't just backed off. She'd backed off and moved thousands of miles away, leaving him alone to deal with his issues.

She couldn't imagine Sam doing that to someone in his life, ever.

They both jumped at the knock on the door.

"That's not my door," Olivia said. "It's yours." She got up and looked out her peephole. "Well, well, speaking of the devil."

"Oh, my God," Becca whispered. "Back away from the door!"

Olivia kept her eye glued to the peephole. "You know, he's got a really fantastic ass. And I'm only looking at the profile—"

"Shhh! He'll hear you."

Olivia turned to her in surprise. "You're not going out there?"

Earlier, that'd been all she'd wanted. A late-night visit from her sexy surfer. Now...now she didn't know what the hell she thought *that* would accomplish.

"It'll accomplish plenty," Olivia said, making Becca

realize she'd spoken out loud. "You'd probably get boinked, for one. And nothing personal, but you're wound pretty tight. You could use it."

Becca came up on her knees, waving wildly for Olivia to shut up. "The walls," she whispered. "Thin. You can hear me breathing. I can hear you swearing. Which means *he can hear you.*"

"No, he can't."

"Yes, I can," Sam said.

Becca and Olivia went stock-still at the sound of his voice, right on the other side of her front door now.

Shit! "Don't let him in!" Becca hissed.

"I have a tin of ranch-flavored popcorn," Sam said through the wood.

"From the pier?" she asked, unable to help herself.

"Yep." The sound of the tin being shaken came through the door. "And it's good," he said, mouth sounding full.

"Hey," she called out, straightening up. "Are you eating my popcorn?"

"You bet your sweet ass. Lance warned me it was damn good, but I had no idea. You'd best hurry before I eat it all."

He'd bought her popcorn. Oh, God. She was a dead woman.

"He's funny, hot, *and* he likes you enough to buy you popcorn," Olivia whispered.

"Don't let him in!" she whispered back.

"Don't listen to her, Olivia, let me in."

Just his voice, calm but steely, made Becca's nipples hard. Damn it. And Olivia was looking at her like Santa Claus had just shown up. Knowing she was too weak to be trusted, Becca leapt to her feet and looked for somewhere to hide. Unfortunately she tripped over the coffee table and went down with a thud.

That's when she realized she was maybe more than half-baked. She might be fully baked. Disoriented, she stayed there on her hands and knees a moment—until suddenly two hands slid beneath her armpits and lifted her to her feet.

"You gave my dad your car?" Sam asked.

She blinked. "Um."

"You gave my dad your car."

"A little bit, yeah." When Sam shook his head, she hurried on, "He's bringing it back tomorrow."

"Do you give anyone anything they ask for?" he asked.

"Not anymore," she said. "I'm on a break from doing that. Your dad just really needed the ride, and I'm not driving tonight anyway, so—" She hiccuped and covered her mouth. "Excuse me."

Still holding on to her, Sam peered down at her, a very small smile on his lips now. "You're shit-faced."

"Nope." Although there did seem to be two of him...Which was nice since both of him were smiling all sexy-like. "I'm not shit-faced. I don't get shit-faced. I don't drink."

Olivia lifted the two bottles of wine they'd decimated. Both empty.

"Who drank those?" Becca asked her.

"That would be us," Olivia said, and laughed. "Sexy Surfer's right, babe. We're shit-faced. We've gotta hit the sack, we both have to work early tomorrow."

"Huh," Becca said. She went to jab a finger at one of the two Sams in front of her, but missed. "Huh," she said again.

Sam was still grinning. "Need help getting home and to bed?"

"No!" she said at the exact same time that Olivia said "Yes!"

Becca whirled on Olivia to give her a very dirty look, but her world began to spin, and didn't stop. "Uh-oh," she whispered, and would've slithered to the floor again except that Sam hooked an arm around her waist. It was a really great forearm, too, all tanned and corded with strength. But it was the big, warm hand that landed just beneath her breast that really grabbed her attention.

"Here's her key," she heard Olivia say, and then her world was upside down because Sam had hoisted her up and over his shoulder in a fireman's hold, his arm wrapped around the backs of her thighs.

"Hey," she said to his ass. His very fine ass.

"Hay's for horses," Olivia said cheerfully, whacked Becca's ass, and opened the front door.

"*Hey*," Becca said again.

But she was talking to no one. Well, other than Sam's ass, of course.

"So romantic," Olivia said on a sigh.

Still upside down, Becca tried to imagine Sam being romantic. But she couldn't picture him giving a woman roses. "Do you?" she asked.

"Do I what?"

"Do you ever bring your women roses?"

"I'm not exactly a flowers type," he said. "But I do have the popcorn." He rattled the tin with his free hand.

The truth was, Becca would rather have popcorn any day of the week over roses. She might even have said so, but her world was spinning even more now, so she squeaked, slammed her eyes shut, and held on for dear life. And what she held on to was his butt—with both hands—earning her a chuckle from the guy who owned the butt. He balanced her and the popcorn with ease while unlocking her front door. Kicking the door closed, he strode across the open space, bypassing her bathroom, and dumped her on the bed.

She sat up, blew the hair out of her eyes, and focused on him standing there, hands on hips, looking sexy as all hell. "Come here," she said.

"You feeling sick?"

"No." She tugged him down over the top of her and pressed her face into that male throat she loved so much and inhaled him deep.

"Becca, I need a shower."

"Oh, boy," she said. "I've heard this story before."

He snorted, then rolled off the bed. She blinked as he leaned over her and pulled off her sandals. "Whatcha doing?"

"Putting you to bed," he said.

"But I thought you were going to shower and then do me."

He went still a moment, then tipped back his head and laughed. The sight was so beautiful she just stared at him for a long moment. "Wow," she breathed. "You're so damn pretty. Does Lucille know? She should pin pics of you in your board shorts, the blue ones that have the white stripe down the side, the ones that show off your butt, all over her Pinterest."

"If you suggest that to her, I'll..." He paused.

"What?" she asked.

"I don't know. I can't think of anything that wouldn't

leave you scarred for life." He reached for the hem on her sweatshirt. "Lift up."

"Please," she said. "You mean lift up *please*."

He gave her an alpha look and she lifted up, and then the sweatshirt vanished, leaving her in a cami top and a gauzy skirt.

He stared down at her, scrubbed a hand over his jaw, muttering something to himself about "being a fucking saint," and then he tugged down the blankets. "Get in," he said.

"Okay." She scrambled in, then waited for him to climb in as well. He didn't. "Hey," she said when he tugged the blankets up to her chin. "What are you doing?"

"Putting you to bed," he repeated, not quite as patiently now.

In fact, he was sounding downright strained.

"Without you?" she asked, confused.

"Without me. Becca, you're not paying attention to me."

Yes, she was. That was always the problem. She looked down at herself. "I'm still dressed."

"Yeah," he said, and again ran a hand over his rough jaw, which made a very male sound that turned her on even more. "I don't trust myself with you undressed."

"I do," she said.

At that, his eyes softened and he placed a hand on either side of her hips. Leaning in, he kissed her softly. "So fucking sweet," he murmured against her lips. "So damn sweet."

"But you still aren't doing me, are you?"

He actually lowered his head, closed his eyes, and groaned from deep in his throat. "I'm trying to be a good guy here, Becca."

"I don't want you to be good. Well, I do. The *good* kind of good, you know?"

He kissed her again. "Go to sleep."

"But I do trust you."

"Not all the way, you don't," he said. "Not yet." Then he kissed her again, and this time he gave her what she wanted, which was heat and lots of tongue. Then he tore himself away, breathing unsteadily. "Stop me," he said.

"No."

Sam groaned. "If I have to be the strong one here, we're in trouble."

"So don't be the strong one." She paused, and remembered. "When!" she yelled. "When, when, *when*!"

"You," he said, backing away, "are a menace to my self-control."

"Why the self-control at all? Forget the self-control! I just said *When*. That was our code word."

He looked pained. And strained. "You're under the influence. It doesn't count."

"Why?" she asked.

"You know why."

She gave him her I'm-not-impressed-with-that-excuse look, and he let out a laugh. "Look, we both know that intimacy between us is...inappropriate," he said.

"Hey, we crossed the intimacy barrier a long time ago."

"Yeah. Shit," he muttered, his voice a low, incredibly sexy growl that wasn't helping the situation one little bit.

"Tell me the truth," she said. "Is it because you're no longer attracted to me?"

"No. Christ, no." He dropped his head back and stared up at the ceiling for a beat, then came back to her. He let his weight cover her and rocked his hips, proving that he wasn't lying. He was absolutely attracted to her, in a big way if the erection he was sporting was any indication.

"I don't get it," she said, clinging to him. "I'm not asking for a marriage proposal. I mean, I'm not exactly relationship material, either."

He went still, then lifted his head. "You don't think I'm relationship material?"

She stared up into his beautiful green eyes, surprised by the fact he seemed insulted by this. "Are you?" she asked.

He didn't take his gaze from her. "Well, no."

"Are you a commitment-phobe?"

"No, definitely not," he said.

She slid her fingers into his silky hair. "So why are you complicating things by holding back?"

"It doesn't matter why," he said. "I said no. And as your boss, whatever I say goes."

She shivered at that, and laughed as she nudged her good spot to his. "Maybe I like that, you being all bossy."

He tightened his grasp on her hips to hold her still, but his eyes were so heated she was near melting point. "You need to stop playing with me."

She stared up at him. "Just tell me this—are you holding back because of me?"

"What?"

"Olivia said maybe it wasn't just the job, that maybe it was me, you were holding back for me." She was worried about this. "That's it, isn't it? You've got some misguided notion that I'm not ready for the likes of you, or something equally macho and alpha and stupid."

The truth was in his eyes.

He *was* holding back for her. Damn it. She hated that. "I hate that, Sam."

He kissed her again. Becca tried to remain unmoved but he was such a good kisser, and in two seconds she was kissing him back. Just when things started to get deliciously out of hand, he pulled back. "You're going to be the death of me," he whispered against her lips.

And then he was gone.

"Ditto," she said into the silent room.

The next morning, Becca staggered out of bed. Moving slowly so her throbbing head didn't fall off, she showered, dressed, and made her way to work.

The hut was open, lights on, coffee made, computer booted up. On her counter sat a mug of steaming coffee, three aspirin, and a whole tin of ranch-flavored popcorn.

Damn, he *was* romantic after all.

Chapter 19

♥

Sam stayed in his warehouse most of the day, figuring that both he and Becca could use a little space.

At least he could.

So why he found himself watching the big, open doorway of his warehouse as if that was his job, he had no idea. But he was still watching when his dad pulled up in the alley with Becca's car. Mark got out and walked toward the beach hut, undoubtedly to return her keys.

Sam rolled his eyes, thinking Becca should consider herself lucky his dad hadn't sold the thing and pocketed the money.

A few minutes later, Mark was back in the alley, and when he caught sight of Sam, he waved. "Son, hey."

"Hey."

Mark came to the doorway. "So…what's your policy on letting houseguests drive your spare car?"

Sam's spare car had been Gil's and was a '68 Camaro. "My policy is fuck no."

Mark sighed. "Yeah. I get it. It's not like I deserve to borrow shit, especially since you've been letting me stay with you and eat your food and everything I should have done for you all those years ago, right?"

It was Sam's turn to sigh as he fished out his truck keys.

Mark grinned. "Thanks. Love ya."

And then he was gone.

Much later, Sam looked up from the boat he was working on and blinked, realizing hours had gone by and he hadn't been interrupted by a single thing. It had to be a record.

The phones had rung, but they'd been picked up. Apparently Becca was doing fine since she knew to call him if she needed anything.

She hadn't.

Which was great. After all, the whole point of hiring her had been so that he could be left alone.

His favorite state.

But Cole and Tanner were still out, and she'd been on her own all day.

Maybe something was wrong. Maybe she'd fallen and hit her head.

Maybe he was an idiot.

"Shit." He gave up wondering and headed toward the hut.

He heard her before he saw her, that bubbly, infectious laugh. When he turned the corner and saw the open hut, Becca was sitting behind the counter. She'd kicked off her sneakers and rolled her jeans into capris. She wore a red tank and a straw hat, which Sam recognized as the one Tanner occasionally wore in the bright afternoon sun, and a welcoming smile.

"That's perfect, Yvonne," she was saying to a customer. "You'll have such a wonderful time. The guys are all so great, you'll want to book another trip right away, I'm sure." She pointed to a spot on the iPad screen in front of her—onto which she'd loaded all their forms. "And don't forget to leave your email addy. You don't want to miss any specials we have going on."

She'd been right—she was a fast learner. She had a gift, a different one from anyone he'd ever met. She had the gift of curiosity and empathy, and of bringing people out of themselves, charming them, getting them to open up.

He knew that firsthand. He hated that she seemed to think her self-worth was wrapped up in her past, because that was bullshit. The smart, determined, resourceful Becca Thorpe could do anything she set her mind to.

He wished she knew that.

Yvonne was beaming when she walked away, and Becca immediately turned her attention to the next person waiting.

It was Anderson, the guy who ran the local hardware store. He was in his mid-thirties, and had been in Lucky Harbor since he was a kid. He was an okay guy, Sam supposed, but he was a known dog when it came to women. And sure enough, he leaned on the counter and flashed Becca his on-the-prowl smile like he was God's gift. "Hey," he said smoothly. "I know you. I sold you some stuff a few weeks back."

"You most definitely did, thank you," Becca said. "What can I sign you up for today? A snorkel? A deep-sea fishing expedition?"

"Which one of those do *you* do?"

"I take your money," she said.

Anderson laughed. "How about I take you instead."

"Um, what?" she asked.

"Out to dinner." Anderson clarified this with a smile, leaning in closer.

"Like…on a date?" Becca asked.

"Yes," Anderson said. "A date. What are you doing later?"

"She's busy," Sam said, stepping inside the hut and coming up behind Becca, laying a hand on her shoulder.

Anderson stopped drooling over Becca and straightened. "Hey there. I like your new front person. She's a whole lot cuter than any of you three. No offense," he said, and smiled.

Sam did not.

Anderson's smile faded. "Right, well, okay then. I'll just be on my way."

When he was gone, Becca very slowly, very purposefully turned to Sam. "What was that?"

Sam shrugged. "He thinks you're cute."

"No, I meant what was that, as in what were you doing just now?"

"Stopped him from harassing you. I came up to see how you were feeling after last night. And to see…" What, genius? "How you're working out."

He knew his mistake immediately, even before she narrowed her eyes. "I'm working out just fine," she said. "But *you* not so much."

"Excuse me?"

She moved closer and lowered her voice without lowering her annoyance level, which was blasting from her eyes. "You just acted like…a caveman."

"A caveman," he repeated.

"Yes! You chased him away from asking me out. You might as well have dragged me back to your cave by the hair."

He stared at her and then turned and tugged down the hut's rolling door for privacy, intending to show her his inner caveman.

But though Becca's eyes were still fiery, she took an immediate step back.

Sam swore beneath his breath and shoved the door back up again, giving her the space she clearly needed.

Becca held her own. She'd crossed her arms, but looked more pissed than anxious. Which was infinitely better, but not ideal. He still had no idea what made her tick. All he knew was that she made *him* tick.

And that was a first for him.

Also, he wanted a few minutes alone with whoever had made her anxious in small spaces. He wanted that badly. "Okay," he said slowly. "You're going to have to make a lot more sense for me here. Are you saying you actually *wanted* to go out with Anderson?"

"You're missing my point on purpose."

"Maybe because you're not speaking English." He dipped his head so that they were eye-to-eye. "Tell me in English, Becca."

"All right," she said, nose-to-nose with him, toe-to-toe. "I want to date *you*, you big, stubborn lug. But you don't want to date me back. You have all these…" She waved a hand. "Stupid rules."

"No, just the one," he said. "And it's not stupid. It's to protect you."

"From what?" she demanded, then blew out a breath when he just looked at her. "Whatever," she said, unimpressed as she tossed up her hands. Then she drew in a deep breath, like she was searching for patience, which was a new one for him. Normally *he* was the one searching for patience. And here she was looking at him like *he* drove *her* crazy. Which made no sense since he was being perfectly reasonable and she was not.

"I'm new to town," she finally said. "You know this."

"Yeah," he said. "So?"

"So maybe I'm lonely."

He stared at her, and he could admit, that hadn't occurred to him. He liked to be alone.

But this sweet, tough, beautiful woman in front of him wasn't wired the same as he was, and he should have gotten that. "Becca."

"Oh, no." She waggled a finger in his face. "Don't you dare feel sorry for me. I'm a big girl, and I take care of myself. You don't want to be with me that way, I get it. We did it once, and maybe it was so awful for you that you can't bear to repeat it, maybe—"

"You *know* that's not the case."

"Fine. But it doesn't matter. You won't *let* yourself be with me, for whatever secret reason—"

"It's not a secret, Becca."

"Yes, it is. I mean, you *say* it's because I work for you, and also because you think I'm not ready, but you know what I think? I think that's just an excuse. Which leaves me to believe you're afraid of me and what we had during our one night together."

He let out a low laugh. "I'm not afraid of shit."

"No?" she challenged, hands on hips. "Then prove it."

He stared at her and then drew in a deep breath and tried again. "I don't feel sorry for you."

"Great. But if you could not put on your scary alpha-man face and shoo away the next person who might want to be my friend, that would be great, too."

She couldn't be that naive. Could she? "Becca, Anderson didn't want to be your *friend*. He wanted to be in your pants."

She lost some of her bluster at that. "Well…that was for *me* to decide."

"So you *do* want to go out with him."

"Nooooo," she said slowly and clearly, as if he was a huge idiot. "As already established, I want to go out with *you*. But you're turning out to be an ass, and I try very hard not to date asses anymore."

"Anymore?" he asked.

And just like that, her expression closed. This got to him, in a bad way. "I think it's time we talk about you," he said quietly.

She turned away.

Reaching out, he gently snagged her hand and pulled her back around.

"I'm on the clock," she said. "We're not talking about this now."

"Becca—"

"Or ever."

He disagreed, vehemently, and began to reel her in, but her cell phone rang. It was sitting on the counter, which is how he saw it was a FaceTime call from Jase.

Becca stared at the thing as if it were a snake poised to strike.

"You going to answer?" he asked.

"Yeah. Sure." Taking a deep breath, she slid her thumb across the screen to answer. "Hey, Jase," she said, back to her friendly smile. It was the one she gave out to his clients, Sam realized, which was different from the smiles she gave him. The smiles for him were…real.

"Becca." A guy's face filled the screen. He looked like Becca, with the same big, soulful brown eyes and easy smile. He also looked incredibly relieved. "You're hard to get ahold of."

"Yes," she said. "I know."

"Too busy to call me back?"

Becca didn't look at Sam. "I'm sorry." Her cheeks were red. Her ears were red, too. Her eyes weren't. They were just plain unhappy.

Jase's smile faded as he took in this fact as well. "Bex," he said, until he caught sight of Sam. "Who's that?"

"He's my boss," Becca said before Sam could answer. "I…got a job."

Jase's gaze came back to Becca. "A job?"

"Yes."

"But you have a job in New Orleans, close to home."

"I lied when I told you I'd taken a leave of absence," she said. "The truth is, I quit. And now I…answer phones."

"I'd have given you money," Jase said. "Bex, you should be playing, going for your dream of music. Not…answering someone's phones. Jesus."

"It's more than phones," Sam said. "She's running a charter company."

Jase didn't look impressed, nor did he take his eyes off Becca. "Let me help you—"

"No. *No*," she repeated, more gently, reaching behind her to give Sam a shove. "I told you when I left. I'll worry about me. You worry about you."

"There was a time when we worried about each other," he said sadly.

Becca shook her head. "I can't do that anymore, Jase. You know that."

"Yeah," he said softly. "I know that. I miss you, Bex."

"Jase—"

"No, I get it." Jase's face closed up, much as his sister's had. "You have to worry about you."

"Jase," she said again, more softly now.

But the connection had ended. Becca went still for a minute, then pulled her heels up to her chair, hugging her bent legs and dropping her forehead to her knees.

Sam slid a hand down her back.

"I'm okay," she said.

"Yeah. That's why you're curled in a protective ball."

Closing her eyes, she shivered at his touch, and hoping that meant he was doing the right thing, Sam curved his palm around the nape of her neck and crouched at her side. "Talk to me."

"I'm fine."

Amelia had long ago schooled him in the fine art of *fine*. He knew that if a woman used the word *fine*, it actually meant the polar opposite of *fine*.

"You made it sound like I was running the free universe, rather than basically being a gofer," she said.

"You're more than a gofer, Becca. But Jase is right. You should be doing something with your talent, your dream—"

She lifted her head and leveled him—slayed him—with her big, luminous eyes. "You firing me?"

"No, of course not."

She drew in a deep breath and let it out again, purposefully, like she was releasing some tension. "You should know that, while I find your whole caveman thing really annoying, I realize you were just trying to protect me. For some reason, that's…arousing, but I don't need protecting. I can take care of myself."

"I know." Sam paused. "Arousing?"

She snorted and turned her head to look at him. "Is that all you heard?"

"I'm a guy."

"Yeah," she said. "I've noticed."

Before Sam could even begin to interpret that statement, Cole strode in.

Looking like she'd been given a reprieve from her own execution, Becca jumped up. Sam snagged her wrist before she could move off and put his mouth to her ear. "We're not done."

"Tell me something I don't know," she muttered, giving him a shoulder nudge that didn't need translation—she wanted space.

Cole, one of the most intuitive people Sam knew, took in both Sam and Becca and stopped short. "What did I interrupt?"

"Just a little show of Neanderthalism, that's all," Becca said.

Cole grinned. "He dragging his knuckles again?"

Becca slid Sam a look. "Just a little."

Cole nodded. "Runs in the family, along with our good looks."

"She knows we're not real brothers," Sam said.

"Hell if we're not," Cole said, losing his good humor. "When you first came to stay at my house—what were we, thirteen? You were a stick, half-starved and always sick, but you still beat the shit out of those assholes who kept jumping me after school. You said we were brothers, and no one messed with your brother."

Damn. Cole was even touchier than Amelia about this family shit. "Listen, I just meant—"

"You said it, man." Cole turned to Becca, who was probably soaking up this new information like a dry sponge. "And then our first year on the Gulf," Cole went on, "that massive storm hit, remember?"

"I remember," Sam said. "You don't need to—"

"We huddled in that fucking tiny room the size of a postage stamp, the four of us," Cole said. "And when that lantern fell and hit Gil on the head and sliced Tanner's leg, I got cut trying to clear the glass. We were bleeding like stuck pigs. Tanner decided we were all going to die, and we were trying to keep him from bleeding out—"

"Jesus," Sam said. "Dramatic much?"

"You kept your head," Cole said. "Even when the blood was everywhere, even when you slashed open your hand trying to get the glass out of Gil. You got us through that night, and the next morning when we got outta that shithole, we all had each other's blood on us and you"—He jabbed a finger at Sam like there might be any question of who he was talking to—"you said again that we were blood brothers. So go ahead, say we're not."

Cole had the patience of a saint, and a very long fuse to a nearly nonexistent temper. But one thing that pissed him off was whenever Sam brought up that they weren't really family. Cole was Amelia's son through and through. Sam shook his head and gave up. He met Becca's gaze.

Hers had softened, and there was something new there.

Like maybe she'd let him in just a little bit more than she had in the past.

Tanner came in and sank to the couch. As he always did after a trip, he immediately began stripping off his wet suit.

"What the hell are you doing?" Sam asked him.

Tanner had gotten the suit shoved down low on his waist. Bare-chested, he stared up at Sam. "Stripping," he said. "What does it look like?" He went to shove the suit off the rest of him, and since Sam couldn't be sure Tanner was actually wearing board shorts beneath—sometimes he went commando—Sam gave him a nudge with his foot. Actually, it was more of a kick. When Tanner looked up with a fight in his eyes, Sam jerked his head toward Becca.

Becca was watching every single movement with avid interest.

Tanner stopped stripping and grinned at her. "Hey, sweetness, how did your day go?"

"Good," she said. "We made a killing today when a group of twenty stopped to kayak. Oh, and as for the Summer Bash, I've looked into some advertising, both online and print for your web presence. You could do better there. I've emailed each of you a suggested plan to up your visibility. I'm not as familiar with Lucky Harbor as I'd like to be, yet, but I'm pretty confident you could also do much better in print ads as well."

Cole smiled. "Are we paying you enough?"

"For now," she said sweetly.

Sam thought about how many different ways she could have answered that, and had to admit it impressed him. She impressed him. She was nosy and curious and frustrating. She was sweet and warm, and sometimes, when he was very lucky, she looked at him like he was the only man on her radar.

And thanks to the intriguing phone call with her brother, he knew she protected her secrets well.

Which only made him want to know all the more what they were.

Chapter 20

Becca found herself enjoying Lucky Harbor more every single day. Twice she'd realized she'd missed another call from Jase, and twice she'd tried to call him back but he'd ignored her return calls.

Not a good sign.

But she couldn't try to live his life for him anymore. Instead, she immersed herself in life here. Lucky Harbor was different from any other place she'd ever lived. She was used to people keeping to themselves. She was used to passing someone on the street and, if accidental eye contact was made, you nodded or smiled briefly and kept moving.

That's not how things worked in Lucky Harbor. People stopped her, wanted to know how her day was, how the jobs were going—and they really, genuinely wanted to know. They also wanted to know how she handled working for the three hottest single men in town.

And yes, that actually happened. But it'd been Lucille asking, so maybe it didn't count.

She spent lots of hours at the rec center with the kids. Just yesterday they'd graduated to putting their five newly learned chords together to make a song.

Of sorts.

They were working on "God Bless America," *working* being the key word. But the hours spent in that classroom were some of her favorite hours ever.

"Think we can have a concert?" Pink asked one afternoon. Her front teeth were starting to grow in, while her twin Kendra's were not, which made it easy to tell them apart. Well, that and the fact that Pink wore only pink.

The truth was, they were about as far from being able to handle a concert as Becca herself was, but who was she to dim their enthusiasm? "Who would we play for?" she asked instead.

"The whole town!" Pink yelled. She yelled almost everything; she couldn't seem to contain her own energy.

"You want to play in front of everyone?" Becca asked, surprised.

Pink nodded vigorously.

Becca looked at Kendra. Kendra nodded vigorously.

Becca looked at the rest of the gang. They all nodded equally as vigorously.

They couldn't play one line of "God Bless America" without breaking up into giggles or a fight, not to mention they had no real skills, and yet they wanted to play in front of the entire town. It was the most awesome show of confidence Becca had ever seen, and suddenly she wished she were a kid again. "Well, I—"

Someone cleared his throat behind her. She turned and

caught Sam, Jack, and Jack's cousin Ben standing in the doorway, each wearing a badass smile. Becca knew that Ben taught "craft hour." He'd been the one to bring in Jack and Sam. The kids raved about them all the time.

Becca didn't know much about Jack or Ben, but the sight of Sam standing there all sexy-cool in jeans and a T-shirt advertising Lance's ice cream shop altered her heart rate. She decided she had to just *not* look at him anymore. Mature, she knew, but this was not a time to visit Lustville.

"How about us?" Jack asked. "Maybe you guys can play for us."

"Oh," Becca said. "I don't think—"

But the kids had all burst out with hopeful "Yays!" and "Yes!" and "Oh, please, Ms. Teacher!"

Becca sneaked a peek at Sam, who gave her a two-hundred-watt grin, damn him.

"Let's hear a few songs," Jack said.

"We only know one," Pink said, and flung herself at the big, bad, silent Ben, wrapping her arms around his waist, giving him a bear hug. Kendra did the same. Ben surprised her by gathering them in and hoisting them up so that their feet dangled above the ground—much to their squealed delight.

Jack ran his fingers along the classroom's xylophone, making a racket that had the rest of the kids giggling.

"Can they play with us, Ms. Teacher?" Pink asked, still hanging from Ben's arm.

"If they want," Becca said, unable to imagine that they did.

But the guys made themselves at home. Pink divvied up the instruments, thrusting a marching drum at Sam.

Shocking her, Sam sat down with the drum. The seats were made for kids, and as a big guy, he should've looked ridiculous stuffed into one. But he didn't look anything close to ridiculous. Actually, he looked pretty damn fine, not to mention sexy-adorable, and she wanted to gobble him up.

He caught her staring at him. "I don't know what I'm doing," he said, not looking bothered by that fact one little bit. It probably never occurred to him to worry about feeling ridiculous or making a fool of himself.

"That's okay," Pink told him. "Ms. Teacher will teach you."

"Yeah?" Sam turned to Becca with mock seriousness, his eyes laughing.

"Can you keep a beat?" she asked with as much teacher-like seriousness as she could muster.

"I don't know," her newest student said softly. "You tell me."

Oh, boy. The kids had given both Ben and Jack cymbals. Everyone was in place and ready, so Becca gave the count. They began playing—out of sync, of course, and off key. Nowhere even close to a beat.

But at the end of the song, when they all burst into applause, Becca took in the sea of happy faces and had to laugh. "Good," she said.

"It was *great*," Pink corrected.

When the class was over, Becca looked for Sam, and found him standing with Jack and Ben. Her heart skipped a beat at all the male gorgeousness in such close range.

"Holy crap," said a female voice from behind Becca. It was Mitzy Gale, the woman who ran the kids' programs at the rec center, and also the principal of the elementary school. She visibly shook herself. "Those three really shouldn't stand together; they're going to blow all the female brain circuits in the building." She looked at Becca. "That was great, by the way."

"It was?" Becca asked.

"Yes. You do so well with the kids. I'd love to hire you to run the after-school music program, both here at the rec center and also at the elementary school."

"You don't have a music program," Becca said.

Mitzy laughed. "Exactly. *You're* going to create one."

"Me?"

"Yes, please."

Becca's heart started beating faster in excitement. Hope. Thrill.

"Now, I should warn you, don't quit your day job yet. The hours are only part-time until our budget kicks in, which might happen for fall, and it might not. It's not a great offer. Frankly, it's a terrible offer, but you're so desperately needed and wanted, Becca, if that counts for anything."

"That counts for everything," Becca said.

She marveled over it for a few days.

Only a few weeks ago, she'd have described herself as an introvert. But here, in Lucky Harbor, working at the charter company, she'd come to realize that she was actually an extrovert. The job demanded it, really, and so did Music Hour with the kids, but…she liked it.

She liked the kids. She liked the guys, too. She liked all of it. Everything. Here, she didn't obsess so much over her career—or lack thereof. Here she got out and met new people every day.

Lived for the moment.

She had Sam to thank for that.

One afternoon, he showed up just as she was closing up the hut. The pattern was that one of the guys was always there at closing. They were there anyway, cleaning up the boat, the gear, whatever, but one of them would grab their cash from the day and get it to Sam. Or Sam would come get it himself.

Today he stuck his head in the door. His hair was windblown, his face tanned, his eyes crinkled to go along with the rare smile on his face as he crooked his finger at her.

She looked behind her.

No one.

"Me?" she asked.

"You."

"Is this going to be lesson number four?" she asked, unable to keep from sounding hopeful.

He met her gaze. He hadn't shaved that morning, and maybe not the morning before, either. His unruly hair had been finger-combed at best. He looked like maybe he had questionable motives. He looked like he didn't care what anyone thought of him. He looked hot.

"Becca, when I give you lesson number four, you'll know it."

Her entire body reacted. But she was beginning to think that he talked the talk of a badass, and walked the walk, but he didn't have the true heart of a badass or he'd have taken advantage of her by now.

Damn it.

Against her better judgment, she followed him outside and down the dock to where a gorgeous, sleek boat was moored. "Wow," she said. "It's beautiful."

"I made it for a client a few years back," he said. "He's

gone into town to grab a drink with some friends. He wanted me to take it out and take a listen to the motor."

"I thought Cole was your mechanic."

"Yeah but he's gone, and I'm good, too." While he was speaking, he was giving her the bum's rush down the ramp, his hand low on her back, then lifting her onto the boat with seemingly no effort at all. Before she could recover from the brief but very welcome feel of being held against his chest, he was tossing her a life vest.

She stared down at it. "You planning on dumping me in the water?"

"Only if you piss me off." He came close, and then closer still, and she pressed her hands to his chest to keep her balance.

She wasn't opposed to pissing him off if it would make him kiss her again. "We going now?"

"In a minute." He ran his hands down her spine, over the backs of her thighs, and then up again, copping a feel of her bottom while he was at it.

"Sam." She was having some trouble getting her cognitive skills to fire with his hands on her like that, roaming, his eyes all hot and liquidy, making his intentions more than clear. "You can't be thinking—"

"About taking you on the galley table below? Yeah," he said, voice whiskey-smooth. "That's pretty much exactly what I'm thinking."

She actually looked to the door that led belowdecks. "Really?" she asked breathlessly.

He laughed, low and sexy. "Yes. Later."

She blew out a sigh. "You don't mean it. You're still just a tease."

He checked the clasps on her vest and adjusted them.

There were several layers between his fingers and her skin, but her nipples got perky anyway.

"That good?" he asked, hands still on the vest, resting lightly against her breasts.

She had to clear her throat to answer. "Fine. But why—"

His gaze met hers. "I'm not taking any chances with you."

A squishy feeling settled low in her belly. "Why are you taking me with you at all? You've been avoiding—"

"I need a second body on board."

So much for the squishy feeling.

He walked through the cockpit to the bridge. He stood behind the controls, feet wide, the sexiest man she'd ever seen. "You need help?" she asked.

He flashed her a quick grin that affected her pulse.

No, he didn't need help.

"Hang on," he said.

Sam revved the engine, watching as Becca grabbed the oh-holy-shit hand bar in front of her with a cute little squeak of surprise as the boat leapt forward.

He loved that feeling, the power beneath him, the surge of the boat as it roared to life. The very first time he'd stood behind the controls of a boat and hit the gas, he'd felt free, and that had never lessened, not once in all these years.

The wind whipped, the salty air slapping them in the face as he took Becca out to the open water for some speed. A little while later, he slowed at a hidden cove where he'd once learned to fish.

He set anchor there.

The sun was low but not down, creating long lines of fire on the ocean, bisecting the swells. The scent of the early evening was pure, fresh air, and he watched with amusement and not a little amount of lust as Becca stood there and closed her eyes. "You okay?" he asked.

"Shh. I'm giving myself a *Titanic* moment."

He laughed, and she opened her eyes to smile at him. "You've seen the movie," she said.

He had, years ago under duress—a date who'd insisted on watching the DVD. He'd slept through most of it, but he knew the scene Becca meant, where the hero had stood behind his woman, her back plastered to his front at the bow so she could feel herself fly across the water.

Becca was still standing at the front of the boat just like that, face to the last of the sun, when he came up right behind her. His hands settled on her hips, then her hands, which he lifted out high to her sides as the wind teased and brushed over their bodies, so close together that a piece of paper couldn't have fit between them.

"You did see the movie," she murmured.

He could feel her every curve as she leaned back into him, her sweet ass snuggled against his crotch. She shifted a little, and clearly felt the reaction she got out of him because she let out a shaky breath that went right through him. She shifted again, more purposefully this time, and he tightened his hands on her hips. "Watch it," he warned.

"I'm tired of watching," she said, "and never doing. You once told me not to play with you, but you're playing with me. If you really wanted me, you'd have had me again by now. Stop doing this, stop making me feel things for you."

He pulled her around, stared into her soft, warm, *hurt* eyes, and saw she really meant it. "Are you talking about the fact that I'm not using you for sex?" he asked incredulously.

"Yes," she said. "I *want* you to use me for sex, damn it!"

"Becca." He slid his fingers into her hair and stared into her face. "I'm not using you for sex because this isn't just sex between us."

"We've only done it once," she said—as if he didn't know, didn't relive it every single night. "*Of course* it's just sex," she said, sounding pissy.

"Okay. That's it." He'd been holding back for…shit. None of his reasoning seemed valid at the moment. So he yanked off her life vest and hauled her into him.

"Hey," she said. "Don't I need that?"

"Not where you're going." He tossed her over his shoulder and headed belowdecks.

"Wait—what are you doing?" she shrieked from upside down.

"I warned you."

She was quiet for a beat, either because she was upside down, or because he'd stunned her. "You'd *better* mean it," she finally said, "'cause last time I ended up in my bed alone, all hot and bothered, and I had to handle my own business."

Now it was *his* turn to go quiet for a beat, imagining just that, Becca in her bed, hot and bothered, handling her own business. It was a really great image. "You hot and bothered now?" he asked.

"Mostly just bothered." Each word was a breathless murmur since she was bouncing up and down with his stride as he brought her into the small bedroom below.

"And anyway," she said, "I'm not getting naked with you now. I don't even like you anymore!"

"I'm going to change your mind about both of those things," he said, and slid his hand from her thighs to her ass.

"I'm going to need that in writing—" she started, and ended with another shriek as he tossed her to the bed.

Chapter 21

Hey—" Becca started, but the air was knocked from her lungs upon impact with the mattress.

Sam was kicking off his sneakers, but she, running on pure adrenaline, bounced up off the bed and gave him a little push until he was up against the wall. With an *oomph* of surprise, he let her have her way. For a beat. But then he took control, turning them so that *she* was pinned between his hard body and the even harder wall, her breasts crushed to his chest. He thrust a thigh between hers and rubbed it against her.

And damn if she didn't moan. This made his eyes heat with both triumph and a hunger that took her breath.

"Hold on," he said.

"For what?" she asked breathlessly.

"The ride." And then, still holding her to the wall, he kissed her.

And God. God, he had a way of kissing like she was his entire world. He was right. She needed to hold on for this. So she did, to him, gripping his hard biceps, his broad shoulders, his back, clutching at everything she could reach because she was starved for this, for him.

When they needed air, he easily switched from her mouth to her neck, licking, biting, sucking, moving against her the whole time. Becca could feel the pressure building inside her, and a wild thrill skittering on the surface of her skin as he drove her body right where he wanted it to go.

She was out of control, and he had plenty of control. Hell, he had all of it, but this wasn't about pressure, or forcing her. She'd been in that position before, and this was different. Like always with Sam, she was fully, definitely, willingly on board, and absolutely willing to take what he was giving.

And in turn give him everything she had.

It was a new sensation, and she wanted to revel in it, the utter feminine power that came with the surrender, but she couldn't do anything but *feel*. He was still moving against her, his hands rough and yet arousing, his mouth taking little love bites as he held her still. She probably should think about being mad at the manhandling, but the truth was, it excited her. She wasn't mad; she wasn't afraid. She was so damn aroused she could hardly stand it. So when he paused, she clutched at him. "I swear," she gasped, "if you're just teasing me again—"

Planting his forearms on the wall on either side of her head, his big hands captured her face for another long, hard, deep kiss as he rocked into her. "Does this feel like a tease?" he asked.

"I don't know yet," she panted. "Depends on what comes next."

"You do. You come next, Becca."

Oh, God. She could feel the quivers start in her body at just the words. "Not on someone else's bed."

"No," Sam said. "Right here. Like this." And then he slid down her body, dropping to his knees on the floor below her. He spread her legs to suit him and then shoved her denim skirt up to her waist. "Hold this."

"Um," she said, but did as he commanded, and held her skirt up past her pink lace, cheeky-cut panties, hoping to God she looked good. She must have, because he let out a gruffly uttered "Fucking hot, babe," scraped the lace to the side, and put his greedy mouth on her. With a soft cry, she sank her fingers into his hair and held on for dear life as he drove her right to the edge, held her there until she mewled his name in entreaty, and then shoved her over. The orgasm broke hard and fast, and she shuddered against his mouth.

"Again," he demanded, and then made it happen.

Still gasping for breath, she opened her eyes as he slowly rose, kissing her hip, her belly, first one breast and then the other on his way to her mouth.

She could feel him pulsing through the thick cotton of his cargo shorts. He needed to get out of the cargoes and work his magic. Of that she was sure. Goal-oriented, she reached for his top button.

He growled deep in his throat as she shoved the cargoes down far enough to spring him free. She wrapped her fingers around him and stroked, eliciting another growl, a wild, primitive sound that vibrated around her body, through her nipples, and into her core as he throbbed and leapt to her touch. She wanted to taste him, but that would mean moving and there wasn't time for that. She wanted him inside her, pounding into her, touching the parts of her body and soul that no man had ever managed to reach.

Except him. "Please, Sam. Now."

Apparently on board with the demand, he rolled a condom down his length. "The condom's not blue," she whispered.

He huffed out a laugh. "No."

"But still extra large."

He snorted. Then his mouth closed on hers, drinking in her moan as he slid up between her legs. His hands came up to tug her skirt, top, and bra away, the material fluttering to the floor. He pulled her panties down her legs and slid his hand between them, his fingers creating exquisite sensations against her wet flesh as he caressed every inch of her. Then he slid his hands around her thighs to cup her butt, lifting her. "Wrap your legs around me, babe—Yeah, like that—" His breath hissed out in a long inhalation as he filled her with one thrust, stretching her to the limit.

The quivers began in her body and echoed in his, letting her know he was as close to the edge as she. Sheathed to the hilt, he began to rock, using his hips and hands to move her as he chose. She tightened her legs around him and met each of his upward strokes, racing for the pleasure, growing frantic for it.

Fisting a hand into her hair, Sam tugged her face up to his. "Look at me."

It was a struggle. She felt drugged, high on him, but she met his searing, intense gaze and something happened: They synced, and then she was free falling…

So was he. One of his hands slapped onto the wall beside her head, palm flat against the surface for balance as he emptied himself into her with a powerful thrust that drove the breath from her lungs. Still spinning, still coming, she felt the shaking of her own body and the tremors in his as he worked to keep them both upright.

His legs gave out and they slid down the wall to the floor, the both of them sucking in air for all they were worth. She lay on her side and Sam flat on his back on the floor, not moving.

"Christ," he finally muttered, and reached over to snag her by the leg. Boneless, she let him haul her in, across the floor to him. Bracing himself on one elbow above her, he tucked her in so that her head lay in the hollow of his shoulder.

Turning her face into his warm skin, she kissed him. "Okay, so maybe I like you a *little*."

He looked down at her with eyes gone warm and soft. "Yeah?"

Reaching up, she touched her fingers to his smile and he gently rubbed his lips across her palm, his gaze never leaving hers. With a sated sigh, she traced his lips, the line of his jaw. "Or a lot. Which leaves me hanging out..." She smiled a little self-consciously with the irony. "Naked."

Leaning over her, he gently kissed the spots he'd nibbled at only moments before, his hand stroking her hair from her sweaty face, smoothing down the tangled mass. He made a sound low and deep in his chest, which vibrated against her nipples. "You're not alone in that," he said. Bringing a hand up to her chin, he once again turned her face to his.

He let her see what he was thinking. Desire, hot, liquid, consuming desire.

Affection, too. Which made her all warm and fuzzy.

But it was the *need* that reached her. Need wasn't the same thing as desire. It was even more awe inspiring. This big, tough, self-made man *needed* her.

And in a very scary way, she felt the same.

Becca awoke first. It definitely wasn't dawn yet but there was a lightening of the sky. That wasn't unusual. What was unusual was that she wasn't her usual morning chilly. In fact, she was downright toasty. That was because she was cozied up to a furnace.

A furnace named Sam. They were in her apartment; he'd brought her here late last night, and then surprised her by staying. He was on his back, the blanket riding low. She was plastered up to his side, one arm flung over his chest, a leg hitched over his. He had his arm snug around her, one big hand palming her butt possessively.

His breathing was slow and even. He was still deeply asleep, and at the thought a smile curved her mouth. She'd worn him out.

She liked that. A lot. Awake, Sam Brody was like a cat, all contained energy, controlled, steady. Asleep, he was boneless and completely relaxed in a way she rarely got to see. He had stubble that was at least twenty-four hours past a five o'clock shadow, and she had no complaints because she'd loved the way it'd felt on her skin. Her face heated as she remembered where some of those places were. She was pretty sure she had the marks to prove it.

If she could, she'd keep him here, right here in her bed, forever. And at that thought, she knew the truth. This wasn't casual. This wasn't about easy sex, or friendship, though both those things absolutely existed.

This was about the fact that she was in deep. Too deep. Her head was still cradled in the crook of his shoulder, and she realized she was rubbing her jaw against him like she was marking him as hers. Stilling, she lifted her head.

His eyes were open and on hers, sleepy...sexy. "You finished looking?"

She blushed and bit her lower lip. "Maybe. Maybe not..." She playfully tugged the sheet down and exposed...yay!...a part of him *very* happy to see her. "I like to look," she said.

"Good to know." And that's when she found herself rolled flat to her back and pinned by 180 pounds of testosterone.

"Turnabout's fair play," he said, and proceeded to get his fill of looking at her.

And then touching.

And then tasting...

Sam barely got to the docks on time. They had a big group waiting—twelve fishermen in from Phoenix. He smiled at the clients as he pushed off, ignoring both Tanner and Cole giving him long looks. "What?" he said, leaping on board.

"You're smiling," Cole said. "In the early morning, pre-coffee."

"It happens," Sam said.

"When?" Cole asked. "When does that *ever* happen?"

Tanner, eyes narrowed, got up into Sam's space and studied him. "What's that?" he asked, touching Sam's throat. "Is that a *hickey*?"

Sam smacked his hand away. "No."

"Yeah, it is," Tanner said. "You totally have a hickey."

"Let me see," Cole said, pushing close. At the sight, he grinned. "Nice. I wouldn't mind one of those," he said, sounding wistful.

Tanner snorted.

Sam stalked to the bridge, rolling his eyes at their laughter behind him.

It wasn't until that night, kicking off his shoes in the foyer of his house, that he caught sight of himself in the mirror.

He totally had a hickey on his throat.

"Son, you can have the hot tub tonight," his dad said, coming in behind him without knocking as usual. "I'm tuckered *out*." He plopped himself on the couch.

Sam moved closer and looked him over. Pale. Even a little gray. He knew he'd been taking his medicine; he'd made damn sure of it every morning. But the meds were no guarantee. "You okay?"

"Always," Mark said.

"Dad."

Mark opened his eyes. "I'm fine. I'm just overtaxed, that's all."

"Maybe it's not a great time to be screwing a woman two decades your junior."

Mark grinned. "But what a way to go, right?"

When Sam just looked at him, he sighed. "And that's not what I've been doing."

"What have you been doing then?" Sam asked.

Mark hesitated.

Never a good sign. "Christ," Sam said. "Gambling?"

"No!" Mark shook his head. "Still got a real high opinion of me, I see." He paused. "I've been working."

"Working," Sam repeated.

"Yeah. I took a job at the arcade, running some of the games, okay?"

"That's a teenager job," Sam said.

"Or the job of a man with no résumé," his dad said.

Sam didn't get it. "Why?"

"I'm going to pay my own way," Mark said.

"Since when?"

"Goddamn it, I'm tired of being a mooch off you."

Sam sighed and sank to the couch next to his dad. "Well, if you're going to take all the fun out of my resentment…"

Mark laughed, but it was hollow. "You've worked so hard all your life," he said. "And people here love you. I want to be a better man, son. Like you."

Sam took the unexpected hit to his solar plexus, heart, and gut. "You can't work, not right now."

"Yes, I can. I am. I already have twenty hours. I'm going to pay you rent and get my own car. And you're not the only one who can build shit, you know. I'm going to make you shelves so all your CDs and DVDs aren't on the damn floor all the time."

Sam stared at him, but his dad looked serious. And sincere. "How about you wait until after you get better?"

Suddenly looking older and very tired, Mark closed his eyes again. "Yeah. Okay. Hey, you got stuff for sandwiches?"

"I think so," Sam said. "You want one?"

"You got any potato chips to put in it?"

Sam blew out a breath. "Yeah."

Sam fed his dad, watched him carefully for a while, and determined he really was just tired and not ill enough for a call to Josh.

"Stop hovering," Mark muttered, eyes closed from his position prone on the couch. "I'm not dying tonight."

"That's not funny," Sam said.

"You're right, it's not. It's sad as hell that you're watching me instead of being with your woman. Go be with your woman."

"Dad—"

"Jesus." Mark pulled out his phone and hit a number. "Hey, darlin'," he said. "Yeah, I'm fine, but I've got some-one here who's not. I'm sending him to you, okay?" Mark slid his gaze to Sam. "Okay, I'll tell him." He clicked off. "She says to be ready for lesson number five. What's she teaching you?"

Sam managed to keep a straight face, but Christ, she cracked him up. "I have no idea," he said evenly.

His dad shrugged. "Well, when a woman looks like that, with a heart like that, you ignore the crazy, son, and get ready for lesson number five."

Two days—and two extremely long, hot, erotic nights later—Becca was in the hut, opening for the day, when the man single-handedly responsible for the perma-smile on her face walked in. She was surprised, seeing as she'd left him boneless and facedown on her bed only half an hour earlier. Knowing he was leaving today on a two-day fishing expedition, she'd let him sleep.

"You got up early," he said, heading for the coffee.

"So did you."

"Twice," he said.

She laughed. It was true. And once the night before as well. "Did I wake you when I left? I tried to be quiet and not talk."

"I wouldn't have minded some talking," he said. "I really liked the *More, Sam, oh please more*."

She threw her pencil at him.

He caught it in midair and grinned.

"I got up thinking I'd try to work on my next jingle," she said.

"You haven't said what your next assignment is." He caught her grimace and smiled. "It can't be worse than your last few."

"Yeah, it can. It's diapers. But at least it's for *baby* diapers." She blew out a breath. "It's because I'm not doing anything spectacular. I keep waiting for my muse to really kick in, but the truth is, I think I've lost my talent." She caught something in his expression. "What?"

"It's not because you're not talented," Sam said. "It's the importance you're attaching to it."

That this was true didn't help. "I need to be successful at something," she said. "At *this*," she corrected when he opened his mouth. "I'm going to be successful at this if it kills me."

"You know," he said. "It wasn't all that long ago when you got mad at me for blaming shit on myself, like when I got my dad and me kicked out of that apartment."

"You were thirteen," she said. "I'm not a minor by any stretch of the imagination. I run my own life, and I take the fall for it."

He brought her a mug filled with lots of sugar and a little bit of coffee, and that he knew the exact right formula warmed her heart. Not enough to ward off the unease at the intimacy of this conversation, but enough that she didn't make a run for the door. Apparently sharing orgasms was easier than sharing her soul. She stared down into the steaming brew, wishing it held the answers to her life.

"Becca."

With a sigh, she looked at him, and found her gaze locked in his, held prisoner.

"You're successful just as you are," he said.

"If you think that's true, you haven't been paying attention."

"Wrong," he said. "I've been paying attention better than you. You came into this job to answer phones and you've so completely fixed us up that now *anyone* could run our place with the blink of an eye."

"In my past," she clarified. "I want to have been successful at stuff in my past."

"Fuck the past. Move on to something that suits you right now."

She stared at him. "Fuck the past? Is that how you live your life? Not thinking or looking back at all, just forward?"

"Hell yeah."

She nodded. This was true. She knew it. She'd seen it. She'd just conveniently forgotten it.

Sam's eyes were warm as his hand curled around the side of her neck, where his thumb gently stroked. "You should try it sometime."

What she wanted to try was him. She wanted to try him out for as long as they both could take it. She almost said so, but saying it out loud twice wouldn't make it so. Her life was in flux. She needed to focus, and focusing around Sam was proving all but impossible. Still, she stepped into him, meeting him halfway when he lowered his mouth and kissed her, an effective kiss that shut down her ability to think and cracked through her defenses.

Of course that's when their morning clients showed up—a group of ten fishermen—and just like that, Sam was gone.

Over the next two days, Becca ran the hut and loaned out the rental gear. She finalized Summer Bash plans. She had dinner with Olivia at the Love Shack on Country Night, and even got talked into dancing a little bit. She was having fun—until she realized Lucille was snapping pics.

Lucille told Becca not to worry her pretty little head about it because the pics would only be posted on Lucky Harbor's Pinterest page, and there weren't many followers yet.

Olivia went home shortly thereafter because she had to work early the next day. The crowd thinned considerably, and Jax sent Becca a long look and a jerk of his chin toward the piano.

Like a moth to the flame. There were still a few stragglers in the place but she sat anyway. Only a few weeks ago, she could not have done so. Still, her heart began to thump. She looked around.

No one was paying any mind at all.

So far so good. She set her fingers on the keys, closed her eyes, and began to play.

When she'd finished one song, she drifted into another, and after three, a movement caught her eye.

Mark.

"Hey," she said, startled, jerking her hands back from the piano. "What are you doing here?"

He set down a full shot glass.

She looked at the glass and then into his face, and her heart softened at the inner turmoil she saw there. "You're struggling."

"Seems like I'm not the only one," he said. "Scooch over, darlin'."

She scooted over, and to her surprise he sat on the bench next to her. "You play the same way you make sandwiches," he said. "Like heaven on earth."

She choked out a laugh. "I don't like it when people listen to me play."

"Is that true, really?"

She thought about it and slowly shook her head. "No, actually. The truth is that I don't like worrying about making a fool of myself."

"Honey, the only foolish act is keeping that talent to yourself." Then he placed his fingers on the keys and began to play "Don't Go Breaking My Heart."

Becca laughed and joined in, and when they were done, she heard a single pair of hands clapping.

Jax, and he was grinning. "You two are hired," he said.

Becca looked at Mark.

"Yeah," he said. "I know. Call me a fool, right?"

She grinned. "You play."

"Nah. I dated a woman who taught me that one, eons ago now. Other than that, I've no idea what I'm doing." He paused, looked at the shot glass. "With anything."

"Me either," Becca said and nudged the shot glass away from him. "But I know that won't help either of us."

"You're right."

"It's not often I hear that," she said. "I like the sound of it. You going to tell me what you're doing here?"

"Maybe I came to make sure I could stay off the booze.

But then I saw you and thought to myself that you looked beautiful. And sad. And since you've helped me so much, I wanted to do the same for you."

She met his gaze. "How do you plan to do that?"

"By imparting wisdom," he said. Then he sighed. "Shit's hard."

She nodded. "Really hard."

"But not having shit…that's harder," he said. "Know what I mean?"

"Yes." She paused. "No."

"We're still breathing."

"Yes," she said. "Last I checked, I was still breathing. You too by the looks of you."

"Right. And not breathing, that would be worse," Mark said.

She stared at him. "That's it? That's the wisdom you're going to impart?" Becca said. "Keep breathing?"

"And don't sweat the small stuff," he said. "Both good bits of advice."

"True enough," she said, and stood up. "Need a ride?"

"Nah. I want to walk. No worries, I didn't drink."

"You going to?"

"No, ma'am."

She kissed him on his cheek and went home and sat on her bed, which reminded her of Sam, and work. By dawn, she'd sent off a jingle for the diaper campaign, but she wasn't thrilled with it, and she was a little bit afraid she knew why.

She was sweating the small stuff.

She was also sweating the big stuff, but one thing at a time.

Chapter 22

By early evening, Becca had closed the hut and was eating ice cream after snorkeling with Olivia when the guys came back in.

She hurriedly popped the last bite of cone into her mouth and pulled on her denim shorts over her still-damp bathing suit.

"Look at you move," Olivia said, amused.

"My bosses are back. They might need something."

"Uh-huh," Olivia said. "Or you want to pull a *Baywatch* and run down the beach toward your man. Or maybe I should say *Babe-watch*."

Becca ignored her and…ran down the beach.

Cole and Tanner were unloading gear to the dock. She didn't see Sam, and thought maybe he'd somehow gotten by her. She slowed her footsteps, and tried to slow her heart down as well.

After all, he didn't owe her a special hello. He owed her nothing.

"Hey," she said, greeting Cole and Tanner. "Everyone good?"

"Sure." Tanner tossed some more gear to the docks. "We hardly ever kill anyone anymore."

Cole turned to look at him. "Seriously? You're allowed to joke about it, but not me?"

Tanner shrugged.

Cole shook his head and pulled Becca in for a hug. "Everything holding up here?" he asked her.

"Of course."

His gaze said he knew otherwise, but he let her get away with it. "Saw you and Anderson all hot and heavy on the dance floor. You really gotta watch that guy, okay?"

Becca stared at him. "You were there?"

Tanner laughed. "No, he wasn't there. But *please* ask him how he knows."

Becca looked at Cole.

Cole grimaced. "It's not a big deal."

"Then tell her," Tanner said.

Cole sighed. "Pinterest."

Tanner coughed and said "pussy" at the same time.

"Hey, my mom sent me the link to the pin," Cole said.

Tanner grinned. "Gets better and better."

Cole had accessed the pic on his phone and showed it to Becca. It was her and Anderson dancing, and from the angle the shot had been taken, Anderson appeared to be holding her very close and whispering a sweet nothing in her ear. "Okay, that is not what it looks like," she told them, and in the interest of a subject change she waved the iPad she held and went through her list of things to go over. "The decorations for the Summer Bash," she said to Cole as he did something fancy with the ropes in his hands.

"Whatever you want," he said.

She sighed and looked at Tanner, who was straddling the dock and the boat with circus-like balancing ability as he hosed down the bow.

"What he said," Tanner said.

"You guys are too easy," she said.

They both shrugged. "You could ask the boss," Cole suggested, jerking his head toward the figure coming out of the cabin, heading to the helm.

Sam.

He wore no shirt, no shoes, nothing but a pair of low-slung board shorts, a backward ball cap, and dark lenses as he did something with the controls and the engine roared to life.

He took her breath.

"He's not the only boss," she managed.

"No, but he likes to think he is," Tanner said.

"He's not exactly crazy about this whole shindig," she reminded them.

Cole laughed.

"What?" she asked.

"Honey, what he's crazy about is *you*."

This startled her. She'd really believed that she and Sam had been doing a great job at keeping…whatever this was under wraps. Not that she was ashamed of what they were doing, although thinking about it did make her blush.

But there was the unprofessional factor. She was, after all—and despite his best efforts to the contrary—sleeping with her boss. She glanced at Sam, still behind the helm, his back to them. "You really think he's doing this party just for me?"

"Did he not hire you when he didn't want to?" Cole asked.

"Yes, but—"

"And did he let you into his Man Cave without bloodshed?"

"Well, yes. But…"

They were both just looking at her.

"Come on," she said. "This is silly. Sam doesn't do anything he doesn't want to. Not unless…" She thought about how he did whatever his dad needed done, just to keep the man afloat, even though it'd be easier to walk away. How much he did for Cole's mom, which she knew he felt was payback, just as she knew that Amelia didn't feel he owed her a thing. How much he did for these guys right in front of her, though that was mutual. How much he'd done for her…

Tanner went brows-up.

"He cares," she whispered. "He cares a lot."

Tanner touched a finger to the tip of his nose.

Cole nodded.

"Well, I know that," she said. And she did know how Sam felt about her; it was in every touch, every kiss, every word he murmured against her late at night in her bed.

But still, hearing it out loud in the light of day from the two people closest to him in the whole world gave her a warm glow. She smiled at them and turned to go to the hut.

"Hey," Cole said, and she looked back. "Take it easy on him."

"What do you mean?"

Tanner chuckled. "He means the guy plays at being tough as hell, but the truth is—"

"I'm tough enough to beat the shit out of the both of you ladies," Sam said from behind Cole and Tanner.

"You're so dead," Cole murmured to Tanner.

Tanner didn't look worried as he leisurely took off toward the hut. Cole followed, leaving Becca alone with Sam.

"So," she said into the awkward silence. "You only *play* at being tough and hard?"

He surprised her by laughing, and then tugged her onto the boat and into his arms. "You tell me." He nuzzled her neck. "Do I *play* at being hard?"

She thought about how deliciously "hard" he'd been the other morning before he'd left and let out a sigh of pleasure.

Holding her close, Sam opened his mouth on her neck. "Love that sound."

"Sam," she murmured, going soft. And damp...

"And that," he said, and nibbled. "Come onto the boat; I want to show you something."

She snorted against his chest. "I've already seen it."

"Smart-ass," he said, his hand sliding down her back to lightly smack her butt. "You've been busy," he said casually as he nudged her into the cabin.

"Yeah." The quarters were tight here but she didn't feel threatened, not with Sam. "Summer Bash is in four days and there's a lot of last-minute stuff. Plus, I've been working with the kids, and we're really nailing down the rest of the song. Sort of." She laughed a little. "Actually, that might be wishful thinking on my part."

"Cute," he said. "But I meant at the Love Shack."

She stared at him. "You saw the pic, too."

"My little sister showed it to me."

"You don't have a little sister," she said.

"Cole."

She laughed. "You should know, the angle of the picture made the dance look a little…more than it was."

He nodded. "He ask you out?"

"He did."

"You tell him you're busy?" he asked, pushing her into the galley.

"Didn't know I was," she said.

"You are." His voice was raspy rough and teasingly sexy—a deadly combo. "Very busy."

"Doing?"

"Me."

She tried to look outraged, but the truth was that the ridiculously alpha statement made her go all warm and mushy. Before she could decide how to respond to the cocky possessiveness, he turned her to face the table. On it were the music books she'd been eyeing online.

"Sam," she said with surprise, and tried to turn to him, but he pinned her still.

"We docked in Seattle with our clients," he said in her ear. "They had lunch downtown, and I picked these up for you." His lips brushed the skin of her neck as deft fingers tugged at the string ties of her bikini top.

With a gasp, she whirled around, holding up her top with her hands. "Hey."

Sam smiled.

Her heart stuttered.

He looked down at the way her nipples pressed against the thin material of her suit and let out a low, very male sound of approval. "Miss me?" he asked.

"No."

"Liar." He slid a hand to the nape of her neck and

rubbed the chafed spot where her bathing suit ties had made her skin raw. When her lips parted on a soft moan, he tangled his fingers in her hair, tipping her face up, his lips inches from hers. He had really great lips.

"Okay," she said. "Maybe I missed your mouth." *And the things you do with it...*

He kissed her again, then used his hips to shift her legs apart. "Only my mouth?"

"Mmm," she said, as if she needed to think about it.

He gripped her hips and rubbed her against a most impressive erection. She dug her nails into his back as he rocked into her.

"Mmm. Maybe some other things, too," she managed.

That made him laugh as he slid his hands down her back to her bottom. "I missed *you*," he murmured against her lips.

The statement was unexpected, and made her melt into him. She looked into his eyes and found herself looking into pure desire. Maybe she had no idea what the future would bring for them, but the next few minutes would be damn good. She slid her hands up ripped abs and around to his warm, sleek back. "Now, Sam?"

"No," he said, surprising her. "Much as I'd love to know if this table would hold, I've been thinking all day about the things I want to do to you. I'm going to need a while. Hours."

She quivered, and felt herself get wet. "Hours?"

"All night."

"Tonight then," she agreed.

"And maybe tomorrow night, too," he said.

She quivered again. "As many as you want."

Chapter 23

Sam nudged Becca back above deck, his eyes on her sweet ass as it moved up the narrow stairs in front of him, his mind on how she'd smiled at him when she'd first seen him. She'd been happy to see him.

He'd had women be happy to see him before. He'd had women want him. But that wanting had usually been purely sexual in nature, and although he'd reciprocated, he hadn't spent too much time delving deeper.

Becca was different. He liked her in a bathing suit, no doubt. He also liked her with their clients. He liked her with his partners.

He liked *her*.

He was so lost in thought that he didn't realize when Becca stopped, frozen in her tracks at the sight of the guy standing on the docks staring at them.

"Jase," he heard her whisper.

Jase had gone still as stone as well. "Hey, sis."

Becca glanced back at Sam, a look on her face that he

couldn't quite interpret. "Sorry," she said softly. "But I've got to talk to him."

Sam got that she wanted privacy for this reunion, and he should have left the area.

But fuck that. He didn't get off the boat, but instead busied himself with the ropes, an ear cocked to the conversation behind him.

That was the thing about water. Sound carried. Voices carried. From the middle of the harbor on a still day, he'd once heard a conversation between two illicit lovers in a cove, clear as a bell.

"How did you find me?" Becca asked.

"Remember how you made me upload that Find Your Friends app so you could always see where I was?" he asked. "That thing goes both ways."

Becca stared at him. "So all this time I thought I was free, you knew exactly where I was. Why are you here, Jase?"

"Maybe I missed you," he said.

Becca stared into her brother's face, looking like she didn't buy that excuse one bit. "Your eyes aren't yours," she finally said.

"What the hell does that mean?" Jase asked.

Becca stared at him for another beat, then took a step back, her voice shaky. "Damn you, Jase. You promised."

At this, Jase shoved his hands into his pockets and hunched his shoulders, staring out on the water, mouth grim. "Yeah, well, you know I've never been good at keeping promises."

She made a sound of disbelief. "So that's it, your whole explanation?" she asked. "You're not good at promises, so that frees you up to not keep them? For God's sake, Jase, grow up!"

Sam couldn't help but think of his dad. Becca had been nothing but accepting of his dad. It told him there was much more to this story.

Jase closed his eyes, like looking at her was too painful. "I've never been as strong as you," he said. "You expecting different from me is like…believing in Santa Claus until sixth grade."

Becca let out a mirthless laugh. "I didn't believe in Santa that long," she said. "I only pretended—for you."

Jase's gaze snapped to Becca's.

"Yeah," she said. "You wanted to believe so bad, I kept up the pretense. For you. You idiot." She gave him a shove that might have landed him in the water if he hadn't been on his toes.

"Jesus, Bex."

"You promised me," she said fiercely with another shove. "You promised me you could do this, get through rehab, stay clean. You wanted a life, you said, your *own* life. You weren't going to need me, lean on me; you were going to do this on your own."

"And *you* said you were drowning from trying to save me," Jase snapped, just as fiercely. "You said you couldn't breathe. Christ, Bex, what was I supposed to do with that?"

"So you lied to me?"

"No. *No*," he repeated when Becca made a sound of soft angst, and then he reached for her.

She evaded, stabbing a finger into his chest. "I tried to save you," she said. "God, I tried. For years, Jase."

"I know," her brother whispered.

Another sound ripped from Becca's throat and tore Sam in two. This was killing her slowly, and he wanted, needed, to fix it for her.

"So why are you here?" Becca asked her brother. "Why now?"

Jase looked away.

"Truth, Jase," she implored. "You owe me that."

He nodded, a muscle twitching in his jaw. "My concert's tonight, in Seattle. I was hoping to get my big sis to play with me."

"Oh, my God. You're kidding, right?" She stared into her brother's face and let out another mirthless laugh. "You're not kidding. You actually think I can—" She laughed again and bent over at the waist. "My throat's closing up," she said to her knees. "Hopefully I'll suffocate quick."

Jase actually smiled. "Still dramatic."

Becca whipped upright, eyes flashing at him. "Don't do that. Don't you dare make me feel like it's all in my head."

"It is all in your head," Jase said. "That's what stage fright is. Ignore it."

"You can't ignore a panic attack," she said through her teeth.

"Bex—"

"No. Damn it! See, *this* is why I left. Look, I get that you don't believe in panic, that you never even feel nerves before a show at all. I don't know if that's because you truly never get nervous or if you've been self-medicating so long that you can't feel it!"

Jase took a step back like she'd slapped him, and brother and sister stared at each other.

"I'm sorry," Becca finally said. "That was out of line."

"No." Jase shook his head. "I deserved it. And I'm the sorry one. I'm sorry I upset you by coming here without warning. Besides the concert, I wanted to see you, and for once make sure you were okay, the way you always used to do for me." He hesitated. "Mom and Dad are flying in. I promised I'd come get you and bring you to the concert tonight."

Becca shook her head slowly. "You shouldn't have promised that."

"No doubt, given how all my other promises have turned out." He let out a long, shaky breath. "I guess you also think I shouldn't have come."

"You shouldn't have, no," she said. "I asked you for time. It's the only thing I've ever asked of you."

Jase stared at her for a long beat, and then nodded.

Becca rubbed the heels of her hands over her eyes, which were filled with a hollow, haunted devastation that just about killed Sam. He had no idea how Jase could even look at her without doing everything in his power to fix this.

"I'm sorry," Jase whispered, but it wasn't enough; it didn't change Becca's expression. If anything, it made it worse. "I'm sorry I wasn't there for you after…Nathan—"

Becca snapped upright, eyes glossy. "Stop."

He didn't stop. "I didn't get what happened. I honestly thought you two were back together, so I didn't think—" He hesitated. "I'm sorry I wasn't there when you needed me most. I know that's why you really left—"

"You're sorry I'm gone."

Jase stared at her for a beat. "Yeah. I'm very sorry you're gone. I wish I'd paid more attention, that I'd really listened—" He broke off when she made a sound like a soft sob and covered her mouth. "Too little too late?" he whispered.

"No, I…I don't know." She closed her eyes. "Yes."

Jase closed his eyes. "I shouldn't have come," he said again, and when Becca didn't contradict this, Jase blew out a breath. "I'm going to text you the venue info for tonight, okay? Please, just think about it."

Becca unlocked the hut and stared at nothing, vibrating with so much energy she didn't know what to do with herself. She couldn't get her mind to wrap around anything, but surely there was plenty to do. Their Summer Bash was in a few days. There were a *million* things she could be doing.

She didn't do any of them.

Footsteps sounded behind her, and she forced herself not to move. She knew Jase wouldn't follow her in here, not after the things she'd said to him.

He'd run tail.

That was what he did. He'd wait her out and eventually come back, not referring to their fight or the things she'd said. He'd smile charmingly, sweet-talk, give her the I-can't-help-myself eyes, and she'd sigh and forgive him. Help him. Whatever he needed. She'd seen Sam do this with his father, and she could do the same.

She strode to the counter and busied her hands, forcing a friendly smile so she could greet their customer. But it wasn't a customer at all. It wasn't Cole or Tanner, either. It wasn't anyone she could fool with her friendly smile at all.

It was Sam.

She didn't say anything. She didn't trust her voice, plus there was nothing to say. She figured he'd heard a whole hell of a lot more than she'd wanted him to, but she couldn't change that. She could, however, do her best to brush it under the table. She was off the clock, in fact. She could go home and lick her wounds in private.

Normally when he showed up, he strode in with that innate, almost cat-like grace, always looking completely in control and completely at ease. But this time, he was still by the door, not moving toward her until she made eye contact. Then he walked to her, took her hand, and tugged her into him.

"I'm not going to talk about it," she said, muffled against his shirt. "There's only one thing I will do, and it is *definitely* not talking."

Lowering his head, he brushed a kiss to the top of hers, and she braced for rejection. But he kept ahold of her hand as he closed the big, sliding front door with his other, even though it always took her two hands and *all* her weight.

"You'd better not be teasing me," she said, as he took her to his warehouse. "Because that'd be just mean."

The big hanging door was closed. He bypassed the front and took her to a side door she'd never noticed before, guiding her down a hallway she'd also never noticed. The first door there was his office. He unlocked it, gently pushed her in, then shut the door behind them.

"Sam—"

"Shh a second."

Oh, hell no. She'd been quiet for most of her life—*all* of her life. She'd been good, and a people pleaser, and all sorts of things she could no longer be because they made her sink. So she opened her mouth to tell him what he could do with his *Shh*, but he kissed her.

Softly.

Gently.

She didn't want soft and gentle, so she did what he'd done to her not all that long ago. She pushed him against the wall, trapped him there with her body, and tugged his face down to hers.

His hands came up to her hips, his fingers tightening on her. He was going to push her away, let go of her, but if he did, she'd go under for the count and drown. She could feel it. "Sam," she whispered, unable to say more.

He must have heard it in her voice. That or he knew her well enough to read her mind because his arms immediately came around her, hard and warm. But his eyes. Damn it, his eyes weren't filled with heat. They were worried and concerned.

For her.

The very last two things she wanted. "Hold me," she said. Demanded. "Just for right now, hold me."

"Becca," he said, and oh, God, it was in his voice. So solemn. Sliding a hand up her back and into her hair, he fisted the strands, pulling her head up to look into his face. He stared down at her, searching her expression, his own steady.

"I'm not fragile." She kissed a corner of his mouth, moving along his rough jaw to his ear, which she nipped, liking when he sucked in a harsh breath. "Don't you dare treat me like I am. I'm not going to break, Sam."

"Maybe you should."

No. Hell no. "I just want to feel something good for a change," she said. "Please, Sam, make me feel something good. Make us both feel something."

"I can't."

She froze for a beat and then tried to shove free but he

held on with a grip of inexorable steel. "I can't do good," he said softly, his mouth against hers, "but I can do *great*."

As payback, she nipped his throat. And then the crook of his neck.

He let out a shuddery groan, lowered his head, and played her game. He took her lower lip between his teeth while she wrapped a leg around him and tried to climb him like a tree.

He slid his hand beneath her other thigh and hoisted her up with ease.

Then he turned and dropped her on the couch, following her down.

"Now?" she whispered hopefully, flinging her arms around his neck.

"Yeah. Now."

And he kept his word. He wasn't good. He was great.

Chapter 24

♥

It took a while, but when Becca finally retained enough muscle memory to move, they dressed, and Sam brought her into the small kitchen. Kicking a chair from the wood table, he gestured for her to sit and strode to the fridge.

Still a little shaky—the aftershocks of emotional trauma compounded by really great sex—she sat and looked around. "You're being awfully generous with the Man Cave today."

"Maybe I like the sight of you in it." He brought her a soda and a cup of ice, setting them on the table in front of her. Then he kicked out a chair for himself. "Drink," he said.

She looked at the soda. "You got anything stronger? Say, a hundred proof?"

She expected a smile but didn't get one. "No," he said. "I don't keep it here anymore."

She opened the soda and poured it over the ice. "Anymore?"

He held her gaze. "I used to like it too much."

"AA?"

"No. Cold turkey."

She let out a breath and gulped down some soda. She set the glass to the table and wiped her mouth. "You decided to quit, and you quit. Problem solved. Why can't everyone do that?"

"You have to quit for the right reasons," he said.

Her gaze slid back to his. "What were your reasons?"

"I decided I wanted to stick around for the rest of my life."

She huffed out a breath. "That's a good reason." She played with the condensation on her glass until Sam nudged it out of the way, hooked a foot around the leg of her chair, and dragged her in closer so that she was caged between his thighs.

"Talk to me, Becca."

"I'm not going to Seattle tonight to play in the concert with Jase."

"I got that," he said.

"I'll have a panic attack if I do."

"I got that, too." His hands came up to her arms. Gently. Softly stroked up and down. And the gesture made her open her mouth and say more. More than she wanted to.

"The first time it happened," she said, "I was seventeen. I'd just grown about eight inches in six months and was so awkward that my fingers didn't work. I embarrassed everyone. My parents, Jase..." She shook her head.

"Stage fright at seventeen sounds perfectly normal," he said. "Stage fright at *any* age is normal."

"Maybe." She blew out a breath. "I fought it. I managed to keep playing for ten more years, and though I loved it, it was a really difficult time. I used to take anxiety meds to play." She paused. "Jase started stealing them. I let him. And then he moved on to...other stuff. Pain meds that he got from one of the other musicians. He got addicted."

"Not your fault," he said quietly.

She stared at him. "I stopped playing when he needed me most. I missed playing, but not enough to get over my fear."

He covered her hand with his, entwined their fingers. "The Becca I know isn't afraid of shit. Well, except for spiders."

"And things that go bump in the night," she added with a low laugh. She stared at their hands, his big and capable.

He squeezed her fingers gently. "Who's Nathan?"

The question startled her—or maybe it was the sound of Nathan's name on his lips. She pulled free of him too quickly and spilled her soda. "Oh, shit, I'm sorry!" She jumped up but Sam grabbed her hand.

"It's nothing," he said and, ignoring the mess, pulled her into his lap.

Becca curled into him and pressed her face to his throat. He cuddled her and let her settle, but not for long because this was Sam, and he never ran from a problem. Nope, he faced it head-on, however he felt was best—and that was never the easy way, or the fast way.

It was the *right* way.

She usually admired the hell out of that. "He was our manager," she finally said, "and then, when I stopped playing, Jase's manager."

He stroked a hand down her hair. "He's the one who hurt you," he said.

She pressed her face harder into his throat and concentrated on just breathing him in. He smelled like the sea, like the wood he'd sanded earlier. He smelled like her, too, and that actually made her smile, but then suddenly she was all choked up.

Sam merely tightened his hold on her in a way that made her feel safe and warm and cherished, and gave her the moment she so desperately needed.

"He was a longtime family friend," she said. "I had this big, fat, painful crush on him. Always did, from the time I was seventeen. He was the one who talked me into staying in music when I had that growth spurt and kept fumbling."

"How old was he back then?"

"What?"

He gently pulled her face from its hiding zone and looked into her eyes. "You were seventeen, and he was…?"

"Twenty-seven."

"Big age difference for a crush."

"Maybe that was part of it for me," she said. Compared with Jase, or the boys her own age, Nathan had been a grown-up. He'd been smart and funny, and so damn handsome…

"He went for you," Sam said. Not a question, a statement of fact.

"Not until I turned twenty-one. We…dated, a little bit. Nothing serious." That hadn't come until later.

"He kept you playing."

"Yes," she said. "Until after we broke up. After that, not even God could have kept me playing. But Nathan gave it his best shot."

"Tell me," he said, his dark, mossy-green eyes never leaving hers.

She drew an unsteady breath of warm, protective Sam and found the courage to keep speaking about it. "We'd been dating again," she said. "More serious then, much more. We were exclusive. And I did try to play. I tried for Nathan, for Jase, for everyone. But I couldn't do it."

"Let me guess. Nathan didn't like that."

"It frustrated him. I frustrated him," she admitted. "He got…different. Unhappy." Mean, she thought. "I left him," she said. "And it got a little ugly."

Sam gently tilted her face and looked down at her, his expression quiet, steady. "How ugly?"

She closed her eyes, the memories she'd managed to mostly bury over the years coming back to her. She swallowed hard. "*Ugly.* I refused to give in to pressure and stay with him. But he was a family friend, and our paths continued to cross. A lot. He was big in my parents' life, in Jase's life, and he was important to his career as well, so I did my best to keep things as friendly as possible."

"It's bullshit that you had to do that."

She opened her eyes. Sam's gaze wasn't his usual calm now. "I don't know a lot about family," he said, "but I do know that the loyalty should have gone to you."

"Yes, but you don't understand. We were all like family. Nathan's mom and dad had gone to college with my mom and dad. All of us were tight, real tight—"

"Still bullshit," Sam said. "Tell me more about the ugly business."

She stared at his chest. His broad chest. There was a lot of strength in his body, and he'd honed it well, both on and off the water with physical labor. And yet she wasn't afraid of that strength because he knew he'd never use it against her. He'd never push her around in anger and try to take what he wanted, especially if it wasn't what she wanted. He'd never—

"Becca," Sam said, cupping her face, drawing her attention back to the here and now.

"There were a lot of family gatherings," she said. "My parents throw a big shindig on Sunday nights, and everyone goes. After I left Nathan, I stopped attending so he wouldn't have to."

Sam's mouth tightened, telling her what he thought of her family allowing *that* to happen, but he didn't say a word, just waited for her to continue.

"Last year, on my twenty-eighth birthday," she said, "Mom and Dad and Jase talked me into having a party at their house."

"Tell me they didn't invite your ex to your own birthday party."

"Like I said, he was a family friend, a really good one."

"Shouldn't have happened, babe."

They were the words she hadn't realized she needed to hear, and she let out a shuddery breath. "Nathan came. He said he wanted to hook up again, but I knew what he really wanted."

"Which was?"

"Jase had been floundering since the last rehab attempt. He'd been showing up late to gigs, missing some altogether…"

Sam dropped his head, swearing softly beneath his breath before looking at her again. "Nathan wanted you to keep Jase in line."

"Yes."

"Not your job."

"But it was. It *was* my job, Sam," she said when he swore again, not so softly. "That's been my job my whole life. But Nathan also wanted me to try to play again. He thought that would help."

"And you couldn't," Sam guessed.

"Neither one," she said. "I tried to explain this to Nathan at the party, but he was drunk."

Sam went very still. "So you kneed him in the nuts and left him singing soprano on the floor, right?"

She shook her head. "I'd like to say yes, but no, that's not what happened."

"What did happen?"

Her breath hitched, but she kept it together. "He didn't get that we weren't going to be a thing again. He wasn't listening, all he was seeing was me standing between him and the success he wanted—" She closed her eyes at the harsh memory, but that was unwise because then she saw it happening again, so she opened her eyes and kept them on Sam. "He said I owed him. He said that if nothing else, I needed to pretend to be together with him in front of Jase so Jase would feel we were all just one big, happy family again. He said he was going to kiss me and I was going to kiss him back."

"Becca," he murmured, with far too much understanding.

Again she pressed her face into his neck, and realizing she hadn't said any of this out loud to anyone except her family. "I said I'd do it, I'd kiss him in front of Jase. I couldn't do anything else, Sam. I was worried sick about my brother, and feeling all this pressure from my family. I—"

"Babe," he said, moving his hands up and down her back. "*Not* your fault." Calm hands, calm voice, royally pissed-off eyes. "Can you tell me what happened?" he asked very softly.

Could she? She had no idea, but she gulped in some air and tried. "Jase saw us kissing and toasted us, and then went inside. So I thought it was over. But Nathan pushed me into the pool house, which was really just a storage room for the pool equipment. And he— We—" She broke off and shook her head. Nope. As it turned out, she couldn't tell him.

Sam's fingers tightened on her for a beat. Then he let out a long breath and loosened his fingers with what felt like great effort. "He raped you."

She lifted her face, her mouth open to say it wasn't rape because she'd known Nathan. Hell, she'd slept with him many times before, but she'd been to counseling and knew the truth. It had been rape.

Sam had kept his hands lightly on her back, stroking up and down. "I don't hate men," she said inanely.

Sam's arms tightened on her in a bear hug as he brushed his mouth to her temple. "For which I'm eternally grateful," he murmured, voice a little gruff, like he was still fighting his own emotions. "Though I get where your distaste for closed, tight spaces comes from. Where's Nathan now?"

"I was stupid," she said into his chest.

"Where is he now?"

She shook her head. She wasn't sure he understood. "I tried to tell my parents what had happened, but they didn't really get it. They knew I'd been intimate with him before, so—"

"Are you telling me that they didn't want you to press charges?" he asked incredulously.

"He was the son of a family friend. His parents—"

"Fuck that," Sam said harshly.

"I underplayed it, Sam. I did. Jase was so fragile then. If I'd pressed charges and put Nathan in jail, I'd have taken away even more from Jase. I didn't want to make things worse, and I just kept thinking it was true, I *had* willingly slept with Nathan before, so I could handle this. I'd just stay away." She closed her eyes, because she knew that she'd been weak and cowardly to go that route and didn't want to see the disappointment in his eyes. "I just wanted it to go away, Sam. I wanted that so much."

"Becca, where is that asshole now?"

"He's dead. Nathan's dead."

"You killed him," he said, his voice and eyes reflecting no judgment at all as he ran his hands up and down her arms.

"No," she said with a horrified laugh. "I didn't kill him. A Mack truck did." She gulped in more air and tried to breathe calmly. Sam's hands on her helped. "He was out on the freeway on his motorcycle, and he got hit. He died instantly."

"That's too bad." Sam said this almost wistfully, like he'd really have liked the opportunity to kill Nathan himself.

Becca choked out a laugh but it backed up in her throat when Sam slid his fingers into her hair, lifted her face to his, and stared into her eyes. "You're pretty damn incredible," he said fiercely.

"Not really," she said, trying to joke. "Just your average screwup."

He didn't smile. He didn't look away; he just stared into her eyes. "Incredible," he repeated, softly but with a fierce intensity that made the knot in her chest loosen for the first time in…as long as she could remember.

He took her home, and to bed, where he made slow, sweet love to her. And then not so slow, or sweet. But after, as she drifted off to sleep, she was absolutely sure of two things. One, Sam might indeed think she was incredible, but she thought the same thing about *him*.

And two, she wasn't just falling for him. She *had* fallen. She'd fallen deep.

The next morning Becca woke up alone. This wasn't unusual after a night in Sam's arms. Despite him not being a particularly great morning person, he liked to get up before dawn and run with Ben, or surf.

She showered, her mind whirling with images from the night before. Sam in her bed, his erotic whispers in her ear, the small of his back slick with sweat as he took her right out of herself, over and over again…

All really great memories, but she had to shove them from her mind because she had a lot to do at work today, much of it Summer Bash–related. She crossed the alley and headed to the hut.

Normally at this time of morning, the only sounds were the waves hitting the shore with a rhythmic, soothing regularity that had become as familiar to her as breathing. The seagulls usually had something to say as well, and once in a while the guys were out there on the dock or boat, their low, masculine voices carrying over the water.

But this morning she heard a familiar woman's and man's voice, and Becca rounded the corner to stare in shock at Sam talking to…her parents.

Chapter 25

Becca took in the sight of Sam and her parents, clearly in the middle of a very intense conversation, and went still with shock. "Mom? Dad?"

Evelyn and Philip Thorpe whirled around and stared at her.

"What's going on?" Becca asked. "What are you all doing here?"

"We got your address from Jase," her mom said, taking in Sam's move and the way he brushed a kiss to her temple. "But we got lost trying to find your apartment." She moved forward, arms reaching out, and Becca stepped into her for a hug. Her father pulled her in next, but it felt awkward and stilted. What didn't feel awkward or stilted was the way Sam slid an arm around her waist afterward, holding her against him.

Surprised at the public display, she looked up into his face. He'd either just gone swimming or surfing or was fresh from a shower because his hair was wet, curling along his neck. His T-shirt stretched taut across his shoulders. He looked alert and tough as hell, his arm around her saying he was in protective mode.

There was a definite tension in the air, making her wonder what the hell had been said just before she'd arrived.

"Jase had really hoped you'd come to the concert last night," her mom said.

Becca met her mom's gaze. "I...couldn't."

"I know." Evelyn glanced at Sam. "Or I know better now."

Sam remained silent, keeping his own counsel as usual. Becca narrowed her eyes at him, but he didn't respond to that, either, just held her gaze, his own steady and calm. Damn it, he was good. She'd never once been able to beat him in an eye contact contest.

"We rented a car from Seattle," her mom said. "We wanted to see you before our flight out." She glanced at Sam again. "Sam was just...chatting with us," she said carefully. "You didn't tell us you had a boyfriend." Her smile faltered, and her eyes got misty. "I wish you could've told us, Becca. I've been so worried about you being out here alone, with you saying you didn't want anyone to visit you, that you needed time. If I'd known you had a boyfriend, I'd have felt so much less worried about you."

"Mom." If she said the word *boyfriend* one more time, Becca was going to have a stroke. "Sam's my boss."

"*And* your boyfriend," Evelyn said, turning to Sam for confirmation. "Right?"

Sam gave a single nod, and when Becca stared at him, his eyes smiled. Not his mouth, just his eyes.

She didn't know exactly what to make of that, but,

definitely feeling a warm fuzzy, she turned to her mom. "I'm sorry you've been worried, but I'm fine. And a boyfriend—or not—doesn't change that." As she said this, Becca realized that for the first time in a very long time, the automatic *I'm fine* statement was actually true. She *was* fine. In fact, she'd truly never been better. She smiled and caught Sam's gaze, which touched over her features possessively, and then warmed.

So did her heart.

"Sam said maybe we could get some breakfast at the diner," her mom said.

"Oh," Becca said, not sure she wanted to commit to an hour of being grilled about Jase.

"Honey." Her dad took her hands and squeezed gently. "Please? We have some things to say to you, your mom and I, things we hope you'll hear."

Becca stared into his eyes, saw pain and regret, and steeled herself against the wave of guilt. "Okay," she said. "Breakfast."

So they went to the diner, an unlikely foursome.

It was early, but the locals were a hardworking bunch, and some were breakfast regulars. Becca found herself being waved at by a few.

"People know you," her mother said, sounding surprised.

Becca understood the sentiment. Her mother had never lived in a small town, either, and had a healthy respect for privacy. But there was no privacy in Lucky Harbor. As Jax had told her one night, you could leave a pot of gold in your backseat and it wouldn't get stolen, but you couldn't keep a secret. "I like it here," she said, and caught Sam's eye.

He smiled at her.

She smiled back, knowing that this was going to be okay. Somehow.

"Jase had a fantastic show last night," her mom said. "He went out with the promoters afterward and stayed up late. He has a second show tonight, or he'd have been here."

There'd always been excuses for Jase, and Becca had long ago accepted that. But she couldn't do it anymore. "Mom, Jase has a problem. He needs rehab." She'd said this in the past, and it had gotten her nothing but more excuses and arguments. But this time her mom didn't rush in to dispute the fact that Jase did indeed need rehab. This time her eyes filled with tears, and she put a shaky hand to her mouth.

Her father hugged her. Evelyn gave him a watery smile but shook her head and reached for Becca's hand across the table. "I know," she said simply.

"You...do?" Becca asked in surprise.

"Yes." Her mom swiped at a tear that slipped and looked around the café self-consciously. She didn't like to show a lot of emotion unless she was on stage. "I've known for a while," she went on softly. "I just didn't want to accept it. After you left..." She stopped to blow her nose. "It became more clear."

"You protected him, Becca," her dad said. "We didn't realize how much because you were also protecting us, when we should have been protecting you."

Becca gave up staring into her water like it held the secrets of life and looked at Sam. "What did you say to them?"

"Don't be upset with him," Evelyn said. "Everything

he said was true. Painful to hear, but true. And last week, the Seagals came to us."

Nathan's parents.

"They confessed their knowledge of how...terribly he'd treated you in the end—" She broke off, her eyes filling. She reached for a napkin from the table's dispenser, but she couldn't get one out. "Damn it."

Sam opened the dispenser and handed her a huge stack.

"I'm...devastated," Evelyn said, dabbing at her eyes. "I didn't understand—" She shook her head. "Honey, I need to know something."

Becca had to swallow the lump in her throat to speak. "What?"

"That you'll...you'll forgive us. Can you? Forgive us?"

"No," her father said to Evelyn firmly. "We don't get to ask that. Remember, actions, not words. We just want her to be okay."

And from the way he looked at Sam as he said it, Becca knew exactly where those words had come from. She hesitated and felt his hand gently squeeze her thigh, infusing her with strength. Not his, which he had in spades, but her own, and it welled up from within her. "Mom," she said softly. "I'm okay." She marveled that it was the utter truth, thanks in no small part to Lucky Harbor. To her friends here. To the peace and joy she'd found here.

To Sam himself...

"I know it's late for this," her mom said, "but I promise you I won't offer any more excuses for Jase. Ever. We did you wrong, Becca. We let you suffer rather than rock our boat. I can't ask you forgiveness for that, but..." She sucked in a breath along with a short sob. "But we are sorry, baby. So very sorry."

Becca felt her throat tighten, her eyes burn. "Thank you," she whispered.

Her father cleared his throat, his own eyes suspiciously red. "In realizing our mistakes," he said, "we realized something else—we've done Jase wrong, too. We've enabled him. That will stop. We came out here to talk to him, to see if he'd go to rehab."

"How did that go?" Becca asked.

Pain crossed her dad's features. "He's not ready. And we don't know if he will be. All we can do now is stand back and let him come to the realization himself."

"We've lost you both," Evelyn whispered. "Our own fault. Love you, baby. So much."

Beside her, she felt Sam stiffen. She didn't know what that was about, but she took her mom's hand. "You haven't lost me. I'm still yours, Mom. Always."

Sam tried to watch over Becca as much as he could, but he must not have been too subtle about it because by noon she'd told him that if he was going to hover around like a protective mama bear, she was going to call in Lucille and the rest of the geriatric gang for snorkel lessons and book him as the instructor.

That's when he figured Becca wasn't in danger of having a meltdown. That she was dealing in the only way she knew how—by burying her shit deep and moving forward. And he left her to it.

So he was relieved when, at the end of the day, she poked her head into his warehouse, looking good. "I'm off to the rec center," she said, and was immediately on the move.

He barely caught her, snagging her wrist and pulling

her back inside. Gently he pushed her up against the wall and cupped her face, tilting it up to his.

She met his gaze, hers clear and remarkably calm. He slid the pad of his thumb across her full lower lip, and it tipped into a smile.

"I'm really okay," she said.

"Yeah?"

"Yeah," she said, and pulled him down for a quick but very hot kiss before shoving at him. "Gotta go."

Not budging, he pulled out his phone and looked at the time. "You've got half an hour."

"Ten minutes of that is drive time."

"Twenty minutes then," he said. "You've got twenty minutes."

Her eyes softened. "For?"

"For whatever comes to mind," he said, and kissed her neck "What comes to mind, Becca?"

When his mouth got to the sweet spot beneath her ear, she moaned. "Everything that comes to mind takes more than twenty minutes," she whispered.

"Let me prove you wrong," he whispered back, and ran his hand from her hip to the underside of her breast, his thumb gliding over her already hardened nipple.

Eyes closed on another moan, her head thunked back against the wall as she arched her back, pressing herself into his palm. "Here? Against the wall?" she asked hopefully.

"No," he said with a laugh, mouth open on her throat. "Last time I nearly killed you when my legs gave out."

She pointed to his worktable across the vast expanse of the room. Then she began to pull him toward it. Halfway there she apparently gave up on trying to walk and kiss at the same time because she threw herself at him. He carried her to the worktable, where he kicked the stool out of his way and, holding her with one arm, swiped a hand across the surface, sending the tools, everything, to the floor.

"Sam," Becca gasped on a laugh, a thrill racing through her entire body as he lifted her to the table. "It'll hold, right?"

"Yeah." He stepped back to look at her sprawled out on the table. "Oh, yeah," he said, voice thick. "It's perfect." He yanked his shirt over his head, as always rendering her stupid with the sight of his bare torso. He made quick work of her shirt as well, and then her shorts and her senses with equal aplomb. Between his mouth and his hands, she was quivering from head to toe in two minutes flat.

She knew she was supposed to be keeping track of time, but honestly she couldn't do anything except melt over what he was doing with his tongue between her legs. In fact, she might have fallen right off the table with all her writhing but Sam had a firm grip on her thighs, preventing her from moving anyplace but closer to his mouth. "Sam—" She stopped when he swirled his tongue over an exceptionally good spot. "Oh, my God. I love that."

He did it again.

And then again.

And then he added a well-placed stroke with the pad of his callused thumb, and she just about screamed his name. "And *that*," she gasped. "I love that, too."

"How about this?" He slid a long finger into her, timed with another swirl of his tongue.

"Yes! God, Sam—I love that so much—"

"And this…?" Another finger, and another pass of his tongue, all of which melted her into a puddle of desperation. "Tell me, Becca," he commanded.

"Yes," she whispered, shuddering. "I love it when you do that—" She'd been trying to last, straining to hold on, but she couldn't. She came, just as he'd intended.

When she could breathe again, she realized he'd set his head in her lap and was pressing a soft, hot, open-mouthed kiss low on her belly.

"In me," she whispered. "I love it when you're in me."

Lifting his head, he looked right into her eyes as he pulled a condom from a pocket and protected them both before sliding into her. "This?" he asked, voice thick with his own need.

Half-delirious with desire, on the edge of yet another orgasm, her mouth disconnected from her brain. "Yes," she gasped. "That. I love that. And you, Sam. God, I love *you.*"

Chapter 26

Becca heard the words escape her but she was too far gone. With one of Sam's hands fisted in her hair, the other possessively on her ass holding her close, buried deep inside her as he was, she felt it when every inch of him froze.

Felt it, but couldn't stop the freight train of the orgasm hitting her full blast. She rocked into him, clutched him hard, and let go.

From some deep recess of her mind she was aware that she took him with her, felt him shudder in her arms. She let herself get lulled by that into a puddle of sated bliss.

But then Sam didn't lift his head and flash his sexy smile, as he usually did. He didn't press his mouth to her temple, or drag it along her throat. Or cuddle her in close.

He didn't do any of things he normally did postcoital. In fact, he slid out of her, pulled his jeans back up, and vanished down the hall, presumably into the bathroom since she heard the click of the door shutting.

Letting out a breath, Becca hopped down off the worktable. It took her a moment on shaky legs to straighten and fix herself, not to mention gather her wits. Scratch that, she couldn't gather her wits, not even a little bit.

She opened her eyes and startled. Sam was there, right there in front of her, big and silent. Too silent. "I didn't hear you come back," she said inanely.

He held out her keys, which she'd clearly dropped.

Taking them, she stared up into his face, which was utterly cool and composed.

"You've got to get to the rec center," he said.

"What's wrong?"

He didn't answer. Or move.

"Sam," she said, heart in her throat. "I said I love you, and you…well, I don't know what exactly, but one minute you were right here with me, and now you're gone."

He slowly shook his head. "You shouldn't say things that you can't possibly mean."

She stared at him. "And how do you know I don't mean it?"

"Look, I get it," he said. "You were in the heat of the moment. But you need to be more careful."

There were so many things wrong with those two sentences, she wasn't sure where to start. "And you weren't in the heat of the moment?"

"I was," he said. "You know I was."

She moved onto the more problematic statement. "And…careful?" She was as confused as hell, and hurt because he was maintaining his distance with a cool ease she couldn't begin to match. "I just told you that I love you. Love isn't *careful*, Sam."

He looked at her for a long beat. "You called Lucky Harbor a pit stop. You don't fall in love with a pit stop."

"Are you kidding me?" she asked. "When did I say that? When I first came here? I wouldn't have recognized love then if it'd hit me in the face. But you know as well as anyone that things change. *Feelings* change. And you said you weren't a commitment-phobe."

"I'm not."

"Just as long as the L-word doesn't come into play?"

Turning his back to her, he shoved his hands into his pockets and looked out the window. "I'll ruin this," he said softly.

"This?"

He shrugged. "I've ruined a lot of relationships. Just about every one of my father's while growing up. And then my own."

She stared at his tense shoulders. "You can't possibly believe that." But clearly, he did. Shocked, she shook her head. "Sam, any woman your father was seeing while you were growing up, whatever happened was on them. You were just a kid; you don't get to be blamed for adult relationships going bad."

"My own then," he said. "I'm not good at long-term relationships. They don't work out."

He was grasping at straws now, and she knew it. "It only takes one," she said. "The right one."

Unable, or unwilling, to believe her, he shook his head, and then walked out.

Sam woke up and stared at the ceiling of his bedroom. *I'm not good at long-term relationships*, he'd said, and here he was alone.

A self-fulfilled prophecy.

He rolled out of bed and went for a long, hard run with

Ben. The problem with running, especially predawn, was that it allowed a lot of thoughts to tumble through his brain.

So he cranked his iPod higher and did his best to drown those thoughts out.

They leaked in anyway, and at the forefront was the memory of the sweet, open look on Becca's face when she'd said it. *I love you.* He knew she'd expected to hear it back, but he hadn't been able to say it.

Christ.

Why she'd had to say it at all was beyond him. Love wasn't in the damn words. Love was in the showing. And if he'd gone there with Becca—which, he could admit, he maybe had—then she should know it without him saying it.

And actually, her using those words, especially when she had, was selfish. Thoughtless.

Because now it was over.

He and Ben normally didn't say much on their runs but after running to the pier and back, Ben stopped and looked at him.

"What?" Sam asked.

"You tell me what. You're talking to yourself."

"The fuck I am."

"You said you don't need this shit."

"I don't," Sam said.

Ben nodded, and looked a little bit amused. "What shit are we talking about exactly?"

"Nothing."

"This have anything to do with the pretty new music teacher?"

When Sam narrowed his eyes, Ben shrugged. "Hey,

man, you know Lucky Harbor. There's no need to bolt your door at night, but you've gotta keep your secrets under lock and key. And anyway, you being into the pretty music teacher isn't much of a secret."

Sam shook his head. "Don't you have your own problems to worry about? Seems to me it wasn't all that long ago that you made news when a certain blonde stood outside your house yelling all of *your* secrets for the world to hear."

"Yeah." Ben smiled. "I was pretty sure I didn't need that shit, either. I was wrong. You're wrong, too." And with that asinine, ridiculous statement, he turned and walked away.

"I don't," Sam said to the morning. "I don't need that shit."

The morning didn't answer.

He walked into his house to shower, and found his dad at his kitchen table on the laptop.

And Becca at his stovetop cooking breakfast.

Sam stopped short. Hell, his heart stopped short, despite the possible hostility in her gaze. He started to smile at her, so fucking happy to see her that it had to be all over his face, but she gave him a blank face and turned away from him.

Yeah. Definite hostility.

"I felt sick," his dad said. "Weak. I called you, but you didn't answer."

Sam pulled his cell phone from his pocket. No missed calls.

"So anyway," his dad said, not meeting his eyes. "My blood sugar was low or something."

Sam gave him a long look.

"*Real* low," Mark added.

"So you call Cole," Sam said. "Or Tanner."

"Uh…they didn't answer, either."

Becca brought a plate over to Mark, nudging Sam out of the way to do so. Actually, it was more like a shove. "Leave him alone," she said to Sam. "He has low blood sugar."

"He always has low blood sugar in the morning," Sam said. "That's why I've got a fridge full of food for him. All he had to do was take a bite of something, and in less than sixty seconds he'd have been fine."

Becca turned to him, hands on hips, face dialed to Stubborn, Pissed-Off Female. "It's no bother for me to help him."

"Of course it's a bother," Sam said. "You had to get up even earlier than usual, which you hate. You had to drive here. He's not your responsibility, Becca."

"I didn't mind," she said.

"Well you should have."

"Why?" she asked, eyes narrowed. "Just because *you* don't feel anything doesn't mean I can't."

Okay, there it was. The two-ton elephant in the room. Finding his own mad, he stared at her, hard. "You don't want to go there with me right now."

She lifted her nose to nosebleed heights. "You're absolutely right."

"I mean it, Becca."

Mark started to rise with his plate. "You know what? I'll just go eat in the other room—"

"You'll do no such thing," Becca said, and pointed her wooden spoon at him like she meant business. "Sit," she commanded. "Eat."

"Go in the other room, Dad," Sam said.

Mark gave them a look like *You're both crazy*, grabbed his plate, and walked out of the kitchen—but not before bending to drop a kiss on Becca's cheek.

She sighed, softened, and gave him a quick hug.

And then Sam and Becca were alone. Perfect. Just where he didn't want to be.

Becca looked at him for a moment, shook her head, muttered something to herself that sounded suspiciously like "jackass idiot," and then walked out of the kitchen.

He followed after her just in time to catch the double doors as they closed.

In his face.

"Damn it." He managed to catch her in the living room by the front door—barely. She was ticked off, and she was quick.

But he was quicker.

"Knock it off," she said, pushing at him. "I'm only here to check on him, not to see you. You're here now, you can take over, I'm out."

"You're out," he repeated.

"Yep," she said, popping the *p*. "Out. As in all the way out."

He pinned her to the front door. "Not before we discuss this like adults."

"Seriously?" she asked incredulously, fighting to free herself, nearly catching him in the jaw with her elbow until he leaned in and flattened her to the wood.

Panting, she blew her hair out of her face and glared up at him. "Is *discuss like adults* what you did yesterday when you flung my own words back in my face? *Damn it*," she said, struggling. "Let me go!"

"I didn't fling your words back in your face."

"You basically said I didn't mean them," she said. "Same thing. I mean honest to God, Sam, you reacted to my *I love you* like I'd tried to kill you!"

"You don't tell your summer fling in the town you just happened to 'pit-stop' in that you lo—" He fumbled over the word that she seemed to have no trouble with at all.

"My God, you can't even say the word?" She shoved him again. "And you're not a pit stop, not for me, and you damn well know it so stop saying it."

"*You're* the one who said it in the first place."

"I say a lot of things, especially when I'm pissed off," she snapped. "In fact, I have another thing to say to you—I quit."

Well, hell. "Becca—"

"Don't worry, I won't leave you in the lurch, that's not how I operate. But I'm giving you notice, Sam. I'll spend the next two or three weeks finding my replacement and training them before I go, because it turns out you were right, we can't work together, and do…whatever it was that we were doing."

The past tense killed him. "You're not quitting."

"I need to," she said. "It's for me. And you're going to let me go, because you didn't want me to work for you in the first place."

Christ. She was killing him.

The soft knock on the other side of the door galvanized them both.

"Sorry," came Cole's sheepish voice. "I kept waiting for a good time to interrupt, but it never came. I missed a call from your dad, wanted to make sure everything was okay."

Becca wriggled out from between Sam and the door, but he caught her hand. "We're done here," she said, trying to pull free.

He held on and studied her face, taking in the misery and pain he'd caused her. "I don't think we are," he said quietly.

"Think again." And without looking back, she tore loose and headed back to the kitchen. A minute later, he heard the back door slam as she made her escape.

Sam swore as he hauled open the front door.

Cole was arms-up on the door frame, and gave him a long look. "She said *I love you* and you flung it in her face?"

Sam started to shut the door on Cole's nose but Cole was quicker than he looked, and stronger too, and shoved his way in.

Sam turned to ignore him and go after Becca, but Cole got in his way and in his face.

"Don't," Sam warned him.

"You going to say it back?" Cole wanted to know.

"We're not discussing this."

Cole stared into Sam's eyes and saw the truth: No, he wasn't going to say it back. "You're a fucking idiot," Cole said, but he wasn't done. Hell, no. Cole always did have plenty to say, and no one, not man, woman, or God himself, could shut the guy up when he had something on his mind.

"You're not good with letting people in, I get that," his oldest friend said. "We *all* get that, but—"

"You don't get shit," Sam said.

Cole ignored this, because he knew, as did Sam, that no one knew Sam better than Cole himself.

No one.

"You go so far with trust and no further," Cole said, "and I get that, too. You got it from your dad. He let you in and then let you back out again how many fucking times? I can't imagine it, going through all that, except I can, since I watched you go through it."

"Drop it, Cole."

Of course he didn't. Cole was incapable of dropping a damn thing. "But," he went on as if he hadn't been interrupted, "you landed at a damn good home when you needed one, and we never threw you away, not once. So you do know real trust, and that it can be good." He paused, waiting for his words to sink in. "That woman you just chased out of here, she's got eyes for only you. And she's the kind of woman that loves down to her toes, with her entire heart and soul. You're safe with her, Sam. You get me? You're as *safe* with her as she is with you."

"Shut up or I'll shut you up."

"You know, it's funny," Cole said casually, unperturbed by the threat. "We all think of you as the guy always willing to risk whatever it takes. And it's true. Physically."

"Gee, thanks, Dr. Phil."

"But the one thing you never risk is your emotions. You hold them close to the vest," Cole said. "I think it's because you're afraid they'll be taken away. You're too stubborn to realize otherwise, and now after listening to your conversation with Becca, I think you're also a little bit stupid as well."

Sam shoved free without a word, mostly because he was fresh out of words, and maybe a little afraid that Cole was right—about everything.

"You want to be an idiot, be my guest," Cole said, lifting his hands like he surrendered. "It's certainly your turn after all these years of keeping our shit together for us. But if that's your plan, you've got to stop reeling her in, man. She deserves more than that from you. Hell, *you* deserve more from you."

Before Sam could respond to this, Cole added one more thing. "And if she really quits because of you, I'm going to kick your ass. I might need Tanner to help me, but I will do it."

Chapter 27

♥

Sam actually agreed with most of what Cole had said. Becca deserved more from him. As for what *he* deserved, the jury was still out on that one. So he went to work. He opened his shop and stood in the middle of it, wondering when the hell he'd stopped enjoying the solitude of his warehouse, instead looking forward to the moments Becca spent in here with him. But he'd blown that one.

I love you, Sam...

The words mocked him. He'd heard those exact same words from his dad throughout his life, and they'd never meant a damn thing. Those three words had never gotten him anywhere, not once. The only thing to do that was hard work. He had a lot to show for hard work, and absolutely jackshit to show for love.

But at the thought, he felt only a sense of unease. Because it wasn't strictly true. Cole and his family had taken him in every time he'd needed it. They'd fed and housed him. That had been love.

Without the words.

He liked it a whole lot better that way.

He needed to talk to Becca. Make her understand that they didn't need the damn words. But, typical of the season, the day was crazy, and she was swamped, giving him the stink eye every time he showed up in the hut.

A busy business was great, he told himself. After the way he'd grown up and the long years on the rigs where he'd worked 24/7 in conditions he wouldn't wish on an enemy, he knew more than anyone just how good he had it. He enjoyed chartering, enjoyed the work—which didn't really feel like work at all—enjoyed the people, and their bottom line had been more than decent. He'd made sure of it.

But today, he didn't enjoy shit. By midafternoon, he was over pretending to work and headed back to the hut. He had no real plan. He was hoping one would come to him.

Becca was in denim shorts, a halter top, her little name tag pinned to it, a straw hat on her head, with her hair loose and tumbling around her shoulders. It'd gotten sun-streaked over the past weeks, and her shoulders and toned arms were tanned, as were her mile-long legs. She had a few freckles, too. She hated them, but he didn't. In fact, he enjoyed connecting the dots.

With his mouth.

As if she could feel his presence, she looked up. She was busy with several clients, but as she gave him yet another Come-closer-and-die look, he realized that beneath her temper, she was hurt as hell.

That was all on him.

"Ouch," Tanner said, coming up beside him, slipping

an arm around his shoulders. "Looks like you've been served."

Sam gave him an elbow to the ribs that Tanner returned.

Normally Sam would've been ready for it but he'd caught sight of a guy skulking off to the side of the hut, just out of Becca's sight. Waiting. And because Sam was concentrating on that, Tanner's elbow to the ribs nearly sent him sprawling into the water.

Tanner started to laugh, but the smile died on his face at the sight of Sam's expression. "What?"

"Keep Becca occupied," he directed, and strode for Jase.

Jase saw him coming and straightened. "Hey, man." He lifted his hands. "I just want to borrow your employee for a minute, that's all."

"She know you're here?" Sam asked.

"No."

"Good. Get the fuck off my property."

Jase's good-natured smile slipped. "What?"

"You heard me."

"Hey, wait a minute," Jase said with a shake of his head. "I need to talk to my sister."

"Yeah? You ever think about what *she* needs?"

Jase blinked. "What the hell is this?"

"It's me telling you one last time to leave," Sam said. "*Now.*"

Jase shoved his hands in his pockets. "Listen, I don't know what she's told you about me, but we're cool, her and I, so—"

Sam grabbed him by the collar. "Are you? Cool?"

"Yeah. I mean…" Jase closed his eyes and shook his

head. "Okay, so we're not cool, but it's not what you think."

"You know what I think?" Sam tightened his grip on Jase to make sure he had his full attention. "I think you let her take care of *you* all your life, and then when she needed the favor returned one time, you failed her. You let her get hurt. You let her feel guilty for being raped." Christ, he wanted to squeeze until Jase stopped breathing. And indeed, Jase choked and brought his hands up, but Sam was beyond giving a shit. He heard Cole and Tanner calling his name, felt them trying to pull him off Jase, but he held on.

Until he heard her voice. Becca's.

"Sam! Sam, let go!"

Shocked, Becca clutched at Sam's cement biceps. "Please, Sam," she said, heart in her throat, but as if *please* had been the magic word, Sam did indeed let go.

Jase slid to the ground, gasping for air. Letting out her own tense breath, Becca dropped to her knees at her brother's side, running her gaze over him. Realizing he was indeed mostly in one piece, she tilted her head to Sam's. "What the hell?"

Eyes shuttered now, Sam took a step backward and said nothing.

Becca shook her head and turned back to Jase. "What are you doing here?"

Still holding his throat, Jase slid a cautious look up at Sam.

Becca couldn't blame him. Sam had backed up, but he still had a feral look of fury in his eyes. He was breathing steadily, calm even, but his hands were in fists. On either side of him stood Cole and Tanner. Probably to back up Sam, but maybe also to keep him from killing Jase. Hard to tell.

"I was trying to see you," Jase said, "but then I was assaulted."

Tanner made a sound from deep in his throat that should have been a warning, but Jase had never been good at warnings.

"I mean, Jesus," he went on. "I didn't do shit; he just came after me."

This time the growl came from Cole. Clearly, neither he nor Tanner had any idea what this was about, but it didn't matter. Brothers of the heart, they stood united with Sam. "Jase," she said softly. "This isn't the time or place. I'm at *work*. Go home."

"I…can't."

She stared into his eyes, saw shame and guilt, and felt her heart clutch. "Why, Jase?" Oh, God. "What have you done?"

"I…need your help." He clutched at her hands and held her gaze in his own red-rimmed one. "This one last time, Becca. *Please.*"

At his words, the years fell away. She could see him at age five to her seven, needing her to chase away his night terrors after he'd been bullied at school. At age twelve needing her to hide him after he'd stupidly shoplifted a metronome from the music store. Then over a decade later, coming out of rehab and still looking broken. And she felt herself waver. "Jase—"

"Just this one last time," he promised in a broken whisper.

She pulled her key from her pocket. "Go to my place. I'll be off in a few hours. Wait there."

He took the key.

"Jase," she said. "Promise me."

"I promise," he said woodenly.

She rose and watched him do the same. He straightened his shirt, gave her three bosses a very wide berth, and left.

She let out a breath and turned to the small crowd gathered. "Show's over," she said briskly. "We've got a sale on water equipment for the next hour only, twenty-five percent off. Who wants to snorkel or kayak? Line up, first come, first served."

A murmur rose from the crowd. Lucky Harbor was filled with good people, but they were also hardworking and loved a bargain.

"Does the snorkel gear come with a hottie instructor?"

This came from Lucille. She had her hand raised, her gaze on Tanner. "Because I wouldn't mind getting… instructed," she said.

Tanner winced but everyone else laughed, dispelling the tense atmosphere.

Satisfied that things would go back to normal, or as normal as it got around here, Becca started back around to the front of the hut.

"Becca."

The softly spoken single word was from Sam. She considered ignoring him, but the problem with that was she'd never been able to ignore Sam. Not when he'd been her Sexy Grumpy Surfer, not when he'd become her boss, and certainly not now that he'd become so very much more. She was going to have to do something about that, and she knew it. It was one thing to put herself out there and fall in love with someone. It was another entirely to be the only one of the two of them putting herself out there. "I've got work," she said.

And then she got to it.

Becca sat in the reception room of the "recovery" center in Seattle and watched her brother walk away from her toward the nurse who'd just called his name.

She'd gone home after work and found Jase pacing, looking more than a little crazed, and in desperate need of a fix.

"I fucked up," he said straight off. "I stole Janet's Vicodin."

She blinked. "Who's Janet?"

"Someone I met after last night's concert."

Becca just stared at him. "Are you crazy?"

"Yes, apparently. She could've called the cops on me, but she didn't. Jesus, Becca." He shoved his fingers into his hair and looked at her wild-eyed. "I *stole* from her. I sneaked out of her bed and into her purse and I took her pain pills." He dropped his hands to his sides, leaving his hair standing on end. "I'm a fucking thief now?" he whispered.

"Actually, you've been a thief for a while," she said, desperate to lighten his mood. "Remember when you stole makeup from the department store at the mall? They called Mom and Dad, and you gave them the story that you were thinking of becoming a drag queen. Which," she went on, "was bullshit. You'd just already spent your allowance on pot, and wanted the makeup for your girlfriend."

He stared at her, then scrubbed his hands over his face, letting out a half laugh, half groan. "Christ, Becca. I'm trying to be dramatic here and have a moment, and you're making light of it all."

She'd opened her laptop then, and they'd looked up rehab centers together. Jase had settled on one in Seattle. And now, there in the Seattle waiting room watching him go, her eyes filled. "I love you, Jase," she said. "Be safe."

He was too thin, very pale, and maybe a little bit terrified to boot, but there was one thing Jase had known since birth, and that was how to put on a show. He smiled and blew her a kiss.

She rubbed her aching chest but smiled, keeping up the brave pretense until he'd vanished behind the door of the thirty-day rehab center.

Besides her, Olivia grabbed her hand. "He'll be okay."

"He will," Becca said, because she wanted to believe it.

"No, I mean really," Olivia said. "He had a really determined look."

Becca decided to put her faith into that being true. She squeezed Olivia's hand in return and, for the second time in her life, walked away from Jase.

Halfway back to Lucky Harbor, Olivia said casually, "You going to tell me why you're over there crying while pretending not to cry?"

Becca sniffed. "It's smoggy. My eyes are burning."

Olivia looked out at the clear blue sky and raised an eyebrow at Becca.

"Okay, well, then I have allergies."

"To what?" Olivia wanted to know.

"Your nosiness."

Olivia laughed. "That I could almost buy." She glanced over at Becca. "I'd bet my last dollar that you're not crying about Jase anymore. That you've moved on to crying about something else. Someone else. Sam."

Becca stared out the window. "Don't ever bet your last dollar."

"What did he do?"

"He didn't do anything." Which was the problem. "I just thought I knew him, but as it turns out, I didn't."

"Yes you do," Olivia said. "Guys are simple. There's only three things you need to see a guy deal with to know exactly who he is."

"Like?"

"One, slow Internet."

Becca thought back to her first day on the job when she'd first discovered the slow Internet in the hut. Sam hadn't lost his collective shit as her old boss would have. Nope, he'd simply gotten around the problem by writing things down on napkins, pieces of wood, whatever was handy. Not patiently, exactly, because Sam had a lot of great qualities, and patience wasn't one of them. But he had a depthless reservoir of steady calm. After the craziness of her family and her life, that never failed to bring *her* to a steady calm.

Well, until very recently.

"Two," Olivia said, "untangling Christmas tree lights."

She remembered the tangled strings of white lights she'd found, the ones Sam had replaced, and smiled despite herself.

"What?" Olivia asked.

"I had a bag of tangled dock lights, and Sam handled the situation." She shook her head. "By buying new ones."

Olivia laughed out loud. "Honey, that man's a keeper."

Well, she'd tried to keep him…"That's only two out of three things you need to see a guy deal with," she said. "What's the third?"

Olivia slid her a look. "How he deals with over-wrought female theatrics."

Oh, boy. Becca had seen this, too, the night she'd heard a noise outside her door and gone into a full-blown panic attack. Sam hadn't thought her ridiculous or made her feel stupid. He'd been too far away for his own comfort and had sent Cole to stand in for him until he could arrive. And then there'd been the unexpected visit from her parents. Whatever she'd faced, Sam had been there for her.

Two hours later, Becca came home and found a stack of boxes waiting for her. An assortment of brand-new instruments for the kids, including a horn, a percussion set, and a bass.

For your new music program, the card read. Nothing else, no name, no address, nothing.

An anonymous donation.

But there was nothing anonymous about how she felt. Overwhelmed. Cared for.

Loved.

And as she sat there, surrounded by the boxes of brand-new instruments, she realized something. She didn't need a card. She knew exactly who the instruments were from. Damn, stubborn, stupid, wonderful man.

Chapter 28

On the morning of their Summer Bash, Sam got up extra early, knowing the day would be crazy. He was an hour earlier than usual, but he wasn't the only one. Standing in front of his warehouse door, waiting for entry, were both Amelia and Mark.

They'd squared off and were glaring at each other, Amelia with her arms crossed over her chest, Mark looking guilty as hell.

"What's going on?" Sam asked.

"Just making sure you don't need anything today, honey," Amelia said, tearing her hard gaze from Mark and moving toward Sam to hug and kiss him. "Summer Bash has taken over town," she said, "and everyone's so excited. I thought I'd come offer to help."

"Me too," Mark said.

Amelia snorted.

Mark frowned at her. "What the hell was that?"

"Dad," Sam said.

"No, I mean it," Mark said, staring at Amelia. "You got something to say?"

"I sure do," Amelia said. "I came here to give whatever I could. Time. Encouraging words. Whatever it takes. And you—"

"I what?" Mark asked, eyes narrowed.

"Coffee," Sam said. "Clearly, we need coffee."

"You think I didn't come to help," Mark said to Amelia. "You think I came to take."

"Isn't that your MO?" Amelia said.

"Breakfast even," Sam tried. "From the diner—"

"Shut up, Sam," Mark said. "The lady's got something to say."

"Don't you tell him to shut up," Amelia said.

Sam moved to step between them but Mark pointed at Amelia. "No, son, I want to hear what she thinks of me."

"You know what I think of you," Amelia said. "I—"

"Caffeine," Sam said. "The hut's got—"

"Sam, baby," Amelia said, eyes sharp on his father, "shut up."

Sam opened his mouth, but Mark pointed at him. "Do what she says, son."

Christ. Sam rubbed a hand over his jaw and wondered if this is how Cole and Tanner felt dealing with his grumpy ass in the mornings. "You know, usually I'm the one snarling at people before sunrise," he said.

This didn't lighten the tension.

"Maybe things change," Mark said to Amelia. "Maybe people change."

The words hit Sam. They were close to what Becca had said to him. He stared at his father. "What did you just say?"

"Maybe it's not just my liver I'm working on healing," Mark said, but he was speaking directly to Amelia. "I know what I've got here, Am. You've got to trust me on that. He's given me everything. I know it, but I'm trying to give back now. Trying to be what he needs."

Wait a minute. "I don't need anything," Sam said.

"You're wrong, son."

"Very wrong," Amelia agreed, but she hadn't taken her eyes off Mark. "What is it that you think he needs?"

"Nothing," Sam said. "I don't need shit."

"He needs to learn to be happy, Let people in."

"And depend on people," Amelia piped up.

"Becca could make him happy," Mark said to her.

"Which brings us to love," Amelia said.

"I didn't do a great job there," Mark said. "I admit it. I'm trying to remedy that."

"I said I don't need anything," Sam said with a frown, but no one spoke to him. Hell, no one looked at him.

"It's a work in progress," Mark said to Amelia. "It's taking time. It took time to get him this screwed up; it's gonna take time to unscrew him."

"Hello," Sam said, waving his hands. "Right here. Am I invisible?"

Amelia didn't move an inch, but there was a very slight lessening of the grim set to her mouth. "You're starting to get it," she said to Mark.

Mark nodded.

"I wonder if I should use my invisibility for good, or for evil," Sam mused.

At that, it was Mark's turn to snort.

Amelia let out a very reluctant, very small smile and hugged Sam again, hard. "It's going to be okay," she said.

"It's all going to be okay. Assuming you don't do anything stupid."

"Wait—me?" Sam asked.

"You," Mark said.

Sam pointed at them. "You've lost it. Both of you, cuckoo for Cocoa Puffs."

"Like I said," Mark muttered to Amelia. "Work in progress." He hugged Sam, too. "I'm proud of you," he said. "Love ya, son."

Sam waited for the usual anger over those words, so casually uttered, to hit. It didn't. Because suddenly the words didn't feel so casually uttered.

He wasn't sure what to make of that. "Cuckoo," he repeated, and tossed his dad the keys to the warehouse. "I'm going to check on the setup. Don't kill each other."

Becca was already at the beach when he arrived.

She was a tyrant in white shorts and a white tank top, whistle around her neck, clipboard in hand, a visor on her head, and a militant finger pointing out where she wanted what. She'd hired high school kids to help set up, and they were carrying out the equipment she'd rented. Benches. Trash bins. Awnings.

She'd gotten the Eat Me diner to cater, and they were setting up a food tent.

Cole arrived just behind Sam and watched along with him. "She's really something," he said.

Just then, Becca glanced up and met Sam's gaze from across a stretch of a hundred feet of organized chaos. He stared into those fathomless eyes and felt a piece of him that he hadn't even known was loose settle into place. "Yes," he agreed. "She is something."

"Something that you're going to get back," Cole said. "Right?"

He'd like to say yes, but the truth was, she was a woman who believed in the words, needed the words. She deserved a man who could give them to her. "Stay out of it," he said.

Tanner came up beside them. "Stay out of what?"

"Nothing," Sam said.

"He's being a pussy," Cole said.

"What's new about that?" Tanner asked.

Sam blew out a breath and pushed past them both.

"Where you going?" Cole asked.

"Work. You oughta try it sometime."

"He definitely didn't get laid last night," Tanner said. "He's always an asshole when he doesn't get laid."

Ignoring this, Sam strode out to the beach. Becca was now on top of one of the tables, messing with the umbrella over it.

It shut on her.

He was grinning even before he heard the colorful swearing from beneath the canvas. All he could see of her now was her bare feet and a bit of her shapely calves. He reached beneath the umbrella and got two good handfuls of warm, pissy woman.

She squeaked.

He let his hands slowly glide up the entire length of her body to reopen the umbrella.

Becca turned to face him and stared down at him from her perch. "Did you really just feel me up in front of all these people?"

"It was beneath the umbrella."

"That's not funny."

His smile faded at the pain on her face. "You're right. It isn't funny. Becca—"

"You bought me instruments?"

"I bought the kids instruments," he said.

"Why?"

"Because watching you teach those kids music, anyone can see how much it means to you," he said. "And knowing it makes it mean something to me." He tried to reach her with his gaze but she was closed off to him completely. "I was in a position to help," he said. "So I did."

"It had to be thousands of dollars," she said, sounding worried.

"I had it," he said simply. "And now you have a music program."

"But—"

"Stop." He put a finger to her lips. "Becca, you give your time to the program. You give your heart and soul. You give everything you have. Why can't I give what I have to give?"

She shook her head, muttered something beneath her breath that might or might not have been a well-thought-out commentary on his ability to out-stubborn even her. Then she jumped down, strode to the next table, and climbed up.

Sam followed and leapt on the table with her just as she opened the umbrella. Reaching up, he closed it around them and whipped a still-sputtering Becca to face him.

Now they were nose-to-nose, chest-to-chest, thigh-to-thigh, pressed tight together inside the umbrella like a banana in its peel.

"What the hell are you doing?" she demanded.

"Helping."

"I don't need your help. And FYI—people I fall in love with who don't love me back don't get to cop feels, beneath an umbrella or not."

"Let's talk about that," he said.

She stared at him incredulously. "You have five hundred people pouring onto this beach today. I've got a list of stuff to do a mile long, and—"

"I've had the words all my life," he said quietly. "It was always *I love ya, Sam, go get me my booze.* Or *I love ya, Sam, get lost for a few hours, will you?* Or *I love ya, Sam, where's that money you got from Grandma for your birthday, Dad needs a little loan.*"

Becca let out a long, shuddery breath and put her hands on his chest, her eyes not so closed off to him now. "Sam—"

"I'm sorry for how I reacted," he said. "I was a total asshole. I—"

"Ms. Teacher?" came a little girl's voice somewhere near their feet. "Is that you?"

Becca's eyes flew open, and she stared at Sam wide-eyed. "Pink?" she called out.

"Yes, ma'am. You sure have pretty toenail polish. My daddy just brought me here, along with some of the other girls. The boys are coming soon, too. We're gonna play the games you talked about. Who's that with you? It's a boy. I can tell 'cause he's got hair on his legs, and his toenails aren't painted."

Becca tried to jump down, but Sam held on to her. She gave him a long look. "It's my..." She hesitated. Narrowed her eyes at Sam. "Boss."

"The drummer?"

Sam grinned at Becca, who rolled her eyes. "Yes. The drum player."

"Whatcha doing in there?" Pink wanted to know. "Kissing?"

"No."

"Are you *gonna* kiss?"

"No! We're just—"

"We're totally gonna kiss," Sam whispered in her ear.

Becca gave him another long look, but as they were sandwiched together, he didn't miss her shiver. And it wasn't because she was cold.

"—Setting up the umbrellas," she said to Pink. "I'll be right there." Then she shook her head at Sam. "We're *not* going to kiss."

"Gonna eat those words, babe."

She didn't smile at him, or soften in any way.

His fault. He wasn't done fixing this with her, not by a long shot. He skimmed his hand up her back and into her hair. "You threw me the other day," he admitted.

"I didn't mean to," she said. "The words, they just sort of came out. But I felt it, Sam," she said, the pain in her voice tearing his guts out. "I meant it."

"Becca—"

"No. I need you to hear this," she said. "I was touching you, looking at you, and thinking, All I ever want is to feel like this, surrounded by you, consumed by you, warmed from the inside out by *you*." She punctuated each word with a finger poke to his chest. "I've never felt that way before, and I thought, I honestly believed, you felt the same." She dropped her hand. "And looking back, I can't even say I regret letting you know. I still believe you felt it, too, I saw it in your eyes. I still believe that you'd have gotten there, that you'd have said it to me, too, eventually."

Sam closed his eyes until he felt her body go still and then opened them again to see a look of defeat on her face.

"You were never going to get there," she said flatly. "You were never going to say it."

Chapter 29

♥

Heart pounding, eyes stinging, Becca started to climb down off the table, but Sam caught her. He wrapped one arm low on her back to hold her against him, the other tilting her jaw.

She did her best not to be moved by his proximity, and failed spectacularly.

"It's true," Sam admitted. "I never intended to say the words."

Oh, God. Face burning with humiliation, she began to struggle in earnest, knowing only that she had to get away.

Between them a phone began vibrating. Hers. She slapped a hand down to it, hitting IGNORE. The moment she did, Sam's phone began ringing. He hit IGNORE, too. "Becca—"

"I let you in," she said. "All the way in. I told you everything, things I've never told anyone, and you held back. You kept yourself distant—God forbid anyone walk into the Man Cave."

"You didn't walk in," he said. "You blasted your way in."

"Well, I'd have waited to be invited, but I'd still be waiting!" She drew a breath with what appeared to be great difficulty. "And you telling me to stop living in the past is bullshit, Sam. Your entire present is lived the way it is because of your past. And you know what?" She got right up in his face. "That's just as bad as me being unable to get past my own past. Which means we're *both* screwed up!"

She began to fight the umbrella to get down, completely ignoring the six-foot-plus of testosterone and bad attitude still trapped inside the umbrella with her. And then all that testosterone and attitude spoke, and his words stopped her cold.

"I'm not good with trust."

Like a knife to the heart, she thought, and dropped her head to the pole of the umbrella, squeezing her eyes shut at the pain in his voice. "I've never given you any reason to doubt me," she said softly. "I was yours before you even knew what you had." She looked at him. "I'd never have stepped out on you, Sam."

"I don't mean that," he said, and drew in a deep breath. "I—"

"Hey," Tanner said, his voice floating up to them from below. "Trust me, this conversation is fascinating, but you need to shelve it for later. We've got other problems."

"Problems can wait," Sam said, eyes still on Becca.

"Becca isn't going to think so," Tanner said.

Crap, what now? Becca ducked low, beneath the umbrella, hopping off the table to face Tanner. "What is it?" She was aware of Sam hopping down behind her and standing at her back, but she ignored him. She planned to ignore him until forever. Or until the time she got over him, whichever came last.

"That was fun," Tanner said. "Four legs, two female, two male, poking out beneath the umbrella. Lots of yelling. I think Lucille got video of it if you want to revisit it later."

Sam gave him a hard look.

"No? Okay." Tanner shrugged. "The band Becca hired just canceled."

Becca gasped. "What?"

"Yeah, apparently they went out last night and had all-you-can-eat sushi. They're currently in the B and B puking their guts out."

"Oh, my God," she said.

Sam shook his head. "It's going to be okay."

She stared at him. "How?" she demanded. "How is not having music at the Summer Bash going to be okay?"

"We have games, food, and the ocean right here," he said reasonably. "Trust me, Lucky Harbor knows how to have a good time. There's no need to panic."

"It's a party, Sam." She could feel her voice rising along with her anxiety. "A big one, the biggest of the year. I set this whole thing up, I strong-armed you guys into having this party in the first place, and I want it to be perfect. So of course I have to panic. Join me, won't you?"

He had the nerve to smile at her, like her hissy fit was cute.

"We need music, Sam," she said tightly. "Music makes the damn world go around."

"I thought that was love."

She narrowed her eyes. "So you *can* say the word."

Tanner snorted, then turned it into a cough when Sam gave him another hard look. "Maybe I should give you two a moment," he said, and flashed a grin at Becca. "Give him hell, sweetness."

When he was gone, Sam put his hands on her and turned her to face him. "Babe, seriously, it's going to be okay."

Shaking her head, she looked away, to the sand. Her kids were out there—not the entire class yet, but many. Playing in the sand, chasing each other, having a ball. She felt a pang for the simplicity of youth.

"Becca."

When she looked at him again, he was no longer smiling, but his eyes were gentle. Warm.

Fierce.

"I know how much this means to you," he said. "And that you've had a lot of shit dumped on you—"

"I'm fine," she said, not enjoying the reminder of her shitty week. "This is my problem. I'll take care of it." *Somehow*.

He slid his hands to her hips. "I want to ask something of you."

"What?"

"I want you to trust me to help," he said. "Trust me to fix the bash for you. And then after, I fix us," he said, voice low. Determined.

Still fierce.

Her heart caught. "Sam—"

He slanted his head and gave her one quick, hot kiss, and then he was gone.

She stood there a moment, then realized the beach was filling quickly. The air was hot, salty, and ringing with the laughter and sounds of people fully enjoying themselves. It seemed that all of Lucky Harbor had come.

She let out a breath and went back to supervising the setup. An hour later, everything was going amazingly well. The food was plentiful; the drinks were flowing. The younger kids were playing games near the water, supervised by the teens from the rec center whom Becca had hired to do exactly that.

A little later, the pyrotechnic team arrived and set up for the night's show. The crowd thickened some more. There was face painting and a hula-hoop contest. Older kids were bodyboarding, or flirting with each other. Adults were eating, drinking, relaxing in the late-afternoon sun.

There was music after all. It came from Sam's quick-thinking setup with his iPod, a speaker, and a long extension cord from the hut. As night began to fall, Becca walked through the crowds for the umpteenth time. She was hot and tired and exhausted, but exhilarated as well.

She'd pulled it off.

Well, everything except the live music. That was still needling her. It was the only thing lacking. But then she saw movement in the area that she'd originally blocked off for the band. Sam was there, directing the high school boys she'd hired to help set up. They were dragging chairs onto the makeshift stage, and...

"Oh, my God," she whispered to herself.

Instruments.

From her classroom.

The instruments Sam had bought. And more than that, there was her keyboard as well. She started walking over there, ended up running, and skidded to a halt behind him. "What the hell are you doing?"

"Not supposed to swear in front of the kids," he said, waving them in.

"But—" She broke off as the kids sat with their instruments.

Sam smiled at them.

They beamed back.

"Sam," Becca said, her heart rate accelerating to near-stroke levels. "What's going on?"

Sam moved closer to her, pulling her into him.

"Don't," she said.

"Don't what?"

She pushed free. "I can't think when you touch me."

He just looked at her, like she was still cute but also a colossal pain in his ass. "Or look at me," she added.

So what did he do? He tightened his grip, stepped into her, and cupped her face up to his. "Couple of things we have to get straight," he said.

"Now isn't exactly the time—"

"You were right before," he said over her. "I never intended to say the words to you."

She went still, absorbed it, decided she hated it, and tried to back away.

He tightened his grip. "I never was going to say them," he went on, "because they'd never meant anything to me, never gave me anything but a headache. They've always cost me one way or another. I thought this, with you, was different, that somehow my actions would be enough."

At that, she stopped fighting him and stared up at him. "Oh, Sam."

"I've had the words all my life and they meant nothing.

I thought love was in the showing." He let out a low laugh and shook his head. "But then you came out of nowhere. I didn't expect you, Becca."

"I know, I—"

He put a finger to her lips. "I'm still getting past the surprise that I was willing to go there with you at all."

"There," she said, needing a translation.

"*Here*. You've become a part of me," he said. "As important and basic as breathing. I feel things for you that I can't even name." His lips twitched. "And a few that I can."

She sucked in a breath and looked around to see if anyone was listening. When the kids had gathered on stage, the crowds had shifted in and were settling around the stage. Her keyboard sat up there, mocking her, and a new pit of panic gripped her, but Sam took her hands in his.

"You can do this," he said softly.

"Do what?"

But he let her go and moved to the edge of the stage, facing the crowd. "Welcome to the first annual Lucky Harbor Charters Summer Bash!" he called out.

The crowd cheered.

He grinned at them, and Becca could hear the collective hearts of every woman in the place sigh.

"Here at Lucky Harbor Charters," he said, "we've appreciated your business all year. We appreciate your *future* business as well. And today is mine, Tanner's, and Cole's thanks to you. But first, I'd be remiss if I didn't ask you to help me thank Becca Thorpe for…" He met her gaze. "Well, everything."

Everyone whooped and hollered for her, and Becca

found herself staring at them all, cheeks hot as she gave a little wave.

Sam nodded to the pyrotechnic guys waiting for their cue. "We hope you enjoy the show—"

"Sam!" Becca whispered.

Sam held up a finger to the crowd, grinned at them again, effectively paralyzed them with the gorgeousness of his good humor, and then stepped close to Becca, as if they were alone instead of with every single person in town.

"What are you doing?" she hissed.

"Getting ready to start the fireworks display."

"Why are all my kids sitting in those chairs holding their instruments?" she asked, already knowing the answer as the blood began to roar in her ears.

"You can do this," he said again, so damn sure. Of course he was sure; it wasn't *his* ass on the line here.

"What do you mean? Why do you keep talking in some language that I don't understand! I can't—" She broke off and put a hand to her chest, which was pounding, pounding, pounding. "Oh, my God. I'm going to have a stroke; I'm not kidding. I can't do this. Sam, you know that I can't play in front of strangers."

He ran his hands up and down her arms. "They're not strangers, babe. They're your friends."

She looked out at the crowd. She saw Cole and Tanner. Mark. Jack, and Ben. Jax. Lucille. Amelia. Lance. Mark. Olivia...

Sam was right. These were her friends. They cared about her. And she cared about them. "But..." She swallowed. The lump in her throat—the one the size of a regulation football—didn't go anywhere. "We haven't practiced anything for this."

"Yes we have, Ms. Teacher!" Pink called out, bouncing in her seat so hard her little-girl legs swung with each word. "We've been practicing for weeks, remember?"

"'God Bless America,'" Becca whispered.

Sam nodded. "'God Bless America.'" He nudged her to her keyboard.

"You sneaked into my apartment for the keyboard?" she asked.

"Nope," he said. "I used a key."

"You don't have a key."

He smiled.

He had a key. He had a key to everything, including her heart. Damn it. "Sam—"

"Just try it, Becca, I promise you'll do great. And afterward, I've got ranch-flavored popcorn waiting."

She paused. "You bought me more ranch-flavored popcorn?"

"A brand-new tin," he promised, and then lowered his voice. "And more condoms. None of them blue." He gave her another nudge, gestured to the pyrotechnic guys, and a hush came over the crowd. "We welcome our own Lucky Harbor band," he called out. "Give them a hand as we start the show!"

The crowd hooted and hollered, and Becca gave one last panicked look in Sam's direction.

Tanner was standing with him now, beaming. "I can't believe you bribe your woman with popcorn," he said to Sam.

"And sex," Sam said, his voice low and serious. "Don't forget the sex."

Becca stifled a half-hysterical laugh and turned to her kids. They were all grinning widely, excited, and she could only hope to God they actually remembered the song this time. "One, two, three," she prompted, and waited for them to jump in.

Silence. As if suddenly overcome by shyness as one, the kids had gone suddenly still as stone, staring out at the audience like a pack of deer caught in the headlights.

"One, two, three," she repeated.

Nothing.

Oh, God.

The crowded shifted but remained quiet. These people were mothers, fathers, friends...they *wanted* these kids to achieve their dreams. Which meant that there was no sense of impatience or irritation that the ticket price was too high for the value of the show or that she was disappointing anyone. Lucky Harbor wanted this, them, *her*, to succeed. Becca drew a breath and spoke softly. "Hey," she called to her precious class. "Guys, look at me."

The anxious faces turned her way. God. God, she knew just how they felt. The panic was clawing its way up from her own gut to her throat, choking her until it was all but impossible to breathe. But they were looking at her, eyes wide. Counting on her. She walked to the keyboard.

You can do this, Sam had told her. And Sam was always right. She ran her gaze over the kids, taking in each and every one of them, and smiled. "Just me," she said softly, for their ears only. "Just me and a few friends and family. That's all. Everyone knows this song. If we start, they'll join us, okay?"

Like bobbleheads, the kids nodded in unison.

And she smiled at them again, feeling her heart warm and fill with love and pride. "One, two, three," she prompted, and this time she began to play first, an intro, not taking her gaze off the kids.

Just her and the kids...

As she played, she settled. Her heart still threatened to burst out of her chest, but the fear receded a little bit, replaced by a familiar tingle that was so old she hardly recognized it.

Excitement.

She ran the intro again and held her breath, but the kids joined in this time—though not exactly smoothly. Several of them were half a beat behind, and Pink and Kendra were at least half a beat ahead.

Just like in real life.

The fireworks began as they entered the chorus. The town indeed joined in, and by the end of "God Bless America," everyone was in sync, and Becca could hardly keep in time herself because the lump in her throat was back.

I thought my actions would be enough.

The entire song, Sam's words floated in her head, and in her heart. He'd never said he didn't love her, only that he'd hoped his actions would be enough. And his actions did speak pretty loudly. He'd given her a job. He'd supported her, encouraged her to follow her heart, whether that be music or whatever floated her boat. He'd helped her get over the past. He'd backed her up with her family. He'd come running when she'd gotten scared. He'd been there for her, through whatever she needed, at the drop of a hat.

His actions *had* spoken for him—loud and clear. He'd *shown* her he loved her, with every look, every touch, every move he made.

The song ended, the fireworks ended, and everyone burst into a roar of applause. The kids bowed. Becca started to bow, too, but was pulled into a brick wall.

Sam's chest. "So proud of you," he murmured in her ear.

She was shaking. Adrenaline, she knew. But Sam had her, his arms locked tight around her. "Look at me," he said, voice low and serious.

She tilted her face to his.

"I hold people at a distance, I know it. I do it because I also know that anyone or anything can be ripped away from you at any time. But you, Becca..." He shook his head. "I can't—you're in, babe. You're past my walls, past my defenses. If I have to deal with that, so do you."

The crowd was still cheering as she stared up at him. "What are you saying?"

He got serious. Very serious, very intent, his eyes focused on hers. "It means I'm in love with you." He slid his thumb over her jaw in a gesture so sweetly powerful that she had to close her eyes at the sensation. "It means I love you so fucking much I ache with it. All the time. It means I want you to stay here in Lucky Harbor and be with me for as long as you'll have me, which I'm hoping is a damn long time because I've carved out a damn fine life for myself and I want you in it. All the way in it."

She stared up at him. "You...you said the words."

"I did," he agreed.

"You said the words," she whispered again, marveling. "Right?"

From the front, Lucille leaned in. "Honey, yes," she called up to her. "He said he loves you. You might want to see Dr. Scott on Monday about that hearing problem."

Becca wasn't about to be distracted from Sam. "You didn't want to say them, but you did. For me."

"Always for you," Sam said, and, ignoring their avid audience, he bent her over his arm and kissed her, a long, slow, deep one that meant business. It was there in his kiss how much he loved her, and it had been all along.

When he was done, he lifted his mouth from hers and slid his thumb over her wet lower lip. "We good?" he asked.

Lucille cupped her hands around her mouth and shouted to Becca, "Honey, he wants to know if you're good!"

Becca gave her a thumbs-up before turning to Sam. "Considering all I want is you, we're perfect."

Epilogue

♥

One month later, Becca got a call. Her agency had been steadily sending her new assignments, and she'd done well on all of them. This time they were offering her one of their largest accounts, an American car company.

Finally.

Becca hung up and laughed, and then did a little dance right there on the boat.

The guys were sprawled out enjoying the last of the Indian summer as September came to a close.

After a crazy summer, the best summer of Becca's life, they'd all taken a rare day off and were fishing. Or at least making a semblance of fishing, as in the lines were cast. But she doubted any of them, slouched in various positions on deck, each with a beer, dark sunglasses on, bodies relaxed and still, was worried about his catch.

It'd been Sam's idea to take Becca out today. He'd been unhappy when Cole and Tanner had tagged along without invitation, but he'd given in to the inevitable invasion, and they'd had a great day.

Cole was smiling at her little dance. "Probably you shouldn't ever teach dance classes," he said.

"I think she dances kinda cute," Tanner said. "It's white-girl rhythm, but it's the enthusiasm that counts. Although I could tell better if you'd do it again, in a bikini this time," he said with some hopefulness and a sidelong glance at Becca's tee and shorts. "Maybe we should instill a new uniform code. A bikini code."

Sam smacked him upside the back of his head. "My woman," he said. Then he tugged Becca onto his lap.

"Hey," Cole complained. "No PDA on this boat."

"You tagged along," Sam reminded him. "Deal with it." He smiled at Becca. "What's up, babe?"

"I got a big assignment."

His smile was slow and sure. "Proud of you," he said, and leaned in for a warm kiss.

She cupped his scruffy jaw. "Do you have any idea how much I love you?"

Sam nipped her bottom lip and slid his palm to the nape of her neck to hold her still for another kiss. "Show me," he murmured against her lips.

"Christ," Tanner mumbled to Cole. "They're like bunnies."

Cole sighed, rose to his feet, and headed for the helm. "Time to head in." He pointed at Sam. "And that wasn't one of those double entendre things. You can wait until we get back."

Sam smiled into Becca's eyes. "I'll try."

She smiled back. It'd been a great month, maybe the best month of her life. She was teaching, writing jingles,

sometimes still playing late at night at the Love Shack…
when she wasn't sleeping in Sam's arms. They stayed at
his house sometimes, but more often than not Sam left his
place to his father and stayed with Becca in her warehouse
apartment.

She loved it.

She loved him.

She loved life.

As a bonus, Jase had just gotten out of rehab. She'd
talked to him the day before, and he sounded good, real
good. He wasn't going to go straight back out on the concert rounds but was going to stay with their parents and
do some studio work and see how things went.

She was hopeful about that, and as Sam pulled her sunglasses off and kissed her, she realized she was hopeful
about a bunch of things.

Thirty minutes later they pulled up to their dock.

Becca had placed an ad in the paper for help at the hut,
freeing her up to teach music classes to the rest of the
grades in the district. She'd hired someone who was perfect for the job.

"Hey, son." Mark caught the ropes Sam tossed him and
helped tie down the boat.

Becca looked him over carefully. He'd had a rough
month health-wise, and they'd had to change up his meds,
but he was looking good today at least, and she'd take
that. She knew he was happy to be working, and that he
loved feeling helpful, and most of the days he was even
on time.

"You do it yet?" Mark asked Sam.

"Do what?" Cole wanted to know.

Mark blinked at Cole, then looked at Sam. "I thought

you were going to do it today. How did you do it with
these clowns with you?"

Sam's mouth tightened.

"She didn't like it?" Mark asked. He turned to Becca.
"You didn't like it?"

"Dad, drop it," Sam said. "Jesus."

Becca grabbed her small backpack and the tin of
ranch-flavored popcorn Sam had given her that morning
as she'd boarded. Clutching all her stuff, she stepped off
the boat. "Like what?" she asked Mark.

He tapped on the tin.

"Oh, I *love* it when he buys me the popcorn," she said.
"I just didn't get a chance to eat any yet. Sam distracted
me every time I tried."

Sam looked pained.

Becca stared at him, wondering what the odd tremor
in her belly was. She couldn't help but feel like she was
missing something.

Something big.

Mark looked at Sam and laughed. "You poor, dumb
bastard. I almost feel sorry for you."

Sam scrubbed a hand over his face and let out a sigh.

Becca set her backpack down and opened the tin.

Popcorn.

"Becca," Sam said, and reached for the tin.

She shoved a handful in her mouth, and the delicious
flavor exploded against her taste buds. Cole reached into
the tin as well, but she smacked his hand away. "Mine."

"Man, never get between a woman and her popcorn,"
Tanner told Cole.

Becca shoved down another few bites, leaving enough
room to push the popcorn aside. At the bottom was a

little velvet black box, dusted with popcorn crumbs. She stopped breathing.

"I knew you'd get hungry enough eventually," Sam said. "I was just trying to avoid a crowd when it happened." He leveled the guys with a look. "I should've known better."

She just stared at him, her heart pounding.

Sam reached into the tin.

"Hey," Cole bitched. "You'll share with him and not me? I thought we were friends."

Tanner wrapped an arm around Cole's neck, clapping a hand over his mouth.

Sam pulled the small black box from the tin. He nudged a gobsmacked Becca to the dock bench and then crouched at her side. "I might be a little slow," he said, "but luckily I learn from my mistakes." He opened the box and revealed a diamond ring that dazzled her and left her speechless.

It spoke of forever and stability and calm acceptance. It was a testament to his life, proof of his love and commitment. "Oh, Sam," she breathed.

"Is that *Oh, Sam*, you done good?" Mark asked. "Or *Oh, Sam*, you're an idiot? 'Cause there's a big difference, darlin'."

Tanner wrapped his other arm around Mark's neck and muzzled him as well.

"It's so beautiful," Becca whispered, throat tight, eyes misting.

Sam smiled at her. "I love you. Be mine, Becca. Marry me."

Mark tore Tanner's hand from his mouth. "Son, you're supposed to ask, not tell."

Sam slid his dad a dark look.

Mark grimaced. "Right. Don't butt in. I almost forgot that part, sorry." He then lifted Tanner's hand back to his own mouth.

Becca let out a laugh and stared down at Sam, the big, tough, stoic man who was so good at coming in under the emotional radar that she'd never seen him coming at all. He had his heart out on the line, and she knew he wasn't all that patient about such things. So she touched his face, feeling the rough day-old stubble beneath her fingertips as she leaned in. "Yes," she whispered against his mouth. "I'll be yours. And that makes you mine as well, you know. You ready for that?"

He grinned. "It's all I ever wanted."

About the Author

New York Times bestselling author **Jill Shalvis** lives in a small town in the Sierras full of quirky characters. Any resemblance to the quirky characters in her books is mostly coincidental. Look for Jill's bestselling, award-winning books wherever romances are sold and visit her website for a complete book list and daily blog detailing her city-girl-living-in-the-mountains adventures.

You can learn more at:

JillShalvis.com
Twitter @JillShalvis
Facebook.com/JillShalvis